The Complete and Original
Norwegian Folktales
of Asbjørnsen and Moe

The Complete and Original

Norwegian Folktales

of ASBJØRNSEN AND MOE

Peter Christen Asbjørnsen and Jørgen Moe

Translated by Tiina Nunnally
Foreword by Neil Gaiman

UNIVERSITY OF MINNESOTA PRESS
Minneapolis   London

NORLA
NORWEGIAN LITERATURE ABROAD

This translation has been published with the financial support of NORLA.

The translator is grateful to *Norsk biografisk leksikon* for its comprehensive biographical information on Asbjørnsen and Moe.

PAGE viii Theodor Kittelsen, *Skogtroll*, 1907. 36 × 28 cm. National Gallery, Norway. Photograph by Jacques Lathion/Nasjonalmuseet.

PAGE xii Theodor Kittelsen, *Husmand*, 1911. 84 × 56 cm. Blaafarveværket Collection, The Th. Kittelsen Museum at The Cobalt Mines. Photograph by Blaafarveværket.

Published by the University of Minnesota Press
111 Third Avenue South, Suite 290
Minneapolis, MN 55401-2520
http://www.upress.umn.edu

Design by Nancy Koerner and Michael Starkman
at Wilsted & Taylor Publishing Services

ISBN 978-1-5179-0568-2
A Cataloging-in-Publication record for this book is available from the Library of Congress.

Printed in the United States of America on acid-free paper

The University of Minnesota is an equal-opportunity educator and employer.

25 24 23 22 21 20 19   10 9 8 7 6 5 4 3 2 1

Contents

❧   ❧   ❧

Foreword

Neil Gaiman

I KEEP TRYING TO WRITE a measured and sensible introduction to this book, and I keep failing. I keep failing because in order to find out what I think I pick up the proofs and start to read—or rather, at this point, to reread and to rerereread—any one of the Norwegian folktales waiting between these covers, and then I'm swallowed by them. I don't read them critically. I don't even put my compare-this-story-from-this-tradition-to-this-other-story-that-it-somehow-resembles hat on. I just start to read, and I'm following the adventures of Ash Lad, or the Girl Whose Godmother Was the Virgin Mary, and I feel satisfied.

Someone is telling me a story.

I first went to Norway in July 1998. I landed in a tired daze: I had flown to Oslo from Reykjavik, where the sun did not set and my hotel had no curtains, so I had spent most of the past three days awake. I managed a day in Oslo of seeing people, of drinking my tea where Ibsen drank his coffee, and eventually I was taken to my room in the Grand Hotel where the curtains, lined with black, closed, and in the glorious darkness I finally slept.

I woke refreshed, and had days of joy.

I was introduced to the art of Theodor Kittelsen (1857–1914), who drew trolls and the Norwegian countryside. Kittelsen was more than an illustrator or a folk artist, but he was not as well known as Arthur Rackham or John Bauer. His trolls made sense: they were as much a part of the world as the trees and the hills. His drawings and paintings felt as though they had paused in their travels for Kittelsen to create their portraits. I learned that Kittelsen was once told that a rival had decided to start painting trolls, and he had been puzzled and upset by this. "How can he draw a troll?" he asked. "He's never seen a troll!"

The cover of this book features a painting by Theodor Kittelsen.

I was driven across the country, from Oslo in the southeast to Bergen in the southwest, passing through the Hardangerfjord region with its remarkable waterfalls, each a scenic joy. I found myself loving Norway. There was a wildness to the landscape that appealed to me, but it was a restrained wildness. I resolved to return.

And return I do, when I can. I love Norway. There is a gloom in Norway that creeps out in the oddest places. I delight in the Emanuel Vigeland Mausoleum in Oslo, a candle-lit chapel where people sit in silence and wait for their eyes to become accustomed to the darkness, then they stare at the naked people and skeletons painted on the shadowy walls. Part of my delight is that the windowless red-brick mausoleum is quietly just another building in a pretty, tree-lined, residential neighborhood.

I encountered Asbjørnsen and Moe's *Norwegian Folktales* sometime in the 1990s, and really enjoyed them. They were story types I was familiar with, but there was a focus and a chill, a way of bringing characters on stage, and a canny use of what W. S. Gilbert called "corroborative detail, intended to give artistic verisimilitude to an otherwise bald and unconvincing narrative" that engaged me. Still, the translation I read then was a century old, and it creaked at the edges, sometimes.

I was already in love with Norse mythology, and one can feel the shadows of the Frost Giants in some of these stories, or echoes of the tale of Thor and the Loki and the Thialfi of the contest with the giants: Asbjørnsen and Moe also sensed this and drew attention to it. Our sacred mysteries become myths become folktales, and Frost Giants and gods become trolls and heroes, given enough time.

In a translation as crystalline and pellucid as the waters of the fjords, Tiina Nunnally takes the stories that Asbjørnsen and Moe collected from the people of rural Norway, translates them, and gives them to us afresh. Each story feels honed, as if it were recently collected from a storyteller who knew how to tell it and who had, in turn, heard it from someone who knew how to tell it.

There are a great many sensible people in these stories. Quests are undertaken, disguises adopted, treasures returned with, royalty wed, yes. But there's an ease and a community I love, as well as a way with stories. People seem—many of them—to want to help, and experiencing how information is doled out is a pleasure. Watch the young girl who cannot spin or weave or sew be rescued by three old women who can; all they ask is that she call each of them "aunt" on her wedding day. I have read dozens of versions of this story, but this is the first to conceal the information about the old women's deformities until the dramatically perfect moment in the story.

You will meet youngest sons and foolish farmers, clever women and lost princesses, adventurers and fools, just as in any collection of folk stories from anywhere in Northern Europe. But the *Norwegian Folktales* come with trolls, and if Asbjørnsen and Moe did not see them, as Kittelsen did, then they got their stories from people who had, people who had seen the trolls walking in the mist at dawn.

Translator's Note

THERE ONCE were two Norwegian boys who loved listening to stories, especially folktales. One was named Peter Christen Asbjørnsen, and the other was Jørgen Moe. At the age of fourteen, the boys met at school in 1827 and formed a lasting friendship that would prove auspicious for both of them.

Ten years later, influenced by the folklore work of the Grimm brothers in Germany, Asbjørnsen and Moe set off separately into the mountainous countryside of southern Norway. They were in search of storytellers who might be willing to share the tales that had been passed down in their families for generations. Over the course of more than twenty years, the two young men intermittently continued their work with folktales, even as they pursued completely different interests.

What Asbjørnsen and Moe discovered on these expeditions turned out to be more precious than any hoard of gold and silver, more bountiful than any feast conjured up by a magic tablecloth, and more impressive than a giant twelve-headed troll. What they discovered was a cultural treasure trove. The folktales that Asbjørnsen and Moe wrote down and later collectively published as *Norske folkeeventyr* (Norwegian Folktales) would nurture Norway's emerging national identity. And the tales would make their names legendary—not just in their own country but around the world.

◆ ◆ ◆

Peter Christen Asbjørnsen was born in Christiania (present-day Oslo) in 1812. He was the son of a glazier whose family had roots in the Gudbrandsdal region. As a child, Peter often suffered long periods of illness. In his father's workshop, he would listen to local shopkeepers and tradesmen recounting traditional legends and tales. He read widely and had a keen interest in nature, which prompted him to take frequent hikes in the nearby countryside.

After he finished school, Asbjørnsen spent three years in Romerike as a private tutor before going on to study natural history and medicine. During these years he laid the groundwork for a literary outpouring that would one day include not only the famous folktale collections but also Christmas stories, regional legends, scientific treatises (he introduced Darwin's ideas to Norwegian readers in an article published in 1861), and even a seafaring novel.

Eventually Asbjørnsen focused his considerable energy and zeal on zoology, receiving several grants to conduct research along both Oslo Fjord and Hardanger Fjord. There he discovered a new type of starfish, which he named *Brisinga endecacnemos*, after the necklace called "Brísingamen" that belonged to the goddess Freyja in Nordic mythology. Later he turned to forestry and studied in Germany, where he met Jacob and Wilhelm Grimm.

On returning to Norway, Asbjørnsen was appointed chief forester in Trøndelag. He also became an expert on Norwegian peat production, and both vocations provided him with a steady income for the rest of his life. He died in 1885.

Jørgen Moe took an entirely different course in his life. He was born in 1813 in the Norwegian municipality of Hole in the southern region of Ringerike. His father was a prominent landowner and farmer who often represented the area in Stortinget, Norway's parliament. He was determined that his son should study law, but Jørgen had no interest in that field. His passions were literature and the philosophy of aesthetics. Eventually he would become a respected author and write some of Norway's most beloved poems and songs, including the classic children's story "I Brønden og i Kjæret" (In the Well and in the Lake).

In 1832, recognizing that his literary interests were unlikely to provide him with a living, Moe made the practical decision to study theology. Seven years later he passed his exams, having weathered a broken engagement and a debilitating period of depression. He wasn't yet ready to become an ordained Lutheran pastor and settle into clergyman duties; instead, he supported himself by taking various teaching positions as he continued to publish poetry and ballads in the National Romantic style.

During this period, Moe was corresponding with his longtime friend Peter Christen Asbjørnsen about topics such as the retelling of traditional tales by the German author Ludwig Tieck. More significantly, they discussed the groundbreaking work of Jacob and Wilhelm Grimm. The brothers' emphasis on the historical and cultural importance of folklore reignited the enthusiasm the two friends had always felt for Norwegian folktales. The influence of the Grimm brothers led Moe to write an extensive Introduction to the second edition of *Norske folkeeventyr*, published in 1852. The first half of Moe's Introduction was a lengthy commentary on folktale scholarship in diverse cultures around the world; the second half (now translated into English for the first time and included in this book) presents a fascinating look at Moe's own views of the Norwegian tales and, in particular, how they relate back to the sagas and Norse mythology.

Moe wrote:

> Like the dwarves Austri, Vestri, Nordri, and Sudri in the *Edda*s, the winds are personified in the tales "About the Boy Who Went to the North Wind and Demanded the Flour Back," "Soria Moria Castle," and "East of the Sun and West of the Moon." In the story "Lillekort," the title character is given a ship that is one and the same with the ship called Skiðblaðnir of Norse mythology. And you might even deduce that the hunchbacked and one-eyed old woman is reminiscent of the god Odin, whose divine power is manifested in the description of the ship.

Asbjørnsen and Moe decided to remove this scholarly introduction from future Norwegian editions in favor of allowing the tales to "speak for themselves" to readers of all ages.

In 1850, Moe lost the research grant that had offered him some measure of financial security, and the following year he married. It was finally time for him to assume his pastoral duties in order to provide for himself and his family. He held positions in Bragernes and Vestre Aker, and in 1876 he was appointed bishop of the Kristiansand diocese. He was known as a masterful preacher, a conservative theologian, and a man who always showed great kindness and devotion to his congregations. Throughout his long career, Moe continued his literary projects, although his clergyman obligations meant that he had to give up further folklore research. In 1872 he became a member of the Royal Norwegian Society of Sciences and Letters. He died in 1882.

◆　◆　◆

The publication of Asbjørnsen and Moe's *Norske folkeeventyr* began in December 1841 with the appearance of a slim, ninety-six-page unbound pamphlet. The pamphlet garnered praise from both Peter Andreas Munch, the influential historian and saga translator, and Johan Sebastian Welhaven, the respected author and literary critic. This positive reception motivated the two young folklorists to continue their expeditions throughout southern Norway, usually going to separate regions in order to collect the most tales for more pamphlets. In 1843, a volume of forty-one tales was published in Christiania by Johan Dahl, followed in October 1844 by a second volume of twelve tales by the same publisher. Together, these two volumes would make up the "first edition" of *Norske folkeeventyr*. Eight years later, in 1852, a second edition was published that expanded the number of tales to fifty-eight, and then finally, in 1866, the third edition included sixty tales, with Asbjørnsen and Moe each adding one new tale.

In his Foreword to this second edition, Asbjørnsen explained their methodology:

> The very effort of persuading the nation's storytellers to make themselves known, openly and without reservation, requires approaching them in a unique manner. A direct appeal does not get you far, and even the promise of payment is wasted on the best of them, meaning those who have a love for what has been handed down to them. To convince such people to remove the lock from their lips, it is necessary to possess an innate tact, which is then further developed through practice and by studying the Norwegian people. But above all, it is necessary to allow a true love for these traditions to shine through; you need not bother with any dissembling, for it will have either no effect or the opposite effect in terms of what you wish to achieve.

When Asbjørnsen and Moe set off for Norway's deep mountain valleys, they took with them their great love for the traditional tales they had already heard from family, friends, and local storytellers. They were energetic, passionate, and determined young men who wanted to discover and record stories that were part of their cultural heritage. As Moe explained in his Introduction to the 1852 edition:

> Although the tales may be similar in content to stories from other nations, they are nevertheless not the same. They are clearly manifestations of our country's unique setting and commonly shared conditions.
>
> In this sense, the setting—the entire stage on which a simple and ordinary story is played out while at the same time a colorful and richly varied imaginary performance takes place—is always the familiar

mountainous landscape of Norway. We see the dense forests with the small green clearings where you can rest after a journey; the ridge after ridge of mountains that you must traverse; the heights where Dappleband is raised; the big, high mountain that casts a shadow over the king's courtyard; the steep, mirror-smooth slope that Ash Lad has to ride up; the sheltered cleft where the old woman sits and lures in the weary herder. These and thousands of other small details tell us that we are at home in Norway, no matter how amazing the events may be that capture our attention.

Just as momentous as their decision to collect the tales was their resolve not to write them down in the distinctive dialects of each region. Instead, they gave the tales a consistent, literary voice, while maintaining the vitality and immediacy of oral storytelling. They opted for a syntax and word choices that were clearly Norwegian at a time when the Danish language still weighed heavily on literary and linguistic endeavors in Norway. Asbjørnsen and Moe were initially criticized for dramatically veering away from the established (and more formal) conventions deemed necessary for written texts. Yet their volumes of folktales soon sparked a national surge of interest in what was uniquely Norwegian.

Asbjørnsen wrote in the Foreword to the second edition:

At the time we began our collections, there were undoubtedly few in Norway who regarded the tales as anything more than mere nursery-room chatter, with most viewing our attempt to collect and publish them as childish foolishness. We think that we have contributed in some manner to a recognition of what is meritorious about bringing to light everything that belongs to the nation.

Certainly most Norwegians would agree. Generations of Nordic writers, artists, illustrators, and musicians have been influenced by the stories that Asbjørnsen and Moe collected and published in the mid-1800s. Generations of children have grown up shivering with awe and anticipation as they read tales about magic spells, mountain-sized trolls, resourceful princesses, and the intrepid young boy named Ash Lad.

Nearly 180 years after the publication of the first slim volume, *Norske folkeeventyr* is still considered a national treasure. Countless editions have been published in Norway and the rest of Scandinavia, and the names Asbjørnsen and Moe have become synonymous with this sparkling example of Norway's proud cultural traditions.

◆   ◆   ◆

It didn't take long for the work of Asbjørnsen and Moe to make its way to other parts of the world, thanks to early translations. The first English translation was published in 1859 under the title *Popular Tales from the Norse*. It was based on the fifty-eight tales presented in the second edition of *Norske folkeeventyr* and included a lengthy Introduction by the translator, Sir George Webbe Dasent (1817–96). Dasent had developed an interest in Nordic tales and mythology after meeting Jacob Grimm in Stockholm. He went on to publish many translations from the Scandinavian languages and was especially known for his English renderings of Icelandic sagas.

What is most remarkable about this first translation is that it has remained the *only* English translation to include the initial collection of all fifty-eight folktales. (When Asbjørnsen and Moe added two tales to their third edition, a total of sixty stories then became the standard number in later Norwegian volumes.) Subsequent English translations have presented only a handful of stories. Even the publication of *Norwegian Folk Tales* in 1960, translated by Pat Shaw and Carl Norman, contains only thirty-five tales, and less than a third of these are from the original *Norske folkeeventyr*.

Several years ago, Erik Anderson, editor at the University of Minnesota Press, mentioned to me that he had long wanted to publish a new translation of the folktales collected by Asbjørnsen and Moe. I have always loved translating classic literature, so I was intrigued by the idea, but I was busy with other books, and the timing wasn't right. In 2017, generous funding opportunities from Norway and an opening in my work schedule suddenly made the folktale project feasible.

Before I agreed to take on what would be a very challenging endeavor, I decided to look at several stories translated by Dasent. His *Popular Tales from the Norse* has been reprinted many times (even quite recently), and I wanted to be sure that there was a need for a new English translation.

I quickly concluded that although Dasent's translation may have been suitable for a nineteenth-century audience, it would not appeal to modern-day readers. The style is uneven and inconsistent, there are misunderstandings, and the wording seems clumsy and old-fashioned. Certain details are more identifiable as British rather than Norwegian. Dasent chooses "bannock" instead of "*lefse*," "Boots" instead of "Ash Lad"—and, strangely enough, he describes Norway's majestic mountains as "hills." Of greatest concern is the loss of the storytelling voice that Asbjørnsen and Moe were so careful to instill in the Norwegian. Accuracy is essential in any translation, but just as important is capturing the voice or tone of a literary work. The translator must try to convey in her own language the rhythm and cadence—what I call the music—of the original. This is one of the most difficult tasks a translator must accomplish.

Asbjørnsen and Moe adopted a clear and deceptively simple narrative style that was meant to be read aloud. They used repetition and alliteration to mimic the tradition of oral storytelling. The tales are filled with humor, rhymes, and an abundance of detail. Sometimes they chose words specific to the old farming way of life in Norway, using terms no longer common today. Payments are made in *daler* and *skillinger,* reflecting the monetary system of the time. And there is a lot of dialogue, which has to sound natural—not too archaic and not too modern. Throughout the stories, the towering mountains and dense forests of the Norwegian landscape are always vividly present.

I would need to consider all these stylistic issues, but clearly it was time for a new English translation of Asbjørnsen and Moe's Norwegian folktales. I happily delved into the project.

I wanted to go back to the original source, so I chose to work from the fourth Norwegian edition. (This turned out to be doubly daunting, because the book was printed in the old Gothic script with almost no paragraph markings.) With each of the previous editions, Asbjørnsen and Moe had made changes to the Norwegian language in terms of syntax, spelling, and word choice. The fourth edition was the last time the two friends decided together which revisions should be made to the text. Subsequent revisions (occasionally even in the storyline) were largely made by Moe's son, Moltke. Later Norwegian editions continued the process, begun by Asbjørnsen and Moe, of making the language more Norwegian.

I grew up in a Finnish American family, and from an early age I was familiar with the trolls and the elves *(tonttu)* that inhabit the forests of Finland. I was also familiar with the more benign Danish elves, called *nisser.* My siblings and I used to scare ourselves silly by looking at John Bauer's illustrations in our mother's book of Swedish fairy tales. As a child I read Tove Jansson's Moomin books, *Alice in Wonderland,* the fairy tales of Hans Christian

Andersen, and many other books filled with magic and enchantment. I read a tame version of "The Three Billy Goats Gruff" and a few other Norwegian stories. And of course I'd seen pictures and carvings of Norwegian trolls. But I had never actually read Asbjørnsen and Moe's *Norske folkeeventyr*.

What a joyous discovery! All those gigantic trolls are both ferocious and strangely endearing. They lumber through the dark forests and hunker down inside the mountains. Some of the trolls bellow and roar, while some of them wheedle and whine. They matter-of-factly lop off heads, turn princes into stone, and whisk folks away into the mountains. Yet none is a match for the bold and inventive Ash Lad, who has no compunction about chopping off troll heads, even twelve at a time.

As Moe explained in his Introduction to the second edition:

> Everywhere we can see, as in the sagas, *the direct and ruthless way* in which everything is described—a means of expression that stems not from cruelty but from naïveté and lack of guile. We find the same bold and magnificent sense of humor that—like the hero in a German tale—seems to be "presented in order to teach fear." We discover everywhere *the pure epic narrative style whose sole purpose is the joy of observation*. Hence, it dwells as much on the sorrowful and terrible as it does on the bright and cheerful, but it rarely if ever reveals the disposition of the narrator as events unfold.

There are observant princesses who know the secrets to wielding a magic sword and servant girls who use their wits to marry a prince. A sister persists in an impossible task to rescue her brothers. A brave maiden rides the North Wind to save the prince who had been turned into a polar bear. There are talking horses, clever foxes, and steadfast roosters.

I was astonished by the lively humor and the sheer variety of the stories. Some show the virtues of kindness ("The Husband's Daughter and the Wife's Daughter") or integrity ("The Honest Four-*Skilling* Coin"). Some explain aspects of the natural world ("Why the Bear Has a Stump of a Tail"). And some are just plain odd ("The Rooster and the Hen").

Translating these sixty tales into English has been an honor and a delight. I hope that many more generations of readers, both young and old, will now enjoy the treasure trove that Norwegian storytellers long ago entrusted to Peter Christen Asbjørnsen and Jørgen Moe, those two young men who loved folktales.

❖   ❖   ❖

I thank Norwegian author Nan Bentzen Skille for explaining some of the words and phrases that puzzled me. Thanks also to author Lise Lunge-Larsen for her helpful comments on an early version of the manuscript. Special thanks to research librarian Anne Kristin Lande at the National Library of Norway for her help in clarifying the regional collection site names. I'm grateful to my colleagues at NORLA, the office of Norwegian Literature Abroad in Oslo, for their continuing support of my work. And I thank everyone at the University of Minnesota Press, especially Erik Anderson, who had the foresight to realize that Asbjørnsen and Moe's *Norske folkeeventyr* deserved a new English translation that would speak to readers today.

This translation is dedicated to the memory of Steven T. Murray, translator extraordinaire.

Tiina Nunnally
April 2019
Albuquerque, New Mexico

The Complete and Original
Norwegian Folktales
of Asbjørnsen and Moe

About Ash Lad,
Who Stole the Troll's Silver Ducks,
Coverlet, and Golden Harp

here once was a poor man who had three sons. When he died, the two older sons were about to set off into the world to try their luck, but they refused to take the youngest with them.

"You!" they said. "The only thing you're good for is sitting here and digging in the ashes."

"Then I suppose I'll have to go alone," said Ash Lad.

The two sons left. They came to a royal palace, and there they found jobs as servants. The first was hired by the stablemaster and the other by the gardener.

Ash Lad also set off. He took along a big bread trough, which was all they had left from their parents, though his brothers had no use for it. The trough was heavy to carry, but he didn't want to leave it behind.

After he'd walked for a while, he too arrived at the royal palace and asked to be hired as a servant. They told him that they had no need for him, but he pleaded so sincerely and politely that finally he was allowed to go to the kitchen. There he could carry firewood and water for the kitchen maid.

He was hardworking and clever, and it didn't take long before everyone grew quite fond of him. But his two brothers were lazy, and for that reason they were beaten and received only meager wages. They grew jealous of Ash Lad when they saw that things were going much better for him.

Right across from the royal palace, on the other side of the lake, lived a troll who had seven silver ducks that swam about in the water and could be seen from the palace. The king had often wished he might own those ducks, so the two brothers said to the stablemaster, "Our brother has boasted that if he wanted to, he could get those seven silver ducks for the king."

As you might expect, it wasn't long before the stablemaster told the king about this. The king then summoned Ash Lad and said, "Your brothers say that you can get the silver ducks for me, so that is what you must do."

"That's not something I've thought or said," replied the boy.

But the king insisted. "You did say it, and you shall do it," he said.

"All right," said the boy, "seeing as I have no choice. Give me a quarter barrel of rye and a quarter barrel of wheat, and I will try."

He was given the rye and wheat, which he put in the bread trough that he'd brought from home. Then he got in the trough and rowed across the lake. When he reached the opposite shore, he began walking along, scattering the grain here and there. Finally he managed to lure the ducks into the trough, and then he began rowing back as fast as he could go.

When he reached the middle of the lake, the troll appeared on shore and caught sight of him. "Are you making off with the seven silver ducks that belong to me?"

"Yes, I am!" said the boy.

"Will you be back this way again?" asked the troll.

"That may be," said the lad.

When he brought to the king the seven silver ducks, everyone at the royal palace grew all the more fond of him, and even the king said it was a job well done. But his brothers grew more resentful and envious. They decided to tell the stablemaster that Ash Lad had boasted that if he wanted to, he could bring to the king the troll's coverlet, which had a silver pane and a golden pane and another silver pane and golden pane. Once again the stablemaster didn't hesitate to report this to the king.

The king then told the boy what his brothers had said, that he had boasted he could get the troll's coverlet with the silver and golden panes. So that was what he had to do, or else he would lose his life.

Ash Lad replied that this was not something he had thought or said, but it did no good. So he asked for three days in which to consider the matter. When the time was up, he again rowed across the lake in the bread trough and then walked back and forth on shore, keeping an eye out. Finally he saw that those who lived inside the mountain had come out to hang up the coverlet to air. When they were safely back inside the mountain, Ash Lad grabbed the coverlet and began rowing back as fast as he could go. When he was in the middle of the lake, the troll appeared and caught sight of him.

"Are you the one who took my seven silver ducks?" shouted the troll.

"Yes, I am!" said the boy.

"And are you now making off with my coverlet with one silver pane and one golden pane and another silver pane and golden pane?"

"Yes, I am!" said the boy.

"Will you be back this way again?" asked the troll.

"That may be," said the boy.

When he got back with the golden and silver coverlet, everybody grew even more fond of him than before, and he became the king's personal servant. That made his two brothers even more resentful. To seek revenge, they said to the stablemaster, "Our brother has now boasted that he can get for the king the golden harp the troll owns. It's a harp that will make everyone happy when they hear it, no matter how sad they might be."

The stablemaster reported this at once to the king, who said to the boy, "Since you said that, you must do it. If you succeed, you shall have the princess and half my kingdom. But if you don't succeed, you shall lose your life."

"That is not something I have either thought or said," replied the boy. "But I suppose there is nothing to be done about it, and I will have to try. I will need six days to consider the matter."

He was granted the six days, but when they were up he had to set off.

He put in his pocket a nail, a birch twig, and a candle stump and rowed across the lake. Then he crept about, walking back and forth. After a while the troll came out and caught sight of him.

"Are you the one who took my seven silver ducks?" shouted the troll.

"Yes, I am!" replied the boy.

"Are you also the one who took my coverlet with the silver and golden panes?" asked the troll.

"Yes, I am!" said the boy.

Then the troll grabbed him and took him inside the mountain.

"So, daughter of mine," he said, "I've got him now, the one who took my silver ducks and my coverlet with the silver and golden panes. Put him in the sty to fatten him up. When we slaughter him, we'll invite all our friends."

She gladly did so at once. She put Ash Lad in the sty, where he stayed for eight days and was given the very best food and drink he could ever wish for, and as much as he wanted. When the eight days were up, the troll told his daughter to go out and cut into the boy's little finger to see if he was fattened up. So she went over to the sty.

"Give me your little finger!" she said. Instead, Ash Lad stuck out the nail, which she tried to cut.

"Oh no! He's still as hard as iron," said the troll's daughter when she went back to her father. "We can't take him yet."

After another eight days the same thing happened, only this time Ash Lad held out the birch twig.

"He's a little better," she said when she went back to the troll. "But he'll be as tough as wood to chew."

After eight days the troll again told his daughter to go and see if he was fattened up.

"Give me your little finger!" said the troll's daughter when she got to the sty. This time Ash Lad held out the candle stump.

"Now he's ready," she said.

"All right then!" said the troll. "I'll be off to invite our guests. In the meantime you must slaughter him. Then fry half of him and boil the other half."

After the troll left, his daughter set about sharpening a big, long knife.

"Is that what you're going to use to slaughter me?" asked the boy.

"That's right!" said the troll's daughter.

"It's not sharp enough," said the boy. "Why don't you let *me* sharpen it. Then it will be easier for you to take my life."

So she let him have the knife, which he began honing and sharpening.

"Let me try it on your braid," said the boy. "I think it's ready now."

She agreed to let him do that. But the instant he grabbed hold of the troll daughter's braid, he yanked her head back and cut it right off. Then he boiled half of her and fried the other half and set the food on the table. After that he put on her clothes and sat down in the corner.

When the troll came home with the folks he'd invited, he asked his daughter—for he thought it was her—to come and eat dinner with them.

"No," replied the boy. "I don't want any food. I feel very grumpy and sad."

"Well, you know what to do about that," said the troll. "Get the golden harp and play it!"

"Yes, but where exactly is it?" said the boy.

"You know very well where it is. You were the one who played it last. It's hanging over there above the door."

The boy didn't have to ask twice. He took down the harp and played it as he walked in and out of the house. All of a sudden he pushed the bread trough out into the water and began rowing so fast that the water surged around the trough.

After a while the troll thought his daughter had been gone a long time, and he went outside to see what had become of her. Then he saw the boy in the trough far, far away on the lake.

"Are you the one who took my seven silver ducks?" shouted the troll.

"Yes!" said the boy.

"Are you the one who took my coverlet with the silver panes and golden panes? Was that you too?"

"Yes!" said the boy.

"And have you now taken my golden harp?"

"Yes, that I have!" said the boy.

"But didn't I just eat you?"

"No, it was your daughter you ate," replied the boy.

When the troll heard that, he grew so angry that he burst.

Then Ash Lad rowed back to shore and gathered up a big heap of gold and silver, as much as the trough could carry. When he got back to the royal palace with the golden harp, he was given the king's daughter and half the kingdom, just as the king had promised. But he treated his brothers well, for he thought that everything they'd said was only because they'd wanted the best for him.

The Gjertrud Bird

*B*ack in the day when our Lord and Saint Peter wandered here on earth, they once came upon a woman who was baking. Her name was Gjertrud, and she wore a red cap on her head. Since they had been walking for a long time and they were both hungry, our Lord asked her ever so politely if he might have a bite of *lefse*.

Oh yes, he certainly might. She broke off a stingy little piece of dough and rolled it out. Yet it grew so big that it covered the entire griddle. No, the *lefse* was too big now, and he couldn't have any of that one. She broke off an even smaller piece, but when she rolled it out and spread it on the griddle, that *lefse* also grew too big. He couldn't have any of that one either. For a third time she broke off an even smaller piece, a teeny tiny bit, but again the *lefse* was much too big.

"So I have nothing to give the two of you," said Gjertrud. "You might as well go on your way without having even a taste, for all the *lefse* I make is too big."

Then our Lord grew angry and said, "You have treated me so badly that you will be punished in this manner: You will become a bird, forced to find your dry nourishment between bark and wood. And you will receive something to drink only when it rains."

Hardly had he uttered the last word than she turned into the Gjertrud bird, a black woodpecker, and flew from her bread board straight up through the chimney.

Even today you can see her flying around, wearing her red cap, her body completely black from the soot in the chimney. She picks and pecks at the trees in search of food, and she whistles for rain, for she is always thirsty and waiting for something to drink.

The Griffin

There once was a king who had twelve daughters, and he was so fond of them that he always kept them close. But every afternoon, while the king slept, the princesses would go out for a stroll. One day when the king was having his afternoon nap and the princesses had gone out, they suddenly disappeared and did not return.

Then a great sorrow came over the whole country, but the king was the most sorrowful of all. He sent out word to all the churches both in his own kingdom and abroad, saying that he was searching for his daughters. And he ordered the bells to toll for them everywhere in the land.

But the princesses were gone, and gone they stayed. No one knew where they were. It was thought that they must have been taken inside the mountain. And it wasn't long before this was rumored far and wide, both in towns and in villages and in foreign realms as well.

Then the rumor also reached a king in a faraway land who had twelve sons. When the princes heard about the twelve royal daughters, they asked to be allowed to set off to search for them. The king was reluctant to grant his sons permission to leave, for he was afraid he might never see them again. But they fell to their knees before the king and pleaded for so long that he finally relented and let them set off.

He outfitted a ship for them and assigned the Red Knight to be their helmsman, for he was a skilled seaman. They sailed around for a long time and went ashore in all the lands they neared, searching for and inquiring about the princesses, but no one had seen or heard from them.

By now the princes had been sailing for a few days short of seven years. One day a big storm blew in, and the weather was so foul that they thought they would never see land again. Everyone had to work very hard, and no sleep was possible for as long as the storm lasted. On the third day the wind subsided, and suddenly everything was utterly still. They were all so worn out from the work and the terrible weather that they fell asleep at once. But the youngest prince was restless and couldn't sleep.

As he walked back and forth on deck, the ship came to a small island, and on the island was a little dog running about and barking and whining at the ship, as if it wanted to come on board. The prince called and called and whistled to the dog, which barked and whined all the more. He felt bad that the dog would have to stay there and die. He thought it must have come from a ship that had gone down in the storm. Yet he didn't think he could help the dog, for he wasn't sure he was capable of putting the rowboat in the water. The others were all sleeping so soundly that he didn't want to wake them just because of a dog.

The weather was now clear and calm, and the prince thought to himself: You could go ashore and save that dog. He decided to put the rowboat in the water, and it was easier than he'd expected. He rowed ashore and went over to the dog, but every time he reached for it, the animal would leap aside. The dog kept on like that until, before he knew it, the prince had entered a big, splendid castle. Once inside, the dog changed into a lovely princess, and on the bench sat a man so big and so ugly that the prince was truly frightened.

"You have no need to be afraid," said the man. Yet the prince grew even more frightened at the sound of the man's voice. "I know full well what it is you want. You and your brothers are twelve princes, and you are searching for the twelve princesses who disappeared. I know where they are. They are with my master. There they sit, each on a golden chair, each of them picking the lice from one of his heads, for he has twelve of them. You have been sailing for seven years, but you will have to sail for seven more before you find them. You're welcome to stay here," he said, "and I will give you my daughter. But first you will have to kill my master, for he treats us all harshly, and we have grown tired of that. When he's dead, I will be king in his place. But let's see if you can wield that sword," said the troll.

The prince reached for the old and rusty sword that hung on the wall, but he could hardly budge it.

"Take a swig from this flask," said the troll.

After he did that, the prince was able to move the sword. After another swig, he could lift it, and after yet another swig, he could swing the sword as easily as a stick for turning *lefse*.

"When you get back on board," said the troll prince, "you must hide the sword in your bunk so the Red Knight won't see it. He's not skilled enough to wield the sword, yet he will be furious with you and try to kill you. When there are three days short of seven more years," he went on, "the same thing will happen again. Terrible weather will bring a storm upon you, and after it passes, all of you will be very sleepy. Then you must take the sword and row ashore. You will come to a castle protected by all sorts of guards—wolves and bears and lions—but don't be frightened by them. They will all fall at your feet. When you enter the castle, you will see my master sitting in a splendid chamber, gilded and bejeweled. He has twelve heads, and the princesses each sit on a golden chair, picking the lice from one of his heads. And that is not work they enjoy, let me tell you. You must hurry up and chop off one head after the other. If he wakes up and sees you, he will swallow you alive."

The prince went back on board the ship, taking the sword and keeping in mind what he'd been told. The others were still asleep, so he hid the sword in his bunk to make sure that neither the Red Knight nor anyone else would see it. Now the wind picked up again, and he woke the others. He told them he didn't think it was right for them to sleep any longer, for they now had such a good wind. No one had noticed that he'd been gone.

When it was three days short of seven years, everything happened just as the troll had said. Terrible weather brought a storm that lasted for three days, and when it passed, they were all so tired from working hard that they lay down to sleep. But the youngest prince rowed ashore. There the guards fell at his feet, and he was able to enter the castle.

When he entered the chamber, he found the big troll sitting there asleep, just as the troll prince had said. And the twelve princesses each sat on a chair, picking the lice from his heads. The prince motioned for the princesses to move out of the way. They pointed at the troll and motioned for the prince to turn around and leave. But he kept on gesturing for them to move out of the way, and then they understood that he wished to rescue them. Quietly, one by one, they moved aside. Quickly he chopped off all the heads of the troll king until blood gushed out in a great torrent.

After killing the troll, the prince rowed back to the ship and hid the sword. He thought that he'd done his share. He wouldn't be able to remove the body, and he wanted the others to offer a little help. So he woke them up and said it was a shame they should be lying there asleep while he'd found the princesses and rescued them from a troll. The others laughed at him and said he'd probably been asleep just like them. He'd probably slept even more soundly and merely dreamed he was such a man. If anyone was going to rescue the princesses, it would more likely be one of them.

Then the youngest prince told them everything that had happened, and they agreed to go ashore with him. As soon as they caught sight of the torrent of blood and saw the castle and the troll and the twelve heads and the princesses, they realized he'd been telling the truth. Then they helped him throw the heads and the body into the sea.

Everyone was happy. Yet none was happier than the princesses, who no longer had to sit and pick lice off the troll all day long.

Of all the gold and precious items to be found in the castle, they took as much as the ship would hold. Then they went on board, both the princes and the princesses.

After they had sailed a good distance out to sea, the king's daughters said that in the midst of their joy they had forgotten their golden crowns, which were kept in a cupboard. They would dearly like to have them. When none of the others offered to go back to get the crowns, the youngest prince said, "I've already ventured so much that I can certainly go back to get the crowns too. Just take down the sails and wait for me to return."

His brothers agreed to do that. But when the youngest prince had gone so far that they could no longer see him, the Red Knight spoke up. He wanted to be the foremost of them all and claim the youngest princess for himself. He said that it would do no good to lie at anchor and wait for the prince, for surely they realized that he would never come back. They knew, he said, that the king had given him (the Red Knight) power and authority to sail wherever he liked. Now he told them to say that he had rescued the princesses, and if anyone said otherwise, that person would lose his life. The princes didn't dare do anything except what the Red Knight wanted, and so they sailed off.

In the meantime, the youngest prince rowed ashore, went up to the castle, and found the cupboard with the golden crowns. He rolled and trundled the cupboard down to shore and lifted it into the boat. But when he rowed to the spot where he should have seen the ship, it was gone. It was nowhere in sight, and he realized what must have happened. It would be no use to try and go after the ship, so he had to turn around and row back to shore.

Of course he was afraid to spend the night alone in that castle, but there was no other shelter. He mustered his courage, locked all the doors and gates, and went to lie down in a room where a bed had been made up. But he was frightened. He grew even more fearful after he'd lain there for a while and the walls and roof began to creak and groan, as if the whole castle was about to split apart.

Suddenly something landed next to his bed, like a load of hay. Then it was quiet again. A moment later he heard a voice saying:

Don't be afraid,
I've come to your aid—
I am the griffin.

"As soon as you wake up in the morning," said the griffin, "you must go to the storehouse and get me four barrels of rye. That's what I need for my breakfast, or else I can't do a thing."

When the prince awoke, he saw an unbelievably big bird with a feather at the back of his neck that was as thick as a medium-sized beam. The prince went out to the storehouse to get four barrels of rye for the griffin. After the bird had eaten, he asked the prince to hang the cupboard with the golden crowns on one side of his neck and then take as much gold and silver to counter the weight and hang that on the other side. Then he told the prince to climb onto his back and hold on tight to his neck feather.

The bird took off, whooshing through the air, and it didn't take long before they flew near the ship. The prince wanted to go on board to get the sword. He was afraid someone might see it, and the troll had told him this must never happen. But the griffin told him to leave it be for now.

"The Red Knight won't see it," said the bird. "But if you go on board, he'll try to kill you. He wants to have the youngest princess for himself, though you needn't worry about her. She places a bare sword blade beside her in bed every night."

Finally they came to where the troll prince lived, and there the youngest prince received a reception beyond all measure. The troll couldn't think of enough to do for him, for he had slain his master and made him king. He would have gladly given the prince his daughter and half his land and kingdom.

But by now the prince had grown so fond of the youngest of the twelve princesses that he could find no peace. He wanted to set off at once. The troll begged him to remain calm for a little while longer. He told him that the ship would have to sail for almost seven years before it arrived home. About the princess, the troll said the same as the griffin. "As for her, you needn't worry. She places a bare sword blade beside her in bed. If you don't believe me," said the troll, "you can go on board when they sail past here and have a look around while you pick up the sword, for I do need to have it back."

When the ship sailed past, another storm arose, and when the prince went on board, they were all asleep. Each of the princesses lay with her prince, but the youngest of them slept alone with a bare sword blade beside her in bed. On the floor next to her bed lay the Red Knight. The prince took the sword and rowed back to shore without anyone noticing that he'd been on board.

But the prince was still restless, and he kept wanting to set off.

When the end of the seven years finally approached, with only three weeks remaining, the troll king said, "Now you can get ready to leave, seeing as you don't wish to stay here with us. You can borrow my iron boat, which travels on its own. All you have to say is: 'Boat, get going!' In the boat you'll find an iron club, which you should hold up when you see the ship appear. Then they'll have such winds that they won't even think to look for you. When you come alongside the ship, hold up the iron club again, and such a storm will arise that they'll have other things to do than keep an eye out for you. When you've passed the ship, hold up the club for a third time. But take care to always put it back down, or else such bad weather will arise that both you and they will perish. When you go ashore, you needn't concern yourself with the boat. Just shove it back in the water, turn it around, and say: 'Boat, go back the way you came!'"

When the prince was ready to leave, he was given heaps of gold and silver and other precious things, along with all the clothing and linen that the troll princess had sewn for him during so many long years. Now he was much richer than any of his brothers.

No sooner had he sat down in the boat and said, "Boat, get going!" than the boat took off.

When he caught sight of the ship right in front of him, he held up the club.

Then the winds were so fierce that his brothers forgot to keep an eye out for him. When he came alongside the ship, he once again held up the club. Then there was such a storm and such foul weather that white foam surged around the ship and the waves washed over the deck. His brothers had other things to think about than looking for him. And when he was past the ship, he held up the club for a third time. Then those on board had enough to do, and there was no time to pay attention to who he might be.

The prince reached land long, long before the ship arrived. After he'd taken all his belongings out of the boat, he shoved it back in the water, turned it around, and said, "Boat, go back the way you came!" And the boat took off.

Then he dressed as a seaman and went up to a wretched hovel where an old woman lived. He convinced her that he was a poor sailor who had been on a big ship that had gone down. He was the only one to survive. Then he asked her if she could offer shelter for both him and the things he had rescued.

"God save me," said the woman, "I can't offer anyone shelter. You can see how things are here, with nowhere to sleep even for me, much less for anyone else."

"Well, that's neither here nor there," said the seaman. If only he had a roof over his head, it didn't matter where he slept. She couldn't very well refuse him shelter when he was willing to put up with what little she could offer.

That evening he moved in all his belongings. No sooner were they inside than the old woman, who wanted to hear some news she might share with her neighbors, began asking him what sort of person he was, where he was from, where he'd been, where he was headed, what things he'd brought with him, what the purpose of his journey was, and whether he'd heard anything about the twelve princesses who had disappeared so many years ago. She asked many other questions too, for there was now plenty of time to discuss and recount. But the seaman told the woman that he was so miserable and had such a bad headache from the vile weather he'd been through that he could hardly think about anything else. She would have to allow him to rest for a few days and recover from all the hardships he'd endured. Then he'd tell her what she wanted to know, and more.

The next day the old woman again began to question and pester him, but the seaman still had such a terrible headache from the storm that he couldn't think about anything else. Yet he suddenly let slip a few words. He said that maybe he did know something about the princesses after all.

The old woman left at once to tell all the gossipmongers what she'd heard.

One after the other, they came running to ask for news of the princesses. Had he seen them, would they be coming back soon, were they on their way? And more such questions. But the seaman complained that he had such a headache from the bad weather that he couldn't make sense of anything. Yet this much he did say: If the princesses hadn't perished in the fierce storm that had raged, then they would arrive in fourteen days' time or maybe even sooner. But he couldn't say for certain whether they were still alive. Even though he'd seen them, they might have later gone down with the ship.

One of the old women rushed off to the royal palace with the news. She reported that there was a seaman staying in the hovel of a certain old woman, and he had seen the princesses, and they would probably be returning in fourteen days' time or maybe even in eight. When the king heard this, he sent word to the seaman to come and speak to him in person.

"I can't go there looking like this," said the seaman. "I don't have the proper clothes to appear before the king."

But the king's messenger said he must come. The king wanted and needed to speak to him, no matter how he looked. Until now, no one had ever been able to bring him word of the princesses.

So the seaman went to the royal palace and was brought before the king, who asked him if it was true that he had actually seen the princesses.

"Yes, I have," said the seaman, "but I don't know whether they are still alive. When I saw them, the weather was so bad that my ship went down. But if they *are* still alive, they will probably arrive in fourteen days' time or maybe sooner."

When the king heard this, he was almost beside himself with joy. As the time approached when the seaman had said his daughters might return, the king put on all his finery and went down to the shore to greet them. There was great joy in all the land when the ship arrived carrying the princesses and the princes and the Red Knight. But no one was happier than the old king, who now had his daughters back.

All eleven of the older princesses were also lively and merry, but the youngest of them, who was to have the Red Knight as her husband, wept and was filled with sorrow. The king was not pleased by this. He asked her why she was not merry and cheerful like the other princesses. There was no reason for her to sulk. After all, she had escaped the troll and was to wed a fine man, the Red Knight. She didn't dare say anything, for the Red Knight had warned the princesses that he would kill anyone who recounted what had really happened.

But one day when the princesses were sewing their wedding finery, a man came in wearing a big sailor's coat and carrying a peddler's cupboard on his back. He asked the princesses whether they'd like to buy some of his wares for their wedding. He had many exquisite and precious things, made of both gold and silver. Oh yes, they'd like to see what he had. They looked at his wares, and they looked at him, for they thought they recognized both him and many of the things in his possession.

"A man who has such costly things," said the youngest princess, "must have something that is even more precious, something that would suit us even better."

"That might well be," the peddler said.

But the others told her to shush. They reminded her what the Red Knight had threatened to do.

One day, a short time later, the princesses were sitting next to the window when the prince again appeared, wearing the big sailor's coat and carrying the cupboard with the golden crowns on his back. When he entered the great hall of the royal palace, he opened the cupboard for the princesses, and each of them recognized her crown. Then the youngest said, "I think it's only fair that the one who rescued us should have the reward he deserves. That person is not the Red Knight but this man who has brought back our golden crowns. He was the one who rescued us."

The prince cast off his sailor's coat and stood there looking much more splendid than all the others. So the old king had the Red Knight killed.

Only then was there true joy at the royal palace. Each princess married her prince, and news of their weddings spread far and wide, throughout twelve kingdoms.

The Quandary

here once was a king whose daughter stubbornly talked without ceasing, and no one was able to silence her. So he decreed that anyone who could do so would be given the princess and half the kingdom.

Three brothers heard about this and wanted to try their luck. First to try were the two older brothers, who thought they were the most clever. But they made no headway with her, and after that they were punished.

Then Ash Lad set off. After he'd gone partway, he found a loop made from a willow bough, and he picked it up. When he'd gone a little farther, he found a broken piece of crockery, and he picked that up too. When he'd gone farther still, he found a dead magpie, and a short distance away was a twisty goat horn. A bit farther on he found the matching horn. As he was approaching the royal palace, he walked across the fields where manure had been spread. There he found the worn-out sole of a shoe that had fallen off. All these things he took with him to the royal palace, where he was brought before the princess.

"Good day," he said.

"Good day," she said, squirming a bit.

"Would you mind if I fried my magpie here?" he asked.

"I'm afraid it would burst," replied the princess.

"Oh, don't worry about that. I'll wrap this loop around it," said the boy, taking out the willow bough.

"The fat will run off it," said the princess.

"I'll hold this underneath," said the boy, showing her the broken piece of crockery.

"You have such a twisty way of talking," said the princess.

"No, I'm not twisty, but this is," he said, taking out one of the horns.

"Well, I've never seen the like!" said the princess.

"Here, I'll show you the like," said the boy, and he took out the other goat horn.

"So, are you worn out from trying to silence me?" said the princess.

"No, I'm not worn out, but here's something that is," replied the boy, and he took out the shoe sole.

And with that the princess had no idea what to say.

"So now you're mine," said the boy. Then he was given the princess, along with half the realm and kingdom.

Richman Peddler Per

There once was a man they called Richman Peddler Per, for he traveled about peddling his wares and had taken in a great deal of money. This had made him a wealthy man. Richman Per had a daughter, and he was so fond of her that anyone who came to court her was turned away, for he thought none of them was good enough.

This happened to all of them, until finally no one came anymore, and as the years passed, Per feared that she would never marry.

"I'm truly puzzled," he said to his wife. "Why does no one come to court our daughter when she is so rich? It would be very strange if no one wanted to marry her. She has plenty of money, and she will have even more. I think I will go and visit the stargazers and ask them who she is meant to marry, for not a soul is coming here."

"How can the stargazers know the answer to that?" asked his wife.

"Oh, they can read everything in the stars," said Richman Per.

Taking a great deal of money with him, he set off to see the stargazers. He asked them to look at the stars and tell him which man his daughter was supposed to marry.

The stargazers looked at the stars, but they told him they couldn't see what he wanted to know. So Per urged them to look harder, and if they told him, he would pay them well.

The stargazers looked harder. Then they told him that his daughter would marry the miller's child, who had just been born at the mill, which stood below Richman Per's estate.

Per gave the stargazers a hundred *daler* for what he had learned and went back home. He thought it unreasonable that his daughter should take as her husband a man who had just come into the world and someone who was of such lowly birth. He said as much to his wife. Then he added, "I wonder whether they would sell the boy to me. Then we could get rid of him."

"Oh, I'm sure they would," said his wife. "They are poor folks, after all."

So Peddler Per went down to the mill and asked the woman whether she would sell him her son. If so, he would pay her a great deal of money. No, she wouldn't do it.

"I can't understand why you won't," said Peddler Per. "I see nothing but misery here, and I doubt very much the boy will make things any easier."

But the woman was very fond of her son, and she didn't want to lose him.

When the miller came in, Per said the same thing to him and promised to give them six hundred *daler* for the boy. Then they would be able to buy themselves a farm and give up having to grind grain for others or starve when there was no mill water. The miller was pleased with this. He talked to his wife, and then Richman Per was given the boy. The mother wept and carried on, but Per consoled her by saying that the boy would be treated well. Yet they had to promise not to ask after him, for Per intended to send him far away to other lands where he would learn foreign languages.

When Peddler Per came home with the boy, he had a small chest made that was so finely crafted it was a pleasure to behold. He filled the cracks with pitch and placed the miller's boy inside. Then he put the lid back on and set the chest in the river, where the current carried it away.

Now I'm rid of him, thought Peddler Per.

But when the chest had floated a great distance along the river, it shot into the waterway of another mill. There it got stuck in the waterwheel and caused the mill to stop turning. When the man went down to see what had happened to stop the mill, he found the chest and took it back with him. When he came home to his wife at midday, he told her, "I certainly wonder what could be inside this chest. It came racing down to the waterwheel through the mill stream today and stopped the mill."

"Well, we'll soon find out," said his wife. "The key is sitting in the lock. Let's open it."

When they opened the chest, they found inside the most beautiful child anyone had ever seen, and they were so happy that they wanted to keep the boy. They had no children of their own, and they were so old by now that they couldn't expect to have any.

After some time had passed, Peddler Per again began to wonder whether anyone would ever come to court his daughter, for she was so rich and had so much money. But no one came.

Again he went to see the stargazers and offered them a great deal of money if they could tell him who his daughter was to marry.

"We've already told you that she will marry the miller's boy from below your estate," said the stargazers.

"You may well have said that," Peddler Per replied, "but something has happened to him, and he's no longer alive. So if I could find out who my daughter will marry, I will gladly give you two hundred *daler*."

The stargazers looked at the stars again, but then they grew angry and said, "Nevertheless, she will marry the miller's boy, the one you set in the river. You hoped to put an end to him, but he is still alive. He is living at the mill that is a certain distance away."

Peddler Per gave them two hundred *daler* for this prophecy while he pondered how to get rid of the miller's boy.

When he got home, the first thing Peddler Per did was to pay a visit to the other mill. By now the boy was old enough that he had been confirmed. He helped out at the mill, and a handsome lad he was.

"Couldn't you let me have that boy?" Peddler Per asked the miller.

"No, I can't," he replied. "I've brought him up as my own son. He has turned out so well that now he can be useful and help me at the mill, for I'm starting to grow old and frail."

"Oh, the same thing is happening to me," said Peddler Per. "That's why I'd like to have someone I could train as a peddler. If you would let me have the boy, I'll give you six hundred *daler*. Then you can buy yourself a farm and spend your old age in peace and quiet."

Well, when the miller heard that, he let Peddler Per have the boy. The two of them then traveled far and wide, peddling their wares, until they came to an inn that stood at the edge of a great forest. From there Per sent the boy home with a letter for his wife—it wasn't far through the woods. He told the boy to tell his wife to do what it said in the letter as quickly as possible.

The letter said that she should light a big bonfire at once and throw the miller's boy onto it. If she didn't do this, she herself would be burned alive.

The boy took the letter and set off through the woods. Toward evening, he came to a farm deep in the forest, and he went inside. He found no one at home, but in one room a bed had been made up, so he stretched out on top of it. He had stuck the letter in his hatband, and he placed the hat over his face.

When the robbers came home—for twelve robbers lived on that farm— they saw the boy lying on the bed. They wondered who he could be. One of them picked up the letter, tore open the envelope, and read what it said.

"Hmm, hmm," he said. "This is Peddler Per's handiwork. Let's play a trick on him. It would be a shame for that old scoundrel to put an end to such a handsome young boy."

So the robbers wrote another letter to Peddler Per's wife and stuck it back in the hatband while the boy slept. The letter said that she should hold a wedding at once for her daughter and the miller's boy. She should also give them horses and cattle and all manner of tools and set them up properly on the farm that Peddler Per owned on the mountainside. If this was not done before he arrived home, she would be punished.

The next day the robbers sent the boy off. When he came to the peddler's house, he gave the woman the letter. He told her he brought greetings from Peddler Per, who said she should do what it said in the letter, and as quick as could be.

"You must have served him well for him to write this to me," the peddler's wife told the miller's boy. "When the two of you set off, he was so angry that he couldn't get rid of you fast enough."

Then she held the wedding at once and set him up with horses and cattle and all manner of tools on the farm on the mountainside.

Not long afterward Peddler Per returned home. The first thing he asked his wife was whether she'd done what he'd written in the letter.

"Well, I thought it was strange, but I didn't dare do anything else," she said.

Then Per asked her where his daughter was.

"You know very well where she is," said his wife. "She's with the boy on the farm on the mountainside, just as it said in your letter."

When Peddler Per heard what had happened and had a look at the letter, he was so furious that he was about to explode. He set off at once for the farm where the young folks lived.

"It may well be, my son, that you've won my daughter," he told the miller's boy. "But if you plan to keep her, you have to go to the dragon of Dybenfart and bring me back three of his tail feathers. Whoever has those feathers can get whatever he wants."

"Where will I find him?" asked his son-in-law.

"You'll have to figure that out for yourself, for I have no idea," said Peddler Per.

The boy confidently set off.

After he'd walked for a while he came to a royal palace. I think I'll go in here and ask, he thought to himself. These sorts of folk are more familiar with the world than others, and they may be able to tell me where to go.

The king asked him where he was from and what was the purpose of his journey.

"I must go to the dragon of Dybenfart and get three tail feathers from him. If only I knew where to find him," said the boy.

The king wished him luck with that. "I've never heard of anyone who has come back from there," he said. "But if you do see the dragon, you might ask him from me why I can't get fresh water in my well. I've pondered it time after time, but I've never had fresh water."

"I'll do that," said the boy.

He enjoyed a good visit at the royal palace, and he was given money and provisions when he left.

Toward evening he came to another royal palace. When he went into the kitchen, the king came to him and asked where he was from and what was the purpose of his journey.

"I'm going to the dragon of Dybenfart to get three tail feathers from him," said the boy.

"I wish you luck with that," said the king. "I've never heard of anyone coming back from there. But if you do go there, could you ask the dragon where my daughter is? She disappeared many years ago," he said. "I've had inquiries made through the churches, but no one has been able to tell me anything about her."

"I'll do that," said the boy.

He enjoyed a good visit at the royal palace, and when he left, he was given money and provisions.

When evening approached, he came to yet another royal palace. Here the queen came into the kitchen and asked him where he was from and what was the purpose of his journey.

"I'm going to the dragon of Dybenfart to get three tail feathers from him," said the boy.

"I wish you luck with that," said the queen. "I've never heard of anyone who has come back from there. But if you do meet the dragon, could you ask him from me where I might find the golden keys I've lost?"

"I'll do that," said the boy.

After he'd walked for a while, he came to a big, wide river. He stood there, wondering how to get across or whether he should walk along the shore. Then an old, hunched man appeared and asked him where he was headed.

"I'm going to see the dragon of Dybenfart, if only somebody could tell me where I might find him."

"I can tell you that," said the man. "It's my job to take across the river anyone who wants to see him. He lives right over there. As soon as you get to the top of the hill, you'll see his castle. If you speak to him, you could also ask him from me how long I have to stay here and take folks across the river."

"I'll do that," said the boy.

Then the man put the boy on his back and carried him across the river. When the boy came to the top of the hill, he saw the castle and went inside.

The princess was home alone.

"Oh, my dear sir! How would a Christian man like you dare to come here?" she said. "I haven't seen anyone like you since I arrived. It's probably best you leave as soon as you can, for when the dragon returns home, he will smell you. Then he'll swallow you up at once, and you'll bring misfortune upon me too."

"No," said the boy, "I can't leave until I get three tail feathers from the dragon."

"That you will never get," said the princess.

But the boy refused to leave. He wanted to wait for the dragon and get the tail feathers and the answers to all his questions.

"Well, since you're so stubborn, let me see if I can help you," said the princess. "Go and see if you can lift the sword hanging on the wall over there."

No, the boy couldn't budge it.

"Then take a swig from this flask," said the princess.

After the boy had rested for a while, he tried again, and he was able to move the sword a little.

"Take another swig," said the princess, "and then tell me the purpose of your journey."

He took another swig and then told her that a king wanted him to ask the dragon why he couldn't get fresh water in his well. Another king wanted him to ask what had happened to his daughter, who had been gone for many years now. And a queen wanted him to ask the dragon what had become of her golden keys. Finally, the ferryman wanted him to ask the dragon how long he had to stay there, taking folks across the river. Now when the boy seized hold of the sword, he was able to lift it. After taking yet another swig, he was able to swing it.

"If you don't want the dragon to kill you at once, you need to crawl under the bed," said the princess, as evening approached. "He will soon return home, and you must lie there very quietly so he won't notice you. After we've gone to bed, I will ask him your questions. Listen well and remember what he says. But stay under the bed until all is silent and the dragon falls asleep. Then crawl out quietly and bring the sword with you. When the dragon gets up, you have to chop off his head with one blow. Then quickly snatch off the three tail feathers, or else he'll tear them off himself and no one will be able to make use of them."

A short time after the boy had crept under the bed, the dragon came home.

"I smell the bones of a Christian man!" said the dragon.

"Oh yes, a raven came flying with a man's leg in its beak and landed on the roof," said the princess. "That must be what you smell."

"I see," said the dragon.

The princess served dinner, and after they had eaten, they went to bed. But when they'd lain there for a while, the princess began tossing and turning, and all of a sudden she woke up.

"Oh my!" she said.

"What's wrong?" asked the dragon.

"Oh, I was sleeping so badly," said the princess. "I had such a strange dream."

"What did you dream?" asked the dragon.

"I thought a king came here and asked you what he should do to get fresh water in his well," said the princess.

"Oh, he should be able to figure that out himself," said the dragon. "When he digs out the well and removes the old rotten beam lying at the bottom, then he'll have fresh water again. But go back to sleep and don't dream anymore."

After the princess had lain there for a while, she grew restless again and began tossing and turning in bed. Then she woke up.

"Oh my!"

"What is it now?" said the dragon.

"Oh, I was sleeping so badly, and then I had such a strange dream," said the princess.

"You're certainly having a lot of dreams," said the dragon. "What did you dream now?"

"I thought a king came here and asked you what happened to his daughter, who disappeared many years ago," said the princess.

"That was you," said the dragon. "But he'll never see you again. And now I beg you, let me have some peace tonight. Don't lie there dreaming anymore, or I'll have to break your ribs."

The princess hadn't lain there long before she began thrashing about again. And all of a sudden she woke up.

"Oh my!" she said.

"What is it now! What's going on?" said the dragon. By then he was so wild from lack of sleep that he was about to fly into a rage.

"Oh, you mustn't be mad," said the princess. "I had such a strange dream."

"What a cursed number of dreams you're having! What was it you dreamed this time?" said the dragon.

"I thought a queen came here and asked you where she might find the golden keys that she'd lost."

"Oh, she should take a look in the bushes where she once lay. She's certain to remember that time quite well. That's where she'll find the keys," said the dragon. "Now spare me from any more of your dreams."

They slept for a while, but once again the princess grew uneasy, and all of a sudden she woke up.

"Oh my!"

"You'd better watch out or I'll break your neck," said the dragon. "By now he was so angry that sparks were flying off him. "What is it this time?"

"Oh, you really mustn't be mad at me. I can't help it," said the princess. "I had such a strange dream."

"There seems to be no end to your dreaming," said the dragon. "So what did you dream?"

"I thought the ferryman down at the river came to ask you how long he had to stay there, carrying folks across," said the princess.

"That stupid beast, he can easily escape," said the dragon. "When someone shows up and wants to go across, he should throw the man in the middle of the river and say: 'Now it's your turn to carry folks across until somebody comes to take your place!' But don't tell me any more of your dreams, or you'll be singing a different tune."

So the princess let him sleep.

As soon as it was quiet and the miller's boy heard the dragon snoring, he crept out.

Before daylight, the dragon got up, but he had hardly put his feet on the floor before the boy chopped off his head and snatched off the three tail feathers. Then there was great joy, and both the boy and the princess took as much as they could carry of silver and gold and coins and other treasures.

When they got down to the river the ferryman was very surprised to see everything he had to carry across. That's why he forgot to ask what the dragon had said until the boy and the princess and all their belongings were on the opposite bank.

"Oh, that's right," the ferryman said as they were about to leave. "Did you ask the dragon what I wanted to know?"

"Yes," said the boy. "He said that when someone comes here and wants to go across, you should throw that person into the middle of the river and say: 'Now it's your turn to carry folks across until somebody comes to take your place.' Then you'll be free."

"Oh, blast you!" said the ferryman. "If you'd told me that before, you'd be the one taking my place."

When they came to the first royal palace, the queen asked the boy whether the dragon knew where she could find her golden keys.

"Yes," said the boy, and he whispered to the queen, "He said that you should look in the bushes where you once lay. You're certain to remember that time quite well."

"Shush, shush," said the queen, and she gave the boy a hundred *daler*.

When the boy came to the second royal palace, the king asked whether he'd mentioned to the dragon what he wanted to know.

"Yes," said the boy, "and here is your daughter."

Then the king was so happy that he would gladly have given the princess and half his kingdom to the miller's boy. But the boy was already married, so he was given instead two hundred *daler* and a horse and wagon and as much gold and silver as it would hold.

When the boy came to the third royal palace, the king came out to ask whether he'd mentioned to the dragon what he wanted to know.

"Yes," replied the boy. "He said you should dig up the well and remove the old, rotten beam lying at the bottom. Then you'll have plenty of fresh water."

And the king gave him three hundred *daler*.

From there the boy traveled home. He was so laden with gold and silver and looked so splendid that he practically glowed. Now he was much richer than Peddler Per.

When Per received the dragon feathers he was no longer opposed to the marriage. But when he saw all the wealth, he asked the boy whether he'd gotten all these treasures from the dragon.

"Yes," said the boy. "And there was much more than I could carry away. There's so much left that it would fill many wagons. If you want to go there, I'm sure there's plenty for you too."

Well, Peddler Per did wish to go there.

Then his son-in-law gave him such good directions that he wouldn't have to ask the way.

"As for the horses," said the boy, "it's best if you leave them on this side of the river. The old ferryman can carry you across."

When Per left, he took along many provisions and many horses, but he left everything near the river, just as the boy had told him to do. Then the ferryman hoisted Per onto his back. When they had gone a short distance, he threw Per into the middle of the river and said, "Now it's your turn to stay here and carry folks across until somebody comes to take your place!"

And if no one has come to take his place, then Richman Peddler Per is still out there today, waiting to carry folks across the river.

Ash Lad, Who Competed with the Troll

There once was a farmer who had three sons. He was living in dire cicumstances, he was old and frail, and his sons refused to do any work. A splendid big forest belonged to the farm, and the father wanted the boys to fell some of the trees in order to pay his debts.

At long last he got them to agree, and the eldest was to set off first to chop down trees. When he got to the forest and began hacking at an old and bearded spruce, a monstrous big troll came over to him.

"If you chop down any trees in my forest, I will kill you!" said the troll.

When the boy heard this, he threw down his axe and ran back home as fast as he could go. He arrived out of breath and reported what had happened. But his father said that the boy had the heart of a rabbit. The trolls had never scared him away from chopping wood when *he* was young.

The next day the second son set off, but the same thing happened to him. After he'd made several hacks in the spruce, the troll came over to him too and said, "If you chop down any trees in my forest, I will kill you!"

The boy hardly dared even look at the troll. He threw down his axe and took off, just as his brother had done, running as fast as he could go. When he came back home, his father was angry and said that the trolls had never frightened him away when *he* was young.

On the third day Ash Lad was about to set off.

"You!" said his two older brothers. "How do you think you'll be able to complete such a task? You've never even set foot outside the house."

Ash Lad said nothing in reply. He merely asked for plenty of provisions to take along. His mother had no sour milk to give him, so she leaned over the pot to curdle some into cheese for him. He put it in his sack and left.

After he'd been chopping for a short time, the troll came over to him too and said, "If you chop down any trees in my forest, I will kill you!"

But the boy didn't hesitate. He ran into the forest to get the cheese from his bag and squeezed it so hard that the whey burst out.

"If you don't shut up," he shouted at the troll, "I'll squeeze you just like I'm squeezing water out of this white rock!"

"Oh no, spare me, my friend," said the troll, "and I'll help you chop down some trees."

Well, on that condition the boy spared him. The troll was an expert with the axe, so they felled and chopped dozens of trees that day.

As evening approached, the troll said, "You're welcome to come home with me, for it's closer to my house than yours."

And that's what the boy did. When they reached the troll's house, they had to make a fire in the fireplace and the boy was supposed to get water for the porridge pot. But the two iron buckets were so big and heavy that he couldn't even budge them.

Then the boy said, "It's not worth carrying mere thimbles like these. I'm going to bring back the whole well."

"Oh no, my dear friend," said the troll. "I don't want to lose my well. You make the fire, and I'll get the water."

When he came back with the water, they made a big pot of porridge.

"It's neither here nor there," said the boy, "but if you're like-minded, how about having an eating contest?"

"Oh yes!" replied the troll. He'd always thought he would be good at that.

So they sat down at the table. Unnoticed, the boy picked up his leather sack and held it in front of him. Then he poured more of the porridge into the sack than what he actually ate. When the sack was full, he got out his sheath knife and cut a slit in it. The troll looked at him but didn't say a word.

After they'd been eating for a long time, the troll put down his spoon. "Oh, I can't eat another bite," he said.

"You have to eat!" replied the boy. "I'm only half full. Do what I did and slice a hole in your stomach. Then you'll be able to eat much more."

"But won't that hurt horribly?" asked the troll.

"Oh, it's nothing even worth mentioning," replied the boy.

So the troll did as the boy said, and as you might imagine, that proved the death of him. Then the boy took all the gold and silver he found there inside the mountain and went back home. And of course he now had plenty to pay the debts.

About the Boy Who Went to the North Wind and Demanded the Flour Back

There once was an old woman who had a son. She was very feeble and frail, so the boy was supposed to go out to the storehouse to get some flour for her to make porridge for dinner. But when he came out onto the steps of the storehouse, the North Wind rushed over to him, grabbed the flour, and flew with it through the air. The boy went back inside the storehouse to get some more, but when he came out onto the steps, the North Wind again rushed over to him and grabbed the flour. The same thing happened a third time. That made the boy mad. He thought it was unreasonable for the North Wind to behave like that, so he decided to seek out the wind and demand the flour back.

Then he set off, but it was a long way. He walked and walked, until finally he came to the North Wind.

"Good day," said the boy. "Good seeing you again."

"Good day," replied the North Wind—his voice was rough. "Good seeing you too. What do you want?" he said.

"Oh," said the boy, "I want to ask if you'd kindly return the flour you took from me on the storehouse steps. We don't have much, and when you behave like that, taking what little we have, there's nothing for us to do but starve to death."

"I don't have any flour," said the North Wind. "But seeing as you're in such great need, I'll give you a tablecloth that will bring you whatever you want. All you have to say is: 'Cloth, spread out and let me see all manner of costly foods!'"

The boy was quite happy with that. But it was such a long way back that he wouldn't be able to reach home that day, so he stopped at an inn. When he saw that the folks there were about to eat supper, he placed the cloth on the table in the corner and said, "Cloth, spread out and let me see all manner of costly foods!"

No sooner did he say those words than the cloth did as he asked, and everybody thought it was a wondrous thing. But no one was more pleased than the innkeeper's wife. With that sort of tablecloth, she thought, I wouldn't have to bother with frying and boiling, with placing and setting, or with serving and clearing away.

As night fell and everyone went to sleep, she took the boy's tablecloth and replaced it with another that looked exactly the same as the one the North Wind had given him, though it couldn't produce even oat *lefse*.

When the boy awoke, he gathered up his tablecloth and went on his way. That day he returned home to his mother.

"So," he said, "I've been to see the North Wind. He was a reasonable man, for he gave me this tablecloth. When I say: 'Cloth, spread out and let me see all manner of costly foods!' then I will have everything I could ever want to eat."

"Well, that may be," said his mother, "but I won't believe it until I see it."

The boy hurried to sit down at the table. There he set the cloth and said, "Cloth, spread out and let me see all manner of costly foods!"

But the cloth didn't produce so much as a scrap of crispbread.

"Well, there's nothing for it. I'll just have to go and see the North Wind again," said the boy. And he set off. Late in the afternoon he arrived at the home of the North Wind.

"Good evening," said the boy.

"Good evening," said the North Wind.

"I want payment for the flour you took from me," said the boy. "That tablecloth you gave me wasn't worth much."

"I don't have any flour," said the North Wind, "but here is a goat that will make gold ducats. All you have to say is: 'My goat, make coins!'"

The boy was happy with that, but it was such a long way back that he wouldn't be able to reach home that day, so he again took lodging at the inn. Before he asked for anything, he tried out the goat, for he wanted to see if it was true, what the North Wind had said. And it turned out to be true enough. But when the innkeeper saw what happened, he thought it was a splendid goat. So when the boy was sound asleep, the innkeeper put in its place another goat that did not make gold ducats.

The next morning the boy went on his way. When he returned home to his mother, he said, "The North Wind is a kind man after all. He gave me a goat that can make gold ducats. All I have to say is: 'My goat, make coins!'"

"Well, that may be," said his mother, "but it could be nothing but talk. I won't believe it until I see it."

"My goat, make coins!" said the boy, but what the goat made was not coins.

Again he went to see the North Wind. He told him the goat was worthless and he wanted payment for the flour.

"Well, I have nothing more to give you," said the North Wind, "except for that old stick in the corner. When you say: 'My stick, strike!' it will keep on striking until you say: 'My stick, stop!'"

Again it was a long way home, so the boy stopped at the inn that night as well. He now realized what must have happened to the tablecloth and the goat, so when he lay down on the bench, he began to snore at once and pretended to be asleep. The innkeeper could tell that the stick also had certain powers. He found another stick that looked the same and was about to swap them, for he could hear the boy snoring. But just as the innkeeper was about to take the stick, the boy shouted, "My stick, strike!"

And the stick began hitting the innkeeper, making him jump over tables and benches as he shouted and screamed, "Oh, good Lord! Oh, good Lord! Make the stick stop, or it will beat me to death! I'll give you back the tablecloth and the goat!"

When the boy decided the innkeeper had suffered enough, he said, "My stick, stop!" Then he stuffed the tablecloth in his pocket, picked up the stick, tied a rope around the goat's horns, and took everything home. That was proper payment for the flour!

The Virgin Mary As Godmother

There once was a poor couple who lived far, far away in a great forest. The wife gave birth to a beautiful daughter, but they were so poor that they didn't know how they could afford to have the child christened.

One day the husband went out to seek godparents who might be able to pay for the christening. He walked all day, going from one person to another. All of them said they would gladly be a godparent, though none of them had any money to pay for the christening.

In the evening, as he was headed back home, he met a lovely lady who wore splendid clothing and looked both kind and good. She offered to have the child christened, but afterward she would keep the girl.

The man replied that he must first ask his wife what she wanted to do. When he got home and told his wife, she said no at once.

The next day the man went out again, but no one wanted to be godparent if they had to pay for the christening. No matter how much he pleaded, it did no good.

That evening as he headed for home, he again met the lovely lady who looked so gentle, and she made the same offer. Again he told his wife what had happened. She said that if the next day he could find no godparent, then they would have to let the lady take the child, seeing as she looked so kind and good.

On the third day the man went out, but he found no one to be godparent. In the evening when he again met the kind lady, he promised to give her the child if she would have her baptized and made a Christian.

In the morning the lady came to the man's house. She was accompanied by two gentlemen, and all three carried the child off to church, where she was christened. Then the lady took the child home with her. There the little girl lived for many years, and her foster mother was always good and kind to her.

When the girl was old enough to begin to understand things, her foster mother made ready to go away for a while.

"You're allowed to go into all the rooms, wherever you like," she told the girl, "except for the three chambers that I will show you now."

And then she left.

The girl couldn't resist peeking into one of the chambers. *Whoosh!* Out flew a star.

When the lady came back, she was angry with her foster daughter and threatened to send her away. But the child wept and pleaded, so she was allowed to stay.

After a while the foster mother had to go away again, and once more she forbade the girl to go into the two chambers that she had never entered before. The girl promised to obey, but after she'd been alone for a time, wondering and pondering what there might be inside the second chamber, she couldn't resist opening the door a crack to peek inside. *Whoosh!* Out flew the moon.

When the foster mother came back and saw that the moon had slipped out, she was greatly distressed. She told the girl that she could no longer keep her. She would have to send her away.

But the girl wept so bitterly and pleaded so nicely that once more she was allowed to stay.

After a while the foster mother had to go away again, and this time she sternly warned the girl, who by now was nearly grown, that she must not try to enter or look inside the third chamber.

When her foster mother had been gone for a while, and the girl had been alone for long enough to feel bored, she thought: How fun it would be to look inside the third chamber! At first she didn't think she would do it, for her foster mother had warned her not to. But the second time the idea occurred to her, she could no longer resist. She thought she would, she must, look inside that chamber. So she cracked open the door. *Whoosh!* Out flew the sun.

When the foster mother came back this time and saw that the sun had flown out, she was deeply distressed. She said that now the girl would not be allowed to stay. The foster child wept and pleaded even more nicely than before, but it did no good.

"No, now I will have to punish you," said her foster mother. "I will give you a choice: you can either become the most beautiful woman but unable to speak, or you can become the ugliest woman and able to speak. Either way, leave me you must."

The girl said, "Then I choose to be beautiful." And that's what she was, though from that moment she was mute.

After leaving her foster mother, the girl wandered into a big, big forest. No matter how far she walked, the woods never ended. As evening approached, she climbed up into a tall tree that stood right next to a spring. There she settled down to spend the night.

Close by was a castle, and early the next morning a maid came out of the castle to get water from the spring to make tea for the prince. The maid saw a lovely face in the spring and thought she was looking at herself. Then she threw away the water bucket and ran back, tossing her head and saying, "If I'm that lovely, then I'm much too good to be carrying buckets of water." Someone else would have to go and get the water, and she didn't care who that might be. When she got back, she said she was too beautiful to go to the spring to get water for the prince.

Then the prince went there himself, for he wanted to find out what had happened. When he reached the spring, he too saw the image in the water, and he looked up at once. There he caught sight of the lovely girl sitting in the tree. He enticed her down and took her home with him. He dearly wanted her to be his queen, for she was so beautiful. Yet his mother, who was still alive, was not as certain. "The girl can't speak," she said. "She might well be a troll person."

But the prince refused to be satisfied until the girl was his.

After they'd lived together for a while, she was expecting a child. When she was about to give birth, the prince ordered a big group of guards to watch over her. Yet when the hour of birth neared, all the guards fell asleep. After the child was born, the girl's foster mother appeared and made a cut in the child's little finger. Then she smeared the blood on the young queen's lips and fingers, saying to her, "Now you shall be as distressed as I was when you let out the star." And then she left, taking the child with her.

When those who had been ordered to stand guard awoke, they thought the queen had eaten her own child. The old queen wanted to have her burned at the stake, but the prince was so dearly fond of her. In the end his pleas saved her from punishment, though just barely.

The second time the young queen was about to give birth, twice as many guards were ordered to keep watch. The same thing happened as before, except that the foster mother said, "Now you will be as distressed as I was when you let out the moon."

The young queen begged and pleaded—because when her foster mother was there, she was able to speak—but it did no good. Now the old queen really wanted to have her burned at the stake, but once again the prince's pleas set her free.

When the young queen was about to give birth for the third time, the guards around her were tripled, but the same thing happened as before. The foster mother came while the guards slept, cut the child's little finger, and smeared the blood on the queen's lips. Then she said that the queen would now be as distressed as she had been when the sun was let out.

This time the prince could do nothing to save his young queen. She would and must be burned at the stake.

But just as she was being led to the bonfire, the foster mother arrived with all three children. Two of them held hands as she led them forward. The third child she carried in her arms. She went over to the young queen and said, "Here are your children. I am giving them back to you now. I am the Virgin Mary, and as distressed as you have been, that was how I felt when you let out the sun, the moon, and the star. Now you have suffered enough for what you did, and from now on you will be able to speak."

Everyone can surely imagine, though no one can really say, how happy the young queen and her prince were after that. Since that time they have always been happy, and from that day on, even the prince's mother was fond of the young queen.

The Three Princesses
in White Land

There once was a fisherman who lived close to a castle and caught fish for the king's table. One day when he was out fishing, he caught nothing at all. No matter what he did with his fishing pole and line, he caught not even a bone on his hook. But as the day wore on, a head popped out of the water and said, "If you'll give me what your wife carries under her belt, you will have plenty of fish." The man quickly agreed, for he didn't know that she was expecting a child.

That day he did catch fish after all, as many as he could ever want. When he got home that evening and told his wife how he'd managed to catch so many fish, she began to wail and weep. She asked God to save and preserve her from the promise her husband had made, for she told him now that she carried a child under her belt.

Word soon reached the castle that the woman was greatly distressed. When the king heard about this and asked the cause, he promised to take in the child to make sure it was safe.

The days came and went. When it was time, the woman gave birth to a son. Then the king took him in and raised him as his own until the boy was fully grown.

One day the boy asked for permission to accompany his fisherman father when he went out fishing. He said he had such a deep yearning to do that. The king was reluctant to agree, but in the end the boy was granted permission. He set off with his father, and things went fine all day, until they came ashore in the evening. That's when the boy noticed that he'd forgotten his handkerchief, and he wanted to go back to the boat to get it. But the instant he climbed in, the boat started moving so fast on its own that water surged all around. No matter how hard the boy pulled on the oars, it did no good. The boat kept going all night, and finally the boy ended up far, far away and close to a white beach. There he went ashore. After he'd walked for a while, he met an old man with a long white beard.

"What is this place called?" asked the boy.

"White Land," replied the man. Then he asked the boy where he was from and where he was headed, and the boy told him.

"Well," said the man, "if you continue on along the shore, you'll come upon three princesses who are buried in the ground so only their heads are visible. The first one—she's the eldest—will call to you and ask you ever so nicely to come and help her. The second princess will do the same. But don't go over to either of them. Hurry past them, as if you don't hear or see them. Then go over to the third princess and do as she asks. That will bring you good fortune, yes it will."

When the boy came to the first of the princesses, she called to him and asked him ever so nicely to come and help her. But he walked past as if he didn't see her. He did the same with the second. Then he went over to the third princess.

"If you'll do as I say, you can have any of us you like," said the princess.

He agreed gladly, so she told him that three trolls had buried all three princesses in the ground. Before that, they lived in the castle he could see in the forest.

"Go into the castle and let the trolls beat you—one night for each of us," she said. "If you manage to endure all that, you will rescue us."

"All right," replied the boy, and he agreed to try.

"When you go inside," the princess went on, "you'll find two lions standing in the doorway, but if you walk right between them, they won't harm you. Then go straight ahead into a small, dark room. That's where you must lie down. Then a troll will come and beat you. But take the flask that is hanging on the wall and smear what's inside on the places where he struck you. Then you'll be as good as new. Grab the sword that is hanging next to the flask and strike the troll dead."

He agreed to do as the princess said. He walked between the lions as if he didn't see them and went straight into the small chamber, where he lay down.

On the first night a troll with three heads and three whips came and beat the boy terribly. But he bore it bravely, and when the troll was done, the boy took what was inside the flask and smeared it on himself. Then he grabbed the sword and struck the troll dead.

When he went out the next morning, the princesses were still stuck in the ground, but only up to their waists.

The second night proceeded in the same way. But this troll had six heads and six whips, and he beat the boy even worse than the first one had done.

When the boy came out in the morning, the princesses were still stuck in the ground, but only up to their calves.

On the third night the troll who appeared had nine heads and nine whips, and he beat and lashed the boy for so long that he finally fainted. Then the troll picked up the boy and threw him against the wall, making the flask fall down. What was inside poured all over the boy so he was as good as new. Then he didn't hesitate. He grabbed the sword and struck the troll dead.

That morning when he came out of the castle, the princesses were no longer stuck in the ground. Then he took the youngest of them as his queen, and they lived happily and well for a long time.

But eventually he longed to go home for a while to see his parents. His queen was not pleased about this, but his longing was so great that he'd decided to leave, and leave he must. Then she said to him, "You must promise me one thing. You will do only what your father asks you. Not what your mother asks."

He promised.

Then she gave him a ring and said that anyone who wore such a ring could wish for any two things he liked.

So he wished that he was home. His parents could hardly believe how splendid and handsome he looked.

After he'd been home for a few days, his mother wanted him to go up to the castle to show the king what a man he'd become.

His father said, "No, that's not something he should do, for when he's there, we'll miss the pleasure of his company."

But it did no good. His mother begged and pleaded for so long that the young king agreed to go. When he came up to the castle, he looked more splendid in his clothes and his bearing than the other king, who wasn't terribly pleased about this. He said, "Well, here you can see what my queen looks like, but I can't see yours. Your queen must not be so lovely after all."

"If only she stood here now, you would see for yourself!" said the young king, and in a flash, there she stood.

But his queen was greatly distressed and said to him, "Why didn't you obey me and heed what your father said? Now I'll have to go right back home, and you've used up both of your wishes."

And with that she tied a ring in his hair that was engraved with her name. Then she wished herself home.

The young king was deeply distressed. Day in and day out he thought only about how to get back home to his queen.

I need to see if I can find out where White Land is, he thought. And he set off into the world.

After he'd walked for a while, he came to a mountain. There he met a man who was master of all the animals in the forest—for they came whenever he blew on his horn. The young king asked him about White Land.

"I don't know," the man replied, "but I'll ask my animals." Then he summoned them by blowing on his horn. He asked if any of them knew where White Land was, but none of them did.

Then the man gave the young king a pair of skis. "When you put these on," he said, "they'll take you to my brother, who lives a thousand miles from here. He's master of all the birds in the sky, so ask him! When you get there, just turn the skis around to make the tips point this way, and they'll go home all on their own."

When the young king arrived, he turned the skis around, just as the master of the animals had said, and they went back home.

Again he asked about White Land. The man blew on his horn to summon all the birds, and then he asked if any of them knew where White Land was. No, none of them did. Long after the others had arrived, an old eagle appeared. She had been gone for close to ten years, but even she didn't know.

"Well, well," said the man, "I'm going to lend you a pair of skis. When you put them on, they'll take you to my brother, who lives a thousand miles from here. He is the master of all the fish in the sea, so you should ask him. But don't forget to turn the skis around!"

The young king thanked him and put on the skis. When he came to the master of all the fish in the sea, he turned the skis around, and they went back home just like the others had done. Again he asked about White Land.

The man blew on his horn to summon all the fish, but none of them knew anything. Finally an old, old pike appeared. It had taken the man great effort to summon her. When the young king asked the pike his question, she said, "Oh yes, I know it well. That's where I've been the cook these past ten years. Tomorrow I'll be going back because the queen, whose king disappeared, is going to marry another."

"If that's the case, let me give you some advice," said the man to the young king. "Over in the marsh are three brothers who have been out there for a hundred years, arguing over a hat, a walking stick, and a pair of boots. Anyone who acquires all three things will be able to make himself invisible and wish himself as far away as he likes. Tell them you want to try out the three things, and afterward you'll settle the dispute for them."

The young king thanked the man and did just as he'd said.

"What is it you've been arguing about forever and a day?" he said to the brothers. "Let me try out those things, and afterward I'll settle the dispute for you."

They gladly agreed. But when he'd been given the hat, the walking stick, and the boots, the young king said, "The next time we meet, I'll tell you my decision." And with that he wished himself away.

As he flew through the air, he happened upon the North Wind.

"Where are you headed?" asked the North Wind.

"To White Land," said the young king, and with that he told the North Wind what had happened.

"Well," said the North Wind, "I can certainly get you there a little faster. I'll send blasts and gusts into every corner. When you get there, stand on the steps next to the door, and I'll come rushing over as if I want to blow down the whole castle. When the prince who is supposed to marry your queen comes out to see what's going on, seize him by the scruff of the neck and throw him out. Then I'll do my best to whisk him away."

The young king did just as the North Wind had said. He stood on the steps when the North Wind came in, racing and roaring and pounding against the wall of the castle so it shook. Then the prince came out to see what was going on. Instantly the young king seized him by the scruff of the neck and threw him out. Then the North Wind carried him off.

After the young king was rid of the prince, he went inside the castle.

At first the queen didn't recognize him, for he had grown thin and pale from wandering so long and suffering such sorrow. But when he showed her the ring, she was overjoyed. Then a proper wedding was celebrated, and news of their marriage spread far and wide.

Some Women Are Like That

There once was a man and a woman who were going to sow their fields, but they had no seeds and no money to buy any. All they had was a single cow. The man was supposed to go into town to sell the cow to get money for seeds. But when it came right down to it, the woman didn't dare let her husband go. She was afraid he'd drink up all the money. She decided to set off with the cow herself, and she took along a hen as well.

Close to town she met a butcher. "Are you going to sell that cow, ma'am?" he asked.

"Yes, I certainly am," she said.

"How much do you want for it?"

"I'd need to have a *mark* for the cow, but you can have the hen for ten *daler*," she said.

"Well," he replied, "I have no use for the hen, and I'm sure you can sell it when you get to town. But I'll give you a *mark* for the cow."

So she sold him the cow, and he gave her a *mark*. But nobody in town wanted to pay ten *daler* for a scrawny and mangy hen.

Then she went back to the butcher and said, "I can't get rid of this hen, sir! You'd better take it off my hands, since you already took the cow."

"I'm sure we can manage that," said the butcher. He invited her to sit at the table and gave her food and offered her so much liquor to drink that she ended up in a drunken stupor.

While the woman slept it off, the butcher dipped her in a barrel of tar and rolled her in a pile of feathers.

When she awoke, she was covered in feathers. She began to wonder: Is this me or not me? Oh no, it can't be me. It must be a big, strange bird. But what should I do to find out if it's me or it's not me? Oh, I know how I'll figure that out. When I get home, if the calves lick me and the dog doesn't bark at me, then it's me.

The dog hardly caught sight of this beast before it began barking up a storm, as if thieves and scoundrels had come to the farm.

"So, this can't very well be me," she said.

When she went into the cowshed, the calves refused to lick her, for they smelled the tar.

"So, this can't very well be me. It must be a strange bird," the woman said. Then she crawled up onto the roof of the storehouse and began flapping her arms as if they were wings and tried to fly. When her husband saw this, he came out with his rifle and took aim.

"Oh, don't shoot, don't shoot!" shouted his wife. "It's me!"

"Is that you?" said her husband. "Well, don't stand up there like a goat. Come down and give me a true and proper account of what happened to you."

She climbed back down, but she didn't have even a *skilling*. In her drunken state she'd thrown away the *mark* the butcher had paid her.

When her husband heard this, he said, "You're twice as crazy as you were before." He was so furious that he said he'd leave everything behind and never come back unless he met three women who were just as crazy as she was.

He set off. After he'd gone some distance along the road, he caught sight of a woman running in and out of a newly built hut. She was carrying an empty basin. Before she ran inside each time, she would throw her apron over the basin, as if there was something inside it. Then she dumped whatever it was onto the floor.

"Why are you doing that, ma'am?" he asked.

"Oh, I just want to bring in a little sunshine," she replied. "But I can't figure out how to do it. When I'm outdoors, there's sunshine in the basin, but when I come inside, it seems to have fallen out. When I lived in my old hut, I had plenty of sunshine, even though I never brought even a little bit inside. If only somebody could get me some sunshine, I would gladly give him three hundred *daler*."

"If you have an axe," said the man, "I'm sure I can get you some sunshine."

The woman gave him an axe. Then he chopped holes in the wall to make windows, for that was something the builders had forgotten to do. Instantly the sun shone inside, and he got his three hundred *daler*.

That's the first crazy woman, thought the man, and he set off again.

After a while he came to a house where a terrible screaming and howling was coming from inside. He went in and caught sight of a woman who was hitting her husband on the head with a wooden club. Over his head she had put a shirt that had no neck opening.

"Are you trying to kill your husband, ma'am?" he asked.

"No," she said, "I'm just trying to make a neck opening in this shirt."

Her husband screamed and carried on and said, "God save and preserve anyone who has to put on a new shirt. If somebody could teach this woman of mine to make a neck opening in a shirt in some other way, I would gladly give him three hundred *daler*."

"That is easily done. Just give me a pair of scissors," said the man. With the scissors he cut a hole in the shirt and then set off once again with the money.

"That's the second crazy woman," he said to himself.

At long last he came to a farm. He thought he would rest there for a while, so he went inside.

"Where are you from, sir?" asked the woman.

"I'm from the kingdom of Beven," he replied.

"Oh my, oh my! Are you from the kingdom of heaven? Then surely you must know Per, the second and blessed husband of mine!"

The woman had been married three times. The first and third were horrible men. That's why she called only the second her blessed husband, for he had been kind to her.

"Oh yes, I know him well," said the man as he walked around.

"How is he doing?" asked the woman.

"Oh, he's doing rather poorly," said the man from Beven. "He wanders from farm to farm with no food to eat and no clothes to wear. Not to mention any money."

"God have mercy on him!" cried the woman. "There's no need for him to go around in such a miserable state, for he left so much behind. The big loft is filled with clothes that belonged to him, and there's a big chest of coins too. If you'll take all those things to him, I'll give you a horse and wagon to carry them. He can keep the horse, and then he can drive from farm to farm. There's no need for him to walk."

She gave the man from Beven a whole wagonload of clothes, a chest filled with shiny silver coins, and as much food and drink as he wanted. Then he put everything in the wagon, climbed in, and went on his merry way.

"That's the third crazy woman," he said to himself.

The woman's third husband was out plowing the field. When he caught sight of a stranger leaving with a horse and a wagonful of goods, he went straight home. There he asked the woman about the man who had ridden off with the blue-black horse.

"Oh him," she said. "That was a man from the kingdom of heaven. He said that things were so bad for Per, the blessed second husband of mine, that he walks from farm to farm and has no clothes or money. So I sent the man off with all those old clothes that used to belong to Per, along with the old money chest with the silver coins."

Her husband realized at once what had happened. He saddled a horse and rushed off at full gallop. It didn't take long for him to close in on the stranger, who was driving the wagon.

But when the man noticed this, he drove the wagon into a thicket, grabbed a fistful of horsehair off the horse, and ran up a hill. There he tied the horsehair to a birch tree. Then he lay down under the tree and began gawking and staring up at the clouds.

"No, no, no!" he cried, as if to himself as Per the third came riding up. "No, I've never seen anything so peculiar! No, I've never seen the like!"

Per stood there, looking down at the stranger for a while, wondering whether he was crazy or what he could mean. Finally he asked, "What is it you're gawking at while you're lying there on the ground?"

"Oh, I've never seen the like!" said the man. "Someone is going straight up to heaven with a blue-black horse. Here, have a look. Some horsehair got caught on the birch, and up there in the clouds you can see his blue-black horse."

Per looked up at the clouds and then at the man and said, "Well, I don't see anything but some horsehair on the birch tree."

"No, you can't see it from where you're standing," said the man. "Come over here and lie down and look up. But don't take your eyes off the clouds."

Per the third lay down and stared up at the clouds so hard that tears filled his eyes. Then the man from Beven took Per's horse, mounted it, and rode off with both the other horse and the loaded wagon.

When Per the third heard a rumbling from the road, he jumped to his feet. But he was so confused by the sight of the stranger riding off with his horse that he didn't even think to take chase until it was too late.

Per was not a particularly brave man, let me tell you, so when he came home to the woman and she asked him what he'd done with his horse, he said, "I gave it to the stranger for Per the second. I didn't think it was right for him to sit in a wagon, clattering from one farm to another in the kingdom of heaven. Now he can sell the wagon and buy himself a carriage instead."

"Well, I'm grateful to you for that! Never did I think you were such a kind husband," said the woman.

When the man came home after collecting six hundred *daler* and a wagon-load of clothes and coins, he saw that all the fields had been plowed and sown. The first thing he did was ask his wife where she'd gotten the seeds.

"Oh," she said, "I've always heard that you shall reap what you sow, and I decided to sow the salt that the North Wind brought here. Now if only we get some rain soon, I'm sure it'll sprout again."

"Crazy you are and crazy you will always be, for as long as you may live," said her husband. "But that's neither here nor there, for the others are no better than you."

Everyone Thinks Their Own Children Are Best

A hunter was once walking through the forest when he came upon a woodcock.

"My dear friend, don't shoot my children!" said the woodcock.

"Which birds are your children?" asked the hunter.

"The loveliest ones in the forest are mine!" replied the woodcock.

"All right, those are the ones I won't shoot," said the hunter.

But when he came back he was carrying a whole clutch of woodcock fledglings that he'd shot.

"Oh no! Why did you shoot my children after all?" said the woodcock.

"Are these yours?" asked the hunter. "I shot the ugliest birds I could find."

"Alas!" replied the woodcock. "Don't you know that everyone thinks their own children are best?"

A Tale of Courtship

There once was a boy who set off to find himself a wife. Among the places he visited was a farm where the folks were terribly shabby and poor. As you might well imagine, when the suitor arrived, they wanted to appear well-to-do, of course. So the man managed to get one new sleeve made for his shirt.

"Sit down!" he said to the suitor. "Oh, but there's so much dust everywhere!" And he went around rubbing and swatting at the benches and table with his new shirtsleeve. The other arm he held behind his back.

The woman had managed to get one new shoe, and she kept stretching it out and kicking at everything, at the stools and the chairs. "There are so many things in the way. What a mess it is!" she said.

Then they called to their daughter to come and tidy up. She had managed to get a new cap. That's why she only stuck her head in the door, nodding this way and that. "I can't be everywhere at once, you know!" she said.

Oh yes, the folks were certainly well-to-do on that farm where the suitor came to visit.

The Three Aunts

There once was a poor man who had a hut deep in the forest and lived on whatever he could hunt. He had one daughter, and she was both lovely and fair. The mother had died when the child was quite young, but the girl was now half-grown. She said that she wanted to seek out folks so she could learn to make her own living.

"Yes, my daughter," said her father. "It's true enough that I've taught you only how to pluck and fry birds. You must still learn how to make your living."

So the girl set off to find herself a job. After she'd walked for a while she came to the royal palace, and that's where she stayed. The queen favored her so highly that the other maids grew jealous of her. They told the queen that the girl had boasted she could spin a pound of flax in twenty-four hours, for the queen was especially fond of all sorts of handiwork.

"Well, if you said that, then that's what you shall do," the queen told the girl. "Though I'll grant you a little more time than that."

The poor girl didn't dare say that she'd never learned to spin. She merely asked for a chamber all her own. She was given the chamber, along with a spinning wheel and flax, which were carried inside. There she sat, weeping and distressed, for she had no idea what to do. She studied the spinning wheel, twisting and turning it, but she didn't know how to use it. She'd never seen a spinning wheel before.

As she sat there, an old woman came into the room. "What's wrong, my child?" she asked.

"Oh," said the girl, "it will do no good for me to tell you. I'm sure you won't be able to help me!"

"You don't know that," said the woman. "It may well be that I could give you good advice."

Hmm, thought the girl, I might as well tell her. So she told the woman how the other maids had reported that she'd boasted she could spin a pound of flax in twenty-four hours. "Poor girl that I am," she said, "I've never in all my days even seen a spinning wheel, much less learned how to spin so much flax in a day and a night."

"Well, don't worry about that, my child," said the woman. "If you'll call me your aunt on your wedding day, then I'll spin the flax for you. You can just go over there and lie down to sleep."

The girl gladly agreed. Then she lay down to sleep.

In the morning when she awoke, the spun flax lay on the table, and it looked both fine and lovely. No one had ever seen yarn so beautiful and so evenly spun.

The queen was terribly pleased with the beautiful yarn, and she grew even more fond of the girl than before. But the others grew even more jealous of her. They decided to tell the queen that now the girl had boasted that in twenty-four hours she could weave all the yarn she had spun. Again the girl didn't dare say no. She asked for a chamber all her own and then said she would try her best.

There she sat once more, weeping and carrying on. She didn't know what she was going to do. Then another old woman came in and said, "What's wrong, my child?"

At first the girl didn't want to explain, but finally she told the old woman why she was sad.

"Well," said the woman, "don't worry about that. If you will call me your aunt on your wedding day, I'll do the weaving for you. You can just go over there and lie down to sleep."

The girl gladly agreed, and she lay down to sleep.

When she awoke, the bundle of cloth lay on the table, woven as finely and evenly as any weaving could be. The girl picked up the bundle and took it to the queen, who was very pleased with the weaving. She grew even more fond of the girl. But the others grew even more jealous of her. All they could think of was what they were going to do next.

Finally they told the queen that the girl had now boasted that in twenty-four hours she could sew the bundle of cloth into shirts.

The same thing happened as before. The girl didn't dare say that she couldn't sew. Once again she went to her own chamber and sat there weeping, in great distress. Then another old woman appeared. She promised to do the sewing if the girl would say she was her aunt on her wedding day. The girl was more than happy to promise. Then she did as the woman said and lay down to sleep.

In the morning when she awoke, she found the bundle of shirts lying on the table. No one had ever seen such beautiful seams before. The shirts were finely sewn and lovely to behold. When the queen saw this handiwork, she was practically in stitches with joy, and she clapped her hands.

"Never have I seen or been given such beautifully sewn shirts," she said. By then she was as fond of the girl as if she were her own child.

"If you wish to have the prince, then you shall have him," the queen said to the girl. "For you need never hire out any work. You can do all the sewing and spinning and weaving yourself."

Since the girl was beautiful and the prince found her pleasing, their wedding was held at once. The moment the prince sat down at the wedding table with his bride, an old and ugly woman appeared. Her nose looked to be six feet long.

Then the bride stood up and curtsied and said, "Good day, Aunt!"

"Is she the aunt of my bride?" said the prince.

Yes, she certainly was.

"Well, then she must take a seat at the table," said the prince. Yet both he and everyone else thought she was a vile person to have at the table.

All of a sudden another old and ugly woman came in. Her backside was so fat and wide that she could barely squeeze through the door.

At once the bride stood up to greet her. "Good day, Aunt!"

Again the prince asked if she was the aunt of his bride.

Both replied yes. The prince said if that was the case, she too should take a seat at the table.

Hardly had she sat down before another old and ugly woman appeared. Her eyes were as big as plates and so red and watery that they were a terrible sight to behold.

Again the bride stood up and greeted her. "Good day, Aunt!"

The prince invited her to take a seat at the table too. But he wasn't happy, and he thought to himself, God help me, what horrible aunts my bride has!

After he'd sat there for a while, he couldn't stand it any longer and asked, "How in all the world can my bride, who is so lovely, have such vile and deformed-looking aunts?"

"I will tell you," said one of them. "I was just as beautiful as your bride when I was her age. But the reason I have such a long nose is because I've sat bending and bowing over my spinning wheel. My nose stretched and stretched until it grew as long as you see it now."

"And ever since I was young," said the second old woman, "I've sat and slid back and forth on the bench for my loom. That's how my backside got as big and swollen as you see it now."

Then the third old woman said, "From the time I was a child I've sat and stared as I sewed, all night and all day. That's why my eyes have grown so foul and red, and nothing more can be done about them."

"I see," said the prince. "I'm glad I found out about this. If that's how folks become so ugly and vile, then my bride will never again spin or weave or sew for the rest of her days!"

The Widow's Son

There once was an oh-so-poor widow who had one son. She toiled for the boy's sake until he was confirmed. That's when she told him that she could no longer feed him, and he would have to go out and earn his own living.

Then the boy set out into the world. After he'd walked for a day or two, he met a stranger.

"Where are you headed?" asked the man.

"I'm going out into the world to try and find work," said the boy.

"Would you like to work for me?"

"I suppose so. I might as well work for you as for anyone else," replied the boy.

"I'll treat you well," said the man. "All you have to do is keep me company and nothing else."

The boy went with the man, and he lived well. There was plenty to eat and drink, and he had next to nothing to do. But he saw no one except the man.

One day the man said to him, "I'll be away for eight days. During that time you'll stay here alone, but you mustn't go into any of these four rooms. If you do, I'll kill you when I come back."

Oh no, said the boy, he wouldn't do that. But when the man had been gone three or four days, the boy could no longer resist, and he went into one of the chambers. He looked around but saw only a shelf above the door, and on the shelf was a sweetbriar branch.

I wonder why I was so sternly forbidden to look at that? thought the boy.

When the eight days were up, the man came home.

"You haven't been inside any of the chambers, have you?" he said.

"No, I haven't," said the boy.

"Well, I'll soon see if you have." And with that he went inside the room where the boy had been.

"Oh yes, you've been in here after all," he said. "And now you'll lose your life."

When the boy wept and pleaded, he escaped with his life, but he was given a proper beating. When that was over, they were just as good friends as before.

A little while later the man again had to go away. This time he would be gone fourteen days. He told the boy not to set foot in any of the chambers he'd never been inside, though he was welcome to go into the one he'd already entered.

Well, the same thing happened as before, except that the boy managed to wait eight days before going into another room. In this chamber he again saw only a shelf above the door, but on this shelf was a big rock and a flask of water.

I wonder what's so scary about that? thought the boy.

When the man came home, he asked the boy if he'd been inside any of the chambers.

No, the boy said again, he hadn't.

"Well, I'll soon see if you have," said the man. When he discovered the boy had been inside another room after all, he said, "I'm not going to spare you anymore. Now you'll lose your life!"

The boy wept and pleaded, and again he escaped with only a beating, but a terrible beating it was, almost more than he could bear. After he'd recovered, he lived just as well as before. And he and the man were just as good friends as before.

A little while later the man again had to go away. This time he would be gone for three weeks, so he said to the boy that if he went inside the third chamber, he could give up any thought of living.

After fourteen days had passed, the boy couldn't resist any longer, and he slipped inside. But he saw nothing in the room except a hatch in the floor. When he lifted up the hatch and looked down, he saw below a big copper cauldron, bubbling and boiling, though he could see no fire underneath.

It would be amusing to find out if it's hot, thought the boy, and he stuck his finger in the cauldron. When he pulled his finger out, it was completely gilded. The boy washed and scrubbed the gilding, but it wouldn't come off, so he wrapped a rag around his finger. When the man came home, he asked the boy what was wrong with his finger. The boy said he'd cut himself badly. But the man tore off the rag, and then he saw quite clearly what had happened to the boy's finger.

At first he wanted to kill the boy, but when he wept and pleaded again, the man merely beat him so hard that he lay in bed for three days. Then the man took a pot down from the wall and smeared what was inside on the boy, and he was as good as new.

After a while the man again had to go away, and he wouldn't be back for a month. He told the boy that if he went inside the fourth chamber, he should give up all thought of living.

For one, two, and three weeks the boy resisted, but then he couldn't hold out any longer. He would and must go inside that chamber, and so he slipped inside. There he saw a big black horse in a stall with a trough for embers near its head and a basket of hay near its tail. The boy thought this was wrong, so he switched them around and set the hay basket next to the horse's head.

Then the horse said, "Seeing as you are so good-hearted that you want to make sure I have food to eat, I'm going to rescue you. When the troll comes home and finds you, he will try to kill you. Go now to the chamber right across from this one and take a suit of armor from those you'll find hanging there. But be sure not to take any of the shiny ones. Take the rustiest armor you can find. Do the same with the sword and saddle."

So that's what the boy did, though he found everything heavy to carry.

When he came back, the horse told him to take off all his clothes and get into the cauldron that was boiling in the second chamber. There he should wash himself well.

Oh, how vile I'm going to look, thought the boy, but he did it just the same. After he had washed, he looked both handsome and hearty, as red and white as blood and milk, and much stronger than before.

"Do you notice anything different?" asked the horse.

"Yes," said the boy.

"Try to lift me," said the horse.

Oh yes, he could do that. He could also swing the sword as if it weighed nothing.

"All right, put the saddle on me," said the horse. "And get into the armor. Gather up the sweetbriar branch and the rock and the flask of water and the pot of grease. Then we'll be off."

When the boy was sitting astride the horse, it set off, though he had no idea how they made their way forward. After they'd been traveling for a while, the horse said, "I think I hear a roaring sound. Look behind us. Can you see anything?"

"There's a big group behind us. There must be at least twenty in the group," said the boy.

"Oh yes, that's the troll," said the horse. "He's bringing along his followers."

They kept on riding until those behind began to draw closer.

"Throw the sweetbriar branch over your shoulder," said the horse. "But be sure to throw it far away from me!"

That's what the boy did. Then a big, thick sweetbriar forest instantly sprang up. The boy kept on riding farther and farther, while the troll had to go back home to get something to chop a path through the forest.

After a while the horse said again, "Look back. Can you see anything now?"

"Yes, a big crowd," said the boy. "As big as a crowd on the way to church."

"Oh yes, that's the troll. Now he's brought more followers with him. Throw the big rock, but be sure to throw it far away from me!"

The instant the boy did what the horse had said, a big, big mountain appeared behind them. Then the troll had to go back home to get something to chop his way through the mountain. And while the troll was doing that, the boy kept riding a good distance ahead.

Then the horse asked him again to look back, and he saw what looked like an entire army swarming after them. The group was so shiny that it glowed.

"Yes," said the horse. "That's the troll. Now he's brought all his followers with him. Dump out behind us all the water from the flask, but be very careful not to spill any on me!"

That's what the boy did, but no matter how hard he tried, he couldn't help spilling a few drops on the horse's hindquarters. Then a big, big lake appeared, but the spilled drops meant that the horse ended up standing in the middle of the lake. Yet it was able to swim to shore. When the trolls came to the lake, they lay down and began to drink it dry, but they slurped up so much water that they burst.

"Now we're rid of them," said the horse.

After they had journeyed for a long, long time, they came to a green clearing in a forest.

"Take off all the armor and put on your tattered clothes," said the horse. "Then remove the saddle and let me go. Hang everything inside this big hollow linden tree. Then make a wig for yourself out of spruce lichen and go up to the royal palace you'll find nearby. There you must ask for work. Whenever you need me, just come here and shake the bridle. Then I'll come to you."

The boy did as the horse said. After he'd put on the lichen wig, he looked so wretched and pale and miserable that no one would ever recognize him. Then he went to the royal palace and asked if he might work in the kitchen, carrying water and wood for the cook.

The kitchen maid asked him, "Why are you wearing that ugly wig? Take it off. I won't have anyone so ugly in here."

"I can't," said the boy. "I may have a few lice in my hair."

"Do you think I'd let you stay here near the food if that's how things are?" said the cook. "Go see the stablemaster. You're better suited to mucking out the stables."

But when the stablemaster asked the boy to take off the wig, he heard the same thing. And he didn't want him there either. "Go see the gardener," he said. "You're better suited to digging in the earth."

The gardener allowed the boy to stay, but none of the other servants wanted to share a bed with him. He had to sleep alone under the steps to the gazebo, which was perched on posts. Underneath the boy gathered some moss for a bed, and there he lay down as best he could.

After he'd been at the royal palace for a while, the boy took off the lichen wig to wash himself just as the sun rose one morning. At that moment he was so handsome that he was a delight to behold.

From her window the princess saw the gardener boy and thought she'd never seen anyone as handsome. She asked the gardener why the boy slept under the steps.

"Oh, none of the other servants will share a bed with him," said the gardener.

"Tonight let him come here and lie down next to the door inside my chamber. After that the servants won't think they're too good to share quarters with him," said the princess.

The gardener said as much to the boy.

"Do you think I should do that?" said the boy. "They'll say that there's something between me and the princess."

"Ha! I'm sure you have reason to fear such suspicions," replied the gardener, "a handsome boy like you!"

"Well, since you're ordering me to do it, I suppose I must," said the boy.

As he was making his way up the stairs that night, he stamped and stomped so hard that they had to ask him to move more quietly or the king might hear.

He went inside the chamber and lay down. There he began snoring at once.

Then the princess said to her maid, "Sneak over there and take off the lichen wig."

The maid obeyed, but as she was about to snatch off the wig, the boy held onto it with both hands and said she mustn't do that. Then he lay down again and began snoring.

The princess motioned to her maid to try again. This time she snatched off the wig. There lay the boy, so lovely and red and white, just as the princess had seen him in the morning sun. After that the boy slept in the princess's room every night.

It wasn't long before the king heard that the gardener boy was sleeping in the princess's chamber every night. He grew so angry that he nearly had the boy killed. But he didn't. Instead, he threw the boy into the tower prison. Then he locked his own daughter in her chamber, and she was never allowed to come out, day or night. No matter how much she wept and pleaded for herself and for the boy, it did no good. The king just grew even angrier.

A short time later, war and unrest descended upon the land. The king had to arm himself against another king who wanted to seize his kingdom.

When the boy heard this, he told the prison guard to go to the king and ask that he might be given armor and a sword. He wanted permission to take part in the war.

Everyone laughed when the prison guard delivered this message to the king. They asked if the boy might be given some broken old armor. Then they'd have the fun of seeing him take part in the war. This he was granted, along with a miserable old nag that limped along on three legs, dragging its fourth leg behind.

Then they all set off to battle the enemy. They hadn't gone far from the royal palace before the boy and his nag got stuck in a bog. There he sat, calling and coaxing the nag. "Hey, get moving! Hey, get moving!"

Everyone else thought this was great fun. They laughed and jeered at the boy as they rode past.

No sooner were they gone than he ran over to the linden tree, put on his armor, and shook the bridle. The horse appeared at once and said, "Do your best, and I will do the same!"

When the boy caught up with the others, the battle had already begun. The king was in a dire situation, but in no time the boy had chased the enemy far away. The king and his men all wondered who this stranger could be. He had come to their aid, but no one got close enough to speak to him. And when the battle was over, he was gone.

When everyone rode back, the boy was still stuck in the bog, calling and coaxing the three-legged nag. Again they laughed. "Oh, look, that fool is still here!" they said.

The next day when they set off, the boy was still there. Again they laughed and jeered at him. But no sooner had they gone past than the boy ran over to the linden tree, and everything happened the same way as before. Everyone wondered who this stranger could be, this champion who had come to their aid. But no one got close enough to be able to speak to him, and of course no one guessed it was the boy.

When they went home in the evening and saw the boy still sitting on the nag, they laughed at him again. A man shot an arrow that struck the boy in the leg. He began screaming and wailing so terribly that the king tossed the boy his handkerchief to bind the wound.

When they set off on the third morning, the boy was still stuck in the bog. "Hey, get moving! Hey, get moving!" he said to the nag.

"Ha, ha! He's going to sit there until he starves to death," said the king's men as they rode past. They laughed so hard at the boy that they nearly fell off their horses.

When they were gone, the boy again ran over to the linden tree and joined the battle at a crucial moment. That day he killed the enemy king, and with that the war came to an end.

When the battle was over, the king caught sight of his handkerchief, which the stranger had tied around his leg. Then the king recognized him. With great joy they took the boy back to the royal palace. The princess saw him from up in her window and was happy beyond belief.

"Here comes my sweetheart," she said.

Then the boy took the pot of grease and smeared his leg. He did the same to all those who were wounded, and in an instant they were as good as new. After that he was allowed to marry the princess.

On the day of the wedding, the boy went to the stable to get his horse. He found the animal moping and hanging its head. It refused to eat a thing. Then the young king—for by then he was king and had been given half the kingdom—spoke to the horse and asked what was wrong.

The horse said, "Now that I've done all I could to help you, I no longer want to live. You must take the sword and chop off my head."

"Oh no, that I won't do," said the young king. "But you shall have anything you want, and you will never have to go anywhere again."

"Well, if you won't do as I say, I will find some way to put an end to you," said the horse.

Then the young king had to agree. As he raised the sword and was about to chop off the horse's head, he was so distressed that he looked away. He didn't want to see the sword strike. But no sooner had he chopped off the horse's head than the loveliest prince stood where the horse had been standing.

"Where on earth did you come from?" asked the young king.

"I was the horse," replied the prince. "I used to be king of the land where the other king came from—the one you killed in battle yesterday. He cast a spell over me and sold me to the troll. Now that he's dead, I will have my kingdom back. Then you and I will be neighbor kings, but we must never wage war against each other."

And they never did. They were friends for as long as they lived and visited each other quite often.

The Husband's Daughter and the Wife's Daughter

There once were two people who were married, and they each had a daughter. The wife's daughter was lazy and listless and never wanted to do anything. The husband's daughter was clever and obliging, and yet she could never please her mother. The wife and her daughter wanted to get rid of the girl. One day both daughters sat down near the well with their spindles. The wife's daughter was going to spin flax, but the husband's daughter was given nothing but bristles to spin.

"You're always so clever and quick," said the wife's daughter, "but I'm not afraid to have a spinning contest with you."

They agreed that if the yarn broke, the person who was using that spindle would end up in the well.

All of a sudden, the yarn broke while the husband's daughter was spinning, and she had to go into the well. When she landed on the bottom, she wasn't hurt, and all around she saw a beautiful green meadow.

She walked through the meadow for a while. Then she came to a brush-wood fence, and she had to climb over it.

"Oh, don't step too hard on me," said the brushwood fence, "and I'll help you some other time. I will."

She made herself as light as a feather and stepped so carefully that she barely even touched the fence.

Then she walked some more and came to a brindled cow that had a wooden milk pail hanging from its horns. It was a big, beautiful cow, and its udder was swollen and full.

"Oh, please, won't you milk me?" said the cow. "For I am bursting with milk. Drink as much as you like, and pour the rest over my hooves. Then I'll help you in turn. I will."

The husband's daughter did as the cow asked. The instant she squeezed the teats, milk sprayed into the pail. Then she drank until she was no longer thirsty. The rest she poured over the cow's hooves, and the pail she hung on its horns.

After she'd walked some more through the meadow, she met a big ram. Its woolen pelt was so thick and so long that it dragged behind, and on one horn hung a big pair of scissors.

"Oh, won't you please shear me?" said the ram. "For here I am with all this wool, huffing and puffing, and it's so hot that I'm about to suffocate. Take as much wool as you like, and wrap the rest around my neck. Then I'll help you in turn."

She agreed to help at once. The ram lay very still on her lap, and she sheared its wool so carefully that the animal didn't suffer even the slightest cut. Then she took as much of the wool as she liked and wrapped the rest around the ram's neck.

A little farther on she came to an apple tree. There were so many apples that the branches bent all the way to the ground. Next to the tree trunk lay a slender stick.

"Oh, won't you please pick these apples off me?" said the tree. "Then my branches can straighten up. It hurts to stand here all bent over. But be sure to swing the stick nice and easy so you don't beat me black-and-blue. Eat as many apples as you like, and place the rest next to my roots. Then I'll help you in turn. I will."

Well, she picked all the apples she could reach, and then she took the stick and carefully knocked the others to the ground. After that she ate her fill. The rest of the apples she placed neatly next to the roots of the tree.

Then the girl walked a long, long way. Finally she came to a big farm. That was where a troll woman lived with her daughter. She went inside and asked for work.

"Oh, it's no use," said the troll woman. "We've hired so many, but none of them was ever any good."

But the girl pleaded so politely that they agreed to hire her. Then the troll woman gave her a sieve and asked her to use it to bring back water. The girl thought it was unreasonable to carry water in a sieve, but she went off all the same to do just that. When she reached the well, the little birds sang:

Smear it with mud!
Stuff it with straw!
Smear it with mud!
Stuff it with straw!

And that's what she did. Then it was easy for her to carry water in the sieve. When the girl got back with the water, the troll woman caught sight of the sieve and said, "You haven't figured that out all on your own!"

Then the troll woman told her to go to the cowshed to do the mucking out and milking. But when she got there, she found a shovel so big and heavy that it was useless. She couldn't even lift it, and she had no idea what to do next. But the birds sang, telling her to take the broom and do a little sweeping and everything else would follow. That's what she did, and before she knew it, the cowshed was as clean as if it had been carefully mucked out and swept.

Now she was supposed to milk the cows, but they were so restless that they kicked and strained, and she couldn't get near enough to milk them. But then the birds sang outside:

A spout
A spurt
Give the birds a squirt!

Well, that's what she did. She squirted a little spout of milk out to the birds. Then all the cows stood still and allowed her to milk them, and they didn't strain or kick. They didn't even lift a leg.

When the troll woman saw the girl come in with the milk, she said, "You haven't figured that out all on your own! Now take this black wool and wash it white."

The girl had no idea how she was going to do that, for she'd never seen anyone wash black wool white. But again she said nothing. She took the wool and carried it out to the well. Then the birds sang that she should take the wool and put it in the big basin standing there, and it would turn white.

"Oh no!" said the troll woman when the girl came back with the wool. "It's no use letting you stay here, for there's nothing you can't do. You're going to end up annoying the life out of me. It's best if I let you leave."

Then the troll woman set out three chests—a red, a green, and a blue—and the girl was allowed to take whichever one she wanted. That would be her payment. She didn't know which to take, but the birds sang:

> Not the chest of green
> Not the chest of red
> Take the blue instead
> That's the one we mean!

So she took the blue chest, which the birds had marked with three crosses on the lid.

"A curse upon you!" said the troll woman. "You will have to pay dearly for this!"

When the husband's daughter was about to set off, the troll woman shoved toward her a glowing hot iron bar. But the girl instantly leaped behind the door so it couldn't touch her, for the birds had told her what to do.

Then she took off as fast as she could go. When she came to the apple tree, she heard a roaring start up on the road. That was the troll woman and her daughter coming after her. The girl was so frightened that she had no idea what to do.

"Come over here to me," said the apple tree, "and I'll help you. Slip under my branches to hide, for if they catch you, they'll take away the chest and kill you by ripping you apart."

That's what she did. Suddenly the troll woman and her daughter appeared.

"Have you seen a girl go past?" said the troll woman.

"Oh yes," said the apple tree. "A girl ran past a little while ago. But she's so far away by now that you'll never catch her."

Then the troll woman and her daughter turned around and headed back home.

The girl continued on. But when she came to the ram, a roaring started up, and she didn't know what to do. She was frightened and alarmed because she knew it was the troll woman and her daughter, who had changed their minds.

"Come over here to me, and I'll help you," said the ram. "Hide under my wool, and they won't see you. Otherwise they'll take the chest away from you and kill you by ripping you apart."

Suddenly the troll woman and her daughter came rushing over. "Have you seen a girl walking past?" the troll woman asked the ram.

"Oh yes," said the ram. "I saw one a while ago, but she was running so fast that you'll never catch her."

Then the two troll women turned around and headed home.

When the girl had walked so far that she'd reached the cow, she heard a terrible roaring start up on the road.

"Come over here to me," said the cow, "and I'll help you. Hide under my udder, or else the troll woman will come and take the chest away from you. Then she'll kill you by ripping you apart."

It wasn't long before the troll woman and her daughter arrived. "Have you seen a girl walk past?" they asked the cow.

"Yes, I saw one a while ago, but she must be long gone by now. She was running so fast that you'll never catch her," said the cow.

Then the troll woman and her daughter turned around and headed back home.

After the girl had walked a long, long way, she wasn't far from the brushwood fence. She heard a terrible roaring start up on the road, and she grew frightened and alarmed, for she knew it must be the troll woman and her daughter, who had turned around again.

"Come over to me, and I'll help you," said the brushwood fence. "Crawl under my branches so they won't see you, or else they'll take the chest away from you and kill you by ripping you apart."

She hurried to slip under the branches of the brushwood fence.

"Have you seen a girl walking past?" said the troll woman to the brushwood fence.

"No, I haven't seen any girl," replied the fence, so angry that it sputtered. The fence made itself so big that there was no question of climbing over it. Then the troll woman and her daughter had no choice but to turn around and go back home.

When the husband's daughter arrived home, the wife and her daughter were even more jealous of her than before. Now the girl was much more beautiful, and she looked so splendid that she was a delight to behold.

The girl wasn't allowed to stay in the house with them. Instead they shooed her out to the pig shed. They said that's where she'd have to stay. She washed everything and made the shed nice and neat. Then she opened the chest to see what she'd been given in payment. The instant she opened the lid, so much gold and silver and so many lovely things appeared that they soon covered all the walls and ceiling. Then the pig shed looked more magnificent than the most splendid royal palace.

When the wife and her daughter saw this, they were quite beside themselves. They asked the girl what sort of work she'd found.

"Oh," she said, "surely you can tell, for you've seen the payment I was given. No one can compare to the folks I worked for, especially the woman."

Then the wife's daughter wanted to set off to work there too so she could have her own chest of gold. Again the two daughters sat down to spin, but this time the wife's daughter spun bristles and the husband's daughter spun flax. The first one to have her yarn break off the spindle would end up in the well. It didn't take long before the yarn broke off the spindle belonging to the wife's daughter. Then, as you might well guess, they threw her into the well.

And the same thing happened. She fell to the bottom but didn't get hurt, and there she found herself in a lovely green meadow. After she'd walked for a while, she came to the brushwood fence.

"Don't step too hard on me, and I'll help you in turn," said the fence.

"Oh, what do I care about a pile of branches?" the girl said. Then she made herself so heavy as she stepped on the brushwood fence that it creaked and cracked.

After a while she came to the cow that was bursting with milk.

"Won't you please milk me?" said the cow. "Then I'll help you in turn. Drink as much as you like, but pour the rest onto my hooves."

The girl milked the cow, but then she drank for as long as she could, until there was nothing left to pour on the cow's hooves. The milk pail she tossed on the ground before she went on her way.

After she'd walked some more, she came to the ram that was dragging its wool.

"Oh, won't you please shear me? Then I'll help you in turn," said the ram. "Take as much wool as you like, but wrap the rest around my neck."

That's what the girl did, though she set about the shearing so recklessly that she made big cuts in the ram's hide. Then she carried off all the wool.

A short time later she came to the apple tree that was bending over, weighed down by all the apples.

"Won't you please pick the apples so my branches can straighten up? It hurts terribly to stand here bent over," said the apple tree. "But be careful not to hit me black-and-blue with the stick. Eat as many apples as you like, but put the rest neatly next to my roots. Then I'll help you in turn."

The girl picked the apples that were nearest and then used the stick to knock down those she couldn't reach. But she did it so carelessly that she tore off and toppled big branches. Then she ate apples until she could eat no more, and she tossed the rest under the tree.

After she'd walked for a while, she came to the farm where the troll woman lived. There she asked for work. The troll woman said she didn't want any servant girls. They were either useless or much too clever, and then they cheated her out of all she owned.

But the wife's daughter refused to give up and demanded a job. Then the troll woman said she would hire the girl if she could make herself useful.

The first task she was given was to carry water in the sieve. The girl went to the well and poured water into the sieve, but as soon as she filled it, the water ran out. Then the birds sang:

> *Smear it with mud!*
> *Stuff it with straw!*
> *Smear it with mud!*
> *Stuff it with straw!*

But she paid no attention to the birds' song, and she threw mud at the birds until they flew far away. She had to go back with an empty sieve, and the troll woman gave her a thrashing.

Then the girl was supposed to muck out the cowshed and milk the cows. She thought she was too good to do work like that, but she went to the cowshed all the same. When she came inside, she couldn't use the shovel, for it was too big. The birds told her the same thing they'd told the husband's daughter. They said she should take the broom and do a little sweeping. Then everything else would follow. But she took the broom and swept out the birds.

When she tried to do the milking, the cows were so restless that they strained and kicked, and every time she had a little milk in the pail, they kicked it over. The birds sang:

> *A spout*
> *A spurt*
> *Give the birds a squirt!*

Instead the girl hit and beat the cows. She threw everything within reach at the birds, and she carried on like no other. She didn't do the mucking out or the milking. When she went back inside, she got both a thrashing and a scolding from the troll woman.

Then the girl was supposed to wash the black wool white, but she was no better at completing this task.

The troll woman had finally had enough. She brought out three chests—a red, a green, and a blue. She said she had no need for a girl who was useless at every task. Yet as payment she would still be allowed to choose whichever chest she liked. Then the birds sang:

> *Not the chest of green*
> *Not the chest of the red*
> *Take the blue instead*
> *That's the one we mean!*

The girl paid no attention to the birds' song or the three crosses on the blue chest. She chose the red chest, for it shone the brightest. Then she set off, heading for home, and she was allowed to go peacefully. No one chased after her.

When the girl came home, her mother was overjoyed. They went to the great hall at once and set down the chest. They thought it was filled with gold and silver, and they thought all the walls and ceiling would end up gilded. But when they opened the chest, only snakes and toads poured out. And when the wife's daughter opened her mouth, the same thing happened. Snakes and toads and all manner of vermin poured out, until finally it was impossible to stay in the same room with her. That was her payment after working for the troll woman.

The Rooster and the Hen
in the Nut Forest

The rooster and the hen once went into the forest to gather nuts. Then the hen got a nutshell stuck in her throat, and she lay on the ground, flailing her wings. The rooster went off to get her some water.

When he came to the spring, he said, "My dear spring, give me water, water that I'll give to the chicken, my hen, who is dying in the nut forest."

The spring replied, "You'll get no water from me until I get leaves from you."

So the rooster ran to the linden tree. "My dear linden, give me leaves, leaves that I'll give to the spring. The spring will give me water, water that I'll give to the chicken, my hen, who is dying in the nut forest."

"You'll get no leaves from me until I get a red-gold ribbon from you," replied the linden.

So the rooster ran to the Virgin Mary. "My dear Virgin Mary, give me a red-gold ribbon, a red-gold ribbon that I'll give to the linden. The linden will give me leaves, leaves that I'll give to the spring. The spring will give me water, water that I'll give to the chicken, my hen, who is dying in the nut forest."

"You'll get no red-gold ribbon from me until I get shoes from you," replied the Virgin Mary.

So the rooster ran to the shoemaker. "My dear shoemaker, give me shoes, shoes that I'll give to the Virgin Mary. The Virgin Mary will give me a red-gold ribbon, a red-gold ribbon that I'll give to the linden. The linden will give me leaves, leaves that I'll give to the spring. The spring will give me water, water that I'll give to the chicken, my hen, who is dying in the nut forest."

"You'll get no shoes from me until I get bristles from you," replied the shoemaker.

So the rooster ran to the sow. "My dear sow, give me bristles, bristles that I'll give to the shoemaker. The shoemaker will give me shoes, shoes that I'll give to the Virgin Mary. The Virgin Mary will give me a red-gold ribbon, a red-gold ribbon that I'll give to the linden. The linden will give me leaves,

leaves that I'll give to the spring. The spring will give me water, water that I'll give to the chicken, my hen, who is dying in the nut forest."

"You'll get no bristles from me until I get grain from you," replied the sow.

So the rooster ran to the thresherman. "My dear thresherman, give me grain, grain that I'll give to the sow. The sow will give me bristles, bristles that I'll give to the shoemaker. The shoemaker will give me shoes, shoes that I'll give to the Virgin Mary. The Virgin Mary will give me a red-gold ribbon, a red-gold ribbon that I'll give to the linden. The linden will give me leaves, leaves that I'll give to the spring. The spring will give me water, water that I'll give to the chicken, my hen, who is dying in the nut forest."

"You'll get no grain from me until I get *lefse* from you," replied the thresherman.

So the rooster ran to the baker woman. "My dear baker woman, give me *lefse, lefse* that I'll give to the thresherman. The thresherman will give me grain, grain that I'll give to the sow. The sow will give me bristles, bristles that I'll give to the shoemaker. The shoemaker will give me shoes, shoes that I'll give to the Virgin Mary. The Virgin Mary will give me a red-gold ribbon, a red-gold ribbon that I'll give to the linden. The linden will give me leaves, leaves that I'll give to the spring. The spring will give me water, water that I'll give to the chicken, my hen, who is dying in the nut forest."

"You'll get no *lefse* from me until I get firewood from you," replied the baker woman.

So the rooster ran to the woodcutter. "My dear woodcutter, give me firewood, firewood that I'll give to the baker woman. The baker woman will give me *lefse, lefse* that I'll give to the thresherman. The thresherman will give me grain, grain that I'll give to the sow. The sow will give me bristles, bristles that I'll give to the shoemaker. The shoemaker will give me shoes, shoes that I'll give to the Virgin Mary. The Virgin Mary will give me a red-gold ribbon, a red-gold ribbon that I'll give to the linden. The linden will give me leaves, leaves that I'll give to the spring. The spring will give me water, water that I'll give to the chicken, my hen, who is dying in the nut forest."

"You'll get no firewood from me until I get an axe from you," replied the woodcutter.

So the rooster ran to the blacksmith. "My dear blacksmith, give me an axe, an axe that I'll give to the woodcutter. The woodcutter will give me firewood, firewood that I'll give to the baker woman. The baker woman will give me *lefse, lefse* that I'll give to the thresherman. The thresherman will give me grain,

grain that I'll give to the sow. The sow will give me bristles, bristles that I'll give to the shoemaker. The shoemaker will give me shoes, shoes that I'll give to the Virgin Mary. The Virgin Mary will give me a red-gold ribbon, a red-gold ribbon that I'll give to the linden. The linden will give me leaves, leaves that I'll give to the spring. The spring will give me water, water that I'll give to the chicken, my hen, who is dying in the nut forest."

"You'll get no axe from me until I get charcoal from you," replied the blacksmith.

So the rooster ran to the charcoal burner. "My dear charcoal burner, give me charcoal, charcoal that I'll give to the blacksmith. The blacksmith will give me an axe, an axe that I'll give to the woodcutter. The woodcutter will give me firewood, firewood that I'll give to the baker woman. The baker woman will give me *lefse, lefse* that I'll give to the thresherman. The thresherman will give me grain, grain that I'll give to the sow. The sow will give me bristles, bristles that I'll give to the shoemaker. The shoemaker will give me shoes, shoes that I'll give to the Virgin Mary. The Virgin Mary will give me a red-gold ribbon, a red-gold ribbon that I'll give to the linden. The linden will give me leaves, leaves that I'll give to the spring. The spring will give me water, water that I'll give to the chicken, my hen, who is dying in the nut forest."

Then the charcoal burner felt sorry for the rooster and gave him charcoal. So the blacksmith got his charcoal, the woodcutter his axe, the baker woman her firewood, the thresherman his *lefse,* the sow its grain, the shoemaker his bristles, the Virgin Mary her shoes, the linden its red-gold ribbon, the spring its leaves, and the rooster got water to give to the chicken, his hen, who was dying in the nut forest.

And then she was as good as new.

The Bear and the Fox

Why the Bear Has a Stump of a Tail

The bear once met the fox, who came slinking along carrying a bunch of fish that he'd stolen.

"Where did you get those fish?" asked the bear.

"I've been out angling, Mister Bear!" replied the fox.

Then the bear wanted to learn to angle too. He asked the fox how to go about it.

"It's a simple matter for you," replied the fox. "You can learn it quickly enough. Just go out on the ice, chop a big hole, and stick your tail in the hole. Then stay there a good long time. Don't pay any attention if your tail stings a little. That means the fish are biting. The longer you can hold out, the more fish you'll catch. Then, with a swift tug, yank your tail up!"

Well, the bear did just as the fox had said. He stuck his tail way down in the hole until it froze solid. When he yanked it up, he yanked it right off. And to this day, he goes around with only a stump of a tail.

The Fox Cheats the Bear Out of His Christmas Meal

The bear and the fox once bought a wooden tub of butter. They were planning to eat the butter for Christmas, so they hid it under a big spruce thicket. Then they walked a short distance away and lay down to sleep on a sunny patch of ground.

After they'd lain there for a while, the fox got up and shouted, "Oh yes!" Then he set off, going straight for the tub of butter. He ate a good third of it.

When he came back, the bear asked him where he'd been, for there was grease on his snout. The fox said, "Can you believe it? I was invited to a christening feast!"

"Is that so? What's the name of the child?" asked the bear.

"Barely Started," said the fox.

And they lay down to sleep.

In a little while the fox jumped up again and shouted, "Oh yes!" He raced over to the tub of butter. There he ate a good portion of the butter. When he came back, the bear asked him where he'd been. He replied, "Oh, can you believe it? I was invited to another christening!"

"What's the name of the child this time?" asked the bear.

"Half Eaten," said the fox.

The bear thought that was a strange name, but he didn't wonder about it for long before he yawned and fell asleep. He'd been lying there only a short time when the same thing happened again. The fox jumped up and shouted, "Oh yes!" Then he raced over to the tub of butter. This time he ate all the butter that was left. When he came back, he said he'd again been to a christening. When the bear wanted to know the child's name, he replied, "Licked the Bottom!"

With that, they both lay down to sleep, and they stayed there a good long while.

When they went over to see to the butter, all of it had been eaten. The bear blamed the fox, and the fox blamed the bear. Each said that the other must have been at the tub of butter while he was asleep.

"All right," said the sly fox. "We'll soon find out which one of us stole the butter. Let's lie down over there on that sunny patch of ground. Whoever has the greasiest tail when we wake up must be the thief."

Well, the bear gladly agreed to the test. He knew that he hadn't even tasted the butter, so with great confidence he lay down to sleep in the sun.

Then the sly fox went over to the wooden tub and got a lump of butter that was left in a crack. He went back to the bear and smeared the butter on his tail. Then he lay down to sleep as if nothing had happened.

When they both woke up, the sun had melted the butter. And it turned out that the bear was the one who had eaten the butter after all.

Gudbrand Slope

here once was a man named Gudbrand. He had a farm far away on a mountain slope, and that's why they called him Gudbrand Slope. He and his wife lived together very happily and were in such agreement that she thought everything her husband did was done well and could not be done any better. How he actually handled matters was of no concern to her. They owned their farmland, they had a hundred *daler* lying at the bottom of a chest, and in the cowshed were two cows with halters.

Then one day Gudbrand's wife said to him, "I think we should take one of the cows to town and sell it. Yes, I do. Then we could get ourselves some spending money. We're such respectable folks that we ought to have some *skillinger* as spending money, just like other people. We can't touch the hundred *daler* at the bottom of the chest, but I don't know why we need more than one cow. And we'll actually come out ahead, for I'll only have to take care of one cow, instead of mucking out and gathering hay for two."

Gudbrand thought this was both sensible and fair. He took one of the cows and set off at once to sell it in town. But when he got there, nobody wanted to buy it.

Well, then, thought Gudbrand, I might as well go back home with my cow. I know I have a stall and a halter for it, and the road is just as long back as it was to get here.

And with that he set off to meander his way home.

After he'd walked along the road for a while, he met a man who had a horse he wanted to sell. Gudbrand thought it would be better to have a horse than a cow, and so he traded with the man.

After he'd gone farther along the road, he met a man who was driving a fat pig. Then he thought it was better to have a fat pig than a horse, and so he traded with the man.

Again he walked on, and he met a man with a goat. He thought it would certainly be better to have a goat than a pig, and so he traded with the man who owned the goat.

Then he walked for a long time until he met a man who had a sheep. He traded with the man, for he thought it was always better to have a sheep than a goat.

After he'd walked some more, he met a man with a goose. Then he traded the sheep for the goose.

And after he'd walked a long, long way, he met a man with a rooster. He traded with the man, for he thought to himself: It's certainly better to have a rooster than a goose.

Then he walked on until it was late in the day. He started getting hungry, so he sold the rooster for twelve *skillinger* and spent the money on food. For it's always better to stay alive than to have a rooster, thought Gudbrand Slope.

Then he continued on toward home until he came to the neighboring farm. There he went inside.

"So how did it go in town?" the neighbors asked him.

"Oh, it went so-so," said the man. "I can't boast of my luck, but neither can I sneer at it." And with that he told them the whole story, how things had gone for him from beginning to end.

"Oh, that's going to be some welcome you receive when you get home to your wife," said the farmer. "God help you! I wouldn't want to be in your shoes."

"Personally, I think things could have gone much worse," said Gudbrand Slope. "But whether it went well or not, I have such a nice wife that she never says a word about the way I do things."

"Oh, that may be, but I can't say I believe it," said his neighbor.

"Shall we make a wager?" said Gudbrand Slope. "I have a hundred *daler* in a chest at home. Do you dare to wager the same amount?"

The two men agreed to the wager. Then Gudbrand stayed until evening. When it began to grow dark, they both went over to his farm. There the neighbor man stood outside the door to listen while Gudbrand went inside to his wife.

"Good evening," said Gudbrand Slope when he came in.

"Good evening," said his wife. "Oh, thank God you're home."

Oh yes, he was home now. Then his wife asked how things had gone for him in town.

"Oh, so-so," replied Gudbrand. "There's really nothing to boast about. When I got to town, nobody wanted to buy the cow, so I traded it for a horse."

"Oh, I thank you for that," said his wife. "We're such respectable folks, and now we can drive to church, just like everyone else. We can afford to keep a horse, so we might as well have one. Go out and bring in the horse, children!"

"Well," said Gudbrand, "I don't actually have the horse. After I'd walked along the road, I traded it for a pig."

"Oh my!" cried his wife. "That's exactly what I would have done! I thank you so much for that! Now we'll have pork in the house, and we'll also be able to offer some pork to folks when they come to visit. What would we do with a horse? Folks would just say we'd gotten so full of ourselves that we could no longer walk to church like we used to do. Go out and bring in the pig, children!"

"Well, I don't actually have the pig here, either," said Gudbrand. "After I'd gone a little farther, I traded it for a milk goat."

"Oh my, oh my. You do everything so well!" cried his wife. "When I stop and think about it, what would I do with a pig? Folks would just say that over here we're eating up everything we own. No, now that I have a goat, I'll have both milk and cheese. And I can still keep the goat. Bring in the goat, children!"

"Well, I don't actually have the goat, either," said Gudbrand. "When I went farther along the road, I traded the goat and got a wonderful sheep in return."

"Oh!" cried his wife. "You did exactly what I would have wished, exactly what I would have done myself. What would we do with a goat? Then I'd have to clamber over hill and dale and bring it back down in the evening. No, now that I have a sheep, I'll have wool and cloth in the house and food too. Go out and let in the sheep, children!"

"Well, I no longer have the sheep," said Gudbrand. "After I'd walked for a while, I traded it for a goose."

"Thank you for that!" said his wife. "Thank you so much! What would I do with a sheep? I don't have a spinning wheel or a spindle, and I don't care to sweat and strain to make clothes. We can buy clothes, just like we did before. Now I'll have a goose to roast, and that's something I've been wanting. And I'll have goose down for that little pillow of mine. Go out and let in the goose, children!"

"Well, I don't actually have the goose, either," said Gudbrand. "After I'd gone farther along the road, I traded it for a rooster."

"God only knows how you've managed to think of everything!" cried his wife. "It's exactly what I would have done. A rooster! It's the same thing as if you'd bought us an eight-day clock. Every morning the rooster will crow at four, and we'll be able to get up at the right time. What would I do with a goose, anyway? I don't know how to roast a goose, and I can just as well fill my pillow with sedge. Go out and let in the rooster, children!"

"Well, I don't actually have the rooster, either," said Gudbrand. "After I'd walked some more, I got terribly hungry, and I had to sell the rooster for twelve *skillinger* to save my own life."

"Oh, thank God you did that!" cried his wife. "No matter what you do, it's always exactly what I would want. What would we do with a rooster? We're our own bosses, and we can sleep as late in the morning as we like. I just thank God that I have you back, for you do everything right. I don't need a rooster or a goose or a pig or a cow."

Then Gudbrand opened the door. "Have I won the hundred *daler* yet?" he asked.

And the neighbor man admitted that he had.

Kari Stave-Skirt

There once was a king who was a widower. He and his queen had a daughter who was so kind and so lovely that no one could be kinder or lovelier. For a long time the king grieved for his queen, for he had been terribly fond of her. Finally he grew tired of living alone, and he married a widowed queen who also had a daughter. But this girl was so ugly and mean that no one could be uglier or meaner. The stepmother and her daughter were jealous of the king's daughter, for she was so lovely. Yet as long as the king was home, they didn't dare do anything to her. They knew he was terribly fond of the girl.

Time passed. Then the king went to war against another king and set off on a campaign. And the queen thought she could do whatever she liked. She starved and beat the king's daughter and refused to leave her in peace. Finally the queen decided that everything was too good for the girl, and she sent her out to tend the livestock.

The king's daughter stayed with the livestock, tending to the animals in the forest and on the mountainside. She had hardly any food, she grew pale and thin, and she was almost always weeping, for she was greatly distressed.

Among the livestock was a big, blue-black ox that always looked nice and glossy. He would often come over to the king's daughter to be petted.

One day when she was sitting and weeping again, greatly distressed, the ox came over and asked her why she was sad. She didn't reply as she kept on weeping.

"Well," said the ox, "I can guess why, even though you won't tell me. You're weeping because the queen is so mean and wants you to starve to death. But you don't need to go looking for food. In my left ear there's a cloth. Take the cloth and spread it out. Then you'll have as much to eat as you like."

That's what she did. She took the cloth and spread it on the grass. There appeared the loveliest foods that anyone could ever want—wine and mead and layer cake too.

She quickly regained her health. She looked so plump and pink and white that the queen and her scrawny daughter turned purple and pale with fury. The queen couldn't understand how her stepdaughter could look so lovely on such a poor diet. She told her maid to follow the girl into the woods and keep watch.

There the maid saw how the stepdaughter took a cloth from the ear of the blue-black ox and spread it out. And on the cloth appeared the loveliest foods. Then the stepdaughter ate her fill. The maid went back and told the queen.

Then the king came home after defeating the king he'd been battling. Great joy spread through the whole palace, and no one was happier than the king's daughter. But the queen took to her bed and gave the doctor a great deal of money to make him say that she would not recover unless she was given the flesh of the blue-black ox to eat.

Both the king's daughter and the servants asked the doctor whether something else might help instead. They pleaded for the ox, for everyone was very fond of him, and they said there was no ox like him in the entire kingdom. But no, the animal had to be slaughtered, and slaughtered he would be. There was nothing else to be done.

When the king's daughter heard this, she was quite dismayed. She went over to the stables to see the ox, which stood there, hanging his head. He looked so sad that she began to weep.

"Why are you weeping?" asked the ox.

She told him that when the king came home, the queen had taken to her bed, and she'd persuaded the doctor to say that she wouldn't recover unless she was given the flesh of the blue-black ox to eat. And so he was to be slaughtered.

"If they put me to death, they'll soon kill you too," said the ox. "If you agree with me, then let's be on our way tonight."

The king's daughter thought it would be hard to leave her father behind, but it would be even worse to live in the same place as the queen. She promised the ox she would come.

That night, after everyone else had gone to bed, the king's daughter crept down to the stable to the ox. He told her to climb onto his back, and then he raced off as fast as he could go.

When the servants got up early the next morning and went to slaughter the ox, they discovered he was gone. And when the king got up and asked for his daughter, they discovered she was gone too. He sent messengers far and wide to search for them, and he also sent word to the church hill, but no one had seen any trace of the ox or the girl.

In the meantime, the ox raced through many lands, carrying the king's daughter on his back. They came to a big copper forest, where the trees and branches and flowers and everything else were made of copper.

Before they entered the forest, the ox said to the king's daughter, "When we go into the forest, you must be very careful not to touch a single leaf, or that will be the end of both you and me. A troll with three heads lives here, and he owns the forest."

Gracious! She would certainly make sure not to touch any leaves. She was very careful to bend away from the branches and to push them aside with her hands, but it was such a dense forest that it was almost impossible to make their way through. And no matter how hard she tried, she couldn't help tearing off a leaf, and it ended up in her hand.

"Oh no, what have you done?" said the ox. "Now it's a matter of fighting for our lives. You must hide the leaf well."

A moment later they reached the other side of the forest, and a troll with three heads came rushing toward them.

"Who has been touching my forest?" said the troll.

"It's just as much mine as yours," said the ox.

"We'll soon see about that!" shouted the troll.

"Yes, we will," said the ox.

Then they ran at each other and began fighting. The ox kicked and butted with all his might, but the troll held his own. The battle lasted all day until the ox finally put an end to it.

By then he was so covered with wounds and felt so wretched that he could hardly walk. They had to spend an entire day resting. The ox told the king's daughter to take the horn that hung from the troll's belt and smear the grease from inside the horn on his wounds. Then the ox recovered, and the next day they set off again.

They journeyed for many, many days until at long last they came to a silver forest. The trees and branches and leaves and flowers and everything else were made of silver.

Before the ox went into the forest, he said to the king's daughter, "When we go into this forest, be very careful, for God's sake. Don't touch anything, and don't tear off even one leaf, or that will be the end of you and me. A troll with six heads lives here, and he owns the forest. I think he may be too much for me."

"Oh," said the king's daughter, "I'll be very careful not to touch anything you don't want me to touch."

But when they went into the forest, the trees were so big and set so close together that they could hardly get through. She moved as carefully as she could, bending aside the branches and pushing them away with her hands. But the branches kept slapping at her eyes, and no matter how careful she was, she ended up tearing off a leaf.

"Oh no, what have you done?" said the ox. "Now it's a matter of fighting for our lives. This troll has six heads, and he's twice as strong as the first one. But take good care of the leaf and hide it well."

All of a sudden the troll appeared. "Who has been touching my forest?" he said.

"It's just as much mine as yours," said the ox.

"We'll soon see about that!" shouted the troll.

"Yes, we will," said the ox. Then he rushed at the troll and jabbed out his eyes and stabbed him so hard that his guts spilled out. But the troll held his own, and it took three whole days before the ox managed to kill the troll.

By then the animal was so wretched and miserable that he could barely move at all. And he was so covered with wounds that blood poured off him. Then he told the king's daughter to take the horn that hung from the troll's belt and smear the grease from inside the horn on his wounds. That's what she did, and the ox recovered. But they had to stay there and rest for a week before he was able to go on.

Finally they set off again. But the ox was still weak, and he didn't move as fast as he had in the beginning. The king's daughter wanted to spare him.

She told him she was so young and nimble that she could easily walk. But she wasn't allowed to do that. She had to climb up on his back again.

Then they journeyed for a long time through many lands. The king's daughter had no idea where they were headed, but at long last they came to a golden forest. It was so splendid that gold dripped from everything. The trees and branches and flowers and leaves were all made of pure gold.

Here the same thing happened as in the copper forest and the silver forest. The ox told the king's daughter that she must by no means touch anything. A troll with nine heads lived here, and he owned the forest. He was much bigger and stronger than the other two, and the ox thought this troll would be too much for him.

Oh, she would certainly be careful not to touch anything, he could be sure of that.

But when they went into the forest, it was even more dense than the silver forest, and the farther they went, the worse it got. The trees got bigger and bigger and stood closer and closer together, until finally she thought there would be no way for them to get through. And she was so afraid of tearing off a leaf. As she sat on the ox, she twisted and turned both this way and that to avoid the branches. She had to push them forward with her hands, but they kept slapping at her eyes, so she couldn't see what she was grabbing. Before she knew it, she was holding a golden apple in her hand.

Now she was dreadfully frightened, and she began to weep. She wanted to throw the apple away. But the ox said she should keep the apple and hide it well. He comforted her as best he could, but he thought it was going to be a hard battle, and he doubted it would go well.

All of a sudden the troll with nine heads appeared, and he was so vile that the king's daughter hardly dared look at him.

"Who has been touching my forest?" shouted the troll.

"It's just as much my forest as yours," said the ox.

"We'll soon see about that!" shouted the troll.

"Yes, we will," said the ox.

Then they rushed at each other and began to fight. It was such a horrible sight to behold that the king's daughter almost fainted. The ox jabbed out the troll's eyes and stabbed him so his guts spilled out. But the troll held his own. When the ox chopped off one head, the others quickly blew life into the troll again, and it took a whole week before the ox managed to kill him.

By then the animal was so wretched and weak that he couldn't move at all.

He was covered with wounds, and he couldn't even manage to tell the king's daughter to take the horn from the troll's belt and smear the grease from inside the horn on his wounds. Yet that's what she did, and then the ox recovered. But they had to stay there and rest for three weeks before the ox was able to go on.

Slowly they set off, for the ox said that they still needed to go a little farther. They traveled over many big mountains covered with thick forests. They continued on for a while and then started up a mountainside.

"Do you see anything?" asked the ox.

"No, I see only the sky and the wilderness on the mountain," said the king's daughter.

As they climbed farther, the mountainside leveled out so the view around them was even better.

"Do you see anything now?" asked the ox.

"Yes, I see a little castle far, far away," said the princess.

"It's probably not so little," said the ox.

At long last they came to a big hill at the edge of a steep cliff.

"Do you see anything now?" asked the ox.

"Yes, now I see that the castle's very close, and it's much, much bigger," said the king's daughter.

"That's where you must go," said the ox. "Right below the castle is a pig shed, and that's what you need to find. There you'll see a skirt made from wooden staves. Put it on and go over to the castle. Tell them your name is Kari Stave-Skirt and ask for work. But first you must take your little knife and use it to cut off my head. Then you must flay off my hide, fold it up, and place it over there at the foot of the cliff. Inside the hide you must put the copper leaf, the silver leaf, and the golden apple. Over there near the cliff you'll find a stick. If you need me for anything, just pound the stick against the cliff wall."

At first the king's daughter refused, but when the ox said it was the only thanks he wanted for everything he'd done for her, she had no choice. She thought it was such a terrible thing to do, but she hacked and sawed at the big animal with the knife until she'd chopped off his head and flayed off his hide. Then she placed the folded hide next to the cliff. Inside the hide she put the copper leaf, the silver leaf, and the golden apple.

After she'd done that, she made her way to the pig shed, but as she walked, she wept and was greatly distressed. There she put on the skirt made from wooden staves. Then she went over to the royal palace and into the kitchen, where she asked for work. She said her name was Kari Stave-Skirt.

Yes, said the cook, there was work for her. She would be allowed to wash the dishes, for the one who used to do that had just left. "When you grow tired of being here, I suppose you'll take off too."

Oh no, she would never do that.

And she was very good at washing dishes. On Sunday guests were expected at the royal palace. Then Kari asked for permission to take to the prince a basin of water for washing, but the others laughed at her and said, "Why would you do that? Do you think the prince will pay any attention to you, the way you look?"

But Kari refused to give up. She kept on begging, and finally she was given permission.

As she climbed the stairs, her wooden skirt clattered so much that the prince came out and asked, "Who are you?"

"I'm supposed to bring you water for washing," said Kari.

"Do you think I would want to have wash water from the likes of you?" said the prince. And he dumped the water on her head.

With that she had to leave.

Then Kari asked for permission to go to church. She was allowed to do that, for the church was nearby. But first she went over to the cliff and pounded on the wall with the stick she found lying there, just as the ox had said.

Instantly a man appeared and asked her what she wanted. The king's daughter said that she'd been given permission to go to church and listen to the pastor, but she had no clothes to wear. Then the man brought her a dress that was as shiny as the copper forest. He gave her a horse and saddle as well.

When Kari arrived at the church, she looked so beautiful and splendid that everyone wondered who she was, and almost no one listened to what the pastor said, for they were looking at her. Even the prince was so drawn to Kari that he couldn't take his eyes off her for even a second.

The instant she left the church, the prince ran out and pulled the door closed behind him. He held one of her gloves that she had dropped. When she climbed onto her horse, the prince followed and asked her where she was from.

"I'm from Wash Land," said Kari. When the prince showed her the glove and wanted to return it, she said:

> *Light ahead and dark behind,*
> *the prince won't see where I ride!*

The prince had never seen the likes of that glove. He traveled far and wide, asking everyone about the land of the proud lady, who had left without her glove. But no one could tell him where that land was.

On Sunday someone had to bring the prince a towel.

"Oh, could I be the one to do it?" said Kari.

"What good would that do?" said the others in the kitchen. "You saw what happened last time."

Kari refused to give up and kept on begging until she was given permission. Then she ran up the stairs, making her wooden skirt clatter.

The prince came rushing out. When he saw Kari, he yanked the towel from her hands and threw it right in her face. "Get out of here, you ugly troll!" he said. "Do you think I'd want a towel that you've been clutching in your dirty fingers?"

Then the prince went off to church.

Kari asked for permission to go to church too. The other servants asked her why she wanted to go, for she had nothing to wear except a wooden skirt that was filthy and vile. But Kari said she thought the pastor was such a splendid preacher, and it did her good to hear what he said. Finally she was allowed to go.

She went to the cliff and pounded the stick on the wall. The man came out and gave her a dress that was even more splendid than the first one. It was completely adorned with silver, and it shone as beautifully as the silver forest. He also gave her a magnificent horse with a silver-embroidered saddle blanket and a silver bridle.

When the king's daughter came to the church, all the churchgoers were still standing outside on the church hill. Everyone wondered who she was, and the prince rushed over and wanted to hold her horse as she dismounted. But she jumped off and told him that wasn't necessary. The horse was so docile that he would stand still whenever she wished and also come when she called.

Then everyone went inside the church. But almost no one listened to what the pastor said, for they were looking at Kari. And the prince was even more enchanted by her than he was the first time. When the sermon was over, she left the church and went over to mount her horse. Then the prince again asked her where she was from.

"I'm from Towel Land," said the king's daughter, and she dropped her riding whip. When the prince bent down to pick it up, Kari said:

Light ahead and dark behind,
the prince won't see where I ride!

Again she disappeared, and the prince couldn't find out where she'd gone. He traveled far and wide and asked everybody about the land she'd said she was from, but no one could tell him where it was. The prince had to give up.

On Sunday someone had to take a comb to the prince. Kari asked for permission to do this, but the others reminded her what had happened the last time. They scolded her for wanting to appear before the prince, so dirty and vile as she looked in her wooden skirt. But she wouldn't stop begging until they allowed her to take the comb to the prince.

When she came clattering up the stairs again, the prince rushed out, took the comb, and threw it at her. He shouted at her to get out.

Then the prince went off to church.

Kari asked for permission to go too. Again the other servants asked her why she wanted to go there, for she looked both vile and dirty and she didn't have the proper clothes to appear in public. They said the prince or someone else might see her, and then there would be trouble for her and for them. Kari said the churchgoers had other things to look at, and she wouldn't stop begging until she was given permission to go.

The same thing happened as before. Kari went to the cliff and pounded on the wall with the stick. Then the man came out and gave her a dress that was even more magnificent than the others. It was almost nothing but gold and diamonds. He also gave her a fine horse with a gold-embroidered saddle blanket and a golden bridle.

When the king's daughter arrived at church, the pastor and the churchgoers were still standing on the church hill, waiting for her. The prince came running and wanted to hold her horse, but she jumped off and said, "No thanks, that's not necessary. My horse is so docile that he will stand still whenever I want him to."

Then they all went inside the church, and the pastor took his place in the pulpit. But no one listened to what he said, for they were looking at Kari and wondering where she was from. And the prince was even more in love with her than the first two times. He didn't notice anything else as he stared at her.

When the sermon was over and the king's daughter was about to leave the church, the prince spilled a quarter barrel of tar on the church porch so that he might help her over it. But she paid no attention to him. She set her foot in the middle of the tar and jumped across. One of her golden slippers got stuck in the tar. After she had mounted her horse, the prince came running from the church and asked her where she was from.

"From Comb Land," said Kari. But when the prince tried to hand her the golden slipper, she said:

> *Light ahead and dark behind,*
> *the prince won't see where I ride!*

Again the prince didn't know where she'd gone. He traveled far and wide in the world and asked everyone about Comb Land. When no one could tell him where it was, he decreed that he would marry whoever could wear the golden slipper.

Then women, both beautiful and ugly, came from many lands. But none of them had such a small foot that she could wear the golden slipper. At long last Kari Stave-Skirt's horrible stepmother arrived with her daughter, whose foot turned out to be just the right size for the golden slipper. The girl looked so ugly and nasty that the prince was reluctant to do as he'd promised. But all the arrangements were made for the wedding, and the bride was dressed in her finery. As they rode to the church, a little bird sang from a tree:

> *From out of the heel*
> *and out of the toe,*
> *from Kari Stave-Skirt's shoe*
> *much blood will now flow!*

And when they looked, the bird had spoken the truth, for blood was pouring out of the golden slipper. Then all the servant girls and all the servant women at the castle had to come and try on the slipper. But it didn't fit any of them.

"Where is this Kari Stave-Skirt?" asked the prince after all the others had tried to put on the slipper. He too had heard the bird singing, and he recalled what the bird had said.

"Her?" said the others. "It won't do any good for her to try on the shoe, for she has feet like a horse."

"That may be," said the prince, "but all the others have tried, so Kari should try too." He shouted out the door, "Kari!" and she came up the steps.

Her wooden skirt clattered as if a whole regiment of dragoons was rushing forward.

"It's your turn to try on the golden slipper. Then you'll be the princess," said the other girls as they laughed and made fun of her.

Kari picked up the slipper, put it on her foot as easy as could be, and threw off the wooden skirt. There she stood in her dazzling gold dress, and on her other foot she wore the mate to the golden slipper.

The prince recognized her at once. He was so happy that he ran over and put his arm around her waist to kiss her. When he learned that she was a king's daughter, he was even happier. And then they celebrated their wedding.

Spin, span, spun—now this story's done.

The Fox As Shepherd

There once was a woman who set out to hire a shepherd. Then she met a bear.

"Where are you going?" said the bear.

"Oh, I'm off to hire a shepherd," replied the woman.

"Won't you hire me as your shepherd?" asked the bear

"Yes, I will, if you're good at calling," said the woman.

"Hey-ya!" said the bear.

"No, I don't want you," said the woman when she heard that. And she went on her way.

After she'd walked for a while, she met a wolf.

"Where are you going?" said the wolf.

"I'm off to hire a shepherd," replied the woman.

"Will you hire me as your shepherd?" asked the wolf.

"Yes, I will, if you're good at calling," said the woman.

"Ooooff-ooooff!" said the wolf.

"No, I don't want you," said the woman.

After she'd walked a little farther, she met a fox.

"Where are you going?" said the fox.

"Oh, I'm off to hire a shepherd," said the woman.

"Won't you hire me as your shepherd?" asked the fox.

"Yes, I will, if you're good at calling," said the woman.

"Dil-dal-holom!" said the fox, nice and sweet.

"Oh yes, I will hire you as my shepherd," said the woman. And she put the fox in charge of tending her livestock.

On his first day as shepherd, the fox ate all the woman's goats. On his second day he put an end to all her sheep, and on the third day he ate up all her cows. When he came home in the evening, the woman asked him what he'd done with her livestock.

"The skulls are in the river, and the bodies are in the grove," said the fox.

The woman was in the middle of churning, but she thought she'd better go and see to her animals. While she was gone, the fox slipped inside the churn and ate up all the cream.

When the woman came back and saw what he'd done, she was furious. She picked up the little bit of cream that was left and threw it after the fox so it splashed on the end of his tail.

And that's why the fox has a white tip on his tail.

The Blacksmith They Didn't Dare Let into Hell

During those days when Our Lord and Saint Peter wandered on this earth, they once came upon a blacksmith who had made a pact with the Devil. The man had agreed that he would belong to the Devil in seven years if, until that time, he could be the master of all masters in the art of blacksmithing. Both he and the Devil had signed the pact. And that's why the blacksmith had put a sign above his smithy door that said, "Here lives the master of all masters!"

When Our Lord saw that, he went inside. "Who are you?" he said to the blacksmith.

"Read what it says above the door," replied the blacksmith. "But maybe you don't know how to read. In that case you'll have to wait until someone comes along who can help you."

Before Our Lord could say anything, a man came by with a horse. He asked the blacksmith to shoe the horse.

"Why don't you let me try?" said Our Lord.

"All right, you can try," said the blacksmith. "You can't make so much of a mess of it that I won't be able to fix what you've done."

Then Our Lord went out and took off one of the horse's legs. He placed the leg in the forge and made the shoe glowing hot. After that he sharpened and rasped, and he bent the nail tips. Then he put the leg, as good as new, back on the horse. When he was done, he took off the other foreleg and did exactly the same thing. After he'd put the leg back on, he took off the hind legs, first the right and then the left. He put them in the forge and made the shoes glowing hot. He sharpened and rasped, and he bent the nail tips. Then he put the legs back on the horse.

All the while, the blacksmith watched what he was doing. "You're not a bad blacksmith after all," he said.

"Think so?" said Our Lord.

A short time later the blacksmith's mother came over to the smithy and told her son to come home for dinner. She was very old, her back was terribly stooped, her face was wrinkled, and she could hardly walk.

"Pay attention to what you're about to see," said Our Lord. He picked up the woman, placed her in the forge, and made from her a lovely young maiden.

"I'll repeat what I've already said," said the blacksmith. "You're not a bad blacksmith after all. Above my door it says: 'Here lives the master of all masters.' Yet I honestly have to say that a person keeps learning as long as he lives."

And with that he went over to the house to eat dinner.

When he went back to the smithy, a man came riding up. He wanted to have his horse shoed.

"I'll have that done in no time," said the blacksmith. "I've just learned a new method for shoeing a horse. It's a good way to do it when the day is short." And he began to cut and crack until he had taken all the legs off the horse. "I don't know why I should bother working with only one shoe at a time," he said.

Then he put the legs in the forge, just as he'd seen Our Lord do. He filled it with heaps of charcoal and got the smithy's boy to work the bellows hard.

But things went as you might well imagine. The legs burned up, and the blacksmith had to pay the man for the horse.

He wasn't very happy about that.

Then a poor old woman came walking past, and he thought: If the first method didn't work, the second one surely will.

He picked up the old woman and put her in the forge. No matter how much she wept and pleaded for her life, it did no good.

"You're so old that you don't know what's best for you," said the blacksmith. "In a moment you're going to become a young maiden again, but I won't take even a *skilling* in payment for my work."

Yet it didn't go any better for the old woman, the poor thing, than it had gone for the horse's legs.

"That was a terrible thing to do," said Our Lord.

"Oh, I doubt there are many who will miss her," replied the blacksmith. "But shame on the Devil. He's not doing a very good job of keeping his promise. He needs to remember what it says on the sign above my door."

"If you could have three wishes from me," said Our Lord, "what would you wish for?"

"Try me," replied the blacksmith, "and then you'll find out."

So Our Lord granted him three wishes.

"First and foremost, I wish that when I tell someone to go up in the pear tree next to the smithy wall he will stay there until I tell him to come down," said the blacksmith.

"My second wish is that when I tell someone to sit in the armchair inside the workshop he will stay there until I tell him to stand up again. And, finally, I wish that when I tell someone to crawl inside the steel-wire pouch I have in my pocket he will stay inside until I give him permission to crawl out."

"These are the wishes of a bad man," said Saint Peter. "First and foremost you should have wished for God's mercy and beneficence."

"I didn't dare aim so high," said the blacksmith.

With that, Our Lord and Saint Peter said goodbye and went on their way.

The days flew, and the years did too. When the time was up, the Devil arrived to get the blacksmith, as they'd agreed in their pact.

"Are you ready?" the Devil said, sticking his nose in the smithy door.

"I just need to shape this nailhead first," replied the blacksmith. "In the meantime, why don't you climb up in the pear tree and get a pear to nibble on. You must be both thirsty and hungry after your journey."

The Devil thanked him for the excellent idea and climbed up in the tree.

"Oh, now that I think of it," said the blacksmith, "I won't be able to make a head on this nail for at least four years. This iron is awfully hard. You can't come down from the tree during that time, but you can sit up there and rest."

The Devil begged and pleaded for permission to come down. His voice was as pitiful as a two-*skilling* coin. But it did no good. Finally he had to promise that he wouldn't return until the four years were up.

"All right, then you can come down," said the blacksmith.

When the time was up, the Devil came back to get the blacksmith. "You must be ready by now," he said. "Surely you must have made a head for that nail."

"Oh yes, I certainly have made a head for the nail," replied the blacksmith. "But you're a little bit early, all the same, for I haven't yet sharpened the point. I've never worked with such hard iron before. While I'm sharpening the nail, you could take a seat in the armchair and rest. I'm sure you must be tired."

"Thanks, I'll do that," said the Devil. And he sat down in the armchair.

But no sooner had he taken a seat than the blacksmith said that after he'd thought about it, he wouldn't be able to sharpen the point until another four years had passed.

At first the Devil begged nicely to be released from the chair, but then he grew angry and began to threaten. The blacksmith apologized as best he could, saying that the iron was to blame, for it was awfully hard. He consoled the Devil by saying that he was seated so comfortably in the armchair, and in four years' time on the dot, he would be allowed to get up.

There was nothing to be done. The Devil had to promise not to take the blacksmith away until four more years had passed.

The blacksmith said, "All right, then you can get up."

And the Devil rushed off as fast as he could go.

Four years later the Devil came back to get the blacksmith.

"I know you must be ready by now," said the Devil, sticking his nose in the smithy door.

"Ready and willing," replied the blacksmith. "We can leave whenever you like. There's just one thing," he added. "I've been wondering about this for a very long time. I wanted to ask you if it's true what they say, that the Devil can make himself as small as he likes."

"Of course it's true," replied the Devil.

"Well, then, could you do me a favor and crawl into this steel-wire pouch to see if there's a hole in the bottom?" said the blacksmith. "I'm so afraid that I'll lose my travel money."

"Gladly," said the Devil. He made himself small and crawled inside the pouch. But no sooner was he inside than the blacksmith closed it up.

"Well, there's not a single hole," said the Devil from inside the pouch.

"Oh, I'm glad to hear that," replied the blacksmith. "But it's always better to be safe than sorry. I might as well weld the joints a little, just to be on the safe side." And with that he placed the pouch in the forge and made it glowing hot.

"Ow! Ow! Are you crazy? Don't you know I'm inside the pouch?" shouted the Devil.

"Yes, but I can't help you," said the blacksmith. "There's an old saying: You should strike while the iron's hot."

Then he picked up a big sledgehammer. He set the pouch on the anvil and began pounding it with all his might

"Ow! Ow! Ow!" shouted the Devil from inside the pouch. "Dear sir! Let me out, and I'll never come back again!"

With that the blacksmith opened the pouch, and the Devil took off fast, without a glance back.

After a while it occurred to the blacksmith that it might have been a mistake to make an enemy of the Devil. If I don't get into heaven, he thought, there's a risk I'll end up homeless, for I've quarreled with the one who is the ruler of hell.

He decided it was best to try to get into either hell or heaven, and better sooner than later. Then he'd know how things stood. So he hoisted the sledge-hammer onto his shoulder and set off.

After he'd walked for a good long while, he came to a crossroads where the road to heaven diverged from the one to hell. There he caught up with a tailor who was scurrying along, carrying an iron for pressing cloth.

"Good day," said the blacksmith. "Where are you headed?"

"To heaven, if I can get in," replied the tailor. "What about you?"

"Oh, we won't be keeping each other company for long," replied the blacksmith. "I'm thinking of trying out hell first, seeing as I'm already acquainted with the Devil."

Then they said goodbye, and each went his separate way.

But the blacksmith was a strong and powerful man, and he walked much faster than the tailor. So it didn't take long before he was standing at the gate to hell. He told the guard to announce him by saying there was someone outside who wished to have a word with the Devil.

"Go back and ask him who he is," said the Devil to the guard.

And that's what he did.

"Give the Devil my greetings, and tell him it's the blacksmith with the pouch. He's sure to remember me," replied the blacksmith. "Ask him politely if I could slip inside hell at once, for I worked in the smithy all day until noon, and after that I walked a long way."

When the Devil heard this, he ordered the guard to fasten all nine locks on the gate to hell. "And put on a padlock too," said the Devil. "If that man gets inside, he'll wreak havoc in all of hell."

"Well, I see there's no refuge to be found here," said the blacksmith to himself when he saw the guard locking the gate more securely. "I suppose I'll have to try heaven instead."

With that he turned on his heel and walked back until he came to the crossroads again. There he took the road the tailor had taken.

The blacksmith was angry about the long journey he'd made, for he'd gone to hell and back to no avail. So he strode along as fast as he could go. He reached the gate of heaven just as Saint Peter opened it a crack to let the skinny tailor slip inside. At that moment the blacksmith was still six or seven paces away from the gate.

It's probably best that I hurry up, he thought. Then he grabbed the sledgehammer and threw it at the opening in the gate just as the tailor slipped inside.

And if the blacksmith didn't manage to get through the gate, I don't know what has become of him.

The Rooster and the Hen

THE HEN:	You promise me shoes, year after year, year after year, but I have no shoes!
THE ROOSTER:	Shoes you shall have!
THE HEN:	I lay eggs and do my best, and yet here I am barefoot!
THE ROOSTER:	So take your eggs and go into town and buy yourself shoes, then you'll no longer be barefoot!

For this children's tale, the emphasis is everything, and the sounds of the rooster and hen must be imitated.

The Rooster, the Cuckoo, and the Black Grouse

The rooster, the cuckoo, and the black grouse once bought a cow together. It wasn't possible to divide up the cow, and they couldn't decide how to reimburse each other. So they agreed that whoever woke up first in the morning should have the cow.

The rooster woke up first.

"Now the cow is MINE! Now the cow is MINE!" said the rooster.

When the rooster crowed, the cuckoo woke up.

"My COW! My COW!" said the cuckoo.

When he sang, the black grouse woke up.

"Dear brothers of mine, SHARE, as is right and FAIR, as is right and FAIR! Tsss! Tsss!" said the black grouse.

Can you tell me who should get the cow?

Lillekort

There once was a poor couple who lived in a miserable hovel marked only by dreary poverty. They had neither food nor firewood. Yet even though they had almost nothing else, God had blessed them with children. Each year they had one more, and now they were expecting another.

The husband was not very happy about this. He was constantly grumbling and griping. He said that he thought by now they'd had enough of God's gifts. When the time came for his wife to give birth, he went off to the forest to get firewood, for he didn't feel like hearing the new baby wail. He said there'd be time enough for that when the child started howling for food.

After her husband had left, the wife gave birth to a beautiful baby boy. The instant he entered the world, he looked around the room.

"Oh, my dear mother," he said, "give me some old clothes that belong to my brothers and enough provisions for a couple of days. Then I'll go out into the world to try my luck. I see that you already have enough children."

"Oh, good gracious, my son!" said his mother. "You're still much too little. That will never do."

The boy refused to give up. He begged and pleaded for so long that his mother ended up giving him some old rags and a few provisions wrapped in a bundle. Then, as happy and confident as could be, he set off into the world.

Yet he was hardly gone before the woman gave birth to another boy. He too looked around and said, "Oh, dear mother, give me some old clothes that belong to my brothers and a couple of days' provisions. Then I'll go out into the world to find my twin brother. You already have enough children."

"Good gracious, me! You're much too little, you poor thing," said the woman. "That will never do."

But it did no good. The boy begged and pleaded for so long that in the end he was given some old rags and a bundle with provisions. Then, looking ever so manly, he set off into the world to find his twin.

After the younger boy had walked for a while, he caught sight of his brother up ahead. Then he called to him and told him to stop. "Wait for me!"

he said. "You're racing along the road as if someone were paying you to run. But you should have stayed to have a look at your younger brother before you set off into the world."

Then the older boy stopped and looked back.

The younger boy caught up with him and told him what had happened. There was no question that they were brothers. Then he said, "We had to hurry so much that we didn't have time to meet at home. Let's talk here."

"What do you want to be called?" asked the older boy.

"I want to be called Lillekort," replied his twin. "What about you? What do you want to be called?"

"I want to be called King Lavring," replied the older boy.

So they baptized each other and then continued on. After they'd walked for a while, they came to a crossroads. There they agreed to part and each go his own way. That's what they did, but they'd gone only a short distance when they ended up meeting again. Once more they went separate ways, but after a short time, the same thing happened. They ended up meeting. Before they knew it, for a third time it happened again. Then they agreed that each of them would set off in a different direction, one to the east and one to the west.

"If you are ever in need or suffer misfortune," said the older twin, "just call my name three times and I'll come to help you. But don't summon me unless you're in dire need."

"In that case, I suppose we won't be seeing each other anytime soon," said Lillekort.

Then they said goodbye. Lillekort headed east, while King Lavring went west.

After Lillekort had walked for a good long time, he came upon an old, old hunchbacked woman who had only one eye. Lillekort grabbed that eye from her.

"Ow, ow!" cried the old woman. "What happened to my eye?"

"What will you give me to get your eye back?" said Lillekort.

"I'll give you a special kind of sword that can conquer a whole army, no matter how big it might be," replied the woman.

"All right, hand it over," said Lillekort.

The old woman gave him the sword, and then she got her eye back.

Lillekort continued on. After he'd wandered for a while, he again came upon an old, old hunchbacked woman who had only one eye. And before she knew it, he'd stolen her eye.

"Ow, ow! What happened to my eye?" cried the old woman.

"What will you give me to get your eye back?" said Lillekort.

"I'll give you a ship that can sail on both fresh water and salt water, over mountains and through deep valleys," replied the woman.

"All right, hand it over," said Lillekort.

The woman gave him a tiny little ship, small enough to fit in his pocket. Then the woman got her eye back, and they headed off in opposite directions.

After Lillekort had wandered a great distance, for the third time he came upon an old, old hunchbacked woman who had only one eye. Again he stole the eye. When the woman screamed and carried on and asked what had happened to her eye, Lillekort said, "What will you give me to get your eye back?"

"I'll give you the skill to brew a hundred barrels of malt ale in one batch," she replied.

In return for that skill, the old woman got her eye back. Then they headed off in opposite directions.

After Lillekort had walked a short distance, he thought it might be worthwhile to try out the ship. So he took the ship out of his pocket and stuck first one foot and then the other inside it. No sooner had he put one foot inside than the ship grew much bigger, and when he put the other foot inside, it grew as big as a seagoing vessel.

Lillekort said, "Go now on fresh water and salt water, over mountains and through deep valleys, and don't stop until you reach the king's palace!"

The ship set off at once, moving as fast as a bird through the air, until it came to a spot just below the royal palace. There it stopped. Everyone inside the royal palace had been standing at the windows, and they saw Lillekort come sailing toward them. They were all so amazed that they ran down to see what sort of person had come sailing on a ship through the air.

While they were running down from the royal palace, Lillekort climbed out of the ship so he could stuff it back in his pocket. The moment he stepped out of the ship, it shrank until it was as little as when the old woman had given it to him. The folks from the royal palace saw nothing but a small, ragged boy standing on the shore.

The king asked him where he was from. The boy said he didn't know, nor did he know how he had arrived there. Then he begged sincerely and politely for work at the royal palace. He said if there was nothing else for him to do, he could carry firewood and water for the kitchen maid. And that's what he was allowed to do.

When Lillekort went up to the royal palace, he saw that everything was covered in black, both outside and in, both the roof and the walls. He asked the kitchen maid what this meant.

"Oh, let me tell you," replied the kitchen maid. "A long time ago the king's daughter was promised to three trolls, and next Thursday evening one of them is supposed to come and get her. The Red Knight has vowed to rescue her, but God only knows whether he can. Now you can understand why there is great sorrow and distress here at the palace."

When Thursday evening arrived, the Red Knight accompanied the princess down to the shore, for that was where she was supposed to meet the troll. The knight had vowed to stay there and protect the princess, but I don't think he was going to do much harm to the troll. No sooner had the princess set foot on the edge of the shore than the Red Knight climbed up in a big tree standing nearby and hid as best he could among the branches. The princess wept and pleaded with him ever so earnestly not to leave her, but the Red Knight paid her no mind.

"It's better for one to be killed rather than two," said the Red Knight.

In the meantime Lillekort begged the kitchen maid ever so politely to be allowed to go down to the shore for a while.

"Oh, why do you want to go?" said the kitchen maid. "There's nothing for you to do there."

"Oh yes, my dear mistress. Please let me go," said Lillekort. "I dearly want to go down there and have a little fun with the other children."

"Well, all right. Go ahead," said the kitchen maid. "But make sure you're back before the supper cook pot has to be hung over the fire and the roast has to be put on the spit. And bring back a big armload of firewood for the kitchen."

Lillekort promised to do just that. Then he ran down to the shore.

As soon as the boy reached the spot where the king's daughter was sitting, the troll appeared with a great rushing and roaring. He was so big and stout that he was a vile sight to behold. And he had five heads.

"Scram!" bellowed the troll.

"Scram yourself!" said Lillekort.

"Do you know how to fence?" shouted the troll.

"Even if I don't, I can learn," said Lillekort.

Then the troll swung a big, thick iron bar he was holding in his fist. It made the sand on the ground fly up ten feet in the air.

"Drat!" said Lillekort. "That was something! But now I'll show you what I can do!" Then he grabbed the sword that the old hunchbacked woman had given him and swung it at the troll so that all five heads flew across the sand.

When the princess saw that she'd been saved, she was so happy that she didn't know what to do. She jumped and she danced.

"Lie down on my lap and sleep for a while," she told Lillekort. While he slept, she put on him a golden tunic.

It didn't take long before the Red Knight climbed down from the tree when he saw there was no further danger. He threatened the princess for so long that she had to promise to say he was the one who had rescued her. He then took the lungs and tongues from the troll, wrapped them in his handkerchief, and accompanied the princess back to the royal palace.

The honors that had been bestowed on the Red Knight before were nothing compared to what happened now. The king couldn't do enough for him. And the knight was always seated to the right of the king at the table.

As for Lillekort, he went out to the troll's ship and gathered up a great many gold and silver treasures. Then he scurried back to the royal palace.

When the kitchen maid saw all the gold and silver, she was horrified. She said to him, "My dear, Lillekort, where did you get all this from?" She was afraid that he had not come by the treasures in an honest way.

"Oh," replied Lillekort, "I went home for a while, and all these things had fallen out of some buckets, so I brought them back for you. Yes, I did."

When the kitchen maid heard the treasures were for her, she didn't ask any more questions. She thanked Lillekort, and after that everything was perfectly fine.

On the second Thursday evening, the exact same thing happened. Everyone was sad and distressed. But the Red Knight said that if he could rescue the princess from one troll, he could certainly rescue her from another. Then he accompanied her down to the shore.

Yet he wasn't going to do much harm to this troll either. When the time approached for the troll to arrive, the knight said just as he'd said the first time, "It's better for one to be killed rather than two." And he climbed up in the tree.

Lillekort begged the cook for permission to go down to the shore for a while.

"Why do you want to go there?" said the cook.

"Oh, please let me go," said Lillekort. "I dearly want to go down there and have some fun with the other children."

Again he was allowed to go. But first he had to promise to be back before the roast needed to be turned, and he had to bring back a big armload of firewood.

No sooner did Lillekort reach the shore than the troll appeared with a great rushing and roaring. This troll was even bigger than the first one, and he had ten heads.

"Scram!" bellowed the troll.

"Scram yourself!" said Lillekort.

"Do you know how to fence?" shouted the troll.

"Even if I don't, I can learn," said Lillekort.

Then the troll swung his iron bar—this one was even bigger—so the sand on the ground flew up twenty feet in the air.

"Drat!" said Lillekort. "That was certainly something! But now I'll show you what I can do!" Then he grabbed his sword and swung it at the troll so that all ten heads danced across the sand.

Again the king's daughter said to Lillekort, "Lie down on my lap and sleep for a while." And while he slept, she put on him a silver tunic.

As soon as the Red Knight saw there was no further danger, he climbed down from the tree. Again he threatened the princess for so long that she had to promise to say he was the one who had rescued her. He then took the tongues and lungs from the troll, wrapped them in his handkerchief, and accompanied the princess back to the palace.

There was much joy and elation, as you might well imagine, and the king couldn't do enough for the Red Knight. He showered the man with honors and tributes.

Lillekort gathered up an armload of gold and silver treasures from the troll's ship. Yes, he did. When he got back to the royal palace, the kitchen maid clapped her hands, and she wanted to know where he'd found all the gold and silver. Lillekort replied that he'd gone home for a little while, and these were things that had fallen out of some buckets. He said he'd brought the treasures back for her.

When the third Thursday evening arrived, things went exactly as they had twice before. The whole royal palace was covered in black, and everyone was sad and distressed. But the Red Knight said he didn't think they had much to fear. If he'd rescued the king's daughter from two trolls, he could certainly rescue her from a third.

Then he accompanied her down to the shore, but when the time came for the troll to arrive, he again climbed up in the tree to hide. The princess wept and pleaded with him to stay with her, but it did no good. The Red Knight repeated the same old thing: "It's better for one to be killed rather than two."

That evening Lillekort again begged to be allowed to go down to the shore.

"Oh, why do you want to go there?" replied the kitchen maid.

He begged for so long that he was finally given permission to go. But he had to promise to be back in the kitchen when the roast needed to be turned.

No sooner did he reach the shore than the troll appeared with a great rushing and roaring. This troll was much, much bigger than the first two, and he had fifteen heads.

"Scram!" bellowed the troll.

"Scram yourself!" said Lillekort.

"Do you know how to fence?" shouted the troll.

"Even if I don't, I can learn," said Lillekort.

"I'll teach you!" shouted the troll. And he swung his iron bar so the sand on the ground flew up thirty feet in the air.

"Drat!" said Lillekort. "That was certainly something! But now I'll show you what I can do!"

He grabbed his sword at once and swung it at the troll, so that all fifteen heads danced across the sand.

Then the princess was saved. She thanked and blessed Lillekort, for he was the one who had rescued her.

"Lie down on my lap and sleep for a while," she told Lillekort. While he slept, she put on him a brass tunic.

Later the king's daughter said, "But how will we make it known that you're the one who rescued me?"

"Let me tell you how," replied Lillekort. "When the Red Knight accompanies you back home, he will claim that he was the one who saved you. Then he will be given your hand in marriage and half the kingdom, as you well know. But on your wedding day, when they ask you who should fill the ale bowls, you must say: 'I would like the little boy who works in the kitchen to do it, the one who carries firewood and water for the kitchen maid.' When I fill your bowl, I'll spill a drop on the knight's plate but none on yours. Then he'll fly into a rage and hit me. He and I will do the same thing twice. But the third time you will say: 'Shame on you for striking the one dearest to my heart! He's the one who rescued me, and he's the one I will wed!'"

Then Lillekort ran back to the royal palace just as he'd done before. But first he went out to the troll's ship, and there he gathered up a great deal of gold, silver, and other precious treasures. Again he gave the kitchen maid a whole armload of gold and silver things.

As soon as the Red Knight saw that all danger was past, he climbed down from the tree and threatened the king's daughter until she promised to say that he was the one who had rescued her. Then he accompanied her back to the royal palace.

Now the knight received whatever honors he hadn't already received. All the king could think about was how to reward this man who had saved his daughter from three trolls. He said it was only right that the Red Knight should be given the princess and half the kingdom.

On her wedding day the princess said she wanted the little boy who worked in the kitchen—the one who carried firewood and water for the kitchen maid—to fill the ale bowls at the bridal table.

"Why would you want that dirty, ragged boy in here?" said the Red Knight.

But the princess insisted that she wanted the boy to fill the bowls and no one else. Finally she got her wish.

Then everything happened just as Lillekort and the king's daughter had agreed. Three times he spilled a drop on the Red Knight's plate but none on hers. Each time the Red Knight grew angry and hit the boy. At the first blow, the ragged clothes Lillekort wore in the kitchen fell off. At the second blow, the brass tunic fell off. And at the third blow, the silver tunic fell off. There he stood in a golden tunic so shiny and splendid that it practically gleamed.

Then the king's daughter said, "Shame on you for striking the one who is dearest to my heart! He was the one who saved me, and he is the one I want!"

The Red Knight cursed and swore that he was the one who had rescued her.

Then the king said, "Whoever saved my daughter must surely have some way to prove it."

The Red Knight ran off at once to get his handkerchief with the lungs and tongues, while Lillekort went to get all the gold and silver and other precious treasures he'd taken from the trolls' ships. Each of them placed before the king what they'd brought.

"Whoever has such precious items made of gold and silver and diamonds must be the one who killed the trolls," said the king. "It's impossible to obtain such things from anyone else."

And so the Red Knight was thrown into the snake pit, and Lillekort was to have the princess and half the kingdom.

One day the king and Lillekort went out for a walk. Then Lillekort asked the king whether he'd ever had any other children.

"Oh yes," said the king. "I had one other daughter, but the troll took her, for no one could save her. I have promised you my daughter, but if you can rescue my other daughter, who was taken by the troll, then you can have her too, along with the other half of the kingdom."

"I will certainly try," said Lillekort. "But I will need an iron chain that's a thousand feet long, as well as five hundred men and provisions that will last them fifteen weeks. It will be a long sea voyage," he said.

The king promised him all these things, though he was afraid that he didn't have a ship big enough to carry them.

"I have my own ship," said Lillekort. Then he took out of his pocket the tiny ship the old woman had given him.

The king laughed. He thought this must be a joke, but Lillekort merely asked him for the things that he needed. Then the king would see what was what.

All that Lillekort had asked for was brought to him. The first thing that was supposed to be loaded on board the ship was the chain, but nobody was able to lift it. And there wasn't room for many men to stand around the tiny little ship. Then Lillekort picked up one end of the chain and placed a few links on the ship. As he loaded more of the chain on board, the ship grew bigger and bigger until finally it was so big that there was plenty of room for the chain and the five hundred men and the provisions and Lillekort.

"Go now on fresh water and salt water, over mountains and through deep valleys, and don't stop until you come to the place where we'll find the king's daughter," said Lillekort to the ship.

The ship set off at once. There was a great whistling and whooshing all around as it sailed over land and sea.

After they had sailed far, far away, the ship stopped in the middle of the ocean.

"All right, we've arrived," said Lillekort. "It's another matter whether we'll be able to leave."

Then he picked up the iron chain and wrapped one end around his waist. "I have to go down to the bottom," he said. "When I tug hard on the chain, it means I want to come back up. Then you must all pull as one man, or else it will be the death of both you and me." And with that, he jumped into the water, making a big splash of yellow spray.

He sank and sank until finally he reached the bottom. There he saw a big mountain with a door. He opened the door and stepped inside, and there he found the other princess. She was sewing, and when she saw Lillekort, she clapped her hands.

"Oh, thank goodness!" she cried. "I haven't seen a Christian man since I arrived here."

"Well, I've come to get you," said Lillekort.

"I don't think you'll ever manage that," said the king's daughter. "It won't do you any good even to try. The troll will kill you if he sees you."

"I'm glad you mentioned him," said Lillekort. "Where is he? It might be fun to see that troll."

The king's daughter told him that the troll had gone out to find someone who could brew a hundred barrels of malt ale in one batch. The troll was going to hold a feast, and nothing less would do.

"I can do that," said Lillekort.

"If only the troll wasn't so quick-tempered, then I'd have time to tell him you can," replied the princess. "He's so hot-blooded that I'm afraid he'll tear you to pieces the instant he comes in. But I'll try and think of something. Go hide in the alcove over there, and let's see how it goes."

That's what Lillekort did. No sooner had he crept into the alcove to hide than the troll came in.

"Ugh! I smell the blood of a Christian man," said the troll.

"Yes, a bird flew over the roof carrying a Christian man's leg in its beak. It dropped the leg down the chimney," replied the king's daughter. "I hurried to get rid of it, but that must be what you smell."

"That must be it," said the troll.

Then the princess asked him whether he'd found someone who could brew a hundred barrels of malt ale in one batch.

"No, nobody can do that," said the troll.

"A little while ago, someone came here who claimed he could," said the king's daughter.

"How could you be so stupid?" replied the troll. "Why did you let him leave? You knew I was looking for somebody who could do that."

"Well, I didn't actually let him leave," said the princess. "But you're so quick-tempered that I hid him in the alcove. Seeing as you didn't find anyone else, he's probably still there."

"Tell him to come in," said the troll.

When Lillekort appeared, the troll asked him whether it was true that he could brew a hundred barrels of malt ale in one batch.

"Yes, I can," said Lillekort.

"It's a good thing I found you," said the troll. "Go ahead and do it right now. But God have mercy on you if you don't brew the ale strong enough."

"Oh, it'll be tasty," said Lillekort. And with that he started the brewing.

"I'll need more trolls to carry the brewing liquid," said Lillekort. "The ones I've hired before weren't any good."

Well, he got more trolls—a whole crowd, in fact—and then they set about brewing. When the malt ale was ready, everyone had to taste it, of course. First the troll and then the others. But Lillekort had brewed the ale so strong that after drinking it they fell dead like flies. Finally there was nobody left except a wretched old woman lying behind the stove.

"Oh, you poor thing," said Lillekort. "You should have a taste of the malt ale too." He went over and scraped the bottom of the brew barrel with the wooden ladle and then handed it to her.

At last he was rid of them all.

As Lillekort stood there and looked around, he caught sight of a big chest, so he filled it with gold and silver. Then he tied the chain around the princess and the chest and himself. He tugged on the chain with all his might, and his men hoisted them up safe and sound.

When Lillekort was back on board the ship, he said, "Go now on salt water and fresh water, over mountains and through deep valleys, and don't stop until you come to the king's palace."

The ship set off at once, spraying yellow foam all around.

When everyone at the royal palace saw the ship, they hurried to greet it with song and music. And they welcomed Lillekort with great joy. Happiest of all was the king, whose second daughter had been returned to him.

Now Lillekort found himself in an awkward situation, for both princesses wanted to marry him. But he wanted only the first princess he had rescued. She was the younger of the two. He spent a great deal of time pondering what he should do, for he didn't want to offend the other princess.

One day he was thinking and thinking about this when it occurred to him that if only his brother, King Lavring, was here—and they looked so much alike that no one could tell them apart—then his twin could have the other princess and half the kingdom. The half that Lillekort had already been given was quite enough.

No sooner had he thought of this idea than he went outside the palace and shouted for King Lavring. Nobody came. Then he shouted again, a little louder, but still nobody came. Then Lillekort shouted a third time, with all his might, and there stood his brother.

"I told you not to summon me unless you were in dire need," he said to Lillekort. "Yet there's not a flea here that would do you any harm." And with that, he punched Lillekort so hard that he rolled across the meadow.

"Oh, shame on you for hitting me!" said Lillekort. "First I won one of the king's daughters and half the kingdom, and after that the other king's daughter and the other half of the kingdom. I was thinking of giving you one of the princesses and half the kingdom. So do you think it's reasonable to hit me?"

When King Lavring heard this, he asked his brother to forgive him. They were again good friends and on the best of terms.

"As you know," said Lillekort, "we look so much alike that no one can tell us apart. Switch clothes with me and go up to the palace. The princesses will think you're me. Whoever kisses you first is the one you shall have, and I will take the other."

King Lavring agreed at once. He switched clothes with his brother and went into the palace. When he came to the room where the princesses were sitting, they thought he was Lillekort, and both of them got up and rushed toward him. The older princess, who was bigger and stronger, pushed her sister aside, threw her arms around King Lavring's neck, and kissed him.

So she was the one he won, while Lillekort won the younger of the king's daughters. Then, as you might imagine, they were married. And news of their wedding spread far and wide, throughout seven kingdoms.

The Doll in the Grass

There once was a king who had twelve sons. When they were grown, he told each of them to go out into the world to find himself a wife. She had to be able to spin and weave and sew a shirt in one day, or else the king would refuse to have her as a daughter-in-law. He gave each of his sons a horse and new armor. Then they set off into the world to look for wives.

After they'd ridden some distance along the road, the brothers said they didn't want Ash Lad to go with them, for he was a worthless boy.

Well, there was nothing to be done about it. Ash Lad had to stay behind, and he had no idea what to do or where to turn. He felt so sad that he got off his horse and sat down on the grass to weep.

After he'd sat there for a little while, one of the tussocks in the grass began to move, and out of it emerged a tiny white creature. When it came closer, Ash Lad saw that it was a delicate little maiden. She was so very, very tiny. She came over to him and asked whether he'd like to come and see the doll in the grass.

Oh yes, he would like that very much. And that's what he did.

When he got down in the grass, he found the doll sitting on a chair. She was lovely and beautifully dressed. She asked Ash Lad where he was headed and what was the purpose of his journey.

He told her that he was one of twelve brothers. Their father, the king, had given each of them a horse and armor and told them to set off into the world to find a wife. But she had to be able to spin and weave and sew a shirt in one day.

"If you can do that and you want to be my wife, then I won't journey any farther," said Ash Lad to the doll in the grass.

Oh yes, she would gladly do that. She hurried to spin and weave and sew the shirt. It turned out to be very, very tiny and also very short.

This was the shirt that Ash Lad took home with him. When he arrived, he was embarrassed because the shirt was so small, yet the king said he could take the girl as his wife. Ash Lad was both happy and pleased. He went back to get his little sweetheart.

When he reached the doll in the grass, he wanted her to ride on the horse with him, but that's not what she wanted. She said she would ride in a silver spoon, and she had two little white horses of her own who would pull the spoon.

Then they set off. Ash Lad rode the horse, and the doll in the grass rode in the silver spoon. Both of the horses pulling the spoon were tiny white mice. Ash Lad kept to one side of the road. He was afraid his horse might tread on his sweetheart, for she was so very tiny.

After they had traveled for a while, they came to a big lake. There Ash Lad's horse took fright, veered over to the other side of the road, and tipped over the spoon. The doll in the grass fell into the water.

Ash Lad was terribly dismayed, for he didn't know how he was going to get her out. But a few minutes later a merman brought her to the surface. She was now just as big as any other grown person and even lovelier than she was before. Ash Lad put her on the horse in front of him and rode home.

When Ash Lad arrived, his brothers had also returned. Each had brought a sweetheart, but they were all quite ugly and vile. They were so mean that they'd been fighting with their betrothed all the way home. They wore hats made of mashed tar and soot, which had run down their faces, making them even uglier and more vile.

When the brothers caught sight of Ash Lad's sweetheart, they were all jealous of him. But the king was so overjoyed by those two that he chased the others away.

Then Ash Lad celebrated his wedding to the doll in the grass, and afterward they lived together happily and well for a long, long time. And if they're not yet dead, then they're still living happily today.

Paal Next-Door

There once was a woman who had a deaf husband. He was kindly and simple, and that's why she was more fond of the neighbor. They called that fellow Paal Next-Door.

The deaf husband's servant boy was well aware that something was going on between those two. One day he said to the woman, "Mistress, would you dare wager ten *daler* that I can get you to confess to something that will bring you shame?"

"Yes, I certainly would," she said. And so they wagered ten *daler*.

One day when the servant boy and the deaf husband were in the barn doing the threshing, the boy noticed that Paal Next-Door had come over to see the woman. The servant boy didn't say a word, but a good while before the midmorning break, he turned to face the barn door and suddenly shouted, "All right then!"

"Oh, is it time for us to go in?" said the man. He hadn't noticed a thing.

"Yes, I suppose we should. The mistress is calling us," replied the servant boy.

As they reached the porch of the house, the boy began coughing and clearing his throat so the woman would have time to hide Paal Next-Door. When they stepped inside, a big bowl of porridge made from sour cream stood on the table.

"Oh! Oh, wife!" said the husband. "Are we having porridge and cream today?"

"Yes. Yes, we are," said the woman, but she was hopping mad.

After her husband and the servant had eaten and left, she said to Paal, "That boy is a sly one. This was all his fault. But you'd better go now. I'll meet you at the bottom of the meadow around noon."

The boy was standing on the porch and heard what she said.

"Master," he said. "I think it's best we go to the valley to repair the rail fencing that the wind blew down. The pigs from next door have been rooting around in our meadow."

"All right, let's do that," said the husband, for he did everything anyone told him to do.

Before noon the woman came tottering down to the meadow, lugging something under her apron.

"Oh! Oh, wife! You're certainly not yourself today," said the husband. "Are we having a noon meal too?"

"Oh yes, this is for you," she said, even angrier than before.

They ate their fill of *lefse* and butter and took swigs from the liquor flask.

"I'll take some over to Paal Next-Door, Mistress," said the servant boy. "He probably hasn't had a noon meal today."

"You do that," said the woman, and her good humor was instantly restored.

On his way there the boy got out the *lefse* and dropped a crumb now and then as he walked. To Paal Next-Door he said, "You'd better watch out. The old man has noticed that you keep coming over to see his wife. He's not happy about that. He swore that he'll swing his axe at you the minute he sees you."

Paal was both frightened and dismayed.

The servant boy went back to his master and said, "There's something wrong with Paal's plow. He wants to know if you could bring over your axe and have a look at the plow."

So the husband picked up his axe and went over there.

No sooner did Paal Next-Door catch sight of him than he took off running as fast as he could go.

The husband twisted and turned the plow and looked at it from every angle. When he couldn't find anything wrong, he headed back home. Along the way he picked up the *lefse* crumbs the boy had dropped.

His wife watched him doing this for a while. She wondered what her husband could be picking up from the ground.

"Oh, Master is probably picking up stones," said the boy. "He noticed that Paal Next-Door keeps coming over here, and the old man isn't pleased about that. Now he has sworn that he will stone the mistress to death."

Then the wife took off running as fast as she could go.

"What is the mistress chasing after so fast?" asked the husband when he came back.

"Oh, I think the house is on fire," said the servant boy.

Then the husband set off after her.

As she ran, the wife screamed, "Oh, don't kill me! Don't kill me, and I'll never let Paal Next-Door come visit me again!"

"Those ten *daler* are now mine!" shouted the servant boy.

Soria Moria Castle

There once was a couple who had a son named Halvor. From the time he was a little boy, he refused to do anything but sit and poke at the ashes. His parents kept sending him off to learn a trade, but Halvor refused to settle in anywhere. As soon as he'd been gone for a few days, he'd run away from his apprenticeship and hurry back home. Then he would sit down at the hearth to dig in the ashes again.

One day a ship's captain came and asked Halvor whether he'd like to go to sea with him to visit foreign lands. Oh yes, Halvor said he'd like to do that. It didn't take him long to get ready.

I have no idea how many days they sailed, but eventually a big storm blew in. When it was over and calm was restored, they didn't know where they were. They had been driven toward a foreign coast, and no one on board recognized it.

There was no wind, so the ship was becalmed right there. Halvor asked the captain for permission to go ashore and have a look around. He said he'd rather be walking than lying in his bunk.

"Do you really think you should appear before anyone looking like that?" said the captain. "The only clothes you have are the rags you're wearing."

But Halvor insisted. Finally he was granted permission, though he would have to come back as soon as the wind began to blow.

When he went ashore he found a lovely land. Everywhere he went he found vast plains with fields and meadows, but he didn't see a single person. When the wind began blowing, Halvor didn't think he'd seen enough. He wanted to go just a little farther to see if he could find some folks.

After a while he came to a big road that was so flat you could roll an egg along it. Halvor followed the road, and as dusk fell, he saw off in the distance a big castle, all aglow. He'd been walking all day and he'd brought hardly any provisions, so he was terribly hungry. Yet the closer he came to the castle, the more frightened he felt.

Inside the castle a fire was blazing in the hearth. Halvor went into the kitchen, which looked quite splendid. He'd never seen such a splendid kitchen before. There were wooden basins filled with both gold and silver, but not a soul in sight. After Halvor had stood there for a while and no one came in, he went over to a door and opened it. Inside sat a princess at a spinning wheel.

"Oh, oh my!" she cried. "Why would a Christian boy dare to come here? It's probably best if you leave at once, or else the troll will swallow you whole. A troll with three heads lives here."

"I don't care if he has four heads. I'd like to see that fellow," said the boy. "And I'm not leaving. I haven't done anything wrong. But you must give me something to eat, for I'm terribly hungry."

After Halvor had eaten his fill, the princess told him to try swinging the sword that hung on the wall. But he couldn't swing it. In fact, he couldn't budge it at all.

"Well," said the princess, "take a swig from the flask hanging next to it. That's what the troll does whenever he's going out and needs to use the sword."

Halvor took a swig. With that he could swing the sword as if it weighed nothing.

Let that troll come whenever he likes, he thought.

All of a sudden the troll came rushing home. Halvor hid behind the door.

"Ugh! I smell the blood of a Christian man!" said the troll as he poked his head in the door.

"Yes, you're right about that," said Halvor, and he chopped off all his heads.

The princess was so happy to be saved that she danced and sang. Then she happened to think about her sisters, and she said, "If only my sisters could be saved too!"

"Where are they?" asked Halvor.

Then she told him. One had been taken by a troll to a castle that was forty miles away. The other had been taken to a castle that was sixty miles beyond that one.

"But first," she said, "you have to help me get this carcass out of here."

Well, Halvor was very strong. He dragged the troll's body and heads away. Then he quickly made the whole place neat and clean. He slept soundly, and the next morning he set off at dawn. He was restless, so he walked and ran all day.

When he caught sight of the castle, he grew frightened again. It was much more splendid than the first one, but there wasn't a soul to be seen. Halvor went into the kitchen, but he didn't stop there. He headed straight for the next room.

"Oh, why does a Christian boy dare come here?" cried the princess. "I don't know how long I've been here, but in all that time I haven't seen a single Christian. It's probably best if you leave at once, for a troll with six heads lives here."

"No, I won't go," said Halvor, "even if he has twelve heads."

"He'll swallow you alive," said the princess.

But it did no good. Halvor refused to leave. He wasn't afraid of the troll, but he wanted food and drink because he was hungry after traveling so far.

The princess gave him as much to eat as he liked. Then she again told him to leave.

"No," said Halvor. "I'm not leaving, for I've done nothing wrong, and I have nothing to fear."

"The troll won't care about that," said the princess. "He'll kill you whether or not it's right and fair. But if you refuse to leave, then try to swing the sword that the troll uses in battle."

Halvor couldn't swing the sword. Then the princess told him to take a swig from the flask that hung next to it. When Halvor did that, he could swing the sword.

All of a sudden the troll appeared. He was so big and stout that he had to turn sideways to get in the door. When the troll stuck his first head inside the room he bellowed, "Ugh! I smell the blood of a Christian man!"

Halvor instantly chopped off one of the troll's heads and then all the rest of them.

The princess was overjoyed. But she happened to think of her other sister, and she wished that she too could be saved. Halvor thought it should be possible to do that, and he wanted to leave at once. But first he had to help the princess remove the heads and body of the troll. The next morning he set off.

It was a long way to the castle, and Halvor had to keep walking and running in order to get there in plenty of time. Toward evening he caught sight of the castle. It was much more splendid than the other two. Yet this time he was hardly frightened at all. He went straight through the kitchen into the next room.

There sat a princess who was more beautiful than anyone he'd ever seen. She said the same thing as her sisters, that no Christian had ever appeared in the time she'd been there. And she told him to leave, or else the troll would swallow him alive. She said this troll had nine heads.

"Even if he had twice or three times as many heads, I'd refuse to leave," said Halvor. And he went over to stand next to the stove.

The princess begged him earnestly to leave, or else the troll would eat him whole.

But Halvor said, "Let him come if he wants to."

Then she gave him the troll's sword and told him to take a swig from the flask so he'd be able to swing it.

All of a sudden the troll came rushing home. This one was even bigger and stouter than the others. He too had to turn sideways to get through the door.

"Ugh! I smell the blood of a Christian man!" he said.

Halvor instantly chopped off one of the troll's heads and then the rest. The last head was the toughest of them all. Halvor had to work harder than he'd ever worked before to chop it off, even though he was sure he had enough strength to do it.

Now the other princesses joined their sister at the castle. They were all happier than they'd ever been before. They were very fond of Halvor, and he was fond of them. They said he could have any of the princesses he wanted, but of the three, the youngest was the most fond of him.

Yet Halvor went around acting quite strange. He was both sullen and silent. The youngest princess asked him what he was longing for and whether he was unhappy about staying with them.

Oh, he was happy enough, he told her, for they certainly had plenty to live on, and he was content to stay. But he felt such a longing for home. His parents were still alive, and he dearly wanted to see them again.

The princesses thought this might be easily arranged. "You will be able to go there and back without suffering any harm as long as you follow our advice," they told him.

Oh yes, he would do everything they said.

Then they dressed him in such finery that he looked as splendid as a king's son, and they put a ring on his finger. With this ring he could wish himself there and back. But they told him that he mustn't throw the ring away or mention their names, or else that would put an end to his good fortune. Then he would never see them again.

"I wish I was home, and home was here!" said Halvor, and it happened just as he wished.

Before he knew it, Halvor found himself standing outside his parents' house. Darkness had fallen, and his parents were quite astonished when they saw such a splendid and elegant stranger come in. They began to bow and curtsy.

Halvor asked them whether he might stay the night.

No, they told him, that was impossible. "We're not prepared for that," they said, "for we have nothing that would please such a fine gentleman like you. It would be best if you went up to the manor house. It's not far. You can see the chimney from here. There they have plenty of everything."

Halvor wasn't pleased by this. He wanted nothing more than to stay, but his parents insisted that he go to the manor house instead. There he would find both food and drink, while they didn't have even a chair for him to sit on.

"No," said Halvor, "I won't go there until early in the morning. Let me stay here tonight. I can sit by the hearth."

Well, they couldn't refuse his request. So Halvor sat down by the hearth and began poking at the ashes, just as he used to do when he was idling away the hours at home.

His parents discussed all manner of topics and told Halvor about one thing and another. Then he asked them whether they'd ever had any children.

Oh yes, they'd had a son named Halvor. They didn't know where he'd gone, nor did they know whether he was alive or dead.

"Maybe I'm your son," said Halvor.

"Oh, I doubt that," said the old woman as she stood up. "Halvor was so lazy and idle that he never did a thing. And he was always so filthy that the lice practically knocked each other out as they swarmed all over him. He could never become such a fine gentleman as you, sir."

A little later the woman went over to the hearth to poke at the embers. The light from the fire shone on Halvor's face, just as it used to do when he was home and digging in the ashes. Then she recognized him.

"Oh, but it *is* you, Halvor!" she cried. His old parents were happy beyond all measure. He had to tell them everything that had happened to him. The old woman was so happy to see her son that she wanted to take him at once up to the manor house to show him to the girls. They had always been scornful of him. She led the way, and Halvor followed.

When the woman reached the manor house, she said that Halvor had come back home, and they would soon see what a splendid gentleman he was. "He looks like a prince," she said.

"Oh, we doubt that," said the girls, tossing their heads. "We bet he's the same lousy creature he always was."

At that moment Halvor came in, and the girls were so astonished that they forgot all about the dresses they were mending at the hearth. They fled the room wearing only their shifts.

When they came back, they were terribly shamefaced and hardly dared look at Halvor. They'd always treated him with such arrogance and scorn.

"All of you have always claimed to be so grand and beautiful. That you have. You said no one could be your equal. But you should see the oldest princess that I rescued," said Halvor. "Compared to her, you're nothing but a bunch of goat herders. The middle princess is even more beautiful. But the youngest, who is my sweetheart, is more beautiful than the sun and the moon. If only they were here so you could see them!" said Halvor.

No sooner had he said those words than the three princesses stood right there.

Then he grew dismayed, for he remembered now what they'd told him. At the manor house a feast was arranged for the princesses and a great fuss was made over them, but they refused to stay.

"We want to visit your parents," they told Halvor. "Then we want to go out and have a look around."

He went with the princesses. They came to a big lake outside the manor house, and close to the lake was a beautiful green hill. That's where the princesses wanted to sit down to rest, for they thought it would be lovely to sit there and gaze at the water.

They sat down, and after they'd been there for a while, the youngest princess said, "I suppose I should pick the lice off you, Halvor."

So Halvor lay down with his head on her lap, and she picked the lice from his hair. It wasn't long before he fell asleep. Then she took the ring off his finger and put on another in its place. And she said to her sisters, "Hold my hand as I hold yours. I wish we were at Soria Moria castle!"

When Halvor awoke, he saw that he'd lost the princesses. He began to weep and carry on. He was terribly downhearted, and no one could console him. No matter how much his parents pleaded, he refused to stay. He said his goodbyes and told them he would probably never see them again. If he couldn't find the princesses, he didn't think life would be worth living.

He had three hundred *daler* left. He put the money in his pocket and set off.

After he'd walked for a while, he met a man with a decent-looking horse. Halvor wanted to buy the horse, so he began haggling with the man.

"Well, I hadn't really thought about selling it," said the man, "but perhaps we could reach an agreement."

Halvor asked the man what he wanted for the horse.

"I didn't give much for it. It's a good horse to ride, but it's not much good for carrying anything, though I'm sure it could handle your provisions sack. And you too, if you get off and walk now and then," said the man.

Finally they agreed on a price. Then Halvor put his sack on the horse's back. He walked for a while and rode for a while.

In the evening he came to a green embankment. A big tree stood there, and he sat down next to it. After a while he took his sack of provisions off the horse to let the animal roam free. Then he lay down to sleep.

When the next day dawned, Halvor set off at once, for he was filled with restlessness. He took turns walking and riding all day through a big forest. There were many dazzling green clearings among the trees. He didn't know where he was, nor did he know where he was headed. Yet he allowed himself no time to rest, except when he gave the horse a little to eat. He ate from his own sack of provisions when he came to one of the green clearings. He walked and he rode, and he thought there was no end to this forest.

After dark the next day he saw a light shining through the trees. If only someone is awake so I could warm up and have something to eat, thought Halvor.

A short time later he came to a miserable little hut, and through the window he saw two people sitting inside. They were very old, and their hair was as gray as a dove. The woman's nose was so long that she was using it to poke at the embers as she sat at the hearth.

"Good evening! Good evening!" said the old woman. "And what brings you here? There have been no Christians in these parts for more than a hundred years."

Halvor told her that he was headed for Soria Moria castle. And he asked her whether she knew how to get there.

"No, I don't," said the old woman. "But the moon is about to arrive, so I'll ask him. I'm sure he knows. He must be able to see that castle, for he shines on everything."

When the moon appeared, bright and shiny above the treetops, the old woman went outside.

"Hey, moon! Hey, moon!" she called. "Can you tell me how to get to Soria Moria castle?"

"No, I can't," said the moon. "When I was shining in that direction, a cloud blocked my view."

"Wait a little while," said the old woman to Halvor. "The West Wind is about to arrive. I'm sure he knows, because he gusts and blows into every nook and cranny. Oh! Oh! Did you bring a horse with you?" she said when they went back inside. "Let the poor creature loose in the paddock. Don't make it stand there starving! Wouldn't you like to trade your horse to me?" she said. "We have a pair of old boots, and when you put them on you can cover nine leagues with every step. I'll trade you the boots for the horse, and then you'll get to Soria Moria castle much faster."

Halvor was more than willing to do that.

The old woman was so happy with the horse that she was practically dancing. "Now I too can ride to church," she said.

Halvor was feeling restless and wanted to leave at once, but the old woman told him there was no hurry.

"Why don't you lie down to sleep on the bench, for we have no bed to give you," said the old woman. "I'll keep watch for the West Wind."

All of a sudden the West Wind arrived, roaring so loud that the walls creaked. The old woman went outside.

"Hey, West Wind! Hey, West Wind! Can you tell me how to get to Soria Moria castle? Someone is here who is headed that way."

"Oh yes, I know it well," said the West Wind. "I'm about to go there to dry the clothes for the wedding that's going to take place. If he's quick, he can come with me."

Halvor came outside.

"You'll have to hurry if you want to come along," said the West Wind. Then he headed off.

They traveled a great distance, over moors and ridges and mountains and shores. It was all Halvor could do to keep up.

"Well, I don't have time to stay with you any longer," said the West Wind. "I have to go and tear down part of a spruce forest before I get to the bleaching grounds to dry the wedding clothes. Just keep going along the ridge, and you'll come upon some maids who are doing the washing. From there it's not far to Soria Moria castle."

A while later Halvor came upon the maids who were doing the washing.

They asked him whether he'd seen any sign of the West Wind, who was supposed to come and dry the clothes for the wedding.

"Oh yes," said Halvor. "He has gone to break down part of a spruce forest, but it won't be long before he's here."

Then he asked the maids how to get to Soria Moria castle. They pointed him in the right direction.

When he arrived at the castle, it was practically swarming with folks and horses. But Halvor was so ragged and tattered from traveling with the West Wind through bushes and thickets that he didn't want to step forward. He decided to wait until late in the day, when everyone sat down to eat.

As was the custom, the guests were about to drink a toast to the bride who was leaving her girlhood behind. The man filling the glasses poured some ale for everyone—the bride and the groom, the knights and pages. At long last he came to Halvor.

Halvor joined in the toast. Then he dropped in his glass the ring the princess had put on his finger when he lay on her lap at the lake. He asked the servant to give his greetings to the bride and hand her the glass.

The princess stood up from the table at once. "Who has best earned the right to marry one of us?" she said. "Is it the one who rescued us, or the one who sits here as my bridegroom?"

Everyone agreed there could be only one answer to that. When Halvor heard this, he didn't hesitate to tear off his rags and put on the clothes of a prince.

"Well, he's the one!" cried the youngest princess when she caught sight of him. Then she shoved the other bridegroom aside and celebrated her wedding to Halvor.

Sir Per

There once was a poor couple who had nothing but three sons. I don't know what the two older sons were called, but the youngest was named Per. When the parents died, their children were supposed to inherit their possessions, but there was nothing left except a pot, a griddle, and a cat.

The oldest, who was to have the best, took the pot. "If I loan out the pot, I'll always be allowed to scrape up what's left in the bottom of it," he said.

The second son took the griddle. "If I loan out the griddle, I'll always get to taste the first *lefse* sample," he said.

There was nothing left for the youngest son to choose. If he wanted anything, he would have to take the cat. "If I loan out the cat, I won't get anything in return. No, I won't," he said. "And if the cat gets a little milk, she won't want to share any with me. But I'll take the cat, all the same. It would be a pity for the cat to stay here and die."

Then the brothers set off into the world to try their luck, and each headed in a different direction. After the youngest boy had walked for a while, the cat said, "You will be rewarded, for you refused to leave me behind to die in that old hovel. I'm going into the forest now, yes, I am. There I'll get some wondrous animals. When I come back, you must go up to the royal palace that you can see over there. Tell the king you've brought him a little present. When he asks who it's from, tell him it's from a man named Sir Per."

Per didn't have to wait long before the cat returned with a reindeer from the forest. The cat perched on the reindeer's head, between his ears, and said, "Go straight to the royal palace, or else I'll claw your eyes out."

The reindeer had no choice.

When Per arrived at the royal palace, he took the reindeer into the kitchen and said, "I've brought a little present for the king, yes, I have. I hope he won't refuse it."

The king came into the kitchen, and when he saw the big, splendid reindeer, he was very pleased. "My dear friend! Who has sent me such a fine present?" said the king.

"Oh, it's from a man named Sir Per," said the boy.

"Sir Per?" said the king. "Can you tell me where he lives?" He thought it was a shame that he didn't know such a fine man.

But the boy didn't want to say. He didn't dare, for Sir Per was his master, and he'd warned the boy not to tell.

Then the king gave Per a generous tip and told him to be sure to convey his greetings when he got home, along with many thanks for the present.

The next day the cat again went into the forest. There she jumped onto the head of a stag and perched between the stag's ears. She threatened him until he agreed to go to the royal palace.

Per took the stag into the kitchen and said he'd brought a little present for the king. He hoped the king wouldn't refuse it.

The king was even more pleased with the stag than he'd been with the reindeer. Again he asked who had sent him such a fine present.

"It's from a man named Sir Per," said the boy.

But when the king wanted to know where Sir Per lived, he received the same answer as the day before. This time he gave Per an even bigger tip.

On the third day the cat appeared with a moose. Then Per went into the kitchen of the royal palace and said he had a little present for the king. He hoped the king wouldn't refuse it.

The king came to the kitchen at once. When he saw the big, splendid moose, he was so pleased that he hardly knew which foot to stand on. That day he gave Per a much, much bigger tip—it must have been a hundred *daler*. He dearly wanted to know where Sir Per lived. He kept prodding and asking one question after another. But the boy didn't dare reply, for his master had sternly warned him not to tell.

"Then ask Sir Per if he would come to visit me," said the king.

The boy said he would ask.

When Per came out of the royal palace and again met the cat, he said, "Well, you've certainly gotten me into a real fix. Now the king wants me to visit him, and I have nothing to wear but the rags on my back."

"Oh, don't worry about that," said the cat. "In three days' time you'll have horses and a carriage and splendid clothes dripping with gold. Then you can certainly visit the king."

All right, Per said he'd keep that in mind.

When the three days were up, the cat appeared with a carriage and horses and clothes and everything else that Per needed. It was all so splendid that nobody had ever seen anything like it before. Then he set off, and the cat ran alongside.

The king gave him a warm welcome. But no matter what the king offered or showed his guest, Per said they were certainly fine things, but he had even more magnificent and splendid things back home.

The king wasn't especially happy about this, but Per kept on repeating what he'd said. Finally the king grew so angry that he could no longer hold back. "I would like to go home with you," said the king, "and see whether it's true that things are so much better and more splendid there. But if you're lying, then God help you. And I won't say another word, no, I won't!"

"Well, you've certainly gotten me into a fine fix," said Per to the cat. "Now the king wants to go home with me, but my home won't be easy to find."

"Oh, don't worry about that," said the cat. "Go ahead and set off. I'll run on ahead."

So they set off. Per rode in front behind the cat, who ran on ahead, and the king followed with his entourage.

After they had traveled a good distance, they came to a big flock of lovely sheep. Their wool was so long that it almost touched the ground.

"If you say that this flock of sheep belongs to Sir Per when the king asks you, then I'll give you this silver spoon," said the cat to the shepherd. She had brought the spoon from the royal palace.

The shepherd was happy to do just that.

When the king appeared, he said to the shepherd boy, "I've never seen such a big and beautiful flock of sheep! Tell me, little boy, who owns these sheep?"

"They belong to Sir Per," said the boy.

After a while they came upon a big, big herd of beautiful, stout cattle. They were so fat that their hides gleamed.

"If you'll say that the herd belongs to Sir Per when the king asks you, then I'll give you this silver axe," said the cat to the shepherdess. The cat had also brought the silver axe from the royal palace.

"Yes, I'll gladly do that," said the shepherdess.

When the king arrived, he was quite astonished to see the big, splendid herd. He thought he'd never seen such a beautiful herd before. He asked the girl minding the stout cattle who owned them.

"Oh, they belong to Sir Per," said the girl.

They traveled a little farther and came to a big, big herd of horses. They were the most beautiful horses you could imagine, big and strapping. There were six of each hue—red and dun-colored and blue-black.

"If you say that the horses belong to Sir Per when the king asks you, then I'll give you this silver goblet," said the cat to the herder. She had also brought the goblet from the royal palace.

Yes, he would certainly do that, said the boy.

When the king arrived, he was quite astonished to see the big, splendid herd of horses. He said he'd never seen the likes of them before. Then he asked the herder who owned the red and dun-colored and blue-black horses.

"They belong to Sir Per," said the boy.

After they'd traveled a good distance farther, they came to a castle. First there was a gate of brass, then one of silver, and then one of gold. The castle itself was made of silver, and it was so shiny that it hurt their eyes, for the sun was shining on it as they arrived. They went inside, and the cat told Per that he should say this was where he lived. Inside things were even more magnificent than outside. Everything was made of gold—all the chairs and tables and benches. After the king had walked around and looked at everything, both high and low, he felt quite ashamed.

"Oh yes, Sir Per, your place is more splendid than mine. It would do no good to deny it," he said. And he wanted to leave at once.

But Per asked him to stay and have supper with him. And that's what the king did, though he was sullen and surly the whole time. As they were eating, the troll who owned the castle appeared and pounded on the gate.

"Who is eating my food and drinking my mead like swine?" bellowed the troll.

As soon as the cat heard him, she ran over to the gate. "Wait a minute and I'll tell you how the farmer sows the winter rye," said the cat. And she began rambling on about the winter rye. "First the farmer plows his field," she said. "Then he spreads manure, and then he plows the field again."

All of a sudden the sun appeared. "Turn around and you'll see the most lovely and beautiful of maidens right behind you!" the cat then said to the troll.

When the troll turned around and looked at the sun, he burst.

"All of this is now yours," said the cat to Sir Per. "You must chop off my head, yes, you must. It's the only thing I ask in return for all that I've done for you."

"No," said Sir Per, "I won't do it."

"Yes, you will," said the cat. "If you don't, then I'll claw your eyes out."

Sir Per had to do it. He had no choice. He chopped off the cat's head. At that instant she turned into the loveliest princess that anyone could ever imagine, and Sir Per fell in love with her.

"Yes, all this splendor used to be mine," said the princess. "But that troll over there cast a spell on me so I had to live as a cat with your parents. Now you can do whatever you like, whether you want me to be your queen or not, for you're king of the whole realm."

Well, it turned out that Sir Per did want her to be his queen. So they celebrated their wedding and feasted for eight days. After that I was no longer with Sir Per and his queen, no, I wasn't.

Little Aase Goosegirl

There once was a king who had so many geese that he had to hire a maid whose only job was to tend to them. Her name was Aase, so they called her Aase Goosegirl.

The king's son from England set out to find a bride. Then he found Aase sitting in his path.

"Is that you sitting there, little Aase?" said the king's son.

"Yes. Here I sit, mending and patching. I'm waiting for the English king's son today."

"You can't expect to have the likes of him," said the prince.

"Oh yes, if I'm meant to have him, I will have him," said little Aase.

Artists were now sent to all the lands and kingdoms to paint portraits of the most beautiful princesses. It was from them that the prince would make his choice. He found one of them so much to his liking that he went to see her, and then he decided to marry her. He was both happy and pleased when he won the princess as his sweetheart.

But the prince had brought a flagstone that he placed next to his bed, and that stone knew everything.

When the princess arrived, Aase Goosegirl told her that if she'd ever had a sweetheart before, or if she couldn't rid herself of something that she didn't want the prince to know, then she mustn't step on the stone that he'd placed next to his bed. "For the stone will tell him everything about you," Aase said.

When the princess heard this she felt great sorrow, let me tell you. She asked Aase to take her place and lie down next to the prince that night. After he'd fallen asleep, they'd trade places again, so the right person would be beside him when the day dawned.

That's what they did.

When Aase Goosegirl came in and stepped on the stone, the prince asked, "Who is climbing into my bed?"

"A pure and delicate maiden!" said the stone. Then they lay down to sleep. In the middle of the night the princess came in and took Aase's place.

In the morning, when they were about to get up, the prince asked the stone, "Who is climbing out of my bed?"

"Someone who has had three sweethearts," said the stone.

When the prince heard this, he didn't want the princess anymore, as you might well imagine. He sent her back home and took another sweetheart instead.

When he set off to visit her, little Aase Goosegirl again sat down in his path.

"Is that you sitting there, little Aase Goosegirl?"

"Yes. Here I sit, mending and patching. I'm waiting for the English king's son today," said Aase.

"Oh, he's not someone you can expect to have," said the king's son.

"Oh yes, if I'm meant to have him, I will have him," Aase told him.

Almost the exact same thing happened with this princess as with the first one. But when she got up in the morning, the flagstone said she'd had six sweethearts.

Then the prince didn't want her either, and he sent her on her way. He thought he should try yet again to see if he could find someone who was pure and delicate. He searched far and wide through many lands until he found a princess to his liking. When he set off to see her, Aase Goosegirl had again sat down in his path.

"Is that you sitting there, little Aase Goosegirl?" said the prince.

"Yes. Here I sit, mending and patching. I'm waiting for the king's son from England today," said Aase.

"Oh, he's not someone you can expect to have," said the king's son.

"Oh yes, if I'm meant to have him, I will have him," said little Aase.

When the princess arrived, Aase Goosegirl told her the same thing she'd told the first two. She said that if the princess had ever had a sweetheart, or if there was something else she didn't want the prince to know, then she mustn't step on the stone the prince had placed next to his bed. "For that stone tells him everything," she said.

The princess was dismayed when she heard this, but she was just as sly as the other two. She asked Aase to take her place and lie next to the prince that night. Then, after he'd fallen asleep, they would trade places again so he would have the right person beside him when the day dawned.

That's what they did.

When little Aase came in and stepped on the stone, the prince asked, "Who is climbing into my bed?"

"A pure and delicate maiden," said the stone. Then they lay down together.

In the middle of the night the prince put a ring on Aase's finger, and it fit so snugly that she couldn't take it off. The prince could tell that something wasn't right, and he wanted to have some way of marking the right person so that he would recognize her again.

After the prince fell asleep, the princess came in and chased Aase back to her goose pen. Then the princess took her place in the bed.

In the morning when they were about to get up, the prince asked, "Who is climbing out of my bed?"

"Someone who has had nine sweethearts," said the stone.

When the prince heard this, he grew so angry that he chased her away at once. Then he asked the flagstone what was happening with all these princesses, for he couldn't understand it.

The stone told him what had happened. The princesses had fooled him by sending Aase Goosegirl to take their place.

The prince wanted to know whether this was true. He went out to find Aase, who was tending to her geese. He wanted to see if she was wearing the ring.

If she is, he thought, then it's best I make her my queen.

When he found Aase, he saw at once that she had bound a rag around one finger. He asked her why she'd done that.

"Oh, I've cut myself badly," said little Aase Goosegirl.

The prince asked to see her finger, but Aase refused to take off the rag.

The prince grabbed her finger. When Aase tried to pull it away, the rag fell off, and then the prince recognized his ring.

So he took Aase to the royal palace and gave her all manner of finery and splendid clothes, and then they celebrated their wedding. That's how little Aase Goosegirl won the English king's son after all, simply because she was meant to have him.

The Boy and the Devil

There once was a boy who was walking along the road and cracking nuts. He found one with a worm inside, and at that moment he came upon the Devil.

"Is it true what they say," said the boy, "that the Devil can make himself as small as he wants and force his way through even a pinhole?"

"Yes, it is!" replied the Devil.

"Oh, I'd like to see that. Crawl inside this nut!" said the boy.

And that's what the Devil did.

After he'd crawled all the way inside the wormhole, the boy stuck a twig in the hole.

"Now I've got you," he said, and he put the nut in his pocket.

After he'd walked for a while, he came to a smithy. There he went inside and asked the blacksmith if he would smash open the nut for him.

"Oh, that's easily done," replied the blacksmith. He picked up his smallest hammer, placed the nut on the anvil, and brought the hammer down on it, but the nut refused to break. Then he picked up a slightly bigger hammer, but that one wasn't strong enough either. He picked up one that was even bigger, but that didn't do the trick. Then the blacksmith got angry and picked up the sledgehammer.

"I'll smash you open, that I will," he said. He brought the sledgehammer down with all his might. The nut cracked open with such force that half the smithy roof flew off. And the noise was so loud that it seemed like the entire hut might collapse.

"I think the Devil himself must have been inside that nut, that I do," said the blacksmith.

"Yes, he was," said the boy.

The Seven Foals

There once was a poor couple who lived in a miserable hovel far away in the forest. For them, life meant living hand to mouth and barely getting by. They had three sons, and the youngest was called Ash Lad, for all he ever did was lie around and dig in the ashes.

One day the oldest boy said that he wanted to go out and find work. He was given permission at once, and he set off into the world. He walked and walked all day, and as dusk fell, he came to a royal palace. There stood the king on the steps. He asked the boy where he was headed.

"Oh, I'm out here trying to find work, that I am, sir," said the boy.

"Do you want to work for me and take care of my seven foals?" asked the king. "If you can tend them for an entire day and then tell me in the evening what they eat and drink, you shall have the princess and half the kingdom. But if you can't, I'll lash three red stripes on your back."

The boy thought that would be an easy task. It was something he certainly thought he could do.

The next morning, as the day dawned, the stablemaster let out the seven foals. They ran off, with the boy right behind them. And it so happened that they headed over mountain and valley, through bushes and thickets.

After the boy had been running for a long time, he began to feel tired. And after he'd kept at it for a while longer, he was getting quite fed up with the whole business. All of a sudden he came to a cleft in the mountain. There sat an old woman spinning with a drop spindle. When she caught sight of the boy running after the foals so the sweat poured off him, the old woman shouted, "Come here, come here, my handsome son, and I'll pick the lice from your hair!"

The boy was happy to do that. He sat down in the mountain cleft with the old woman and placed his head on her lap. Then she picked the lice from his hair all day long as he lay there, idling away the time.

As dusk approached, the boy wanted to leave. "I suppose I might as well head straight home," he said. "It will do no good for me to go back to the royal palace."

"Wait a little longer until it's dark," said the old woman. "Then the king's foals will come past here again, and you can follow them home. Nobody knows that you've been lying here all day instead of tending to the foals."

When the horses appeared, she gave the boy a flask of water and a wisp of moss to show the king. She told him to say this was what the foals ate and drank.

"So, did you faithfully tend to the foals all day long?" asked the king when the boy came to him that evening.

"Yes, I certainly did," said the boy.

"Can you tell me what those seven foals of mine eat and drink?" asked the king.

The boy held up the flask of water and the wisp of moss that the old woman had given him. "Here you see their food, and here you see what they drink," said the boy.

Then the king realized that the boy had not tended to the foals properly. He grew so angry that he wanted his servants to chase the boy off at once. But first they had to lash three red stripes on his back and sprinkle salt in the wounds.

When the boy got back home, you might well imagine how he was feeling. He said that he may have gone out to look for work, but he'd never do it again.

The next day the second son said that he wanted to go out into the world to try his luck. His parents said no. They told him to look at his brother's back, but the boy refused to give up. He kept insisting until at long last he was given permission, and then he set off.

After he had walked all day, he too came to the royal palace. There stood the king on the steps. He asked the boy where he was headed. When the boy replied that he was out looking for work, the king said he could work for him by taking care of his seven foals. Then the king offered him the same punishment and the same reward as he'd promised his brother.

The boy was at once ready and willing. He agreed to work for the king, for he thought he could certainly look after the foals and tell the king what they ate and drank.

In the gray light of dawn the next morning, the stablemaster let out the foals. They raced off over mountain and valley, with the boy close behind. But the exact same thing happened to him as to his brother.

After he'd been running after the foals for a long, long time, he was both sweaty and tired. Then he came upon a cleft in the mountain where an old woman was spinning with a drop spindle.

She called to the boy, "Come here, come here, my handsome son, and I'll pick the lice from your hair!"

The boy thought that was a good idea. He let the foals run off while he sat down in the mountain cleft with the old woman. There he stayed, idling away the whole day.

When the foals came back in the evening, the old woman gave him a wisp of moss and a flask of water that he was supposed to show the king.

Then the king asked the boy, "Can you tell me what the seven foals of mine eat and drink?"

The boy held out the wisp of moss and the flask of water and said, "Yes, here you can see their food, and here you can see what they drink."

Again the king grew angry. He ordered his servants to lash three red stripes on the boy's back and then sprinkle salt in the wounds and chase him home at once.

When the boy got back home, he too reported what had happened to him. He said that he may have gone out to look for work, but he'd never do it again.

On the third day Ash Lad wanted to set off. He too wanted to try to look after the foals. His brothers laughed and made fun of him.

"Seeing as what happened to us, how do you think you can accomplish the task, considering the way you look? You're a boy who has never done anything but lie around at night, digging in the ashes!" they said.

"Even so," said Ash Lad, "I still want to try, now that I've got the idea into my head."

No matter how much his brothers laughed and his parents pleaded, it did no good. Ash Lad set off.

After he'd walked all day, he came to the royal palace at dark. There stood the king on the steps, and he asked the boy where he was headed.

"I'm out here looking for work," said Ash Lad.

"Where are you from?" asked the king, for he wanted to know a little more before he hired anyone else.

Ash Lad told him where he was from. He said he was the brother of the other two boys who had taken care of the king's seven foals. Then he asked whether he could try and care for them the next day.

"Oh, blast you!" said the king. He grew very angry, just thinking about those boys. "If you're the brother of those two, you can't be worth much either. I've had enough of your sort!"

"Yes, but seeing as I'm here, couldn't you allow me to give it a try?" said Ash Lad.

"All right, if you really want your back to be lashed, that's fine with me," said the king.

"I think I'd rather have the princess," said Ash Lad.

The next morning, in the gray light of dawn, the stablemaster again let out the seven foals. They raced over mountain and valley, through bushes and thickets, with Ash Lad close behind.

After he'd been running like that for a good long while, he too came upon the mountain cleft. There sat the old woman again, spinning with her drop spindle. She shouted to Ash Lad, "Come here, come here, my handsome son, and I'll pick the lice from your hair!" That's what she said.

"Kiss my behind, kiss my behind!" said Ash Lad. He leaped and ran as he held onto the tail of a foal.

After he'd come safely past the mountain cleft, the youngest foal said, "Climb onto my back, go ahead, for we still have a long way to go."

And that's what he did.

They traveled a long, long way. "Do you see anything?" said the foal.

"No," said Ash Lad.

They traveled even farther.

"Do you see anything now?" asked the foal.

"No, I don't," said the boy.

After they had traveled a long, long way, the foal asked again, "Do you see anything now?"

"Yes, now I think I can see a whitening," said Ash Lad. "It looks like a big, stout birch stump."

"Yes, that's where we'll go inside," said the foal.

When they reached the stump, the oldest foal toppled it over. Where the stump had stood was a door, and inside was a small room. Inside the room were only a fireplace and a couple of stools. But behind the door hung a big, rusty sword and a little flask.

"Can you swing the sword?" asked the foal.

Ash Lad tried, but he couldn't do it. Then he was told to take a swig from the flask, first one swig, then a second and a third. After that he was able to wield the sword as if it weighed nothing.

"Now you must take the sword with you," said the foal. "Use it to chop off the head of all seven of us on your wedding day. Then we'll turn into princes again. That's what we once were. We are the brothers of the princess you shall marry when you tell the king what we eat and drink. A vile troll has cast a spell over us. After you chop off our heads, you must be careful to place each head next to the tail of the body where it once belonged. Then the spell will no longer have any power over us."

Ash Lad promised to do all this. Then they continued on.

After they had traveled a long, long way, the foal asked, "Do you see anything?"

"No," said Ash Lad.

They kept traveling for another good, long while.

"What about now?" asked the foal. "Do you see anything now?"

"No, I don't," said Ash Lad.

Then they traveled many, many miles, over both mountains and valleys.

"How about now?" said the foal. "Do you see anything yet?"

"Oh yes," said Ash Lad. "Now I see what looks like a bluish stripe far, far away."

"Yes, that's a river," said the foal. "And that's where we will cross."

Spanning the river was a long, splendid bridge. After they reached the other side, they again traveled a long, long way. Then the foal asked Ash Lad whether he saw anything. Yes, this time he did. He saw something black far away. It looked like a church tower.

"Yes, that's where we'll go inside," said the foal.

When the foals reached the cemetery, all of them turned back into men. They looked like the sons of a king, wearing clothes so magnificent that they dazzled the eye. They went inside the church and received bread and wine from the pastor, who stood before the altar. Ash Lad followed them inside. After the pastor placed his hands on the princes and blessed them, they left the church. Ash Lad did too, but he took with him the wine flask and the altar bread.

As soon as the seven king's sons left the cemetery, they turned into foals again. Then Ash Lad climbed onto the back of the youngest foal, and they all went back the same way they had come, though they made their way much, much faster.

First they traveled across the bridge, then past the stump, and then past the old woman, who was sitting in the mountain cleft and spinning. They ran by so fast that Ash Lad couldn't hear the words the old woman shouted after him, but he heard enough to know that she was terribly angry.

It was nearly dark by the time they got back to the royal palace. The king himself was standing in the courtyard, waiting for them.

"Have you tended to my foals faithfully and well all day?" the king asked Ash Lad.

"I have done my best, that I have," replied Ash Lad.

"Can you tell me what these seven foals of mine eat and drink?" asked the king.

Ash Lad then held out the altar bread and the wine flask to show the king.

"Here you see their food, and here you see what they drink," he said.

"Yes, you have tended to them faithfully and well," said the king. "And you shall have the princess and half the kingdom."

Then they made plans for the wedding. The king said it was to be so magnificent and splendid that news of the celebration would spread far and wide.

When they were all seated at the table, the bridegroom stood up and went out to the stable. He said that he'd forgotten something there and he needed to find it. When he reached the stable, he did as the foals had said and chopped off the heads of all seven of them—first the oldest and then the others according to their age. Then he carefully placed each head next to the tail of the foal it had belonged to. After he did that, they all turned back into princes.

When Ash Lad returned to the wedding table with the seven princes, the king was so happy that he kissed him and patted him on the back. And his bride was now even more fond of him than she was before.

"I've given you half the kingdom," said the king, "and you shall have the other half when I die. My sons can win their own lands and kingdoms, now that they've become princes again."

As you might well imagine, there was much joy and celebration at the wedding. I was there too, though no one had time to think about me. I was given only a slice of buttered bread, which I placed on the stove. The bread turned black, the butter ran slack, and not a crumb did I get back.

Gidske

There once was a widower who had a housekeeper named Gidske. She dearly wanted to have him as her husband, and she badgered him both day and night to marry her. Finally the man grew annoyed by this, but he didn't know how to get rid of her.

It was between the haying season and the time for cutting grain. That's when the hemp was ripe. They had to go out and shake the hemp. Gidske thought she was so beautiful and clever and capable. She shook the hemp until her head grew dizzy from the strong smell. She toppled over and lay there, asleep in the hemp field.

While she slept, the man came over with a scissors and cut off her skirt. Then he smeared her first with tallow and then with chimney soot so she looked worse than the Devil himself.

When Gidske awoke and saw how vile she looked, she didn't recognize herself. "Can this really be me?" said Gidske. "No, it can't be me, for I've never looked this vile. It must be the Devil himself."

She wanted to find out what was what, so she went over to her master's house and opened the door. Then she asked, "Is your Gidske home today, sir?"

"Yes, blast it, my Gidske is home," said the man. He wanted to get rid of her.

Then I can't be his Gidske, she thought, no I can't. And she lurched off. He was happy to be rid of her.

After she'd walked for a while, she came to a big forest. There she met two thieves.

I'll keep those two company, thought Gidske. If I'm the Devil, then it's suitable for me to keep company with thieves.

But the thieves didn't see it that way. No, they didn't. When they caught sight of Gidske, they took off as fast as they could go. They thought the Evil One himself was after them and would try to catch them. But that didn't do them much good, for Gidske was long-legged and quick on her feet. Before they knew it, she was close on their heels.

"If you're going out to steal things, I'd like to come along and help," said Gidske. "I know this area well."

When the thieves heard this, they thought she'd be good company after all, and they were no longer afraid.

They said they were going out to steal a sheep, but they didn't know where to find one.

"Oh, that's easy," said Gidske. "I worked a long time for a farmer over there beyond the forest. I could find the sheep shed even if it was pitch dark."

The thieves thought this was excellent news. When they got there, Gidske was supposed to go inside the sheep shed and send one animal out to them.

The sheep shed stood very close to the wall of the house, where the farmer was asleep in bed. That's why Gidske was ever so quiet and cautious as she went in. But once she was inside, she shouted to the thieves, "Do you want a ram or a ewe? There's plenty to choose from in here!"

"Shh! Shh! Just take one that's nice and fat," said the thieves.

"Yes, but do you want a ram or a ewe? Do you want a ram or a ewe? There's plenty to choose from!" shouted Gidske.

"Shh! Shush!" said the thieves. "Just take one that's nice and fat. It doesn't matter whether it's a ram or a ewe."

"Yes, but do you want a ram or a ewe? Do you want a ram or a ewe? There's plenty to choose from!" Gidske kept insisting.

"Shut up and just take one that's nice and fat. It doesn't matter whether it's a ram or a ewe," said the thieves.

In the meantime, all the shouting had woken the man inside the house. He came out in his nightshirt to see what was going on. The thieves took off, and Gidske rushed after them so fast that she knocked the farmer down.

"Wait, boys! Wait, boys!" she shouted.

The man saw only a black creature, and he was so frightened that he hardly dared stand up. He thought it was the Devil himself who had been inside the sheep shed. There was only one thing he could think of to do. That's right. He went back inside and woke his servants. Then they all sat down to plead and pray, for he'd heard it was possible to chase away the Devil with prayers.

On the next evening, the thieves wanted to go out and steal a fat goose. Gidske was going to show them the way. When they arrived at the goose coop, Gidske was supposed to go inside and send one bird out to the thieves, for she knew the place well.

"Do you want a goose or a gander? There are plenty to choose from!" shouted Gidske when she was inside the goose coop.

"Shh! Shh! Just take one that's nice and fat," said the thieves.

"Yes, but do you want a goose or a gander? Do you want a goose or a gander? There's plenty to choose from!" shouted Gidske.

"Shh! Shh! Just take one that's nice and fat. It doesn't matter whether it's a goose or a gander. And shut up," they said.

While Gidske and the thieves argued about this, one of the geese began to honk. Then another started honking, and suddenly they were all honking at once.

The farmer came out to see what was going on. The thieves took off as fast as they could go, and Gidske rushed after them. She moved so fast that the farmer thought it was the black Devil himself, for she was long-legged and she didn't hitch up her skirts.

"Don't run off, boys!" shouted Gidske. "You can have whatever you want, either a goose or a gander."

But the thieves didn't think there was any time to waste.

Back at the farm, everyone began to plead and pray, both the old and the young. They were convinced that the Devil himself had been there.

As evening approached on the third day, the thieves and Gidske were so hungry that they didn't know what to do with themselves. They made plans to go over to the edge of the forest, where a rich farmer had a storehouse. There they would steal some food.

And that's where they went. But the thieves didn't dare go inside, so Gidske was supposed to go into the storehouse that was set on posts. Then she would hand food down to the thieves as they waited outside.

When Gidske went in, she found plenty of everything—beef and pork and sausages and flatbread made from peas. The thieves shushed her and told her to toss some of the food outside. She should keep in mind what had happened twice before.

But Gidske insisted on doing the same thing. "Do you want beef or pork or sausage or flatbread made from peas? Look at this lovely flatbread!" she shouted so loudly that her words echoed. "You can have whatever you want. There's plenty to choose from, there's plenty to choose from!"

The man on the farm was awakened by all the arguing, and he came out to see what was going on. The thieves ran off as fast as they could go. Gidske also came running past the farmer, and she was both fast and vile looking.

"Wait, boys, wait!" she shouted. "You can have whatever you want, for there's plenty to choose from here!"

When the farmer caught sight of that ugly beast, he too thought the Devil was on the loose. He'd heard about what had happened on the two nights before. He began to plead and pray, and everyone else on all the farms in the area did the same. They knew it was possible to chase away the Devil with prayers.

On Saturday evening the thieves again set off. This time they were going to steal a fat billy goat for their Sunday meal. As you can imagine, they sorely needed some food, for they hadn't eaten in days. But they didn't want to take Gidske along. They said she did nothing but cause trouble with all her shouting.

While Gidske waited for them on Sunday morning, she grew terribly hungry. She hadn't had much to eat for three whole days. So she climbed up on a pile of turnips and pulled out a few to eat.

When the man who owned the farm with the turnips woke up, he was worried, and he thought he ought to check on his turnips on this Sunday morning. He put on his pants and walked down to the marsh at the bottom of the hill. That's where the turnip pile was. When he got there, he saw something black walking around and tugging and tugging at the turnips. It didn't take long before he too decided it must be the Devil. Then he hurried home as fast as he could go to report that the Devil was in the turnip pile.

Everyone was terribly frightened when they heard this news. They thought it would be best to send for the pastor and ask him to tie up the Devil.

"No, that won't work," said the farmer's wife. "We can't go to the pastor today. It's Sunday morning. He wouldn't come, for he doesn't get up this early. And if he's awake, he'll be reading over his sermon."

"Oh, I'll promise him a steak from a fattened calf, that I will. Then I'm sure he'll come," said the farmer.

He set off for the parsonage, but when he got there, the pastor was still in bed. The maid invited the man to go into the parlor to wait. Then she went upstairs to tell the pastor that a farmer was downstairs and wanted to speak to him.

When the pastor heard that such a respectable man was waiting for him, he got up and went downstairs at once. He was wearing his slippers and nightcap.

The farmer told him why he had come. He said the Devil was loose in his turnip pile, and if the pastor would come over to tie up the Devil, then he'd send him a fat veal steak.

The pastor was not unwilling. He summoned his stable boy and told him to saddle his horse while he got dressed.

"No, sir," said the farmer, "that won't do. I don't think the Devil will linger there long. We don't know when we'll be able to catch him again, once he's on the loose. You'd better come at once."

So the pastor left wearing his nightcap and slippers. But when they reached the marsh, the ground was so wet that the pastor didn't dare walk across it wearing his slippers. The farmer hoisted him on his back to carry him across. He carefully stepped from stump to tussock, but when they came to the middle of the marsh, Gidske caught sight of them. She thought they were the thieves who were bringing her a billy goat.

"Is he fat, is he fat, is he fat?" she shouted so loudly that her words echoed through the forest.

"I'll be damned if I know whether he's fat or skinny," said the farmer when he heard this. "But if you want to know, you'll have to come over and find out for yourself," he said. By then he was so frightened that he tossed the pastor into the middle of the soggy marsh and took off running.

And if the pastor hasn't gotten up, then he's probably still lying there today.

The Twelve Wild Ducks

There once was a queen who was out traveling in winter when new snow began to fall. After she'd gone a good distance along the road, her nose began to bleed, and she had to get out of the sleigh. As she stood there next to a fence and watched the red blood drip onto the white snow, she happened to think about the fact that she had twelve sons but no daughter. Then she said to herself, "If I had a daughter as white as snow and as red as blood, I wouldn't care about my sons."

She had no sooner said these words than a troll woman appeared before her.

"A daughter you shall have," she said. "She will be as white as snow and as red as blood, and then your sons will be mine. But you can keep them until the child is christened."

When the time came, the queen gave birth to a daughter. The child was as white as snow and as red as blood, just as the troll woman had promised. That's why they called her Snow White–Rose Red.

There was great joy at the royal palace, and the queen was happy beyond measure. But then she remembered what she had promised the troll witch. She had a silversmith make twelve silver spoons, one for each prince. And then she had him make one more, and that one she gave to Snow White–Rose Red.

As soon as the princess was christened, the princes were transformed into twelve wild ducks. They flew off, and nothing more was seen of them. They were gone, and gone they stayed.

The princess grew up. She was beautiful and no longer a child, but she often seemed quite strange and sad. No one could understand what was the matter with her.

Then one evening the queen also felt sad. She had so many peculiar thoughts whenever she thought about her sons. Then she said to Snow White–Rose Red, "Why are you sad, my daughter? If there's something wrong, tell me! If there's something you want, you shall have it."

"Oh, I feel very lonely," said Snow White–Rose Red. "Everyone else has siblings, while I'm so alone, for I have none. That's why I'm sad."

"You did have siblings, my daughter," said the queen. "I had twelve sons, who were your brothers, but I gave them all away so that I could have you." Then she told her daughter the whole story.

When the princess heard this, she could find no peace. No matter how much the queen wept and carried on, it did no good. The princess wanted to leave. She had to leave in order to search for her brothers, for she thought she was to blame for what had happened to them.

Finally she set off from the royal palace. She walked and walked far out into the wide world. You wouldn't believe such a delicate maiden would be able to walk so far.

The princess walked for a long time through a big, big forest. Then one day she was very tired. She sat down on a tussock, and there she fell asleep. Then she dreamed that she walked even farther into the forest to a small, timbered house, and that's where she found her brothers.

She woke up at once. Right in front of her was a path leading up from the green marsh. The path led deeper into the forest. The princess set off on the path, and at long last she came to a small, timbered house, just like the one in her dream.

When she went inside, no one was home, but she found twelve beds and twelve chairs and twelve spoons. There was twelve of everything. When she saw that, she was overjoyed, happier than she'd been in years. She could tell at once that her brothers lived here. They were the ones who owned the beds and chairs and spoons.

She set about making a fire and sweeping and straightening the beds. She cooked and cleaned and tidied up as best she could. After she had cooked for all of them, she ate some of the food herself, but she left her spoon on the table. Then she crawled under the bed belonging to the youngest brother and lay down to sleep.

No sooner had the princess lain down than she heard a whooshing and whistling in the air. Then all twelve wild ducks came rushing in. The instant they crossed the threshold, they turned into princes.

"Oh, how nice and warm it is in here!" they said. "God bless whoever made a fire and cooked such good food for us!"

Then each of them picked up his silver spoon to eat. But when each was holding a spoon, there was one more lying on the table. It looked so much like the others that they could hardly tell them apart. Then they looked at each other in surprise.

"This spoon must belong to our sister," they said. "And if her spoon is here, then she must not be far away."

"If that's our sister's spoon, and she's here too, then we should kill her. She's the one to blame for all the harm we've suffered," said the oldest prince.

The princess lay under the bed, listening to this.

"No," said the youngest prince. "It would be a shame to kill her. It's not her fault that we have suffered harm. If anyone is to blame, it has to be our own mother."

Then they set about searching high and low for their sister. Finally they looked under the beds. When they came to the bed belonging to the youngest prince, they found her there and dragged her out. The oldest prince again want to kill her, but she wept and pleaded so earnestly.

"Oh, dear God, don't kill me," she said. "I've been searching for you for many years. I would gladly give my life if I could rescue you."

"Well, if you will rescue us," they said, "we'll let you live. If that's what you want, then you should be allowed to do it."

"Yes, just tell me what has to be done. I'll do whatever it may be," said the princess.

"You must gather marsh sedge," the princes told her. "You must card it and spin it and weave it into cloth. When you've done that, you must cut and sew twelve caps, twelve shirts, and twelve scarves, one for each of us. But while you're doing that, you cannot speak or laugh or cry. If you can manage all this, then we will be saved."

"But where will I find enough marsh sedge for so many scarves and caps and shirts?" said Snow White–Rose Red.

"We will show you," said the princes.

They took her to a big, big marsh that was filled with sedge nodding in the wind and glinting in the sun. The whole place glittered like snow from far away. Never had the princess seen so much marsh sedge before. She began picking and gathering sedge. She worked as fast and as best as she could. When she got back that evening, she set about carding the sedge and spinning the yarn.

That's how things went for a good long time. She gathered sedge and carded it, and in the meanwhile she kept house for the princes. She cooked their meals and made their beds. In the evening they would come whooshing and rushing home as wild ducks. At night they were princes, but in the morning they would fly off again. They were wild ducks all day long.

One day when she was out in the marsh to gather sedge—and if I'm not mistaken, this was actually the last time she had to go there—it so happened that the young king who ruled the realm was out hunting. He came riding past the marsh and caught sight of her. He stopped, for he wondered who this lovely maiden could be. Why was she wandering through the marsh and gathering sedge? He asked her this, but he received no answer to his question. That made him wonder even more.

The young king was so taken with her that he wanted to bring her back to his palace and marry her. He told his servants to set her on his horse.

Snow White–Rose Red wrung her hands and then pointed at the sacks that contained all her work. The king realized that she wanted to take the sacks along, so he told his servants they should bring them too.

Then the princess gave in. The king was both a kind man and a handsome man. He was as gentle and kind toward her as he could be.

When they reached the royal palace, the old queen, who was the king's stepmother, caught sight of Snow White–Rose Red. She grew both angry and jealous, for the princess was quite lovely. She said to the king, "Can't you see that this girl you've brought home to be your bride is a witch? She doesn't speak or laugh or cry."

The king paid no mind to what his stepmother said. He celebrated his wedding and married Snow White–Rose Red. They lived together with great joy and delight. But that didn't stop her from sewing the shirts.

Before the year was over, Snow White–Rose Red gave birth to a little prince. Then the old queen grew even more angry and jealous. When night fell, she tiptoed into the bedroom when Snow White–Rose Red was asleep. There she picked up the child and tossed him into the snake pit. Then she cut her little finger and smeared blood on the mother's lips. After that she went to the king.

"Come and see what sort of woman you've taken as your queen," she said. "She has eaten her own child."

Then the king was filled with such dismay that he practically wept. He said, "Oh, it must be true, for I can see it with my own eyes. But I don't think she'll ever do it again, so this time I will spare her life."

Before the year was over, Snow White–Rose Red gave birth to another son. The same thing happened to him as to the first child. The king's stepmother grew even more evil and jealous. At night she tiptoed into the bedroom while Snow White–Rose Red slept. There she took the child and threw him into the snake pit. Then she cut her finger and smeared the blood on the lips of the mother. She told the king that his queen had eaten this child too.

Then the king was more distressed than you can ever imagine. He said, "Oh, it must be true, for I can see it with my own eyes. But she certainly won't do it again, so I'll spare her life one more time."

Before the year was over, Snow White–Rose Red gave birth to a daughter. The old queen took this child too and threw her into the snake pit. While the young queen slept, the stepmother cut her own finger and smeared blood on the queen's lips.

Then she went to the king and said, "You must come and see if I'm wrong when I say that she's a troll witch. Now she has eaten her third child."

Then the king was filled with sorrow beyond all measure. This time he could no longer spare her life. He was forced to decree that she should be burned at the stake.

When the flames rose up and Snow White–Rose Red was about to be put on the fire, she motioned for the servants to place twelve boards around the fire. On the boards she placed the scarves and the caps and the shirts for her brothers. But the youngest brother's shirt was missing the left sleeve. She hadn't had time to finish it.

No sooner did she do this than a whooshing and rushing was heard in the air, and twelve wild ducks came flying over the forest. Each of them plucked up his clothing and then flew off.

"Did you see that?" said the evil queen to the king. "Now you can truly see that she is a witch. Hurry up and burn her before the wood is gone."

"Oh," said the king, "we have plenty of firewood. We have a whole forest of wood. I want to wait a little longer. I'd like to see how this will end."

At that instant twelve princes came riding up. They looked as lovely and handsome as anyone would care to see. But the youngest prince had a wing instead of a left arm.

"What is happening here?" asked the princes.

"My queen is to be burned at the stake as a witch, for she has eaten her own children," replied the king.

"She has not eaten her children," said the princes. "Speak now, sister. Now that you have saved us, save yourself!"

Then Snow White–Rose Red told the king and her brothers everything that had happened. She said that every time she gave birth, the old queen, who was the king's stepmother, had tiptoed into her room at night and taken the child. Then she had cut her finger and smeared the blood on Snow White–Rose Red's lips.

The princes then took the king to the snake pit. There lay the three children, playing with the snakes and toads. Lovelier children you will never see. The king picked them up and went back to his stepmother. He asked her what punishment she thought would be fair for someone evil enough to betray an innocent queen and three such blessed children.

"That person ought to be tied to twelve wild horses so they could each take a piece," said the old queen.

"You have pronounced your own sentence. That is what you shall suffer," said the king.

Then the evil old queen was tied to twelve horses, and each took a piece of her.

Snow White–Rose Red left with the king and their children and the twelve princes. They all traveled home to see her parents and tell them what happened. Now there was great joy and happiness in the whole kingdom, for the princess had been saved. And she, in turn, had saved her twelve brothers.

The Master Thief

There once was a tenant farmer who had three sons. He had no inheritance to leave them and no work to give them, nor did he know what to do with them. He said they would be allowed to do whatever they liked and whatever they had the most desire to do. They could go wherever they wished. He would gladly keep them company along the way.

And that's what he did.

He went with them until they came to a place where three roads diverged. There each son chose a road. Then their father said goodbye to them and went back home.

I've never heard what happened to the two older sons, but the youngest son walked a long way and for a long time.

One night he was walking through a big forest when a terrible storm came up. The wind gusted and blew so hard that the boy could hardly keep his eyes open. Before he knew it, he'd gone completely astray. He couldn't find either a road or a path. But he kept on going.

Finally he caught sight of a light off in the distance, deep in the forest. He thought he should try to head in that direction, and at long last he arrived. He found a big house, and the fire was burning so brightly inside that he could see someone hadn't yet gone to bed. So he went in, and there he found an old woman tidying up.

"Good evening, ma'am," said the boy.

"Good evening!" said the old woman.

"Whew! What terrible weather we have tonight," said the boy.

"Yes, you're right," said the old woman.

"Could I stay here and take shelter for the night?" asked the boy.

"That probably wouldn't be a good idea," said the old woman. "If the folks come home and find you here, they will kill both you and me."

"What sort of folks live here?" said the boy.

"Oh, they're robbers and awful riffraff," said the old woman. "They stole me when I was little and made me work as their housekeeper," she said.

"I think I'll stay here all the same," said the boy. "Whatever happens will happen. I don't want to go back out into such weather tonight."

"Well, you'll suffer the worst of it then," said the old woman.

The boy lay down on a bed, but he didn't dare fall asleep. And soon enough the robbers came home. The old woman told them that a stranger had appeared, and she couldn't get him to leave.

"Did you see if he has any money?" said the robbers.

"Money? That poor wretch?" said the old woman. "He barely even has clothes on his back."

The robbers began muttering to each other about what they should do with him. Maybe they should kill him, or maybe they should do something else.

In the meantime the boy got up and started talking to the robbers. He asked if they needed a servant, for he might like to work for them.

"Well," they said, "if that's what you want and you're willing to take up our trade, then you can find work here."

"All right," said the boy. "It doesn't matter what trade it is, for when I left home, my father gave me permission to take up whatever sort of work I like."

"Would you like to steal?" said the robbers.

"Yes," said the boy. He didn't think that would be a hard trade to learn.

A man who had three oxen lived some distance away. He was going to take one of them to town to sell, and the robbers had heard about this. They told the boy that if he was able to steal the ox from the man so that he didn't know it was stolen and so the man did him no harm, then he would be allowed to work as a servant for the robbers.

Well, the boy found a lovely shoe with a silver buckle lying on the floor, and he took it with him as he set off. He placed the shoe in the road where the man was going to pass by with his ox. Then he went into the forest to hide under a bush.

When the man approached, he saw the shoe at once.

"What a grand shoe," he said. "If I had the mate to it, I could take it home with me. That would certainly make my wife tenderhearted for once!" His wife was always so angry and mean that there was no time at all between the thrashings she gave him. But he decided there was nothing he could do with just the one shoe if he didn't have the mate, so he left it lying there and continued on his way.

The boy picked up the shoe and hurried off as fast as he could go through the forest to get ahead of the man. Then he again set the shoe in the road.

When the man got there with the ox, he was annoyed that he'd been stupid enough to leave the shoe's mate behind instead of taking it with him. "I suppose

I should run back and get the other one," he said to himself. He tied the ox to a rail fence. "Then I'll have a pair of shoes for my wife, and then maybe she'll turn tenderhearted for once."

He went back and looked and looked for a very long time, but he found no shoe. Finally he had to go back, and he took with him the one shoe that he'd found.

In the meantime, the boy had stolen the ox and gone on his way.

When the man got back and saw the ox was gone, he started to weep and carry on, for he was afraid his wife would kill him when she found out he'd lost the ox. He decided to go home and get the second ox and take it to town, without letting his wife see what he was doing.

And that's what he did.

He went home and got the second ox without his wife noticing, and then he set off for town. But the robbers knew all about this, for they had their spies out. They told the boy that if he could take the second ox so the man didn't know it was stolen and so the man did him no harm, then he would be their equal.

The boy said that would be no problem.

This time he took along a rope. He wrapped the rope under his arms and hung himself from a tree in the middle of the road where the man would pass. When the man appeared with his ox and caught sight of the ghost hanging there, he felt a bit uneasy.

"What heavy thoughts you must have had to hang yourself like that! Oh well, I'll just have to leave you hanging here. I can't blow life back into you," he said. And he continued on with his ox.

The boy got down from the tree and raced along a shortcut to get ahead of the man. Again he hung himself from a tree in the middle of the road.

"I wonder if you really had such heavy thoughts that you hanged yourself here, or is this a ghost I'm seeing?" said the man. "Oh well, I'll just have to leave you hanging here. It makes no difference whether you're a ghost or something else," he said. And he went on his way with his ox.

The boy did exactly the same thing as he'd done before. He jumped down from the tree, raced along a shortcut through the forest, and again hung himself from a tree in the middle of the road.

When the man caught sight of the boy again, he said to himself, "How vile this is! Did these boys really have such heavy thoughts that they hanged themselves, all three of them? No, I can't believe it's anything but phantoms that I'm seeing. But I'm going to find out for sure. If the other two are still hanging there, then they're real. But if they're not hanging there, then I'm seeing nothing but ghosts."

He tied up the ox and ran back to see if the other two boys were really hanging there.

While the man walked around and peered up into the trees, the boy jumped down, took the ox, and went on his way.

When the man came back and saw that the ox was gone, he was beside himself, as you might well imagine. He wept and carried on, but finally he resigned himself to what had happened.

There's nothing to do but go home, he thought. I'll take the third ox without letting my wife see what I'm doing. I'll have to try even harder to sell this one for a good price.

He went home and got the third ox and set off without his wife noticing. But the robbers knew full well what he was doing. They told the boy that if he could steal the third ox the same way he'd stolen the first two, then he would be master of them all.

The boy set off running through the forest. When the man appeared with his ox, the boy began bellowing horribly, sounding just like a big ox inside the forest. When the man heard this, he was happy, for he thought he recognized the voice of his ox. He thought that now he'd find both of them. He tied up the third ox and raced off to search through the forest.

In the meantime, the boy took off with the third ox.

When the man came back and saw that he'd lost that one too, he wept and carried on. For days he didn't dare go back home. He was afraid that his wife would strike him dead.

The robbers weren't very happy either, for now they had to say the boy was master of them all.

One day they thought they would try doing something that the boy couldn't do. All of them set off and left him home alone.

The first thing he did after they'd left was to herd the oxen out to the road so they would go home to the man he'd stolen them from. The farmer was overjoyed, as you can well imagine.

Then the boy took the horses that belonged to the robbers and loaded them with the best of everything he could find of gold and silver and clothing and other magnificent things. He told the old woman to give his greetings and thanks to the robbers, for he was now setting off. And they would have trouble catching him. With that, he left.

At long last he came to the road he'd been traveling when he happened upon the robbers. As he headed for the house where his father lived, he put on a uniform that he'd found among the stolen goods he'd taken from the robbers. It seemed to have been made for a general. Then he rode into the farmyard like some grand personage.

He went inside and asked if he might take shelter there. No, that would be impossible.

"How could I offer lodging to such a fine gentleman? How could I?" said the farmer. "I barely have bedclothes for my own bed, and they're of the most wretched sort."

"You've always been a hard man, that you have," said the boy. "And I hear that you still are, seeing as you refuse to offer lodging to your own son."

"Are you my son?" said the man.

"Don't you recognize me?" said the boy.

Well, then he did recognize him, after all.

"But what have you been doing to become such a fine gentleman and so quickly?" said his father.

"Well, let me tell you," said the boy. "You said I could take up whatever I liked, so I became an apprentice to some thieves and robbers. I've finished my apprenticeship, and now I'm a master thief," he said.

It so happened that a bailiff lived near the house where the boy's father lived. The bailiff owned a big farm and had so much money that he couldn't even count it all. He also had a daughter who was both beautiful and lovely, sweet and kind. The master thief wanted her for his wife. He told his father to go to the bailiff and ask for the daughter to be his bride.

"If he asks you what my trade is, tell him that I'm a master thief," he said.

"I think you're crazy. That I do," said the man. "You can't be very clever if you're suggesting such madness."

The boy insisted he should go to the bailiff and ask for his daughter's hand. There was no getting around it.

"But I don't dare go to the bailiff and speak to him on your behalf. He's a very rich man, and he has so much money," said the farmer.

The master thief said that couldn't be helped. He had to go, whether he wanted to or not. If his father didn't do it willingly, then he'd have to force him to go. Still the man refused, so the boy followed on his heels and threatened him with a big birch club. The farmer was weeping by the time he stepped through the door of the bailiff's house.

"So, my man, what's the matter?" said the bailiff.

He told the bailiff that he had three sons who had set off one day. He'd promised them that they could travel wherever they wished and take up whatever work they liked. "And now the youngest of them has come back home. He threatened me until I agreed to come here and ask on his behalf for your daughter's hand in marriage. I am also supposed to tell you that he's a master thief," said the man as he wept and carried on.

"Rest easy, my man," said the bailiff and laughed. "Tell him from me that first he'll have to prove it. If he can steal the roast from the spit in the kitchen on Sunday while they're all watching, then he shall have my daughter. Go ahead and tell him that!"

And that's what the man did.

The boy thought that would be an easy task. He got hold of three live hares and put them in a sack. Then he dressed himself in rags. He looked so wretched and miserable that he was a pitiful sight to behold. On Sunday morning he crept along the hall like any other ragged boy, carrying his sack.

The bailiff and all the household servants were in the kitchen watching over the roast. All of a sudden the boy let a hare out of the sack. It took off and raced around the yard outside.

"Oh, look at that hare!" they said in the kitchen. They wanted to go out and catch it.

The bailiff saw it too. "Let it go," he said. "It's useless to think of catching a hare that's running away."

It wasn't long before the boy let another hare out of the sack. The servants in the kitchen thought it was the same one, and they wanted to go out and catch it. But the bailiff said it would be no use.

A short time later the boy let the third hare out. It took off and ran around the yard outside. Everyone in the kitchen saw this hare too, and they thought it was the same one as before. They wanted to go out and catch it.

"That's a very strange hare," said the bailiff. "Come on, let's see if we can catch it."

He and everyone else went outside. The hare ran, and they chased after it as best they could.

In the meantime the master thief took the roast and ran off.

I don't know where the bailiff found a roast for his dinner, but this much I do know: he didn't have roast hare, even though he ran until he was both sweaty and tired.

The pastor came to dinner, and the bailiff told him about the trick the master thief had played on him. Then the pastor made fun of him and refused to let up.

"I know I would never allow such a man to make a fool of me," said the pastor.

"Well, you'd better watch out. Yes, you should," said the bailiff. "Before you know it, he may turn up at your place."

But the pastor kept on making fun of the bailiff for allowing himself to be fooled.

Later in the afternoon the master thief arrived to get the bailiff's daughter, as he'd been promised.

"First you'll have to pass a few more tests," the bailiff insisted. "What you did today wasn't very impressive. Why don't you play a clever prank on the pastor? He's sitting inside and laughing at me, for I let myself be fooled by a young man like you."

The master thief said he could easily do that. He dressed himself like a bird by wrapping a big white sheet around his body. He broke off the wings from a goose and fastened them to his back. Then he climbed up in a big maple tree that stood in the pastor's yard.

When the pastor came home that evening, the boy began shrieking, "Mr. Lars! Mr. Lars!" The pastor's name was Mr. Lars.

"Who's calling me?" said the pastor.

"I am an angel sent by the Lord to proclaim to you that you shall be received alive in the Lord's kingdom, for you are such a God-fearing man," said the master thief. "Next Monday evening you must make ready to leave. That's when I will come to fetch you in a sack. And in your parlor you must pile up all your gold and silver and everything else you own of worldly vanities."

Mr. Lars offered his thanks and fell to his knees before the angel.

On the following Sunday he preached a farewell sermon. He said that an angel from the Lord had perched in the big maple tree in his yard and proclaimed that he would be taken alive to God's kingdom, for he was such a God-fearing man. He preached and sermonized so well that everyone in the church wept, both the old and the young.

On Monday the master thief appeared again as an angel, and the pastor offered his thanks and fell to his knees. Then he was stuffed inside the sack. After the pastor was inside, the master thief dragged and hauled him over rocks and tussocks.

"Ow! Ow!" cried the pastor inside the sack. "Where are we going?"

"It's a narrow road that leads to the kingdom of heaven," said the master thief as he dragged him along and practically killed him.

Finally he threw the pastor into the bailiff's goose coop. The geese began hissing and nipping at him so he ended up more dead than alive.

"Ow, ow, ow! Where am I now?" said the pastor.

"You're in purgatory to be cleansed and purified for eternal life," said the master thief. Then he left, taking along the gold and silver and all the other magnificent things the pastor had piled up in his parlor.

The next morning, when the goose girl came to let the geese out, she heard the pastor wailing inside the sack.

"In Christ's name, who are you and what's the matter with you?" she said.

"Oh, if you're an angel from heaven, get me out of here. Let me go back to earth, for this is worse than hell. The little demons are nipping at me with their pinchers," said the pastor.

"Goodness, I'm not an angel," said the girl as she helped the pastor out of the sack. "I just take care of the bailiff's geese. That's all I do. It must be the little goslings that have been pinching you, sir."

"The master thief must have done this! Oh, my gold and silver and all my magnificent clothes!" cried the pastor. He began carrying on, and then he ran back home. The goose girl thought he must have lost his wits.

The bailiff found out what happened to the pastor. When he heard the man had been put in purgatory and traveled the narrow road, he practically laughed himself senseless.

But when the master thief came and asked for his daughter, as he'd been promised, the bailiff insisted, "You'll have to play an even better prank so I can truly see what you're able to do. I have twelve horses in the stable," he said. "I'll put twelve riders on them, one on each. If you're clever enough to steal the horses from under these men, then I'll see what I can do."

"All right, I agree," said the master thief, "if it means that I can have your daughter."

"Yes. If you can do that, you shall have the best that I own," said the bailiff.

So the master thief went to the peddler and bought some liquor in two pocket flasks. In one flask he added a sleeping potion, while the other contained only liquor. Then he ordered eleven men to sleep behind the bailiff's barn that night. For a few coins he persuaded an old woman to lend him a shirt and a skirt made of wooden staves. Then he picked up a walking stick and flung a sack over his back. When evening arrived, he limped off toward the bailiff's stables.

When he arrived, the men were busy watering the horses for the night.

"What the hell do you want?" said one of the grooms to the old woman.

"Oh, brrr! It's so cold!" said the old woman, shivering and shuddering and carrying on. "Brrr! It's so cold that a poor soul might freeze to death!" Then she shivered and shook even more. "Oh, dear God, can I stay here and sit inside the stable door?" she said.

"The Devil take me, no! Get out of here at once! If the bailiff catches sight of you, he'll rake us over the coals," said one of the grooms.

"Oh, that pitiful old hag!" said another, who seemed to feel sorry for her. "Let the old hag sit there. She'll do no harm."

The others didn't want to allow it. They began arguing as they tended to the horses. In the meantime, the old woman retreated farther inside the stable until she finally sat down behind the door. After that nobody paid her any mind.

As night fell, the men found it cold to be sitting so still on horseback.

"Brrr! It's devilishly cold," said one of them, flapping his arms.

"Yes, I'm freezing so much that I'm shaking," said another.

"If only we had some tobacco," said another man.

One of the men did have a quarter wad of snuff, and he divided it up to share. There wasn't much for each of them, but they chewed and they spat. That helped a little, but suddenly things seemed just as bad as before.

"Brrr!" said one of them, and he started shaking.

"Brrr!" said the old woman, and her teeth were chattering so hard that her jaws rattled. Then she got out the flask that held only liquor. Her hand shook so much that some of the liquor spilled out. She took such a long swig that a gurgling sound came from her throat.

"What have you got in that flask of yours, old woman?" said one of the grooms.

"Oh, it's just a drop of liquor, sir," she said.

"Liquor! Can that be true? Let me have a swig! Let me have a swig!" shouted all twelve of the men at once.

"Oh, I have so little," whined the old woman. "There's not even enough to wet your whistle."

But they wanted some, they had to have some, there was no getting around it. So she got out the flask with the sleeping potion and held it to the lips of the first man. She wasn't shaking anymore, and she was careful to keep moving the flask to make sure that each man got what he needed. The twelfth man had barely taken a swig before the first one began snoring.

Then the master thief threw off his rags and easily lifted down one man after the other. He placed them astride the stall partitions. Then he shouted for his own eleven men, and they set off with the bailiff's horses.

When the bailiff came out in the morning and saw his men, they were just beginning to stir. They pounded their spurs against the partitions so splinters of wood flew out. Some of them fell off, while others remained where they were, sitting there like fools.

"Oh yes," said the bailiff, "I can certainly tell who's been here. What a miserable bunch of men you are. How could you sit there and let the master thief steal the horses out from under you!"

And they were all berated for not paying closer attention.

Later in the day the master thief came back and told the bailiff how he'd done it. And now he wanted the man's daughter, as he'd been promised.

But the bailiff gave him a hundred *daler* and said he'd have to do something even better. "Do you think you can steal the horse from under me while I'm out riding?"

"Oh, I'm sure I can," said the master thief, "if it means that I can have your daughter."

The bailiff said he would see what he could do.

One morning he announced that he was going out riding in the big exercise grounds.

The master thief at once got hold of an old, worn-out nag. He made a harness of nothing but reeds and the twigs from a broom. He bought an old, broken-down wagon and a big barrel. Then he told a poor old woman that he'd give her ten *daler* if she would get inside the barrel and open her mouth wide around the plughole. That's where he would stick in his finger. Nothing bad would happen to her, for she would just ride around for a while. And if he took out his finger more than once, she would get ten more *daler*.

Then the master thief dressed in rags and covered himself in soot. He put on a wig and a big beard made from bristly goat hair, so that no one would recognize him. Then he set off for the exercise grounds, where the bailiff had already been riding for a long time.

When the master thief got there, he slowed down to such a snail's pace that the wagon was barely moving at all. He crept forward little by little, then stopped, then again crept forward a little. He was such a sorry sight that the bailiff would never dream that this was the master thief.

The bailiff came riding over to him and asked if he'd seen anyone sneaking through the forest.

No, he hadn't seen anyone like that.

"Listen here," said the bailiff. "If you're willing to ride into the forest to take a look and see if anybody is sneaking around, then I'll loan you my horse. And I'll give you a tip for your trouble."

"No, I can't do that," said the man. "I'm going to a wedding with this mead barrel that I'm supposed to deliver. The plug fell out along the way, so now I have to keep my finger in the hole."

"Oh, don't worry about that," said the bailiff. "I'll look after both your horse and the barrel."

With that, the man agreed to go. But he told the bailiff that he must be quick to put his finger in the plughole when he took his own finger out.

The bailiff said he'd do the best he could. Then the master thief mounted the bailiff's horse.

The minutes flew, the hours did too, and no one came back. Finally the bailiff got tired of sticking his finger in the plughole, and he pulled it out.

"Now I want ten more *daler!*" cried the old woman inside the barrel.

Then the bailiff realized what was happening with the mead barrel, and he set off for home. After he'd walked for a while, his servants came to meet him, bringing a horse, for the master thief had already been to his house.

The next day the master thief came to see the bailiff and asked for his daughter, as he'd been promised. The bailiff gave him two hundred *daler* and again insisted he'd have to pass another test. If he passed, then he could have his daughter.

The master thief agreed. He just needed to know what sort of test it was.

"Do you think you can steal the sheet off our bed and the shift off my wife?" said the bailiff.

"It's not impossible," said the master thief. "If it means that I can truly have your daughter, then I'll do it."

When night fell, he went out and cut down a thief who was hanging on the gallows. He threw the corpse over his shoulder and set off with it. Then he got hold of a big ladder and placed it against the bailiff's bedroom window. He climbed up and shoved the dead man up and down, as if he were outside the window and peering inside.

"There's the master thief, Mother," said the bailiff, poking his wife. "I'm going to shoot him," he said. And he picked up a rifle that he'd placed next to the bed.

"Oh no, don't do that," said his wife. "You're the one who told him to come here."

"Oh yes, I'm going to shoot him, Mother," he said. And he lay there taking aim, but the head kept popping up so he could see a little of it, and then it would suddenly disappear. Finally the bailiff took careful aim and fired. The dead man fell to the ground with a thud. The master thief climbed down the ladder as fast as he could go.

"It's true that I'm the highest authority here," said the bailiff, "but folks like to gossip. It would be a shame if they caught sight of that dead man. It's probably best if I go out and bury him."

"Do as you please, Father," said his wife.

The bailiff got up and headed downstairs. As soon as he stepped out the front door, the master thief slipped inside and went upstairs to the wife.

"So, Father," she said, for she thought he was her husband, "are you already done?"

"Oh yes, I stuffed him into a hole. That I did," he said. "And I scraped some earth on top so he'll be hidden, for the weather is terrible. I'll make a better job of it later. Let me use the sheet to dry myself off. He was covered with blood, and I got some of it on me."

She gave him the sheet.

"You'd better let me have your shift too," he said. "I can see that the sheet isn't enough."

And she did.

Then he remembered that he'd forgotten to close the front door, so he left, carrying both the sheet and the shift.

A little later the real bailiff came back.

"Well, it certainly took you a long time to close the door, Father!" said his wife. "What have you done with my shift and the sheet?"

"What did you say?" said the bailiff.

"I asked you what you've done with my shift and the sheet that you used to dry off the blood. That's what I asked," she said.

"Damn it to hell!" said the bailiff. "Did he actually manage to do that too?"

The next day the master thief appeared, and he wanted the bailiff's daughter, as he'd been promised. The bailiff didn't dare refuse him. He gave her to him, along with a great deal of money, for he was afraid the master thief might steal even his eyes from his head. And if he broke his promise, folks might gossip about him.

The master thief lived a happy and prosperous life. Whether he ever stole anything again, I can't say. But if he did, it was no doubt only for fun.

The Three Sisters Who Were Taken into the Mountain

There once was an old widow who lived with her three daughters far from any village, way up under a ridge. She was so poor that she owned nothing but a hen. She loved that hen dearly. It was the apple of her eye. She clucked to it and tended to it morning and night.

One day the hen disappeared. The woman went out to walk around the house, searching and calling. But the hen was gone, and gone it stayed.

"You have to go out and search for our hen, yes, you must," said the woman to her eldest daughter. "We must get it back, even if we have to go into the mountain to find it."

The daughter set off to look for the hen. She went here and there, searching and calling, but she found no hen. All of a sudden she heard a voice saying from inside the mountain:

> *The hen is skittering inside the mountain!*
> *The hen is skittering inside the mountain!*

The girl went over to see who was speaking. When she came to the mountain wall, she fell through a hatch and landed in a vault deep, deep underground. There she walked through many rooms, each more splendid than the last. In the innermost room a big, hideous mountain man came toward her.

"Will you be my sweetheart?" he asked.

"No," she said. She certainly would not. She wanted to go back up at once to look for the hen that had disappeared.

The mountain man grew so angry that he grabbed the girl and twisted off her head. He threw the body and the head into the cellar.

The woman sat at home and waited and waited, but her daughter didn't come back. She waited a while longer. When she neither saw nor heard from the girl, she told the middle daughter that she would have to go out and look for her sister. "And you can call for the hen at the same time," she said.

So the second sister set off. The exact same thing happened to her. She walked and searched and called, and all of a sudden she also heard a voice speaking from inside the mountain:

The hen is skittering inside the mountain!
The hen is skittering inside the mountain!

The girl thought that was strange. She went over to see who was speaking. She too fell through a hatch and landed in a vault deep, deep underground. There she walked through all the rooms. In the innermost room the mountain man came and asked her if she would be his sweetheart.

No, she certainly would not. She wanted to go back up at once and search for the hen that had disappeared. That's what she wanted.

Then the mountain man grew angry. He grabbed the girl and twisted off her head. He threw the head and the body into the cellar.

The woman sat and waited forever and a day for her second daughter, but she didn't see or hear from the girl. Then she said to the youngest daughter, "Well, now you'll just have to set off to look for your sisters. It was bad enough that the hen disappeared. It's even worse if we should never find your sisters again. You can always call for the hen at the same time."

So the youngest daughter set off. She went here and there, she searched and she called, but she didn't see the hen, and she didn't see her sisters. At long last she too came to the mountain wall. Then she heard a voice saying:

The hen is skittering inside the mountain!
The hen is skittering inside the mountain!

She thought that was strange. She went over to have a look, and then she too fell through the hatch. She landed in a vault deep, deep underground. Down there she walked through many rooms, each more splendid than the last, but she wasn't frightened. She took her time and looked carefully at one thing and another. Then she caught sight of the trapdoor to the cellar. She looked down inside and recognized at once her sisters who were both lying there. As soon as she closed the trapdoor, the mountain man came to her.

"Will you be my sweetheart? Will you?" asked the mountain man.

"Yes, gladly," said the girl, for she realized what must have happened to her sisters.

When the troll heard this, he gave her the most splendid clothes, the loveliest she could ever imagine, along with everything else she might want. He was so happy that someone wanted to be his sweetheart.

One day, after the girl had been there for a while, she seemed more sullen and silent than usual. The mountain man asked her why she was so sullen.

"Oh," said the girl, "it's because I can't go home to see my mother. She's probably hungry and thirsty, and no one is living with her anymore."

"I can't allow you to visit her," replied the troll. "But fill a sack with food, and I'll take it to her."

The girl thanked him. That's exactly what she would do.

In the bottom of the sack she stuffed a great quantity of gold and silver, and then she put a little food on top. She told the troll the sack was ready, but he must not peek inside. He promised not to look.

When the mountain man set off, the girl watched him through a little peephole in the hatch. After he'd gone a short distance along the road, he said, "This sack is so heavy. I want to see what's inside. Yes, I do."

He was about to untie the cord, but the girl shouted, "I can see you! I can see you!"

"I can't believe what sharp eyes you have," said the troll. And then he didn't try to look inside anymore.

When he got to the house where the widow lived, he threw the sack inside the front door. "Here's some food from your daughter. Don't go looking for her," he said.

One day after the girl had been inside the mountain for a good long while, a billy goat happened to fall through the hatch.

"Who asked you to come here, you shaggy-haired beast?" said the troll. He was in such a vile mood that he grabbed the goat and twisted off its head. Then he threw it into the cellar.

"Oh no, why did you do that?" said the girl. "I would have liked to keep that goat to amuse me."

"No need to look so mournful, let me tell you," said the troll. "I can easily bring that billy goat back to life. Yes, I can."

With that he grabbed a flask that hung on the wall. Then he set the head back on the goat and smeared it with what was in the flask. And the goat was as good as new.

Aha! thought the girl. That flask is certainly worth having.

After she'd been with the troll for a good long time, she waited until one day when he went out. Then she put the head back on her eldest sister and smeared her with what was in the flask. The sister instantly came back to life. Then the girl stuffed her into a sack and put a little food on top.

As soon as the troll came home, she said to him, "My dear sir, you need to take some more food to my mother. She must be hungry and thirsty, the poor thing. And she's all alone too. But don't peek inside the sack!"

The troll said he would take the sack to her mother, and he promised not to look inside. But after he'd gone a short distance along the road, he thought the sack seemed awfully heavy. After he'd walked a little more, he decided he would see what was inside. "No matter how sharp her eyes are, she won't be able to see me now," he said to himself.

But the instant he began to untie the cord, the sister who was inside the sack said, "I can see you! I can see you!"

"I can't believe what sharp eyes you have," said the troll. He thought it was the girl in the mountain talking. Then he didn't dare try to look inside anymore. He carried the sack to the mother's house as fast as he could go.

When he came to her front door, he threw the sack inside. "Here's some food from your daughter. But don't go looking for her," he said.

After the girl had been inside the mountain for another good long while, she did the same thing with the second sister. She set her head back on, smeared her with what was inside the flask, and then stuffed her into a sack. This time she put on top as much gold and silver as the sack would hold, and on the very top she put a little food.

"My dear sir," she said to the troll. "You have to take a little food to my mother again, but don't look inside the sack!"

The troll was happy to do as she wished, and he promised not to look inside. But after he'd gone a short distance along the road, he thought the sack seemed awfully heavy, and he couldn't carry it any farther. He set it down so he could rest. He was just about to untie the cord and look inside, but then the sister inside the sack shouted, "I can see you! I can see you!"

"I can't believe what sharp eyes you have," said the troll. Then he didn't dare look inside the sack anymore. Instead, he rushed off as fast as he could go and carried the sack straight to the mother's house.

When he was standing outside the front door, he threw the sack inside. "Here's some food from your daughter. But don't go looking for her," he said.

One day after the girl had been there another good long while, the troll had to go out. Then the girl pretended to be both wretched and ill. She shivered and carried on.

"It will do no good for you to come home before twelve o'clock," she said. "I won't have the meal ready until then, for I'm feeling so wretched and ill."

After the troll left, she stuffed some of her clothes with straw and stood the straw girl in a corner next to the hearth. She put a stirring stick in the straw girl's hand, so it looked as if she was the one standing there. Then she hurried home. She took along a marksman who would have to stay with her in her mother's house.

At twelve o'clock or thereabouts, the troll came home. "Bring me my food!" he said to the straw girl.

She didn't answer.

"Bring me my food!" said the troll again. "I'm hungry!"

She didn't answer.

"Bring me my food!" bellowed the troll for a third time. "Listen to what I'm saying, or else I'll have to shake you awake, yes, I will!"

But the girl stood there, just as silent as before.

The troll was furious. He grabbed her and squeezed her so tight that pieces of straw flew at the walls and ceiling. When he saw that, he got suspicious and began searching everywhere. Finally he went down to the cellar and saw that both of the girl's sisters were gone. He realized at once what had happened.

"Oh, she will have to pay for this!" he said. And he set off for where the mother lived.

But when he came to her house, the marksman fired his rifle. Then the troll didn't dare go inside, for he thought it was thunder.

He set off for home as fast as he could go. Just as he came to the hatch, the sun rose, and then he burst.

There is probably plenty of gold and silver left in the mountain. If only somebody knew where to find the hatch!

About the Giant Troll Who Never Carried His Heart with Him

here once was a king who had seven sons. He was so fond of them that he could never let all of them leave together. One son always had to stay behind.

When they were grown, six of the brothers were going to set off to find wives, but the father wanted to keep the youngest son at home. The others were supposed to bring a princess back to the royal palace for him. The king gave his six sons the most splendid clothes that anyone had ever seen, clothes that cost many, many hundreds of *daler*. And then they set off.

After they had visited many royal palaces and seen many princesses, at long last they came to a king who had six daughters. They had never seen such lovely princesses, and each of them proposed to one of them. After they had won them as their sweethearts, they headed for home. They were so in love with their sweethearts that they'd completely forgotten they were supposed to bring a princess back for Ash Lad, who had stayed behind.

After they had traveled a good distance along the road, they passed very close to a steep mountain wall. That's where the giant troll had his farm. The troll came out and caught sight of the travelers. He turned all of them to stone, both the princes and the princesses.

The king waited and waited for his six sons, but no matter how long he waited, none of them returned. He grew terribly distressed and said he would never be happy again. "If I didn't have you," he said to Ash Lad, "I would not want to live. That's how filled with sorrow I am, for I have lost all your brothers."

"I was thinking of asking your permission to go out and find them. That's what I was thinking," said Ash Lad.

"No, I won't allow it," said his father. "You would just disappear too."

But Ash Lad wanted to go, he had to go. He begged and pleaded for so long that the king had to let him leave. But the king had nothing but an old nag to give him, for the other six sons and their entourage had been given all the other horses he owned. Ash Lad didn't care. He mounted the mangy old horse.

"Goodbye, Father," he said to the king. "I'm sure I'll be back. Maybe I'll bring my six brothers back with me too." With that, he left.

After he'd been riding for a while, Ash Lad came upon a raven lying in the road and flapping its wings. The bird was so hungry that it couldn't even move aside.

"Oh, my dear man! Give me a little food, and I'll help you when you're in dire need," said the raven.

"I don't have much food, and you don't look like you'll be able to offer me much help," said the king's son. "But I can certainly give you something to eat. I can see that you're hungry." And he gave the raven some of the provisions he'd brought along.

After he'd traveled a little farther, Ash Lad came to a stream. There he saw a big salmon that had ended up on dry land. The fish was flapping and flailing and couldn't get back in the water.

"Oh, my dear man! Help me back in the water," said the salmon to the king's son, "and I'll help you when you're in dire need. That I will."

"Whatever help you offer won't be much," said the prince. "But it's a shame for you to lie here and starve to death." So he pushed the fish back in the water.

He traveled a long, long way. Then he came upon a wolf. The wolf was so limp with hunger that he lay stretched out in the middle of the road.

"My dear man, let me have your horse!" said the wolf. "I'm so hungry that my guts are whistling. I haven't had anything to eat in two years."

"No," said Ash Lad, "I can't do that. First I came upon a raven, and I had to give him my provisions. Then I came upon a salmon, and I had to help him back in the water. Now you want to have my horse. I can't do that, for then I will have nothing to ride."

"Oh please, dear sir, you have to help me," said the gray-one. "You can ride on me, and in turn I will help you when you're in dire need," the wolf said.

"Well, the help you can offer me won't be much, but you can have my horse. I can see that you're in great need," said the prince.

After the wolf had eaten the horse, Ash Lad put the bridle bit in the wolf's mouth and the saddle on his back. By now the wolf had grown so strong from eating the horse that he set off as if the king's son weighed nothing at all. The prince had never ridden so fast before.

"After we've traveled a little farther, I'll show you the farm that belongs to the giant troll," said the gray-one.

That's where they finally arrived.

"Look, here is the giant troll's farm," said the wolf. "There you can see all six of your brothers. The troll turned them to stone. And there you can see their six brides. Over there is the troll's door, and that's where you must go in."

"No, I don't dare," said the king's son. "He is sure to kill me."

"Oh no," replied the wolf. "When you go inside you'll find a princess. She will tell you what you should do to put an end to the giant troll. Just do whatever she says. Go ahead."

So Ash Lad went inside, though he was frightened. When he went in, the troll was away. But in one room sat the princess, just as the wolf had said. Ash Lad had never seen a lovelier maiden.

"Oh, God save me, how did you get in here?" said the king's daughter when she caught sight of him. "It will certainly be the death of you. Nobody has ever been able to put an end to the giant troll who lives here, for he never carries his heart with him."

"Well, here I am, so I'll give it a try all the same. That I will," said Ash Lad. "I'll also try to rescue my brothers, who have been turned to stone outside."

"If you really want to try, let me help you," said the princess. "Crawl under that bed over there, and listen closely to what I tell him. But by all means keep very still."

So Ash Lad crawled under the bed, and no sooner was he well hidden than the giant troll came home.

"Ugh! It smells like a Christian man in here!" said the troll.

"Yes, a magpie came flying with a man's leg in its beak and fell down the chimney," said the princess. "I hurried to shoo out the magpie, but it wasn't so easy to get rid of the smell."

Then the troll said no more about it.

When evening came, they went to bed. After they'd been lying there for a while, the king's daughter said, "There's one thing I wanted to ask you, if only I dared."

"What is it?" asked the giant troll.

"I wonder where you keep your heart, seeing as you never carry it with you," said the king's daughter.

"Oh, that's not something you need to wonder about. It's under the doorstep," said the giant troll.

Aha! So that's where we'll find it, thought Ash Lad, who was lying under the bed.

The next morning the giant troll got up awfully early and went off to the forest. No sooner had he left than Ash Lad and the princess looked under the doorstep for his heart. Yet no matter how much they dug and searched, they found nothing.

"This time he fooled us," said the princess. "We'll just have to try again."

Then she gathered up the most beautiful flowers she could find and scattered them around the doorstep after they'd put it back where it belonged. When the time came for the giant troll to return home, Ash Lad crawled under the bed again. The instant he was well hidden, the troll appeared.

"Ugh! It smells like a Christian man in here!" said the troll.

"Yes, a magpie came flying with a man's leg in its beak and fell down the chimney," said the princess. "I hurried to shoo the magpie out, but that must be what you smell, all the same."

Then the troll fell silent and said no more about it.

A little later he asked who had scattered flowers around the doorstep.

"Oh, that was me," said the princess.

"And what's the meaning of that?" asked the mountain troll.

"Oh, it's because I'm so fond of you. I had to do it now that I know that's where you've put your heart," said the princess.

"Is that so? Well, that's not where it is, my dear," said the troll.

After they had gone to bed that evening, the princess asked the troll again where he kept his heart. She said she was so terribly fond of him that she dearly wanted to know.

"Oh, it's over there in the cupboard against the wall," said the troll.

Is that right? thought Ash Lad and the princess. Then that's where we'll try to look for it.

The next morning the troll was up early again and left for the forest. No sooner had he gone than Ash Lad and the king's daughter went to the cupboard to look for his heart. But no matter how much they searched, they found nothing there.

"Well, well. We'll have to try again," said the princess.

She adorned the cupboard with flowers and wreaths, and when evening came, Ash Lad again crawled under the bed.

Then the troll returned.

"Ugh! It smells like a Christian man in here!"

"Yes, a little while ago a magpie came flying with a man's leg in its beak and fell down the chimney," said the princess. "I hurried to shoo the magpie out, but that must be what you smell, all the same."

When the giant troll heard this, he said no more about it. But after a while he noticed the flowers and wreaths hanging all over the cupboard. He asked who had put them there.

The princess said she had done that.

"What is the meaning of such foolishness?" asked the troll.

"Oh, I'm so fond of you, of course, that I had to do it, now that I know your heart is inside the cupboard," said the princess.

"Are you really crazy enough to believe something like that?" said the troll.

"Yes, I have to believe whatever you tell me," said the princess.

"What a fool you are," said the troll. "You'll never find where I keep my heart!"

"It would still be fun to know where it is," said the princess.

Then the troll couldn't stand it any longer. He had to tell her.

"Far, far away in a lake there is an island," he said. "On that island stands a church. Inside that church is a well. In that well swims a duck. Inside that duck is an egg. And inside that egg—that's where my heart is, my dear."

Early the next morning, even before the gray light of dawn appeared, the troll again went off to the forest.

"Well, I'd better set off too," said Ash lad. "If only I can find the way!"

He said goodbye to the princess. When he came out of the troll's farm, the wolf was still waiting for him. Ash Lad told the wolf what had happened in the troll's house. He said he wanted to find the well in the church, if only he knew the way.

Then the wolf told Ash Lad to climb onto his back, for he was certain he could find the way. And they set off, rushing over hills and ridges, over mountains and valleys.

After they'd traveled for many, many days, they came at last to the lake. The king's son didn't know how he would get across it, but the gray-one told him not to be afraid. Then the wolf set off with the prince on his back and swam across to the island.

There they came to the church. The key to the church was hanging high up on the tower. The king's son had no idea how he was going to reach it.

"You must call for the raven," said the gray-one.

That's what the king's son did.

The raven appeared at once and flew up to get the key. Then the prince went inside the church.

When he came to the well, he saw the duck swimming back and forth, just as the giant troll had said. Ash Lad stood there, coaxing and calling, and at last he managed to coax the duck over so he could grab it.

But as soon as he lifted the duck out of the water, it dropped the egg into the well. Then Ash Lad didn't know how he was going to get the egg out.

"You have to call for the salmon," said the gray-one.

That's what the king's son did.

The salmon appeared and brought the egg up from the bottom of the well. Then the wolf told Ash Lad to squeeze the egg. The instant he did that, the giant troll screamed.

"Squeeze it again," said the wolf.

When the prince did that, the troll screamed even more pitifully. He began pleading so earnestly. He said he would do anything the king's son wanted if only Ash Lad wouldn't squeeze his heart to bits.

"Tell him that if he changes back your six brothers he turned to stone, he'll be allowed to keep his life," said the wolf.

That's what Ash Lad did.

The troll agreed at once. He changed the six brothers back into king's sons and their brides into king's daughters.

"Now squeeze the egg to bits," said the wolf.

So Ash Lad squeezed the egg to bits, and the giant troll burst.

After he'd gotten rid of the troll, Ash Lad rode on the back of the wolf to the troll's farm. There stood all six of his brothers, very much alive, along with their brides. Then Ash Lad went inside the mountain to get his own bride. Together they all rode back to the royal palace.

The old king was certainly overjoyed when all of his sons returned, each of them with a bride.

"And yet the loveliest of all the princesses is Ash Lad's bride," said the king. "He will sit at the head of the table with his princess."

Then the wedding feast was joyously celebrated for many a day. If they haven't finished feasting yet, then they're still celebrating today.

Dappleband

here once was a rich couple who had twelve sons. When the youngest grew up, he didn't wanted to stay at home any longer. He wanted to go out in the world and try his luck. His parents thought he had everything he needed at home, so he might as well stay with them. But he was terribly restless. He wanted to leave, he had to leave. Finally, they gave their permission.

After he'd walked a good distance, he came to a royal palace. There he asked for a job, and he was hired.

A troll had taken the king's daughter into the mountain, and the king had no other children. That's why both he and the whole land were suffering great sorrow and distress. The king had promised the princess and half his kingdom to whoever could rescue her. Many had tried, but no one had been able to do it.

After the boy had been there for half a year or so, he wanted to return home to visit his parents. But when he got back, he found that both of his parents were dead, and his brothers had divided up all the family's possessions. There was nothing left for the boy.

"Will I have nothing that belonged to my parents?" asked the boy.

"How could we know that you were still alive? You've been wandering and roaming around for so long," replied his brothers. "But never mind. Up in the heights there are twelve mares that we haven't taken. If you want them for your share, you can have them."

The boy was pleased with that. He thanked his brothers and set off at once for the heights where the twelve mares were grazing. There he found that each of them had a suckling. One of the mares also had a big dappled foal with such a glossy coat that it gleamed.

"You're certainly handsome, my little foal," said the boy.

"If you will kill the twelve other foals, I can suckle from all the mares for a year. Then you'll see how big and handsome I will be!"

That's what the boy did. He killed all the other foals, and then he went home.

The following year he went back to see to the foal and the mares. The foal was now so plump, so plump that his coat glistened. The foal had grown so big that it took great effort for the boy to climb onto his back. All the mares once again had foals.

"Well, I clearly gained by allowing you to suckle from all my mares," said the boy to the yearling. "Now you're big enough to come with me."

"No, I need to stay here for another year," said the foal. "If you kill the twelve other foals, I can suckle from all the mares for one more year. Then you'll see how big and handsome I'll be next summer!"

That's what the boy did.

The next year he went back up to the heights to see to his foal and his mares. All the mares again had their foals. The dappled foal was now so big that the boy could barely reach the horse's neck to feel how plump he was. And the foal's coat was so shiny that it gleamed.

"Big and handsome you were last year, my foal," said the boy, "but this year you're even more splendid. Such a horse is not to be found even at the king's palace. Now you must come with me."

"No," said the dappled horse, "I need to stay here another year. Go ahead and kill the twelve other foals so I can suckle from the mares this year too. Then you'll see me in the summer!"

That's what the boy did.

He killed all the other foals, and then he went home.

When he came back the following year to see to the dappled foal and his mares, he was quite horrified. He would never have believed a horse could grow so big and bulky. Now the dappled horse had to get down on all fours before the boy could climb onto his back. He had a hard enough time getting on even when the horse was lying down. The horse was so terribly fat that his coat gleamed and glittered like a mirror. This time the dappled horse was willing to go with the boy.

So the boy climbed onto the horse's back. When he came riding home to his brothers, they clapped their hands and crossed themselves, for they had never seen or heard of such a horse before.

"If you will give my horse the best possible shoes and the most splendid saddle and bridle," said the boy, "then you may keep all twelve of my mares up there in the heights, along with their twelve foals." That year each of them again had a foal.

His brothers were happy to do as he asked. The horse was given such fine shoes that bits of stone flew high into the air as he galloped across the mountain ridges. And he was given such a fine golden saddle and such a fine golden bridle that they could be seen glowing and gleaming from far away.

"Now we're headed for the royal palace!" said Dappleband, for that was the name of the horse. "But you must remember to ask the king for a good stall in the stable and proper feed for me."

The boy promised not to forget. Then he set off. And as you might well imagine, with such a fine horse it didn't take him long to reach the royal palace.

When he arrived, the king was standing on the steps, gazing and gawking at the approaching rider. "My, my!" he said. "I've never in my life seen such a fine fellow or such a fine horse!"

The boy asked whether he might find work at the palace. That made the king so happy that he was ready to start dancing as he stood there on the steps. Yes, of course, the boy would find work.

"But I will need a good stall in the stable and proper feed for my horse," said the boy.

The king said he would be given meadow hay, as much as the horse wanted. All the other riders would have to take their horses out of the stable so that Dappleband might have the place to himself. Then he would have plenty of room.

It didn't take long before the others at the royal palace grew jealous of the boy. There was no end to the wickedness they wished upon him, if only they dared. Finally they decided to tell the king that the boy had claimed that if he wanted to, he could rescue the king's daughter. A troll had taken the princess into the mountain long ago.

The king summoned the boy at once. He said that someone had heard what he'd claimed, so now he must do it. And as the boy knew, the king had promised both his daughter and half the kingdom to whoever could rescue her. That would be his fair and proper reward if he could do it. If he could not, he would be killed.

The boy denied that he'd made such a claim, but it did no good. The king refused to listen. The boy had no choice but to say he would certainly try.

Sullen and sad, he went down to the stable. There Dappleband asked the boy why he looked so distressed.

He said he didn't know what he was going to do. "It's simply not possible to rescue the princess," said the boy.

"Oh, I'm sure it can be done," said Dappleband. "I'll help you, but first you must shoe me properly. You must demand twenty pounds of iron and twelve pounds of steel for my shoes, as well as one blacksmith to do the forging and one to stoke the fire."

That's what the boy did. And his request was not denied. He was given the iron and the steel and the blacksmiths. Then Dappleband was shod both properly and well. The boy rode off from the royal palace, leaving a haze of dust in his wake.

When he came to the mountain where the princess had been taken inside, he saw he would have to scale the slope in order to reach the top. The mountain rose straight up, as steep as the wall of a house and as slippery as a glass windowpane.

On his first attempt the boy made it partway up the slope, but then the horse's forelegs slid back down. When they landed it caused a great thundering in the heights. On the boy's second attempt, he made it a little farther. But again one of the horse's forelegs slipped, and down they went, sounding like an avalanche.

On their third attempt, the horse said, "Let's go!" And he took off so fast that stones flew high up in the air all around them. This time they made it.

The boy rode inside the mountain at full gallop. There he snatched up the princess and set her on the saddle. Then he rode out before the troll even had time to stand up. And so the princess was rescued.

When the boy got back to the royal palace, the king was both happy and pleased to have his daughter returned, as you can well imagine. Yet somehow or other, the folks at the palace had managed to set the king against the boy, and he was angry with him.

"I thank you for rescuing my princess," the king told the boy when he brought the king's daughter to the palace and then was about to leave.

"She is now supposed to be mine as much as yours, for I'm sure you're a man of your word," said the boy.

"I certainly am," said the king. "And you shall have her, for that is what I promised. But first you must get the sun to shine inside the palace." Right outside the window there was a big, high mountain that cast a shadow so the sun couldn't reach inside.

"That wasn't part of the agreement," replied the boy. "But I suppose no argument will do. I'll just have to try my best, for the princess I intend to have."

He went back to the horse and told him what the king demanded. Dappleband thought they could do it, but first he needed to be newly shod. For that they would need twenty pounds of iron and twelve pounds of steel. Two blacksmiths were also required, one to do the forging and one to stoke the fire. Then they would certainly be able to get the sun to shine inside the royal palace.

When the boy made his requests, they were granted at once. The king was too embarrassed to refuse him. Dappleband was newly shod, and the job was done well.

The boy mounted the horse, and again they set off. For each leap that Dappleband made, the mountain sank thirty feet into the ground. They kept at it until the king could no longer see the mountain at all.

When the boy went back to the royal palace, he asked the king whether the princess would now be his. As far as he could tell, the sun was shining inside the palace.

The folks at the palace had again set the king against the boy. He said that the princess would certainly be his, he had never thought otherwise. But first the boy would have to find her a bridal horse as splendid as the one he owned.

The boy said the king had never mentioned this before. He thought that by now he had earned the princess. But the king insisted, and if the boy couldn't do it, he would lose his life. That's what the king said.

The boy went down to the stable, and as you might well imagine, he was both sad and distressed. There he told Dappleband that the king was now demanding that he should find the princess a bridal horse as splendid as the one he owned. Or else he would lose his life. "That certainly won't be easy," the boy said. "Your equal surely can't be found anywhere in the world."

"Oh yes, my equal can be found," replied Dappleband, "though it will be no easy task to get him, for that horse is in hell. But we'll have to try. Go back to the king and demand that I be newly shod. For that purpose you'll again need twenty pounds of iron and twelve pounds of steel, as well as two blacksmiths, one to do the forging and one to stoke the fire. But make sure the nails and calks are sharpened well. And we'll need to take along twelve barrels of rye and twelve barrels of barley, as well as twelve slaughtered oxen. You also need to get all twelve ox hides, with twelve hundred nails in each. All of these things we will need, along with a barrel that holds four hundred gallons of tar."

The boy went back to the king and demanded everything Dappleband had said. Again the king thought it would be embarrassing to deny these requests. So the boy was given all he'd asked for.

Then he mounted Dappleband and rode off.

After they'd gone far, far away over both mountains and moors, the horse asked, "Do you hear anything?"

"Yes, there's such a vile rushing sound up in the sky. It's frightening me. It really is," said the boy.

"What you hear is all the birds in the forest flying toward us. They've been sent to stop us," said Dappleband. "Cut a hole in the sacks of grain. They'll be so busy with the rye and barley that they'll forget all about us."

That's what the boy did. He cut holes in the sacks of grain, so the barley and rye spilled out in every direction. Then all the wild birds in the forest came flying, so many that they blacked out the sun. But when they caught sight of the grain, they couldn't resist. They landed on the ground and began pecking and picking at the barley and rye until finally they began fighting with each other. But they did nothing to the boy and Dappleband. They'd forgotten all about them.

Again they set off, going far and traveling for a very long time, over hill and valley, over mountains and moors. Then Dappleband began listening once more. He asked the boy whether he heard anything.

"Yes, I hear such a horrible crashing sound coming from every part of the forest. Now it's really frightening me," said the boy.

"What you hear is all the wild animals in the forest," said Dappleband. "They've been sent to stop us. All you have to do is toss out the twelve ox carcasses. The wild animals will be so busy with them that they'll forget all about us."

The boy tossed out the ox carcasses. Then all the wild animals from the forest appeared, bears and wolves and lions and all sorts of vile beasts. But when they caught sight of the ox carcasses, they began to fight among themselves so the blood flowed. They forgot all about the boy and Dappleband.

They set off again, going far and traveling over ridge after ridge, for as you might well imagine, Dappleband didn't move slowly. Then the horse began to whinny.

"Do you hear anything?" Dappleband asked.

"Oh yes, I hear what sounds like a foal whinnying faintly from far, far away," replied the boy.

"It must be a full-grown horse," said Dappleband. "He sounds faint, for he's so far away."

They continued on for a good distance, traveling over ridge after ridge once more. Then Dappleband whinnied again. "Do you hear anything now?" he asked.

"Yes, now I hear him clearly. A grown horse whinnying," replied the boy.

"Well, you'll no doubt hear him one more time," said Dappleband. "Then you'll hear what a voice he has."

They rode again over ridge after ridge. Then Dappleband whinnied for a third time. Before he had a chance to ask the boy whether he'd heard anything, a whinny echoed across the moors. It was so loud that the boy thought the mountains and crags would split apart.

"He's here," said Dappleband. "Hurry and toss over me the ox hides with the nails, and drop the barrel of tar on the ground. Then climb up in that big spruce over there. When the horse appears, he'll be spouting fire from both nostrils. That will heat up the tar in the barrel. Pay careful attention. If the flame rises, I win, but if it falls, I lose. If you see that I win, throw the bridle on the horse—you may take mine—and he will be tamed."

No sooner had the boy tossed the ox hides with the nails over Dappleband, dropped the tar barrel on the ground, and climbed up into the spruce than a horse appeared. He was spewing hot flames. Fire flew into the tar barrel at once. The horse and Dappleband began fighting so hard that stones danced high into the air. They bit and they kicked with both their forelegs and hind legs.

At times the boy watched the horses, and at times he watched the tar barrel. Finally the flame rose, for no matter where the other horse bit and kicked, he struck the hides with the nails. Finally he had to give up.

When the boy saw this, he quickly climbed down from the tree and threw the bridle over the horse. The horse was then so tame he could have used a piece of yarn for reins.

This horse was also a dapple-gray, and he looked so much like Dappleband that no one could tell one from the other. The boy mounted the horse he had caught and rode back to the royal palace. Dappleband ran alongside. When they arrived, the king was standing in the courtyard.

"Can you tell me which horse is the one I caught and which is the one I had before?" said the boy. "If you can't, then I think your daughter belongs to me."

The king came over to look at both dapple-gray horses. He looked high and low, to the front and behind, but there wasn't even a hair that was different on either horse.

"No," said the king, "I can't tell you that. You've brought my daughter a splendid bridal horse, so you shall have her. But there's one more thing we must do to see if it's meant to be. First she will hide two times, and then you will hide two times. If you can find her when she hides, but she cannot find you in your hiding place, then it's meant to be, and you shall have the princess."

"That's not part of the agreement, either," said the boy. "But if that's how it is, I suppose we'll try."

Then the princess had to hide first.

She turned herself into a duck and swam about in the pond that was just outside the royal palace. The boy went straight over to the stable and asked Dappleband where she'd gone.

"Oh, all you have to do is take that rifle over there. Go down to the pond and aim it at the duck you'll see swimming about," said Dappleband. "That will make her appear soon enough."

The boy grabbed the rifle and went down to the water. "I think I'll set my sights on that duck," he said. He took aim.

"No, no, dear sir, don't shoot! It's me!" said the princess. He had found her.

The second time the princess turned herself into a loaf of bread and placed herself on the table with four other loaves. She looked so much like the others that no one could tell them apart.

The boy went over to the stable and told Dappleband that the princess was hiding again. He had no idea where she'd gone.

"Oh, all you have to do is sharpen a good bread knife and pretend that you're going to slice right through the third loaf from the left. It's with the four other loaves on the kitchen table in the royal palace. Then she'll appear soon enough," said Dappleband.

The boy went over to the kitchen and sharpened the biggest bread knife he could find. Then he grabbed the third loaf from the left and set the knife against it, as if he wanted to cut right through the bread. "I'm going to have the first slice of this loaf," he said.

"No, dear sir, don't cut into it! It's me!" said the princess. The boy had found her the second time as well.

Then it was his turn to hide. Dappleband made sure that he would not be easy to find. First the boy turned himself into a horsefly and hid inside Dappleband's left nostril. The princess looked and snooped everywhere, both high and low. She also wanted to search Dappleband's stall, but he began snapping and thrashing about, so she didn't dare go inside. She couldn't find the boy.

"Well, I can't find you, so you'll have to come out on your own," she said.

The boy appeared at once, standing in the stable.

The second time Dappleband again told him what he should do. This time the boy turned himself into a lump of mud and wedged himself between the hoof and the shoe of the horse's left foreleg. Again the king's daughter searched and searched, both inside and outside. Finally she came to the stable and wanted to go into Dappleband's stall. This time he let her come close. She snooped high and low, but she couldn't look under his hooves, for Dappleband had planted them firmly on the ground, yes, he had. She couldn't find the boy.

"Well, you'll just have to come out again on your own. I can't find you," said the princess.

The boy appeared at once, standing beside her in the stable.

"Now you're mine," said the boy to the princess. "For now you can see that it's meant to be," he told the king.

"Yes, if it's meant to be, then that's how it shall be," said the king.

And plans were made, both properly and quickly, for the wedding. The boy mounted Dappleband, and the king's daughter mounted the horse's equal. And as you might well imagine, it didn't take them long to reach the church.

Nothing Is Needed by the One All Women Love

There once were three brothers. I don't really know how it happened, but each of them had been given one wish so they could have whatever they wanted. Two of the brothers didn't take long to decide. They wished that whenever they stuck their fist in their pocket, they would always find money. "For if a person has as much money as he wants, he will always make his way in the world," they said.

But the youngest knew to wish for something even better. His wish was that all women would fall in love with him the instant they saw him. As you will hear, this was better than either possessions or money.

After they'd made their wish, the two brothers wanted to set off into the world. Ash Lad asked whether he could go with them, but they refused to let him come along.

"Wherever we go, we'll be received like counts and princes," they said. "As for a poor boy like you who has nothing and will get nothing, how can you think that anyone will bother with you?"

"You could allow me to go with you all the same," said Ash Lad. "Surely a scrap of roast might fall to me if I'm in the company of such high-ranking gentlemen."

At long last they said that Ash Lad could go with them if he agreed to be their servant. Otherwise they wanted nothing to do with him.

After they'd traveled for a day or so, they came to an inn. There the two brothers who had money went inside. They demanded both meat and fish, both liquor and mead, and all sorts of other good things. In the meantime, Ash Lad had to tend to everything that belonged to the grand gentlemen.

As he went back and forth outside, roaming the yard, the innkeeper's wife happened to look out of the window. There she caught sight of the servant who'd arrived with the two gentlemen. She thought she'd never before set eyes on such a handsome fellow. She looked and looked at him, and the longer she looked, the lovelier the boy seemed.

"What in the name and bones of the Devil are you standing there in the window gaping and gawking at?" said her husband. "It would be better if you made sure the pig was roasted rather than stand there wasting time. You've seen what sort of folks have stopped here today, I know you have."

"Oh, I don't care about those high-and-mighty guests. No, I don't!" said the woman. "If they don't want to stay, they can just go back where they came from. But come over here. You have to see somebody who's out in the yard! Such a handsome fellow I've never seen before in my life. If you agree with me, let's invite him in and give him some food. He probably has little enough to his name, the poor thing."

"Have you lost what little sense you have left, woman?" said her husband. He was so angry that sparks flew off him. "Back to the kitchen with you. Hurry up and tend to the fire. Don't stand here staring at some strange man!"

There was nothing for the woman to do but go to the kitchen and cook the food. She wasn't allowed to look at the boy, nor did she dare offer him anything to eat. But as soon as she was back in the kitchen and had put the pig on the spit to roast, she slipped out to the yard. There she gave Ash Lad a special pair of scissors. All he had to do was snip at the air and the scissors would cut for him the loveliest clothes that anyone would ever set eyes on, clothes made of silk and velvet and everything else splendid.

"I want you to have these scissors, for you're so handsome," said the woman.

When the two brothers had finished eating all the good food, both roasted and fried, they were ready to leave. Once again Ash Lad had to stand behind on their carriage as their servant. Then they set off.

After traveling a good distance, they came to another inn. There the brothers wanted to go inside, but they didn't want to take along Ash Lad, who had no money. He had to stay outside and mind all their belongings.

"And if anyone asks whose servant you are, tell them you work for two foreign princes," they said.

The same thing happened as before. While Ash Lad was wandering about in the yard, the innkeeper's wife went over to the window and caught sight of him. She fell in love with him just as the first innkeeper's wife had done. She stood there looking and looking. She couldn't get enough of looking at him.

Then her husband came rushing into the room carrying something the two princes had demanded. "Don't just stand there gawking like a cow at the barn door. Come back to the kitchen and tend to your fish pot, woman," said her husband. "You've seen what sort of folks have stopped here today, I know you have."

"I don't care about such high-and-mighty rabble. No, I don't!" said his wife. "If they don't like what they get, they can eat whatever they brought with them. But come over here and take a look. I've never before in the world seen so handsome a fellow as the one out there in the yard. If you agree with me, let's invite him in and give him some food. He looks like he needs it, the poor thing. And how very handsome he is!" said the woman.

"You've never had much sense, and I can tell that the little remaining seems to have vanished," said her husband. He was even angrier than the other innkeeper. He chased the woman back to the kitchen. "Get in there! Don't stand around staring at boys!" he said.

So she had to go back to her fish pot. She didn't dare give Ash Lad anything to eat, for she was afraid of her husband. But the minute she had tended the fire, she slipped out to the yard and gave Ash Lad a special tablecloth. When he spread it out, the best food imaginable would appear.

"I want you to have this, for you're so handsome," she said to Ash Lad.

The two brothers ate and drank their fill and paid a fortune for the feast. Then they set off, with Ash Lad standing on the back of the carriage.

When they'd traveled so far that they were hungry again, they stopped at an inn and demanded the most expensive and best food they could name.

"We are two traveling kings, and for us money grows like grass," they said.

When the innkeeper heard that, he ordered so much food to be fried and roasted that it could be smelled at the neighboring farm. The innkeeper couldn't do enough for the two kings. Again Ash Lad had to stay outside and mind everything that was in the carriage.

The exact same thing happened as twice before. The innkeeper's wife happened to look out of the window and catch sight of the servant who stood next to the wagon. Such a lovely fellow she had never seen before. She looked and she looked, and the more she stared at Ash Lad, the more handsome he seemed.

The innkeeper came rushing into the room carrying the food the two traveling kings had demanded. He too did not take kindly to seeing his wife standing at the window and gawking.

"Don't you have anything better to do than stand there gaping when we have such fine folks in the house?" he said to her. "Get back to the kitchen and your sour cream porridge! And be quick about it!"

"Oh, I don't think that's so important. No, I don't. If they don't want to stay until the porridge is done, let them leave," replied his wife. "Come here and take a look! I've never set eyes on such a lovely fellow as the one standing out there in the yard. If you agree with me, let's invite him in and give him some food. He looks like he could use it. What a marvelously handsome fellow he is!"

"You've been chasing after boys all your life, and you still are," said her husband. He was so angry that he hardly knew which leg to stand on. "If you don't go back to your porridge pot, I'll give you a swift kick, that I will!"

The woman had to hurry back to the kitchen as fast as she could go. She knew better than to fool with her husband. But after a moment she slipped out to the yard. There she gave Ash Lad a wooden spigot.

"All you have to do is turn the spigot," she said, "and you'll have the loveliest drinks you could ever want. Mead and wine and liquor. I want you to have this, for you're so handsome."

After the two brothers had eaten and drunk all they wanted, they set off from the inn. Again Ash Lad stood on the back of the carriage as their servant.

They traveled far, and for a very long time, until they came to a royal palace. There the two older brothers presented themselves as the sons of an emperor. They had so much money and looked so splendid that their grandeur was evident even from far away. That's why they were given a gracious and proper welcome. They were to stay at the palace, and the king couldn't do enough for them.

The guards at the king's palace took Ash Lad, who still wore the same rags he'd worn back home and who didn't have even a *skilling* in his pocket, and left him on an island. That's where they rowed out all the beggars and vagabonds who showed up at the royal palace. That's what the king had ordered. He didn't want these people, who looked so ragged and filthy, to disturb the merriment at the palace. Out there on the island they had only enough food to barely stay alive.

Ash Lad's brothers saw the guards rowing him out to the island, but they were glad to get rid of him and didn't mind a bit.

When Ash Lad arrived on the island, he simply got out his pair of scissors and snipped at the air. Then the scissors cut out the loveliest clothes anyone could imagine, clothes made of velvet and silk. Now all the vagabonds on the island looked even more splendid than the king and everyone else at the palace. After that Ash Lad got out his tablecloth and spread it on the ground. Then the vagabonds certainly had food to eat. The likes of the feast that appeared that day on Vagabond Island had never been served at the king's palace.

"I'm sure you must be thirsty too," said Ash Lad. He got out his wooden spigot and turned it just a little. Then the vagabonds certainly had something to drink. Even the king had never in all his life tasted such ale or mead.

When the guards who were supposed to bring food for the ragged vagabonds came rowing out to the island with crusted cold porridge and flasks of whey—that's the food they were supposed to bring—the vagabonds refused even to taste it. The guards from the royal palace were greatly surprised. They were even more surprised when they got a good look at the vagabonds, for they all looked so splendid that they could have been emperors and popes. The guards thought they must have rowed out to the wrong island, but when they took a closer look, they recognized everyone there. Then they realized that the boy they had rowed out the day before must have given the vagabonds on the island such finery and delights.

When the guards got back to the royal palace, they wasted no time reporting that the boy they had rowed to the island the day before had now dressed all the vagabonds in such splendid and magnificent clothes that the finery was practically dripping off them.

"They've become so high-and-mighty that they refused even to taste the porridge and whey we brought," said the guards. One of them had also discovered that the boy owned a pair of scissors that he'd used to cut out all the clothes. "When he holds the scissors in the air and snips, he produces nothing but silk and velvet," said the guard.

When the princess heard this, she could find neither rest nor respite until she was allowed to see this boy and his scissors that could cut silk and velvet from the air. Those scissors would be worth having, she thought. They would give her all the finery she could ever want. She pleaded with the king for so long that at last he had to send for the boy who owned those scissors.

When the boy arrived at the royal palace, the princess asked him whether it was true that he owned a special pair of scissors that could do such things. Would he sell the scissors to her?

Yes, he did own such scissors, Ash Lad told her, but he wouldn't sell them. Then he took the scissors out of his pocket and snipped at the air so that scraps of silk and velvet whirled around the head of the princess.

"Oh yes, you have to sell me the scissors," she said. "You can demand whatever you like for them, but have them I must."

No, he wouldn't sell them for any price, he told her. Such a pair of scissors he would never find again.

As they stood there haggling over the scissors, the princess looked closer and closer at Ash Lad. Like the innkeepers' wives, she thought she'd never seen such a lovely fellow. Then she began haggling over the scissors again, begging and pleading for Ash Lad to sell them to her. He could demand as many hundreds of *daler* as he liked. It didn't matter, as long as she got the scissors.

"No, I won't sell them," said Ash Lad. "But that's neither here nor there. If I'm allowed to sleep on the floor, next to the door, inside the princess's bedchamber tonight, then she may have the scissors. I won't do her any harm, but if she's afraid, she can have two men stand guard in her chamber."

The princess gladly granted his request. As long as she would get the scissors, she was happy.

So that night Ash Lad slept on the floor inside the princess's bedchamber while two men stood guard. The princess didn't get much sleep. She found herself opening her eyes again and again to take another look at Ash Lad. That went on all night. If she did happen to close her eyes, she had to open them at once for another peek at him. That's how handsome she thought he was.

In the morning Ash Lad was rowed back out to Vagabond Island.

When the guards again brought crusted cold porridge and flasks of whey from the royal palace, no one wanted to touch the food. The guards were even more surprised by this. Then one of them discovered that the boy who had owned the scissors also owned a tablecloth. All he needed to do was spread it out and the best food he could ever want appeared.

When the guard got back to the royal palace, it didn't take him long to report what he'd discovered. "The likes of such roasts and such sour cream porridge have never been seen at the king's palace," he said.

When the princess heard this, she went to tell the king. She begged and pleaded so long that he had to send a messenger to the island to bring back the boy who owned the tablecloth. Once again Ash Lad came to the palace.

The princess dearly wanted to have his tablecloth. She offered him gold and green forests in payment, but Ash Lad didn't want to sell it for any price.

"But if I'm allowed to sleep on the bench inside the princess's bedchamber tonight, then she shall have my tablecloth," said the boy. "I won't do her any harm, but if she's afraid, she can have four men stand guard in the chamber."

The princess agreed to his request. Ash Lad slept on the bench in the princess's chamber while four men stood guard. But if the princess hadn't slept much the night before, she slept even less this time. She could hardly close her eyes at all. She lay there looking at the lovely boy all night long, and yet she thought the night was far too short.

In the morning Ash Lad was rowed back to Vagabond Island, though it wasn't what the princess wanted. She had grown very fond of the boy. But there was nothing to be done—he had to go back.

When the guards from the royal palace brought crusted cold porridge and flasks of whey for the vagabonds to eat, not one of them would even look at what the king had sent. None of the guards was surprised by this, but they did think it was strange that the vagabonds weren't thirsty.

Then one of the king's messengers discovered that the boy who had owned the scissors and the tablecloth also had a wooden spigot. If he turned it just a little, the loveliest drinks anyone could imagine appeared—ale and mead and wine.

When the man got back to the castle he couldn't keep his mouth shut any better than on the first two occasions. He told anyone who would listen about the spigot and how easy it was to get all manner of drinks.

"The likes of that ale and mead have certainly never been tasted here at the king's palace," he said. "It's sweeter than both honey and syrup."

When the princess heard this, she wanted to see the spigot at once. And she had nothing against haggling with the boy who owned it. Again she went to the king and asked him to send a messenger to Vagabond Island. She wanted to summon the boy who had owned the scissors and the tablecloth and who owned one more thing that would no doubt be worth having.

The king heard that it was a special wooden spigot that could produce the best ale and the best wine anyone would ever drink. And all it took was a little turn of the spigot. Well, I don't think it took long before he sent off a messenger.

When Ash Lad arrived at the castle, the princess asked him whether it was true that he owned such a special wooden spigot.

Yes, he had it in his vest pocket, Ash Lad told her. But when the princess tried with all her might to buy it, Ash Lad said the same thing as he'd said twice before. He wouldn't sell it for any price, even if the princess offered him half the kingdom.

"But that's neither here nor there," said Ash Lad. "If I'm allowed to sleep on the princess's bed, on top of the coverlet, tonight, she shall have my wooden spigot. I won't do her any harm, but if she's afraid, she can set eight men to stand guard in the chamber."

"Oh no, that won't be necessary," said the princess. She knew him well enough by now.

So that night Ash Lad slept on top of the coverlet beside the princess.

If she hadn't had much sleep on the two previous nights, she slept even less this time. She couldn't close her eyes at all. The whole time she lay there and looked at Ash Lad, who was sleeping beside her on the edge of the bed.

When she got up in the morning and the guards were about to row Ash Lad back out to Vagabond Island, she asked them to wait a moment. Then she ran to the king and begged him earnestly to give her Ash Lad as her betrothed. She said that she was so fond of him that she didn't want to live if she couldn't have him.

"You may certainly wed him, if that's what you want," said the king. "Anyone who owns such special things is just as rich as you are."

So Ash Lad got the princess and half the kingdom—he would be given the other half when the king died. Then everything was both fine and good. But he sent his brothers, who had always treated him badly, out to Vagabond Island.

"There they can stay until they've discovered for themselves who is least needy: the one who has his pockets full of money or the one all women love," said Ash Lad.

I don't think it would help much for them to stick their hands in their pockets and jingle their coins out on Vagabond Island. If Ash Lad hasn't take them off the island, they're still out there today, eating crusted cold porridge and whey.

Ash Lad, Who Got the Princess to Say He Was Lying

There once was a king who had a daughter, and she told such lies that nothing could be worse. Then he decreed that anyone who could tell a big enough lie that the princess would say he was lying could have both her and half the kingdom. Many tried, for everyone wanted to have the princess and half the kingdom, but it didn't go well for any of them.

There were also three brothers who wanted to try their luck. The two older brothers were the first to set off, but it went no better for them than for all the rest.

Then Ash Lad set off. He found the princess in the cowshed.

"Good day, and nice to see you again," he lied.

"Good day," she said, "nice to see you again too. I bet your cowshed isn't as big as ours. When two herdsmen stand at either end and blow on their billy goat horns, they won't be able to hear each other."

"Oh, there you're wrong," said Ash Lad. "Ours is much bigger. When a milk cow starts at one end, she won't give birth to her calf until she gets to the other side."

"Is that right?" said the princess. "Well, I bet you don't have an ox as big as ours. Take a look over there! If someone sits on each horn, they won't be able to reach each other with a goalpost."

"That's nothing!" said Ash Lad. "We have an ox that's so big that when someone sits on each horn and blows on a lur, they won't be able to hear each other."

"Is that right?" said the princess. "I bet you don't get from your cows as much milk as we do from ours," she said. "We use big basins for the milking. Then we bring the milk inside, pour it into big pans, and make big rounds of cheese."

"Oh, we use big vats for the milking," said Ash Lad. "Then we put the milk in carts and wheel them inside. We pour the milk into big washtubs and make cheeses as big as a house. Then we get a mare, pale as a moose, to stamp the cheese into big piles. One time the mare gave birth in the cheese, and after we'd eaten from that cheese for seven years, we found inside it a big horse, pale as a moose. I was once supposed to take the animal to the mill, and suddenly its back flew right off. But I knew just what to do. I picked up a spruce sapling and set it on the horse's back. That's the only back the animal ever had, for as long as we owned it. But the spruce grew. It got so big that I climbed up the tree to heaven. When I got there, I saw the Virgin Mary spinning ropes out of soup grains. All of a sudden the spruce blew away, and I couldn't get back down. But the Virgin Mary lowered me down on one of the ropes, and I landed in a fox den. There sat my mother and your father, mending shoes. Suddenly my mother hit your father so hard that the scabs flew off him."

"You're lying!" said the princess. "My father has never in his life been scabby!"

The Three Billy Goats Gruff, Who Were Supposed to Go to the Mountain Pasture to Fatten Up

There once were three billy goats who were supposed to go up to the mountain pasture to fatten up. All three of them were named Billy Goat Gruff. On the way they came to a bridge over a waterfall, and that's where they were supposed to cross. Under the bridge lived a big, vile troll. He had eyes like pewter plates and a nose as long as a rake handle.

The youngest Billy Goat Gruff was the first to try and cross the bridge. He clip-clopped, clip-clopped on the bridge.

"Who is clip-clopping on my bridge?" yelled the troll.

"Oh, it's the smallest Billy Goat Gruff. I'm going to the mountain pasture to fatten up." He had such a polite voice.

"I'm coming to get you!" said the troll.

"Oh no, don't do that. I'm so little. Just wait a bit and the middle Billy Goat Gruff will come. He's much bigger than me."

"All right then!" said the troll.

In a little while the middle Billy Goat Gruff arrived to cross the bridge. He clip-clopped, clip-clopped, clip-clopped on the bridge.

"Who is clip-clopping on my bridge?" yelled the troll.

"Oh, it's the middle Billy Goat Gruff. I'm going to the mountain pasture to fatten up," said the goat. His voice was not quite as polite.

"I'm coming to get you!" said the troll.

"Oh no, don't do that. Just wait a bit and the big Billy Goat Gruff will be here. He's much, much bigger than me."

"All right then!" said the troll.

All of a sudden the big Billy Goat Gruff arrived. He CLIP-CLOPPED, CLIP-CLOPPED, CLIP-CLOPPED on the bridge. The goat was so heavy that the bridge creaked and groaned under his weight.

"Who is stomping on my bridge?" yelled the troll.

"IT'S THE BIG BILLY GOAT GRUFF!" said the goat, and his voice was vile and coarse.

"I'm coming to get you!" yelled the troll.

Then the goat said,

> WELL, COME ON THEN! TWO SPEARS HAVE I
> TO POKE OUT YOUR EYES
> AND TWO HUGE STONES
> TO CRUSH MARROW AND BONES!

Then he flew at the troll and poked out both of his eyes. He tore apart the troll's marrow and bones, tossed his body into the waterfall, and continued up to the mountain pasture.

There the goats grew so fat, so fat, that they almost had no strength to go back home. And if the fat hasn't worn off them by now, they're still up there today.

Spin, span, spun—now this story's done.

East of the Sun and West of the Moon

There once was a poor farmer who had many children and not much to give them of either food or clothing. They were all beautiful, but the most beautiful of all was the youngest daughter, who was lovely beyond measure.

On a Thursday evening, late in the fall, the weather was terrible and it was dreadfully dark. It was raining and gusting so hard that the walls groaned. They were all sitting near the fireplace, each of them busy with some handiwork. Suddenly there were three knocks on the windowpane. The farmer went outside to see what was going on, and there he saw a big, big polar bear.

"Good evening, my man!" said the polar bear.

"Good evening!" said the farmer.

"If you will give me your youngest daughter, I will make you as rich as you now are poor," said the bear.

The man thought it would be splendid to be so rich, but he decided he should really talk to his daughter first. He went back in and told her there was a big polar bear outside who promised to make them very rich if only he might have her.

She said no. That's not something she wanted.

The man went outside and convinced the polar bear to come back the following Thursday evening to hear his answer.

In the meantime they tried to persuade the youngest daughter. They told her about all the riches they would have and how good she would have it too. At last she agreed.

She washed and mended the rags she wore and made herself as presentable as she could. Then she prepared to leave. She wouldn't be taking much with her.

The next Thursday evening the polar bear returned to get the girl. She climbed onto his back with her bundle, and they set off.

After they'd traveled a good distance, the polar bear said, "Are you frightened?"

No, she wasn't.

"Well, hold tight to my shaggy fur," he said, "and you won't be in any danger."

She rode far, far away. Then they came to a big mountain. When the polar bear knocked, a door opened. They went inside a castle that had many rooms all lit up and glittering with both gold and silver. In a big hall stood a table set for a feast. It looked magnificent. You wouldn't believe how magnificent it was.

Then the polar bear gave the girl a silver bell. If there was anything she wanted, all she had to do was ring the bell and whatever she needed would appear. After she had eaten and it was getting on toward evening, she felt so sleepy after her travels that she thought she'd like to go to bed. She rang the bell.

No sooner did she ring the bell than she came to a chamber with a bed as lovely as anyone could ever want. It was made up with silken comforters and draperies and golden fringe. And everything in the bedchamber was made of silver and gold.

After she lay down and put out the candle, someone came in and lay down beside her. It was the polar bear. He shed his skin every night, though she never saw him, for he always appeared after she'd put out the candle. And in the morning he was gone before daylight.

For a while everything was fine and good, but then the girl grew quiet and sorrowful, for she spent all day alone. She was longing to go home to see her parents and siblings. When the polar bear asked her what was the matter, she said that she found the castle terribly bleak. She was always alone, and she longed to go home to see her parents and siblings. That's why she was so sad.

"I think something can be done about that," said the polar bear. "But you must promise me that you'll speak with your mother only if others are within earshot and not when it's just the two of you. She'll take your hand," he said, "and want to bring you into a room to speak to you alone. You must not do that, or else you'll bring misfortune upon both of us."

One Sunday the polar bear came to the girl and said that today they could go to see her parents. Off they went with the girl sitting on the bear's back. They traveled far and for a very long time until at last they came to a big white manor house. There she saw her siblings running around outside and playing. The scene was so beautiful that it was a delight to behold.

"This is where your parents live," said the polar bear. "But don't forget what I told you, or you'll bring misfortune upon both you and me."

Goodness no, she wouldn't forget.

When she reached the manor house, the polar bear turned around and left, yes he did.

There was no end to the joy when the girl went inside to see her parents. They said they could never thank her enough for what she'd done for them. Everything was now so good, so good. Then everyone asked her how things were going for her where she now lived. She said it was both fine and good. She had everything she could ever want.

What else she told them, I can't say, but I don't think they heard the full story.

That afternoon, after they'd had dinner, things happened just as the polar bear had said. The girl's mother wanted to speak to her in a room alone, but she remembered what the bear had told her and steadfastly refused.

"Whatever the two of us need to say, we can talk about it some other time," she told her mother.

What happened next isn't clear, but at last the girl's mother persuaded her to say how things truly stood. Then she told her mother that at night, after she'd put out the candle, someone would come to lie beside her, though she never saw him. He was always gone before daylight the next morning. This made her sad, for she thought she'd dearly like to see him. In the daytime she was all alone, and it was terribly bleak and lonely.

"Gracious! That could very well be a troll sleeping with you," said her mother. "Let me give you some advice so you'll be able to see him. I'm going to give you a candle stump that you can hide in your bodice. Shine the candlelight on him when he's asleep, but be careful not to drip any tallow on him."

Well, the girl took the candle and hid it in her bodice. That evening the polar bear came back to get her.

After they'd traveled some distance, the bear asked her whether things had happened just as he'd said. And she couldn't deny it.

"If you listen to your mother's advice, you're going to bring misfortune upon both of us. And that will be the end between us."

Oh no, she promised not to do that.

When they got back and she went to bed, everything proceeded as usual. Someone came and lay down beside her. But in the middle of the night, when the girl heard him sleeping, she got up and lit the candle. When she shone the light on him, she saw that he was the loveliest prince anyone would ever see. She fell so in love with him that she thought she couldn't go on living unless she hugged him that very minute. And that's what she did. But the instant she dripped three drops of hot tallow on his shirt, he woke up.

"What have you done?" he said. "Now you've brought misfortune upon both of us. If only you'd waited a year, I would have been rescued, for I have a stepmother who cast a spell over me. She turned me into a polar bear by day and a man by night. But now it's over between us. I'll have to leave you and go back to my stepmother. She lives in a castle that is east of the sun and west of the moon. That's where a princess lives too, and her nose is six feet long. She's the one I will now have to marry."

The girl wept and carried on, but there was nothing to be done. He had to leave. She asked whether she could go with him. No, she could not.

"Can you tell me what road to take? Then I'll come looking for you. Surely I'll be allowed to do that at least?" she said.

Yes, she could do that, he said, but there was no road to the castle. It was east of the sun and west of the moon. She would never find her way there.

In the morning when the girl woke up, both the prince and the castle were gone. She was lying on a little green patch in the middle of a dark and dense forest. Next to her lay the same rags she'd had on when she left home.

After she had rubbed the sleep from her eyes and wept until she could weep no more, she set off. She walked for many, many days until she came to a big mountain. Outside sat an old woman, playing with a golden apple. The girl asked the woman if she knew what road to take to find the prince who was staying with his stepmother in a castle east of the sun and west of the moon. He was going to wed a princess whose nose was six feet long.

"How do you happen to know him?" said the woman. "Maybe you're the one who was supposed to marry him?"

Yes, that was true.

"Ah, so you're the one!" said the woman. "Well, I don't know anything more about him except that he lives in a castle east of the sun and west of the moon. You'll get there either too late or never at all. But I'll lend you my horse so you can ride over to see my neighbor woman. Maybe she can tell you what road to take. When you get there, just tap the horse under his left ear and tell him to go home. And you can take this golden apple with you."

The girl climbed onto the horse and rode for a long, long time. Finally she came to a mountain where an old woman was sitting outside with a golden bobbin. The girl asked her whether she knew which road to take to get to the castle that was east of the sun and west of the moon.

Just like her neighbor, the woman said she knew nothing except that it must be east of the sun and west of the moon. "You'll get there either too late or never at all, but you can borrow my horse to take you to my nearest neighbor. Maybe she knows the road. When you get there, just tap the horse under his left ear and tell him to go home." Then the old woman gave the girl the bobbin, for she might well have use for it.

The girl climbed onto the horse and rode for a long and dreary time. At long last she came to a big mountain where an old woman was spinning on a golden spinning wheel. The girl asked her whether she knew what road to take to find the prince and the castle that was east of the sun and west of the moon.

The same thing happened as before.

"Are you the one who was supposed to marry the prince?" said the old woman.

Yes, that could very well be true.

The woman could tell her nothing more than the other two women had said. She knew only that the castle was east of the sun and west of the moon.

"You'll get there either too late or never at all," she said. "But you can borrow my horse. Then you can ride to the East Wind and ask him. Maybe he knows the place and can carry you there on a gust of air. When you get to the East Wind, just tap the horse under his ear and he'll go back home."

Then she gave the girl the golden spinning wheel. "You might have use for it," said the woman.

The girl rode for many days. It took a dreary long time, but finally she arrived. Then she asked the East Wind whether he could tell her how to find the prince who lived east of the sun and west of the moon.

Oh yes, he'd heard folks talking about that prince, said the East Wind, and about the castle too. But he didn't know how to get there, for he'd never traveled that far.

"But if you like, I'll take you to see my brother, the West Wind. Maybe he knows, for he's much stronger than me. Climb onto my back, and I'll carry you there."

That's what she did. And it certainly didn't take them long.

When they arrived, they went inside. The East Wind told his brother that the girl he'd brought was the one who was supposed to marry the prince in the castle that was east of the sun and west of the moon. She was out searching for the prince, and that's why the East Wind had brought her here. She wanted to ask the West Wind whether he knew where the castle was.

"No, I've never traveled that far," said the West Wind. "But if you like, I'll take you to see the South Wind, for he's much stronger than either of us. And he has wandered both far and wide. Maybe he can tell you. Climb onto my back, and I'll carry you there."

That's what she did. They traveled to the South Wind, and I don't think it took them long.

When they arrived, the West Wind asked his brother whether he could tell the girl how to reach the castle that was east of the sun and west of the moon. She was the one who was supposed to marry the prince who lived there.

"Oh, I see," said the South Wind. "So she's the one? Well, I've roamed just about everywhere in my day," he said, "but that far I've never gone. If you like, I can take you to my brother, the North Wind. He's the oldest and strongest of us all. And if he doesn't know where the castle is, then you'll never, ever find it. Climb onto my back, and I'll carry you there."

The girl climbed onto his back, and he set off at a great speed. They were there in no time.

When they arrived at the place where the North Wind lived, he was so wild and furious that he spewed long, cold blasts of air.

"What do you want?" he shouted from far off. His voice made them shiver with cold.

"There's no need for you to be so fierce, you know," said the South Wind. "It's me, and this is the one who's supposed to marry the prince who lives in the castle east of the sun and west of the moon. She wants to ask you whether you've ever been there. And can you tell her how to get there, for she dearly wants to find the prince."

"Well, I do know where the castle is," said the North Wind. "I once blew an aspen leaf there, though it made me so tired that afterward I couldn't blow anything else for days. If you truly want to go there and you're not afraid to travel with me, then I'll carry you on my back and see if I can take you there."

Yes, if he was willing to try, the girl would and must go with him. And she was not afraid, no matter what bad things might happen.

"All right then. You'll stay here overnight," said the North Wind, "for we need to get an early start. If we do that, we should manage to get there."

Early the next morning the North Wind woke the girl. Then he puffed himself up, and made himself so big and strong that it was terrible to behold. They set off. They traveled high up through the air and went as fast as if they had to reach the ends of the earth at once. In the countryside below, such a storm raged that whole tracts of forests and houses blew down. And when they flew over the sea, ships were wrecked by the hundreds.

That's how they traveled. They went so far, so far that no one would believe how far they went. The whole time they were flying across the sea. The North Wind grew more and more tired, until at last he was so exhausted that he almost had no energy left to blow at all. They drifted farther and farther down until finally they were moving so low that the crests of the waves were striking the girl's heels.

"Are you frightened?" said the North Wind.

"No," she said, she wasn't.

By now they were not far from land. The North Wind had just enough strength left to toss her onto the shore beneath the windows of the castle that was east of the sun and west of the moon. Then he was so tired and so wretched that he had to rest for many days before he could set off again for home.

The next morning the girl began playing with the golden apple outside the castle windows. The first thing she saw was the long nose of the snooty princess who was supposed to wed the prince.

"What do you want for that golden apple of yours?" said the princess, opening the window.

"It can't be bought for either gold or coin," said the girl.

"If it can't be bought for either gold or coin, what do you want for it? I'll give you whatever you want," said the princess.

"I want to be taken to see the prince who lives here. And I want to be allowed to stay with him tonight. Then you shall have the apple," said the girl who had arrived with the North Wind.

Well, that was easily done. And the princess got the golden apple.

When the girl came up to the prince's room that evening, he was asleep. She called to him and shook him, and in between she wept, but she could not wake him. In the morning, when the day dawned, the princess with the long nose came in and chased her away.

That day the girl sat outside the castle windows and began winding yarn on the golden bobbin. The same thing happened as before. The princess asked her what she wanted for the bobbin, and the girl said it could not be bought for either gold or coin. But if she was allowed to go to the prince that night, the princess could have it.

Yet when the girl went up to the prince's room, he was again sound asleep. No matter how much she shouted and yelled and shook him, no matter how much she wept, he kept on sleeping. She wasn't able to wake him. When the day dawned the next morning, the princess with the long nose appeared and chased her out again.

Later in the day, the girl sat down outside the castle windows and began to spin on the golden spinning wheel. That was something the princess with the long nose wanted to have. She opened the window and asked the girl what she wanted for it. The same thing happened as twice before. The girl said that it could not be bought for either gold or coin. But if she was allowed to go to the prince who lived there, and stay with him in the night, the princess could have the spinning wheel.

Oh yes, she was welcome to do that.

It so happened that some Christian folks had been captured and put in the room right next to the prince's bedchamber. For two nights in a row they'd heard a woman in there weeping as she called to him and shook him. They had told the prince about this.

That evening, when the princess brought him soup at bedtime, the prince pretended to drink it. Then he poured it out, for he realized now that it was a sleeping potion.

This time when the girl came in, the prince was awake. Then she told him how she'd managed to find him.

"You've come just in time," said the prince. "Tomorrow is supposed to be my wedding day, but I don't want to marry that snooty princess with the long nose. You're the only one who can save me. I'll tell my bride that I want to find out how clever she is. I'll ask her to wash off the three spots of tallow. She'll agree to do it, for she doesn't know that you're the one who put them there. But it's a task that only Christian folks can do, not troll riffraff like her. Then I'll say that the only person I'll take as my bride is the person who can do the washing. And you can, I know you can."

There was great joy and happiness for the two of them that night.

The next day, when the wedding was about to begin, the prince said, "First I'd like to see how clever my bride is."

That could certainly be done, said the stepmother.

"I have a good shirt that I want to wear to my wedding, but there are three spots of tallow on it. I'd like someone to wash them off. And I've vowed that the only one I'll take as my bride has to be able to do that. If she can't, then she's not worth having."

They all agreed that should be no problem. Even the princess with the long nose agreed to do the best she could to wash the shirt. But the more she washed and scrubbed, the bigger the spots grew.

"Oh, you're no good at washing," said the old troll woman, who was her mother. "Let me have it!"

But no sooner did she grab the shirt than it looked even worse. The more she washed and scrubbed, the bigger and blacker the spots grew.

Then the other trolls wanted to try, but the more time passed, the uglier and more vile the shirt looked. Finally the whole shirt looked as if it had been inside the chimney.

"Oh, none of you is any good," said the prince. "There sits a vagabond girl outside the window. I'm certain that she's much better at washing than any of you. Come in here, girl!" he shouted.

In she came.

"Do you think you can wash this shirt clean?" he said.

"Oh, I don't know," she said, "but I'll give it a try."

And no sooner had she picked up the shirt and dipped it in the water than it was as dazzling white as newly driven snow. In fact, even whiter.

"You're the one I want as my bride," said the prince.

Then the troll woman grew so angry that she burst. The princess with the long nose and all the lesser trolls must have burst too, for I've never heard of them again.

The prince and his bride released all the Christian folks who had been captured. Then they took as much gold and silver as they could carry and moved far away from the castle that was east of the sun and west of the moon.

The Hen Who Had to Go to Dovre Mountain or Else the Whole World Would Perish

There once was a hen who flew up into an oak tree to perch there in the evening. During the night she dreamed that if she didn't go to Dovre Mountain, the whole world would perish. She jumped down at once and set off. After she'd gone some distance, she met a rooster.

"Good day, Roosty Rooster," said the hen.

"Good day, Henny Hen. Where are you off to so early?" said the rooster.

"Oh, I need to go to Dovre Mountain, or else the whole world will perish," said the hen.

"Who told you that, Henny Hen?" said the rooster.

"That's what I dreamed when I was sitting in the oak tree last night," said the hen.

"I'll go with you, I will," said the rooster.

They walked a long way. Then they met a duck.

"Good day, Ducky Duck," said the rooster.

"Good day, Roosty Rooster. Where are you off to so early?" said the duck.

"I have to go to Dovre Mountain, or else the whole world will perish," said the rooster.

"Who told you that, Roosty Rooster?"

"Henny Hen," said the rooster.

"Who told you that, Henny Hen?" said the duck.

"That's what I dreamed when I was sitting in the oak tree last night," said the hen.

"I'll go with you," said the duck.

So they set off and again walked a good distance. Then they met a goose.

"Good day, Goosey Goose," said the duck.

"Good day, Ducky Duck," said the goose. "Where are you off to so early?"

"I have to go to Dovre Mountain, or else the whole world will perish," said the duck.

"Who told you that, Ducky Duck?" said the goose.

"Roosty Rooster."

"Who told you that, Roosty Rooster?"

"Henny Hen."

"Where did you hear that, Henny Hen?" said the goose.

"That's what I dreamed when I was sitting in the oak tree last night, Goosey Goose," said the hen.

"I want to go too," said the goose.

After they'd walked a good distance again, they met a fox.

"Good day, Foxy Fox," said the goose.

"Good day, Goosey Goose."

"Where are you headed, Foxy Fox?"

"Where are *you* headed, Goosey Goose?"

"I have to go to Dovre Mountain, or else the whole world will perish," said the goose.

"Who told you that, Goosey Goose?" said the fox.

"Ducky Duck."

"Who told you that, Ducky Duck?"

"Roosty Rooster."

"Who told you that, Roosty Rooster?"

"Henny Hen."

"Where did you hear that, Henny Hen?"

"That's what I dreamed when I was sitting in the oak tree last night. If we don't get to Dovre Mountain, then the whole world will perish," said the hen.

"Nonsense," said the fox. "The whole world isn't going to perish if you don't get there. No, come home with me to my fox den. That will be much better. It's both warm and nice."

Well, they went home with the fox to his den. When they got there, the fox made a good fire, and soon they were all very sleepy. The duck and the goose sat down in a corner, while the rooster and the hen flew up to a pole where they could perch.

When the goose and duck were sound asleep, the fox put the goose on the fire and roasted him. The hen thought she smelled something burning. She hopped onto a perch higher up and said, half asleep, "Ugh, how it stinks in here! It really stinks!"

"Nonsense," said the fox. "It's just the smoke coming down the chimney flue. Shut up and go to sleep!"

So the hen went back to sleep.

No sooner had the fox eaten the goose than he did the same thing to the duck. He put the duck on the embers, roasted him, and set about eating him.

Then the hen woke up again and hopped onto a perch even higher up. "Ugh, how it stinks in here! It really stinks!" she said. She opened her eyes and caught sight of the fox, who was still eating both the goose and the duck. Then she flew up to the highest perch and sat there, peering up through the chimney.

"My, oh my, look at all the lovely geese flying up there!" she said to the fox.

The sly fox went outside to get himself another juicy roast.

In the meantime, the hen woke the rooster and told him what had happened to Goosey Goose and Ducky Duck. Then Henny Hen and Roosty Rooster flew out through the chimney. And if they hadn't reached Dovre Mountain, then the whole world would certainly have perished.

The Man Who Had to Keep House

There once was a man who was very bad-tempered and stern. He thought his wife never did enough in the house. One evening during haying season, he came home and began grumbling and scolding and cursing so much that sparks practically flew off him.

"My dear husband, don't be so mean," said the woman. "Tomorrow we'll trade jobs. I'll go out with the haying folks and bring in the hay, and you can take care of the house."

Her husband liked that idea, and he gladly agreed.

Early the next morning the woman set her scythe on her shoulder and went out to the meadow with the haying folks to gather in the hay. Her husband stayed behind to keep house.

The first thing he wanted to do was churn some butter. After he'd been churning for a while, he was thirsty, so he went down to the cellar to get himself some ale from the cask. While he was filling the ale bowl, he heard the pig come into the house. He was still holding the wooden spigot in his hand when he raced up the cellar stairs as fast as he could go. He wanted to make sure the pig didn't topple the butter churn. Then he saw that the pig had already knocked it over and was lapping up the cream that had spilled onto the floor.

The man got so mad that he completely forgot about the ale cask and started prodding the pig as best he could. He got the animal as far as the door and then gave it a sharp kick so it dropped to the ground right there.

Then the man remembered that he was holding the spigot in his hand. By the time he got back down to the cellar, all the ale had run out of the cask.

He went back to the cowshed and found enough cream to refill the churn. Then he set about churning, for he wanted to have butter for his midday meal. After he'd been churning for a while, he happened to remember that the cow was still in its stall. The cow hadn't had anything to eat or drink, even though it was now late in the morning. He thought it would be too far to take the cow down to the pasture. He decided to let it climb up on the roof. Their house had a sod roof with splendid, lush grass. The house stood next to a steep hill, and if he placed a board across the roof, he thought he could get the cow up there. But he didn't dare leave the churn again, for his little boy was crawling around on the floor, and he thought the child might well topple the churn. So he hoisted the churn onto this back and went out.

First he needed to give the cow water before letting it loose on the roof. He picked up a bucket so he could get water from the well. When he leaned over the edge, the cream spilled out of the churn, ran down his neck, and landed in the well. It was getting close to mealtime, and he still didn't have any butter, so he thought he would boil some porridge. He hung a pot of water in the fireplace.

After that, he happened to think that the cow might fall off the roof and break its legs or its neck. So he went up on the roof to tether the cow.

One end of the rope he tied around the cow's neck. Then he lowered the rope down the chimney and tied the other end around his thigh, for the water was boiling in the pot, and he needed to put in the porridge.

While he was doing that, the cow did fall off the roof. When that happened, the man was yanked up through the chimney by the rope. There he got stuck, while the cow hung outside the wall of the house, dangling between heaven and earth. It couldn't go either up or down.

The farmer's wife had been waiting forever and a day for her husband to arrive and call everyone in to eat. He still hadn't come. Finally she thought it was taking too long, and she went back home.

When she caught sight of the cow, hanging there so horribly, she went right over and cut the rope with her scythe. At that instant her husband fell back down the chimney. When the woman went inside, there he was with his head in the porridge pot.

Tom Thumb

There once was a woman who had only one son, and he was no bigger than a thumb. That's why he was called Tom Thumb. When he came of age, his mother told him that he needed to go out and court a girl. She thought it was time for him to start thinking of marriage.

When Tom Thumb heard this, he was very happy. So they gathered up what they needed for traveling and set off. The mother held her son on her lap. They were headed for a royal palace where a grand princess lived. But after they'd gone a good distance down the road, Tom Thumb disappeared.

His mother looked for him for a long time. She called his name, and she wept because he was gone and she couldn't find him.

"Hey!" said Tom Thumb. He was hiding in the mane of the horse.

He came out from hiding. Then he had to promise his mother not to do that again. But after they'd traveled some distance, Tom Thumb disappeared. His mother searched for him, she called and she wept, but he was gone.

"Hey!" said Tom Thumb. She heard him laughing and snickering, but she couldn't see him anywhere.

"Hey!" said Tom Thumb, and he crawled out of the horse's ear.

Then he had to promise he wouldn't hide anymore. But after they'd traveled some distance, he again disappeared. He couldn't help himself. His mother searched and wept and called to him, but he was gone, and gone he stayed. No matter how hard she searched, she couldn't find him anywhere.

"Hey!" said Tom Thumb.

His mother couldn't figure out where he was, for his voice sounded so faint. She kept searching. He said, "Hey, here I am!" And he laughed with glee when she couldn't find him. All of a sudden the horse sneezed, and out flew Tom Thumb. He'd been sitting inside the horse's nostril.

This time his mother picked up the boy and stuffed him inside a sack. She didn't know what else to do, for she could tell that he wasn't about to stop his mischief.

When they arrived at the royal palace, a betrothal was soon arranged. The princess thought Tom Thumb was a handsome little fellow, and it wasn't long before the wedding was held.

When they were about to eat dinner at the bridal estate, Tom Thumb was seated at the table next to the princess. But he was in a terrible position, for he couldn't reach any of the food. He wouldn't have had even a bite to eat if the princess hadn't helped him up onto the table. Everything was fine and good as long as he could eat what was on his plate.

But then a big, big tureen of porridge was brought in, and he couldn't reach inside of it. Tom Thumb knew just what to do. He climbed up and sat on the rim.

There was a lump of butter in the middle of the porridge, and he couldn't reach it. He crawled into the tureen and sat at the very edge of the butter. All of a sudden the princess picked up a big spoonful of porridge so she could dip it in the butter.

The spoon came so close to Tom Thumb that he fell into the butter and drowned.

Haaken Speckled-Beard

There once was a king's daughter who was so haughty and sharp-tongued that no suitor was good enough for her. She ridiculed all of them and sent them on their way, one after the other. Yet even though she was so high-and-mighty, suitors kept coming to the palace, for she was beautiful. That nasty witch certainly was.

One day a king's son arrived. He was another suitor, and his name was Haaken Speckled-Beard. The first night he was there, the princess ordered the court jester to cut off the ears of one of his horses and to slash the throat of the other all the way up to its ears.

When the prince went out to go riding the next day, the princess stood on the porch to watch.

"Well! I've never seen the likes of that," she said. "The sharp northern wind that blows through here has sliced off the ears of one of your horses. And the other horse stood there grinning so much that its lips have stretched all the way up to its ears." With that she let loose a great bellow of laughter. Then she dashed inside and let the prince go on his way.

He went back home, but he secretly decided that he would repay her in kind.

The prince put on a big beard made from lichen, pulled on a baggy leather coat, and made himself look like an ordinary beggar. Then he went to a goldsmith and bought a golden spinning wheel. After that he set off.

One morning he sat down outside the princess's window. There he began to file and assemble the golden spinning wheel, for it wasn't quite done, nor did it have any distaffs.

When the king's daughter opened her window in the morning, she called down to the man and asked whether he would sell her that spinning wheel of his.

"No, it's not for sale," said Haaken Speckled-Beard. "But that's neither here nor there. If I'm allowed to sleep outside your bedchamber tonight, you shall have it."

The princess thought that was a good bargain. Surely there would be no risk to her. Then Haakon Speckled-Beard gave her the spinning wheel, and that evening he lay down outside the door to her bedchamber.

In the middle of the night he began to freeze terribly. "Brrr! Brrr! Brrr! It's so vile and cold out here. Oh, let me in," he said.

"You must be out of your mind," said the princess.

"Oh, brrr! Brrr! Brrr! It's so cold. Oh, please let me in!" said Haaken Speckled-Beard.

"Shush, shush! Be quiet!" said the princess. "If my father hears that there's a man in here, I'll suffer a terrible misfortune."

"Oh, brrr! Brrr! Brrr! I'm freezing to death. Just let me come inside and lie on the floor!" said Haaken Speckled-Beard.

There was nothing for the princess to do. She had to let him in. Once he was inside, he lay down on the floor and fell sound asleep.

A while later Haaken came back. This time he brought the distaffs for the spinning wheel. Again he sat down outside the window belonging to the king's daughter and began filing the distaffs, for they weren't quite finished. When she heard the sound of him filing, she opened the window and began talking to him. She wondered what he was doing out there.

"Oh, these are the distaffs for the spinning wheel that the princess got from me. I was thinking that if she had the spinning wheel, she might well need the distaffs too."

"What do you want for them?" asked the princess.

They were not for sale either. But if he was allowed to lie on the floor of the princess's bedchamber that night, she could have them.

He was granted permission to do just that, though she asked him to stay calm and not start freezing and saying "Brrr!"

Haaken Speckled-Beard promised, but in the middle of the night, he began shivering and freezing and carrying on. Then he asked whether he might be allowed to lie on the floor right next to the princess's bed.

There was nothing for her to do but grant him permission, or else the king would hear. Haaken Speckled-Beard lay down on the floor right next to the princess's bed. There he fell sound asleep.

It was a good long time before Haaken Speckled-Beard came back. This time he brought with him a yarn winder made of gold. In the morning he set about filing it after he sat down outside the window belonging to the princess.

The exact same thing happened as before. When the princess heard him, she came to the window and said hello. Then she asked what he would want for the yarn winder.

"I won't sell it for money. But if I'm allowed to lie in your bedchamber tonight with my head resting against the bed frame, then you shall have it," said Haaken Speckled-Beard.

Well, the princess said she would allow him to do that, if only he would stay calm and not cause such a ruckus. He promised to do his best.

But in the middle of the night he began shivering and freezing so much that his teeth began to chatter. "Brrr! Brrr! Brrr! It's so cold! Oh, let me come into your bed and warm up a little!" said Haaken Speckled-Beard.

"I think you're out of your mind, I really do," said the princess.

"Brrr! Brrr! Brrr!" said Haaken Speckled Beard. "Oh, please let me come into your bed. Brrr! Brrr! Brrr!"

"Shush, shush! Be quiet for God's sake!" said the princess. "If my father hears that there's a man in here, I'll suffer a terrible misfortune. I'm certain he'll kill me at once."

"Brrr! Brrr! Brrr! Let me into your bed!" said Haaken Speckled-Beard. He was freezing so much that the whole room shook.

There was nothing for the princess to do. She had to let him slip into her bed. There he fell sound asleep.

But a while later the princess gave birth to a little baby. The king was so furious that he almost put an end to both her and the child.

Sometime after that, Haaken Speckled-Beard came wandering past, as if by chance. He went into the kitchen, just like any other poor beggar would do.

When the king's daughter came in and caught sight of him, she said, "Oh, good Lord, what misfortune you have caused me! My father is so angry he's about to explode. Let me go home with you!"

"I'm sure you're used to much finer things than you'll have if you come with me," said Haaken. "My home is nothing but a hut made from branches. And I don't know how I'll be able to find food for you. I have enough trouble finding food for myself."

"Oh, I don't care how you live," she said. "Just let me come home with you. If I stay here any longer, my father will surely kill me."

Then she was allowed to go with the vagabond, as she called him. They walked a great distance and for a very long time. She didn't find it easy. When they left her country behind and entered another kingdom, the princess wanted to know who owned it.

"Oh, that's Haaken Speckled-Beard, he's the one," said the vagabond.

"I see," said the princess. "He's someone I could have married. Then I wouldn't have to be walking along like some beggar girl."

As they passed all the splendid castles and forests and estates, she asked who owned them.

"Oh, they belong to Haaken Speckled-Beard," said the vagabond.

The princess walked along, feeling miserable. She could have married the man who owned so much.

At long last they came to the royal palace. The vagabond told her that he was known there, and he thought he might well find work for her too. Then they'd have something to live on. He built a hut out of branches at the edge of the forest, at a place where he wanted to stay. He told her that at the king's palace, his job was to cut firewood and carry water for the cook.

Whenever he came back from the castle, he would bring her scraps of food, though they didn't last long.

One day he came back and said, "Tomorrow I'll stay home and look after the child. You need to make yourself presentable and go over to the castle. The prince wants you to come and help with the baking."

"Baking? Me?" said the king's daughter. "I can't bake. It's not something I've ever done before."

"Well, you have to go," said Haaken Speckled-Beard. "He said you must. If you can't bake, I'm sure you can learn. Just watch what the others do. And when you're about to leave, steal some bread for me."

"Stealing is not something I know how to do," said the king's daughter.

"I'm sure you can learn," said Haaken Speckled-Beard. "You've seen how little we have to eat. But be careful and watch out for the prince, for he has eyes everywhere."

As soon as she left, Haaken set off running. He took a shortcut and reached the castle long before she did. There he threw off his rags and lichen beard and put on his princely attire.

The king's daughter helped with the baking and did as Haaken had told her to do. She stole enough bread to fill all her pockets.

When she was about to head for home that evening, the prince said, "We know nothing about this beggar woman. It's best we make sure she hasn't taken anything."

Then he searched all her pockets. He kept digging and rummaging, and when he found the bread he was furious and kicked up a terrible ruckus.

She wept and carried on and said, "The vagabond told me to do it. I had to do it."

"Things could have gone very badly for you," said the prince. "But that's neither here nor there. For the sake of the vagabond, you are forgiven."

After she'd left, he threw off his princely attire, donned the leather coat and put on the lichen beard. He reached the hut made of branches before she did. When she arrived, he was tending to the child.

"Oh, you made me do something I greatly regret," she said. "That was the first time I've ever stolen anything, and it will be the last." Then she told him what happened and what the prince had said.

A few days later Haaken came back in the evening to the hut made of branches. "Tomorrow I'll stay home and take care of the child," he said. "You're supposed to help with the butchering and make sausages."

"Make sausages? Me?" said the king's daughter. "I can't do that. I've certainly eaten sausages, but I've never made any."

Haaken told her she had to go. The prince had said she must. She'd just have to do whatever the others did. Then he told her to steal some sausages for him.

"No, I can't steal," she said. "I'm sure you remember what happened last time."

"You can learn to steal," said Haaken. "It's not certain that things will go badly every time."

As soon as she'd left, Haaken Speckled-Beard ran off along the shortcut and came to the castle long before she did. There he threw off the leather coat and lichen beard. He was standing in the kitchen, wearing his princely attire, when she arrived.

The king's daughter helped with the butchering and made sausages. She also did as Haaken had said and stuffed her pockets full.

When she was about to leave for home, the prince said, "This beggar woman had sticky fingers last time. It's probably best if we make sure she hasn't taken anything." And he began searching and rummaging through her pockets.

When he found the sausages, he was again so angry that he caused a terrible ruckus. He threatened to hand her over to the sheriff.

"Oh, God have mercy, let me go! The vagabond told me to do it," she said as she wept and carried on.

"Things could have gone very badly for you, but for the sake of the vagabond, you are forgiven," said Haaken Speckled-Beard.

After she'd left, he threw off his princely attire, donned the leather coat and put on the lichen beard. Then he raced along the shortcut. By the time she got home, he'd been there for quite a while. She told him what happened. Then she vowed with all her heart that it was the last time he'd get her to do anything like that again.

Sometime later the vagabond went back to the royal palace. When he came home in the evening, he said, "Now our prince is about to be married. But the bride has fallen ill, so the tailor can't take her measurements for the bridal gown. The prince wants you to go up to the royal palace and be measured in her place. He says that you resemble his bride in height and everything else. But after you've been measured, don't leave. Stay right there and watch while the tailor cuts the cloth. Then gather up the scraps and bring them back to make me a cap."

"No, I can't steal," she said. "And I'm sure you remember what happened last time."

"But you can learn," said Haaken. "It's not certain that things will go badly every time."

She thought it was wrong, but she went to the palace and did as he'd said. She stood there and watched as the tailor cut the cloth. Then she gathered up the scraps and stuffed them in her pocket.

When she was about to leave, the prince said, "Let's see whether this woman has again had sticky fingers." He began looking in all of her pockets. When he found the bundle of scraps he grew very angry. He began scolding and raging. There was no end to his fury.

She wept and carried on and said, "Oh, the vagabond made me do it. I had to do it."

"Things ought to go badly for you, but for the sake of the vagabond, you are forgiven," said Haaken Speckled-Beard.

Then the same thing happened as before. When she got back to the hut made from branches, Haaken was already there.

"Oh, God help me!" she said. "I'm going to suffer a terrible misfortune in the end. And you're to blame. You only want me to do things that are wrong. The prince was so furious and fuming that he threatened me with both the sheriff and jail."

A while later Haaken came back one evening to the hut made from branches. "Now the prince wants you to go to the castle to stand in for his bride," he said. "His bride is still ailing and has to keep to her bed. But he insists the wedding should go on. You look so much like her that no one can tell the two of you apart. Tomorrow you must make yourself presentable and go up to the castle."

"Both of you must have lost your minds, you and the prince," she said. "Do you think I look as if I could be a bride? No beggar woman could look worse than I do."

"Well, that's what the prince said you should do. That's what you have to do," said Haaken Speckled-Beard.

She had no choice. She had to go.

When she arrived at the royal palace, she was dressed and adorned so that no princess could look more splendid than she did. Then they went to the church, and she stood in for the bride. When they got back, there was dancing and merriment at the castle.

All of a sudden, as she was dancing with the prince, she glanced out the window and noticed something glowing. Then she saw bright flames shooting out of the hut made from branches.

"Oh no! The vagabond and the child and the hut!" she cried. She was on the verge of fainting.

"Here is the vagabond and there is the child, and let the hut burn!" said Haaken Speckled-Beard. Then she recognized him.

That's when the real merriment and joy began. But after that I've heard not a word about them, nor have I ever asked.

Master Maiden

T here once was a king who had several sons. I'm not really sure how many there were, but the youngest of them could find no peace at home. He wanted with all his heart to go out into the world and try his luck. At long last the king had to give him permission to do just that.

After the boy had traveled for a few days, he came to the estate of a giant troll. There he found work as a servant.

In the morning the troll had to go out to tend to his goats. As he was about to leave, he told the king's son to muck out the stable.

"After you've done that, you won't have to do anything else today. I want you to know that you're working for a kind master," the troll said. "But whatever you're asked to do, you must do it well. And you must never go into any of the other rooms inside the house where you stayed last night. If you do, I will kill you."

"What a kind master he is," the king's son said to himself. He walked back and forth in the house, humming and singing, for he thought there was plenty of time to muck out the stable. Then he thought it might be fun to take a look inside the other rooms, all the same. There must be something in there that the troll was afraid he'd see. And he went into the first room. There on the wall hung a kettle that was boiling, but the king's son saw no heat underneath. I wonder what's inside? he thought. He dipped a lock of his hair into the kettle, and every strand looked as if it was made of copper. "What a strange soup that is! Anyone who tasted it would come away with gilded lips," said the boy. Then he went into the room next door.

There on the wall hung another kettle, bubbling and boiling, but again there was no heat underneath. "I'll try this one too," said the king's son. He stuck a lock of his hair into the kettle, and it came out silvery. "Such a precious soup can't be found even at my father's estate," said the king's son. "But of course it's a matter of how it tastes." And with that he went into the third room.

There on the wall hung a boiling kettle, just like in the other two rooms. The king's son felt an urge to try this one as well. He dipped in a lock of his hair, and it came out such a shiny gold that it gleamed.

"Mercy me! as the saying goes. But I say: Glory be! If the troll is boiling gold in here, I wonder what he's boiling next door?" He wanted to find out, so he went into the fourth room.

There was no kettle in sight, but sitting on the bench was someone who had to be the daughter of a king. Yet no matter whose daughter she was, he had never in all his life seen the likes of her. That's how lovely she was.

"Oh, in Christ's name, what are you doing here?" said the girl sitting on the bench.

"I was hired as a servant yesterday," said the king's son.

"God save you from this place where you've ended up working," she said.

"Oh, I think I've found a kind enough master, I certainly do," said the king's son. "He hasn't given me much of a job for today. All I have to do is muck out the stable."

"And how are you going to do that?" she asked. "If you do the mucking out in the usual way, ten shovelfuls will come in for every shovelful you toss out. I'm going to tell you what you have to do. Turn the shovel around so you're using the handle instead. Then all the muck will fly out on its own."

He would be sure to do just that, said the king's son. Then he stayed with her all day, for it soon turned out that they wished to marry, the king's son and the king's daughter. And, as you might well imagine, he thought the first day he'd spent as the troll's servant hadn't lasted long at all.

As evening approached, the girl told him it would be best if he mucked out the stable before the troll came home.

When the boy got there, he decided he'd like to find out if what she'd told him was true. So he set about mucking out the stalls the way he'd seen the stable boys do it on his father's estate. He quickly had to stop, for after he'd worked for only a short time, there was almost no room left for him to stand. Then he did as the king's daughter had instructed him. He turned the shovel around and used the handle instead. And in no time at all the stable was as clean as if it had been scrubbed.

After that, the boy went back to the house where the giant troll had said he could stay. There he walked back and forth as he hummed and sang. Then the troll came back with the goats.

"Have you mucked out the stable?" asked the troll.

"Yes, now it's spick-and-span, Master," said the king's son.

"That I'd like to see!" said the troll. He headed over to the stable. And it was exactly as the king's son had said.

"You must have talked to Master Maiden, for you would never have figured it out on your own," said the troll.

"Master Maiden? What do you mean by that?" said the king's son. He pretended to be a real numbskull. "It would certainly be fun to see someone like that."

"Oh, you'll see her soon enough," said the troll.

On the morning of the second day the troll again had to go out with his goats. He told the king's son that on this day he had to bring home the horse that was out on the heath. After he did that, he could take the rest of the day off. "I want you to know that you're working for a kind master," the troll said again. "But don't go into any of the rooms I mentioned yesterday, or I'll twist your head right off," he said. Then he left with the herd of goats.

"What a kind master you are," said the king's son to himself. "But I think I'll go inside and talk to Master Maiden, all the same. Maybe she'd rather be mine than yours." Then he went inside to see her.

She asked him what he was supposed to do that day.

"Oh, I don't think it's much of a job," said the king's son. "I just have to go up to the heath to get his horse."

"Well, how are you going to do that?" asked Master Maiden.

"Oh, surely it can't take any great skill to ride a horse home," said the king's son. "I imagine I've ridden wild horses before."

"Well, it's probably not such an easy matter to ride that horse home," said Master Maiden. "I'll tell you what you have to do. When you catch sight of the horse, it will charge at you. Fire and flames that look like burning torches will shoot out of its nostrils. Be sure to take along the bridle that is hanging over there next to the door. Throw the bridle right at the horse's mouth. Then it will become so docile that you can do whatever you like with it."

Oh yes, he would be sure to keep that in mind. Again he stayed there with Master Maiden all day long. They chatted and conversed about one thing and another, those two. Mostly they talked about how splendid and delightful it would be if only they could marry and escape from the troll.

The king's son might well have forgotten all about the horse on the heath if Master Maiden hadn't reminded him as evening approached. She said it would be best if he went out to get the horse before the troll came back.

So that's what he did. He took the bridle that was hanging in the corner and raced up to the heath. It wasn't long before the horse came charging toward him. Fire and red flames were shooting out of its nostrils. The boy saw his chance as soon as the horse came rushing forward, its mouth agape. He threw the bit right into the animal's mouth. Then it stood there as patiently as a lamb. And I don't imagine it took much to get the horse home to the stable. After that the boy went back inside the house and began humming and singing.

That evening the troll came home with the goats. "Did you bring the horse back from the heath?" asked the troll.

"Yes, I did, Master. What a fun horse it was to ride. Even so, I rode straight back home and put it in the stable, yes I did," said the king's son.

"That I'd like to see!" said the troll. He went out to the stable. There stood the horse, just as the king's son had said.

"You must have talked to my Master Maiden, for you would never have figured it out on your own," said the troll again.

"Yesterday you mentioned this Master Maiden, and today you're saying the same thing. God have mercy! Wouldn't you consider showing me this person? I think it would be great fun to see her," said the king's son. He pretended to be just as stupid and ignorant as before.

"Oh, you'll see her soon enough," said the troll.

On the morning of the third day the troll again had to go out to the forest with his goats. "Today you have to go to hell and bring back the fire tax that must be paid, or else I've threatened to burn and plunder the place," he told the king's son. "After you've done that, you can take the rest of the day off. I want you to know that you're working for a kind master." Then he left.

"Yes, what a kind master you are. Yet you ask me to carry out such nasty tasks," said the king's son to himself. "I think I'll go and see your Master Maiden. You may say that she's yours, but maybe she'll tell me what I'm supposed to do." And he went inside to see her.

When Master Maiden asked the boy what the troll wanted him to do that day, he told her that he was supposed to go to hell and get the fire tax.

"How are you going to do that?" said Master Maiden.

"Well, I suppose you'll have to tell me," said the king's son. "I've never been to hell before, and even if I knew how to get there, I wouldn't know how much to ask for."

"All right, I'll tell you. Go to the mountain over there beneath the heath. Pick up the club you'll see lying there, and pound it on the wall of the mountain," said Master Maiden. "The one who appears will have sparks flying off him. Tell him why you have come. When he asks you how much you want, say you'll take as much as you can carry."

Well, he'd surely keep that in mind, said the boy. Then he sat there with Master Maiden all day long, right up until evening approached. He would gladly have stayed there until today if Master Maiden hadn't reminded him that he'd better set off for hell to get the fire tax before the troll came home.

So the boy set off. He did exactly as Master Maiden had told him to do. He went over to the mountain, picked up the club, and pounded it on the wall of the mountain. Then someone appeared with sparks flying out of his eyes and his nose.

"What do you want?" he said.

"The troll told me to come here and ask for the fire tax," said the king's son.

"How much do you want?" said the other.

"I won't ask for any more than I can carry," said the king's son.

"Good thing you didn't want a whole cartload," said the one who had appeared at the mountain wall. "Come on in. Follow me!"

That's what the king's son did. There he saw both gold and silver, you better believe it. The treasure was piled up inside the mountain like heaps of rubble. There he was given a bundle as big as he could carry, and with that he went on his way.

When the troll came back with the goats that evening, the king's son was inside the house. He was humming and singing, just as he'd done on the two nights before.

"Have you been to hell to get the fire tax?" said the troll.

"Yes, I certainly have," said the king's son.

"So where did you put it?" said the troll.

"The sack of gold is over there on the bench," said the king's son.

"That I'd like to see!" said the troll. He strode over to the bench. And there was the sack, stuffed so full that the gold and silver spilled out as soon as the troll loosened the cord.

"You must have talked to my Master Maiden," said the troll. "If you did, I'm going to twist your head right off."

"Master Maiden?" said the king's son. "Yesterday you mentioned this Master Maiden, and today you're talking about her again, and the day before you said the same thing. I wish I could see this person, I really do."

"Well, well. Just wait until tomorrow, and I'll take you to see her," said the troll.

"Oh, thank you, but I'm sure you're only jesting," said the king's son.

The next day the troll took him to see Master Maiden.

"Now you must slaughter him and boil him in that big, huge kettle. You know the one I mean. When the soup is ready, you can call me," said the troll to Master Maiden. He lay down on the bench to sleep. Suddenly he began to snore so loudly that the whole mountain thundered.

Master Maiden picked up a knife, made a cut on the boy's little finger, and dripped three drops on the stool where she'd been sitting. Then she gathered up all the old rags, shoe soles, and other trash she could find. She dumped everything into the big kettle. After that she collected a whole chest of crushed gold, a block of salt, and a water flask that hung near the door. She also took a golden apple and two golden hens. With that she and the king's son set off from the giant troll's estate as fast as they could go.

After they had walked a good distance, they came to the sea. From there they set sail, though where they found a ship, I've never heard.

When the troll had slept for a good long while, he began stretching as he lay on the bench. "Is the soup ready soon?" he said.

"Just started!" said the first drop of blood on the stool.

The troll went back to sleep. He lay there for a long, long time. Then he began stirring again. "Is the soup ready soon?" he said, though he didn't look up. He hadn't done that the first time either, for he was still half-asleep.

"Half-cooked!" said the second drop of blood.

Again the troll thought it was Master Maiden speaking. He turned over on the bench and went back to sleep.

After he'd slept for many more hours, he began moving about and stretching. "Isn't the soup ready yet?" he said.

"Fully cooked!" said the third drop of blood.

Then the troll sat up and rubbed his eyes, but he couldn't see who had spoken. He looked for Master Maiden and called for her. No one answered.

Oh, she probably just slipped out for a moment, thought the troll. He picked up a ladle and went over to the kettle to taste the soup. But there he found nothing but shoe soles and rags and other such trash that had been boiling for a very long time. He couldn't tell whether it was porridge or gruel.

When he saw that, he knew exactly what had happened. He was so furious that he didn't know which leg to stand on. Then he took off after the king's son and Master Maiden, rushing as fast as could be. It didn't take long for him to reach the water, but there he couldn't cross.

"Well, well, I know what to do about this. I'll just have to summon my river swallower," said the troll.

And that's what he did. Then his river swallower appeared and lay down to take two or three slurps. With that the water in the sea went down so much that the troll caught sight of Master Maiden and the king's son on their ship.

"Now you need to toss the block of salt into the water," said Master Maiden.

That's what the king's son did. Then the salt turned into a mountain that stretched so big and tall over the sea that the troll couldn't get across, nor could the river swallower slurp up any more water.

"Well, well, I know what to do about this," said the troll. He sent for his mountain borer to make a hole in the mountain. Then the river swallower would be able to slurp up more water.

But as soon as a hole appeared and the river swallower began to drink, Master Maiden told the king's son to spill a drop or two from the flask. With that the sea was as full of water as it ever was. And before the river swallower could take another drink, they reached land. They were saved.

There they were about to set off for the royal palace that belonged to the king, but the prince refused to allow Master Maiden to walk. He didn't think that would be right, either for her or for him.

"Wait here for a while, and I'll go home to get the seven horses in my father's stable," he said. "It's not far, and I won't be long. I don't want my sweetheart to arrive on foot."

"Oh no, don't do that. When you get back to the royal palace you'll forget all about me. I've seen this happen before," said Master Maiden.

"How could I forget you? Not after the two of us have suffered so much and have grown so fond of each other," said the king's son. He would and he must go home to get the carriage and the seven horses. In the meantime she would have to wait at the shore's edge.

At last Master Maiden had to give in, seeing as that was what he so earnestly wished. "But when you get there, don't take time even to say hello to anyone. Go straight to the stable, get the horses, and harness them to the carriage. Then drive back here as fast as you can go. Everyone will try to greet you, but pretend not to see them. And don't eat anything. If you do, it will mean misfortune for you and for me," she said.

He promised to do as she said.

When he reached the royal palace, one of his brothers was about to celebrate his wedding. The bride and all her kinfolk had arrived at the palace. Everyone crowded around the boy to ask all sorts of questions, and they wanted him to join them inside. But he pretended not to see them and went straight to the stable. There he began harnessing the horses to the carriage.

Everyone followed to watch, but try as they might, they couldn't get him to come inside. So they brought him food and drink and all manner of delicacies that had been prepared for the wedding. The king's son refused to take even a bite. He kept all his attention on harnessing the horses.

Then the bride's sister rolled an apple across the courtyard toward him. "If you refuse to taste anything, you might at least take a bite of this apple. You must be both thirsty and hungry after your long journey," she said.

And that's what the boy did. He picked up the apple and took a bite.

No sooner was the bite of apple in his mouth than he forgot all about Master Maiden and the fact that he was supposed to go back for her.

"I must be out of my mind, I really must. What am I doing out here with the horses and carriage?" he said. He put the horses back in the stable and went inside the king's palace with everyone else. There it was decided that he should marry the bride's sister, the one who had rolled the apple toward him.

Master Maiden sat at the shore's edge and waited forever and a day, but the king's son never appeared. So she set off from there, and after she'd walked a good distance, she came to a little house that stood all alone in a clearing in the woods close to the royal palace. There she went inside and asked if she might take lodging.

An old woman owned the house. She was a mean and bad-tempered witch. At first she didn't want to let Master Maiden stay with her, but at long last, after some persuasion and payment, she changed her mind.

Inside, everything was as horrid and filthy as a pigsty. That's why Master Maiden said she'd fix things up a bit so the place would look more like where other folks lived. The old woman wasn't keen on that either. She complained and fumed, but Master Maiden paid her no mind. She took out her golden chest and tossed almost half the contents on the fire. Then the gold sprayed out over the house so that it was gilded, both inside and out. Yet as soon as the gold began to spray from the fire, the old woman grew so frightened that she took off as if the Evil One himself was after her. But she forgot to duck when she came to the doorway. She ran straight into the lintel, and her head snapped right off.

The next morning the sheriff came riding past. As you might well imagine he was utterly astonished to see the golden house gleaming and glittering in the clearing in the woods. He was even more surprised when he went inside and caught sight of the lovely maiden sitting there. He fell so in love with her that he proposed on the spot. He asked her both politely and sincerely whether she would be his wife.

"Yes, if you have enough money," said Master Maiden.

Oh yes, the sheriff thought he had quite a good sum. He would go home to get the money. That evening he brought back a two-bushel sack stuffed full with coins, and he set it down next to the bench.

Since he had that much money, Master Maiden agreed to marry him. Then they lay down in bed together. But no sooner did they lay down than Master Maiden wanted to get up again.

"I forgot to rake the fire," she said.

"Heavens, do you really have to get up for that?" said the sheriff. "I'll do it." He bounded out of bed and over to the fireplace.

"Tell me when you're holding the poker," said Master Maiden.

"I'm holding the poker now," said the sheriff.

"Then you'll hold that poker, and the poker will hold you. It will shower you with fire and embers until the next day dawns!" said Master Maiden.

The sheriff stood there all night, showering himself with fire and embers. No matter how much he wept and pleaded and begged, the fiery embers grew no colder. When the day dawned and he was finally able to drop the poker, he didn't stay long, as you might well imagine. He set off as if the bailiff and the Devil were both on his heels.

Everyone who saw the sheriff gaped and gawked at him, for he was running like a madman. He couldn't have looked any worse if he'd been flayed and tanned. Everyone wondered where he'd been, but he was too embarrassed to say.

The next day the district judge came riding past the house where Master Maiden was staying. He saw how the place glittered and gleamed from the clearing in the woods. He too wanted to go inside to find out who could be living there. When he went in and saw the lovely maiden, he fell even more in love with her than the sheriff had. He proposed on the spot.

Master Maiden told him, just as she'd said to the sheriff, that if he had enough money, she'd consider it.

The judge said he was not short of money and he would go right home to get it.

That evening he came back with a big sack stuffed with money—I think it was a four-bushel sack. He set the sack on the bench in Master Maiden's house. Then, as agreed, he was to have her as his wife, and they lay down in bed together. But Master Maiden had forgotten to close the door to the porch that evening. She said she would have to get up to close it.

"Heavens, do you have to do that?" said the judge. "No, you stay here, and I'll do it." Then he got out of bed. He moved as lightly as a pea on birch bark and went out to the porch.

"Tell me when you're holding the door latch," said Master Maiden.

"I'm holding it now," shouted the judge from out on the porch.

"Then you'll hold that door latch, and the door latch will hold you. The two of you will slam back and forth until dawn!" said Master Maiden.

And, as you might imagine, the judge had to dance all night. He'd never danced that sort of waltz before, nor did he have a mind to dance it ever again. First he pranced forward. Then it was the door's turn to slide from one end of the porch to the other. The judge was nearly danced to death.

At first he cursed, and then he wept and pleaded, but the door paid him no mind. It kept on moving until the break of dawn. When the door let go of him, the judge took off as fast as if he'd been paid to run. He forgot all about the sack of money and his marriage proposal. He was just glad the door didn't come dancing after him.

Everyone who met the judge gaped and gawked at him as if he were a madman. He looked worse than if he'd been locked up with a bunch of rams all night.

On the third day the bailiff came riding past. He too caught sight of the golden house in the clearing in the woods. Well, he had to go inside to see who lived there. And when he saw Master Maiden, he fell so in love with her that he'd barely said hello before he proposed.

Master Maiden told him the same thing as she'd told the others. If he had enough money, she would agree to have him.

The bailiff said he had quite a lot of money. He would go right home to get it. And that's what he did.

When he came back in the evening, he had an even bigger sack of money than the one the judge had brought—it must have held six bushels. He set it on the bench. And, as agreed, he would then have Master Maiden as his wife.

But no sooner had they gone to bed than Master Maiden said she'd forgotten to let in the calf. She would have to get up to put the calf in the pen.

No, blast it, that's not something she should do. The bailiff told her he would do it. Then he, fat and stout though he was, sprang out of bed as easily as a young man.

"Tell me when you're holding onto the calf's tail," said Master Maiden.

And that's what he did.

"I'm holding onto the calf's tail now," shouted the bailiff.

"Then, God help me, may you hold onto the calf's tail and the calf's tail will hold onto you. The two of you will race everywhere until the day dawns!" said Master Maiden.

Well, as you can imagine, the bailiff really had to get his legs moving. He and the calf raced over land both steep and flat, across mountains and through deep valleys. And the more the bailiff yelled, the faster the calf ran.

By the time it grew light, the bailiff was practically in pieces. He was so happy to let go of the calf's tail that he forgot all about the sack of money and everything else. When he left, he moved a little slower than the sheriff and the judge, but the slower he moved, the more time everyone had to gape and gawk at him. And they made full use of that time, let me tell you, so exhausted and ragged did the bailiff look from running after the calf.

The next day the weddings were to be held at the royal palace. Then the eldest brother would go to church with his bride. And the youngest boy who had worked for the giant troll would wed her sister.

When they were seated in the carriage and were about to leave, one of the axles fell off. They replaced it with one, then another, and another, but all of them fell right off. It didn't matter what kind of wood they used.

This went on and on. It stopped them from leaving, and everyone grew discouraged.

Then the sheriff—for he too, let me tell you, had been invited to the wedding at the royal palace—said that a maiden lived over in the clearing in the woods. "If only you could borrow the poker that she uses to rake the fire, I know it won't break."

Well, they sent a messenger to the clearing to ask ever so politely if they might borrow the poker that the sheriff had mentioned.

The request was granted. Now, as you might imagine, they had an axle that wouldn't fall off.

But the second they were about to leave, the bottom of the carriage collapsed. They had to make a strong new coach bottom, and make it quickly. But no matter how they nailed it together or what sort of wood they used, it didn't hold. No sooner had they put in the bottom and were about to leave than it collapsed again. Now things were even worse than they were with the broken axle.

Then the judge—for, as you might expect, if the sheriff had been invited, then he too was there for the wedding at the royal palace—said, "A maiden lives over in the clearing in the woods. If only you could borrow one of the doors to her porch, I know that it would hold."

Well, again they sent a messenger to the clearing to ask ever so politely if they might borrow the gilded porch door that the judge had mentioned. The request was granted at once.

They were about to set off again, but then the horses weren't strong enough to pull the carriage. Six horses were already harnessed. Now they added two more so there were eight, then ten, then twelve. But no matter how many horses were harnessed to the carriage, and no matter how many grooms used their whips, it was no use. The carriage wouldn't budge.

By now it was getting late in the day. They had to, they must, make their way to the church. Everyone at the royal palace was feeling quite discouraged.

Then the bailiff said that a maiden lived over in the gilded house in the clearing in the woods. If only they could borrow her calf. "For I know that calf could pull the carriage, even if it was as heavy as a mountain," said the bailiff.

They thought it would be embarrassing to drive to church with a calf harnessed to the carriage, but they had no choice. Again they sent a messenger to ask ever so politely, on behalf of the king, if they might borrow the calf that the bailiff had mentioned. And Master Maiden let them have it at once. Again she didn't refuse their request.

After they'd harnessed the calf, the carriage certainly did get moving. It raced over the land, both steep and flat. It raced along so fast that they hardly had time to catch their breath. Part of the time they were on the ground, and part of the time they were in the air. When they reached the church everything began to spin around them like a yarn winder. It was only by the skin of their teeth that they managed to get out of the carriage and go inside the church.

They traveled even faster on their way back, and before they knew it they were at the royal palace again.

When were all seated at the table, the king's son—the one who had been a servant at the giant troll's estate—said that he thought they should invite over the maiden from the clearing in the woods. After all, she was the one who had loaned them the poker and the door and the calf. "If we hadn't had those three things, we would never have been able to leave the palace," he said.

The king thought that was both right and proper. So he sent five of his best men to the gilded house. They said they brought many greetings from the king and asked whether she would be kind enough to come to the royal palace to have dinner.

"Give my greetings to the king, and tell him that if he's too good to come to me, then I'm too good to go to him," replied Master Maiden.

The king had to come in person, and then Master Maiden agreed on the spot.

The king seemed to suspect that she was a little more than she seemed. That's why he invited her to sit in the high seat next to the younger bridegroom.

After they'd been sitting at the table for a short time, Master Maiden took out the rooster and the hen and the golden apple that she'd brought from the giant troll's estate. She placed them on the table in front of her. The rooster and the hen at once began fighting over the golden apple.

"Oh, look how those two have set their sights on the golden apple!" said the king's son.

"Yes, that's how you and I also set our sights on escaping, back when we were inside the mountain," said Master Maiden.

Then the king's son recognized her. As you might imagine, he was over-joyed. He ordered the troll witch, who had rolled the apple toward him, to be ripped apart by twenty-four horses until there wasn't even a shred left of her.

Only then did they truly begin to celebrate his wedding. And no matter how exhausted they still were, the sheriff, the judge, and the bailiff all stayed for the celebration.

Well Done and
Poorly Rewarded

There once was a man who had to go to the forest to get some firewood. Then he met a bear.

"Give me your horse, or else I'll kill all your sheep in the summer," said the bear.

"Oh, God save me, no!" said the man. "There's not even a stick of firewood left back home. You have to let me take home a sled full of wood, or else we'll freeze to death. I'll bring the horse back to you tomorrow."

They agreed that he would do just that. But the bear told the man that if he didn't come back, he would lose all his sheep in the summer.

The man loaded up his firewood and set off for home, though, as you might expect, he wasn't very happy about the agreement he'd made. Then he met a fox.

"What is making you look so dejected?" asked the fox.

"Oh, I met a bear up here," said the man. "I had to promise to give him my horse tomorrow about this same time. If he doesn't get the horse, he said he would tear apart all my sheep in the summer."

"Ha! Is that all?" said the fox. "If you'll give me the fattest ram you own, I'll get you out of the fix you're in, yes I will."

The man agreed. And he promised to stick by his pledge.

"When you bring the horse to the bear tomorrow," said the fox, "I'll call to you from up on the scree, that's what I'll do. When the bear asks you who's calling, tell him it's Hunter Per and he's the best marksman in the world. After that, it's up to you."

The next day the man set off. When he met the bear, a voice began calling from up on the scree.

"Hey! Who's that?" said the bear.

"Oh, that's Hunter Per. He's the best marksman in the world," said the man. "I recognize his voice," he added.

"Have you seen any bears around here, Erik?" the voice shouted from the woods.

"No, I haven't seen any bears," said Erik.

"What's that standing next to your sled?" the voice shouted from the woods.

"Tell him it's the trunk of an old pine tree," whispered the bear.

"Oh, it's just the trunk of an old pine tree," said Erik.

"We usually take pine stumps like that and topple them onto the sled. That's what we do," shouted the voice from the woods. "If you can't manage it on your own, I can come and help you."

"Tell him you can do it on your own. Then topple me onto your sled," said the bear.

"No thanks, I can do it on my own, yes I can," said the man. And he toppled the bear onto his sled.

"We usually tie down pine stumps like that. That's what we do," shouted the voice from the woods. "Do you need some help?"

"Tell him you can do it on your own. Then tie me down tight," said the bear.

"No thanks, I can do it on my own," said the man. Then he set about tightly tying down the bear. He used all the rope he had. After that the bear couldn't lift even a paw.

"We usually shove an axe into pine stumps like that. That's what we do," shouted the voice from the woods. "Then it's easier to steer the sled over the big hills."

"Pretend that you're shoving the axe into me," whispered the bear.

The man picked up his axe and split the bear's skull in two. The bear fell dead at once. Then the man and the fox were great friends and in perfect agreement.

When they reached the man's farm, the fox said, "I have a good mind to come inside with you, but I'm not very fond of your dogs. I'll stay out here until you bring me the ram. I want only one, but it has to be nice and fat."

The man thanked the fox for his help and promised to get the ram. After he'd put the horse in its stall, he headed for the sheep shed.

"Where are you going?" asked his wife.

"Oh, I'm going over to the sheep shed to get a fat ram for the nice fox who saved our horse," said the man. "That's what I promised him."

"Why on earth should we give a ram to that thieving fox?" said his wife. "We have the horse back and the bear too. That fox has certainly stolen more geese from us than a ram is worth. And if he hasn't, he will," she said. "No, put a couple of the meanest dogs in your sack and turn them loose on the fox. Do that, and maybe we'll be rid of that thieving scoundrel," said his wife.

The man thought that was a good idea. He took two mean red dogs and stuffed them in a sack. Then he set off.

"Do you have the ram?" said the fox.

"Yes, come and get it!" said the man. He untied the cord on the sack and let the dogs out.

"Whoa!" said the fox and jumped back. "So it's true what they say: that a job well done is poorly rewarded. And now I see that another saying is also true: your own kind can be your worst enemy." And the red dogs chased after him.

True and Untrue

There once were two brothers. One of them was named True and the other Untrue. True was always honest and kind toward everyone. Untrue was nasty and full of lies, and no one could ever trust a word he said. Their mother was a widow and had little to live on. When her sons were grown, she had to send them off to earn their own living in the world. She gave each of them a little bag of food, and then they had to go.

They walked until evening and then sat down in the forest on a tree that the wind had toppled. They got out their bags of food. They were hungry after walking all day, and they thought it would be good to have a bite to eat.

"If you agree, let's eat what's in your bag first until there's nothing more left. Then we can open mine," said Untrue.

True was happy with that, so they began to eat. But Untrue took all the best pieces and stuffed them into his mouth. For his part, True got only bread crusts and burnt pieces of *lefse* and leftover pork rinds.

In the morning they again ate food from the bag belonging to True, and they did the same at midday. By then there was nothing left in his bag.

They walked until evening, and again it was time for some food. True wanted to have something to eat from his brother's bag, but Untrue refused. He said the food was his, and he had only enough to feed himself.

"Yes, but you ate the food from my bag until there was nothing left," said True.

"Yes, and if you're foolish enough to let other people eat all your food, then it serves you right." That was Untrue's opinion. "So you can just sit there and drool," he said.

"Your name is Untrue, and untrue you are. That's what you've been all your days," said True.

When Untrue heard this, he flew into a rage. He threw himself at his brother and poked out both of his eyes. "Now try and see whether someone is true or untrue, you stupid blind man," he said. With that he ran off.

Poor True now wandered around, fumbling his way forward in the middle of the dense forest. He was blind and alone, and he had no idea what to do. Then he happened to grab hold of a big, stout linden tree. He thought he would climb up and sit there overnight to keep himself safe from the wild animals. He thought to himself that when the birds started singing, it would be daytime and he could try to fumble his way forward again.

So he climbed up in the linden tree.

After he'd sat there for a while, he heard someone come and begin cooking and rustling about under the tree. Moments later others arrived. When they greeted each other, he heard who they were: the bear and the wolf, the fox and the hare. They had all come there to celebrate Midsummer.

The animals set about eating and enjoying themselves. When they were done with that, they began chatting with one another.

Then the fox said, "Why don't we each tell a little story while we're sitting here?"

The others thought that was a good idea. They said it would be amusing. So the bear began, for he was the foremost of them all.

"The king of England has such poor eyesight," said the bear, "that he can hardly see even two feet in front of him. If he happened to climb up in this linden tree in the morning, while there was dew on the leaves, and he took some of that dew and smeared it on his eyes, he'd regain his sight. His eyes would be as good as new."

"Yes," said the wolf. "The king of England also has a deaf-mute daughter. But if he knew what I know, he'd soon figure out what to do for her. Last year when she took communion, she spat out the bread. Then a big toad appeared and swallowed the bread. If only they would dig under the floor, they'd find that toad. It's sitting right there under the altar rail, and the bread is still in its mouth. They should cut open the toad, take out the bread, and give it to the princess. Then she would be just like other folks again. She'd be able to hear and speak."

"Oh yes," said the fox. "If the king of England knew what I know, he wouldn't be so short of water at his palace. Under the big flagstone in the middle of the courtyard is the clearest spring water that anyone could ever want. If only he knew where to dig for it."

"Yes," said the hare. "The king of England has the loveliest orchard in all the land, but the trees don't bear even a sour apple. A heavy gold chain lies buried in the ground, wrapped three times around the orchard. If the king dug it up, he'd have the most splendid orchard in all his realm."

"Well, it's getting late, so we'd better see about going home," said the fox. Then they all set off.

After they'd left, True fell asleep as he sat there in the linden tree. But when the birds began to sing in the morning, he woke. He took some dew from the leaves and smeared it on his eyes. Then he could see just as well as before Untrue poked out his eyes. After that, he went straight to the king of England's estate, and there he asked for work. He was hired at once.

One day the king went out in the courtyard. After he'd walked around for a while, he wanted to take a drink from the water pump. It was a hot day, and the king was thirsty. But when the servants poured him some water, it was muddy and sludgy and disgusting. The king was quite annoyed.

"I don't think there's a man in my whole kingdom who has worse water on his farm, and yet I must go looking for fresh water far away over mountain and valley," said the king.

"Yes, but if you allow me to get the servants to break up the flagstone lying here in the middle of your courtyard, you'll have fresh water and plenty of it," said True.

The king was very pleased to hear this. And no sooner did they take up the flagstone and do a little digging than a stream of water shot into the air. The water was as clear and as steady as if the spigot on a cask had been turned. No fresher water could be found in all of England.

A while later the king went out to the courtyard again. Then a big hawk came flying in to chase after his hens. Everyone began clapping their hands and shouting, "There it goes! There it goes!"

The king grabbed his rifle and was about to shoot the hawk, but his eyesight was too poor. That made him quite distressed.

"By God, if only someone could tell me what to do about my eyes! I think I'll soon be completely blind," said the king.

"I can tell you what to do," said True. Then he told the king what he himself had done.

As you can well imagine, that very evening the king set off for the linden tree. The next morning, all he had to do was smear his eyes with dew from the leaves and his eyesight was as good as new.

After that, the king favored True more highly than anyone else. He always kept True close, no matter where he went, both at home and away.

Then one day they went out to the orchard together.

"I don't know how this happens, I certainly don't," said the king. "No man in England spends as much on his orchard as I do, and yet I can't get a single tree to bear even a sour apple."

"Oh yes," said True. "If you'll grant me what is buried three times around your orchard and get the servants to dig it up, then your orchard will bear fruit."

The king gladly agreed.

Then True had the servants start digging. Finally he got the whole golden chain out of the ground.

After that True was a very rich man—much, much richer than even the king. Yet the king was well pleased, for now the orchard bore so much fruit that the branches of the trees hung all the way down to the ground. And no one had ever tasted such sweet apples and pears.

On another day when True and the king were talking, the princess happened to walk past. The king grew quite distressed when he saw her.

"Isn't it a shame to have a daughter as lovely as mine, and yet she can neither hear nor speak?" said the king.

"Oh, something can be done about that," said True.

When the king heard this, he was so happy that he promised to give True the princess as his bride, along with half the kingdom, if he could make her well again.

True took a couple of men with him to the church. There they dug up the toad that was sitting under the altar rail. They cut open the toad and took out the piece of bread, which they gave to the princess. Then she was just like other folks again. She was instantly able to hear and speak.

Then True was to marry the princess. Great preparations were made for the wedding, and news of the celebration spread far and wide throughout the whole kingdom.

While everyone was dancing at the wedding, a poor boy came in and asked for a scrap of food. He looked so ragged and miserable that everyone crossed themselves when they saw him. But True recognized the boy at once. It was Untrue, his brother.

"Don't you know me?" said True.

"Oh, where would the likes of me have ever met such a grand gentleman as you?" said Untrue.

"Yet we have met," said True. "I was the one whose eyes you poked out a year ago today. Your name is Untrue, and untrue you are. I said it then, and I'll say the same thing now. But you're still my brother, so you shall have some food. Then you can go to the linden tree where I sat last year. If you hear something there that will bring you luck, then so much the better for you."

He didn't have to say that twice. Untrue thought that if True had learned so much from sitting in the linden tree that he could become king of half of England in only half a year's time, then he would go there too.

He set off, and when he got to the linden tree, he climbed up in the branches. He hadn't sat there long when all the animals again arrived to eat and drink and celebrate Midsummer underneath the tree.

After they'd eaten their fill, the fox wanted each of them to tell a story. Then, as you might imagine, Untrue started to listen so hard that his ears practically fell off.

But the bear was angry, yes he was. He growled and said, "Somebody's been gossiping about the stories we told last year, so this time we're going to keep quiet about what we know."

Then the animals all said good night and went their separate ways. And Untrue was none the wiser. That's because his name was Untrue, and untrue he was.

Per and Paal and Esben Ash Lad

There once was a man who had three sons: Per and Paal and Esben Ash Lad. Other than the three sons, the man had almost nothing at all. He was so poor that he could barely even feed himself. That's why he kept telling his sons that they'd have to go out in the world and earn their own keep. If they stayed at home with him, they would starve to death.

Some distance away was the royal palace, and right under the king's windows grew an oak that was so big and so mighty that its shadow blocked out all light from the king's courtyard. The king had promised a great deal of money to anyone who could chop down the oak, but no one had been able to do it. As soon as someone cut off a single chip from the tree trunk, two chips would grow in its place.

The king also wanted to have a well dug that would hold water all year round. His neighbors had wells, but he had none. And the king thought that was a shame. To anyone who could dig a well that would hold water all year round, the king offered both money and more. But no one had been able to do it, for the royal palace stood high up on top of a hill. And no sooner did they dig a few inches in the ground than they struck bedrock.

Now that the king had set his mind on getting these two tasks done, he sent word to all the churches, both near and far. He decreed that anyone who could chop down the big oak in the royal courtyard and dig a well that would hold water all year round would win the princess and half the kingdom.

As you can well imagine, there were plenty who wanted to try, yet no matter how hard they pounded and chopped, and no matter how much they hacked and dug, it did no good. With every blow the oak grew thicker and thicker, and the bedrock never got any softer.

After a while the three brothers wanted to set off and try their luck as well. Their father was happy to hear this. Even if they didn't win the king's daughter and half the realm, maybe they would at least find work somewhere with a good man. That's what their father thought, and that's what he wished. When the brothers presented their father with their plan to go to the royal palace, he gave them permission at once. Then Per and Paal and Esben Ash Lad set off.

After they'd walked a good distance, they came to a spruce-covered slope. At the top was a steep heath. There they heard something chopping and chopping on the heath.

"I certainly wonder what is doing all that chopping up on the heath," said Esben Ash Lad.

"You and your constant wondering," said both Per and Paal. "Is there anything to wonder about when a woodcutter is chopping trees up on the heath?"

"I still think it would be amusing to see what's up there," said Esben Ash Lad. And with that he set off.

"Oh, you're such a child. It would be good for you to learn to follow along with us," shouted his brothers. But Esben paid them no mind, no, he didn't.

He headed up the slope, in the direction of the chopping sound. When he reached the top, he saw that an axe was chopping and chopping at the trunk of a pine tree.

"Good day!" said Esben Ash Lad. "So here you are, doing all this chopping?"

"Yes, I've been here chopping away for a very long time and waiting for you," replied the axe.

"Yes, well, here I am," said Esben. He picked up the axe and took the blade off the handle. Then he stuffed both the blade and the handle in his bag.

When he got back to his brothers, they laughed and made fun him. "So, what sort of strange sight did you find up on the heath?" they said.

"Oh, it was just an axe that we heard," said Esben.

After they'd walked for a while, they came to a mountain crag. From on top came the sound of something hacking and digging.

"I certainly wonder what is hacking and digging up on the crag," said Esben Ash Lad.

"You and your constant wondering," said Per and Paal again. "Haven't you ever heard birds hacking and pecking on trees before?"

"Yes, but I still think it would be amusing to see what it is," said Esben. And no matter how much his brothers laughed and made fun of him, he paid them no mind. He set off for the mountain crag. When he came to the top, he saw that a hoe was hacking and digging in the ground.

"Good day!" said Esben Ash Lad. "So here you are all alone, hacking at a hole?"

"Yes, I am," said the hoe. "I've been hacking and digging here for a very long time and waiting for you," it said.

"Yes, well, here I am," said Esben. He picked up the hoe and took the blade off the handle. Then he hid both in his bag and went back down to join his brothers.

"So, was it something terribly strange that you found up there on the mountain crag?" said both Per and Paal.

"Oh, it was nothing much. It was just a hoe that we heard," replied Esben.

Then the brothers continued on for a good distance until they came to a stream. All three of them were thirsty after walking so far, and they lay down next to the stream to drink.

"I really wonder where this water comes from," said Esben Ash Lad.

"And I certainly wonder whether you're right in the head," said both Per and Paal. "If you're not already crazy, then you certainly will be soon, with all the wondering you do. Where does the stream come from? Haven't you ever seen water come trickling out of a crevice in the ground?"

"Yes, I have, but I still would like to see where the water comes from, that I would," said Esben. And he set off to follow the stream. No matter how much his brothers shouted and laughed at him, it did no good. He went his own way.

After he'd followed the stream a good distance, it began to get smaller and smaller. And after he'd walked some more, he caught sight of a big walnut. Out of the walnut trickled the water.

"Good day!" said Esben. "Are you here all alone, seeping and trickling?"

"Yes, I am," said the walnut. "I've been here seeping and trickling for a very long time and waiting for you."

"Yes, well, here I am," said Esben. He picked up a tuft of moss and stuck it in the hole so the water wouldn't come out. Then he put the walnut in his bag and went back to join his brothers.

"So, did you find out where the water comes from?" said both Per and Paal.

"Yes, it was just coming out of a hole," said Esben.

Then his two brothers laughed and made fun of him again, but Esben Ash Lad paid them no mind.

"At least I found it amusing, that I did," he said.

After the brothers had again walked a good distance, they came to the royal palace. By then everyone in the realm had heard that anyone might win the princess and half the kingdom if they could chop down the big oak and dig a well for the king. So many had come to try their luck that the oak was now twice as big and thick as it started out, for I'm sure you'll remember that two chips would grow for every one that was cut with an axe. That's why the king had decided to punish anyone who tried but failed to chop down the tree. That person would then be sent out to an island, and both of his ears would be sliced off.

The two brothers refused to be frightened away. No doubt they thought they could fell the oak. Per, who was the eldest, was the first to try. But the same thing happened to him as to all the others who had tried to chop down the oak. For every chip he cut from the tree, two grew in its place. Then the king's servants sliced off Per's ears and sent him out to the island.

Now Paal wanted to try, but the exact same thing happened to him. He made one, two, three cuts in the tree. When the king's servants saw the oak grow, they sent Paal out to the island as well. And they sliced off his ears even closer, for they thought he should have learned to be more careful.

Then Esben Ash Lad wanted to try.

"If you really want to look like a branded sheep, we'll slice off your ears at once. Then you won't have to make the effort," said the king. He was angry at Esben after his brothers had failed.

"I still think it would be amusing to try," said Esben. And he was granted permission.

He took the axe blade out of his bag and put it back on the handle. "Go ahead and chop!" Esben said to the axe. It began to chop so the chips of wood flew. It didn't take long before the oak fell.

When that was done, Esben took out the hoe blade and put it back on the handle. "Go ahead and dig!" said Esben. The hoe began to hack and dig so fast that earth and rocks sprayed out. And the well grew deep, as you might imagine.

After he'd made the hole as deep and wide as he liked, Esben Ash Lad took out the walnut and placed it in a corner at the bottom. Then he pulled out the tuft of moss. "Seep and trickle!" said Esben, and the water began to trickle and then gush out of the hole in the walnut. In no time the well was filled to the brim.

Esben had chopped down the oak, which blocked the light from the king's windows, and he'd dug a well in the king's courtyard. So he won the princess and half the kingdom, just as the king had promised. But it's a good thing that Per and Paal had lost their ears, or else they would have kept on hearing everyone say that Esben Ash Lad's constant wondering had not made him crazy after all.

The Mill That Keeps Grinding at the Bottom of the Sea

ong, long ago there once were two brothers. One of them was rich, and one of them was poor. When Christmas Eve arrived, the poor brother had nothing to eat in the house, neither sour milk nor bread. So he went to see his brother and asked him, in God's name, for a little food for Christmas. This was not the first time the man had asked for something from his rich brother, who had always been miserly. Nor was the rich man especially pleased to get another request.

"If you do what I ask you to do, I'll give you a whole ham," he said.

The poor brother thanked him and agreed at once.

"Here it is. Now go straight to hell!" said the rich man. And he tossed the ham to his brother.

"Well, I made a promise, so I'll have to do it," said the poor brother. Then he took the ham and set off.

He walked and walked all day. At dusk he came to a place that shone so splendidly. This must be it, thought the man with the ham. Out in the woodshed stood an old man with a long white beard chopping firewood for Christmas.

"Good evening!" said the man with the ham.

"Good evening to you! Where are you off to so late?" said the man.

"I'm headed for hell, if only I can find the way," replied the poor man.

"Well, you've come to the right place. This is it," said the old man. "When you go inside, everyone will want to buy that ham of yours, for ham is rare in hell. But don't sell it for any price. Instead, trade it for the hand mill that's behind the door. When you come back out, I'll teach you what to do with the mill. It's a useful thing to have, that it is."

The man with the ham thanked him for his good advice and knocked on the Devil's door.

When he went in, everything happened just as the old man had said. All the demons, both big and small, swarmed around him like ants on the ground. One after the other they made offers for the ham.

"It's true that my wife and I were going to have this ham for our Christmas Eve dinner, but seeing as you're all so eager to have it, I suppose I'll let it go," said the man. "But if I'm going to part with the ham, I want the hand mill that's behind the door over there."

The Devil was reluctant to let the hand mill go. He haggled and wrangled with the man. But the man held his ground, and the Devil had to give up the mill.

When the man went out to the yard, he asked the old woodcutter how to work the mill. After he'd learned how to do that, he thanked the woodcutter and set off for home as fast as he could go. Even so, he didn't get back until the clock struck midnight on Christmas Eve.

"Where in the world have you been?" said his wife. "Here I've been sitting, hour after hour, longing and waiting. And I don't have even two sticks to set crosswise under the pot for the Christmas porridge."

"Oh, I couldn't get here any sooner. There was one thing and another I had to do, and it was a long way to go. But take a look at this!" said the man.

He set the hand mill on the table. First he told it to make candles, then a tablecloth, and then food and ale and all the other good things for a Christmas Eve dinner. And whatever he asked for, the mill produced.

His wife crossed herself again and again. She wanted to know where her husband had found such a hand mill, but he didn't want to tell her.

"Where I found it is neither here nor there. You can see that the mill is a good one, and the mill water never freezes," said the man.

Then he made food and drink and plenty of other good things for the Christmas celebration. And on the third day he invited over their friends, for he wanted to share the feast.

When the rich brother saw everything that was being offered at the farm he grew both annoyed and furious, for he refused to wish his brother well.

"On Christmas Eve my brother was in such great need that he came to me and begged for food, in God's name. Yet now he's putting on a feast as if he were both a count and a king," he said. "But where in the flames of hell did you find all these riches? Tell me that," he said to his brother.

"Behind the door," said the man who owned the hand mill. He didn't bother to give any sort of accounting for what had happened, no he didn't. But later that evening, after he'd had something to eat and drink, he couldn't resist, and he brought out the mill.

"Here you can see what has given me all these riches!" he said. Then he told the mill to start grinding, and it produced one thing after another.

When his brother saw this, he dearly wanted to have that mill. And at long last, he got it, though he had to pay three hundred *daler*. In return, he'd be allowed to have the mill when it was haymaking season.

If I can have it then, he thought, I'll be able to get it to grind food for many years to come.

As you might well imagine, in all that time the hand mill did not gather rust. And when the haymaking season arrived, the man gave the mill to his brother, though he was careful not to tell him how to use it.

It was in the evening when the rich brother took the mill home. The next morning he told his wife to go out with the farm folks to gather in the hay. "I'll make the midmorning meal today," he said.

When the mealtime approached, he set the hand mill on the kitchen table. "Grind for me herring and gruel. Do it fast and well!" said the man.

And the mill began making so much herring and gruel that all the dishes and troughs were quickly full. Soon there was enough to cover the entire kitchen floor.

The man fumbled and fiddled with the mill to make it stop, but no matter how he turned and twisted it, the mill kept on grinding. Soon the gruel reached so high that the man was about to drown. Then he tore open the door to the living room, but it didn't take long before the mill had made enough food to fill that room too. Only with the greatest effort was the man able to reach down into the flood of gruel to get to the front door latch. When he got the door open, he didn't stay long in the house. He set off, with the herring and gruel gushing out right behind him, across the yard and the fields.

By now his wife, who was out spreading hay, thought it was taking a long time for their midmorning meal to be ready. "Even though my husband hasn't called us home, let's go. He doesn't know much about making gruel, so I suppose I'll have to help him," the woman said to the haying folks.

Then they started heading for home. After they'd gone a short distance up the hills, they saw a flood of herring and gruel and bread come sloshing toward them. The farmer himself was at the front of the torrent.

"I wish to God that each of you had a hundred wooden lunch boxes! Be careful you don't drown in the gruel!" shouted the farmer. He raced past them as if the Evil One were on his heels and headed for the place where his brother lived.

There he begged his brother, for God's sake, to take back the hand mill, and do it at once. "If it keeps grinding for another hour, the whole countryside will perish under this flood of herring and gruel," he said.

His brother refused to take the mill back unless he was paid another three hundred *daler*. So his brother had to pay him.

Now the brother who used to be poor had both money and the mill. It didn't take long before he'd fixed up his farm, and it was much more splendid than the one his brother owned. He made the mill grind for him so much gold that he could clad the buildings with gold plate. The farm stood close to the shore, so it could be seen gleaming and glittering from far out at sea.

Everyone who sailed past wanted to come ashore to visit the rich man who lived on the golden farm. And everyone wanted to see the wondrous hand mill, for news of the mill had spread far and wide. By now there wasn't a soul who hadn't heard of it.

At long last a ship's captain appeared. He wanted to see the mill, and he asked whether it could grind salt.

"Oh yes, of course it can grind salt," said the man who owned the mill.

When the ship's captain heard this, he dearly wanted to have that mill, cost what it might. He thought that if he owned such a mill, he wouldn't have to sail far away through dangerous waters to fill his cargo hold with salt.

At first the man didn't want give up the mill, but the ship's captain begged and pleaded. Finally, he agreed to sell the mill, and he was paid many, many thousands of *daler* for it.

As soon as the ship's captain hoisted the mill onto his back, he left at once, for he was afraid the man might change his mind. And there was no time to find out how to use the mill before he headed for his ship, moving as fast as he could go.

When they'd sailed a good distance out to sea, the captain got out the hand mill. "Grind salt, and do it fast and well!" he said.

Then the mill began grinding salt so fast that it sprayed everywhere. When the cargo hold was full, the captain wanted the mill to stop. But no matter what he did or how hard he tried, the mill just kept grinding as fast as ever. The salt heap grew taller and taller, until finally the ship sank.

There at the bottom of the sea the mill stands today, grinding day in and day out. And that's why the sea is salty.

The Maiden on the
Glass Mountain

There once was a man who had a hay meadow somewhere high up on the mountain slope. In that meadow was a hay barn where he stored fodder, though I don't imagine there had been much of anything in that barn for several years. Every Midsummer Eve, when the grass was most splendid and lush, the hay meadow would end up grazed bare, as if a whole herd had gnawed at the grass all night.

It happened once, and it happened twice. By then the man was quite dismayed about this. He told his sons—he had three, and the youngest was Ash Lad, as you might well know—that one of them would have to sleep in the hay barn on Midsummer Eve. This couldn't go on. During the past two years the grass had been eaten away clear down to the nub. Whoever agreed to go would have to pay careful attention, the man said.

Well, the eldest boy wanted to go up to tend to the meadow. He said he would keep a close eye on the grass so that neither folks nor livestock nor the Devil himself would get any of it.

As evening approached, the boy went into the barn and lay down to sleep. In the middle of the night there was such a roaring and such an earthquake that the walls and roof shook. The boy jumped up and took off as fast as he knew how. He didn't dare even look back. And that night the hay was eaten up, just as it was the two years before.

On the next Midsummer Eve, the man again said that this couldn't go on. Year after year they were losing all the grass in the outlying meadow. One of his sons would have to go up there and keep watch, keep a very close eye. The second eldest son wanted to try that evening.

He went into the hay barn and lay down to sleep, just as his brother had done. But in the middle of the night, there was a loud roaring and a great earthquake, even worse than on the last Midsummer Eve. When the boy heard this, he was so frightened that he took off as fast as if he were being paid to run.

The next year it was Ash Lad's turn. When he got ready to leave, his two brothers laughed and made fun of him. "Oh, you're certainly the right person to keep watch over the hay. You've learned nothing but how to sit by the fire in the evening and warm yourself," they said.

Ash Lad paid no mind to what they said. As evening approached, he wandered up to the hay meadow, that he did. There he went into the hay barn and lay down. After a while, there was a great roaring and crashing that was vile to hear.

Oh, if that's as bad as it gets, I suppose I can stand it, thought Ash Lad.

After a while there was another crash and an earthquake that made the straw fly all around the boy.

Oh, if that's as bad as it gets, I suppose I can stand it, thought Ash Lad.

The next moment there was more roaring and such an earthquake that the boy thought the walls and roof were going to collapse. But the sound passed, and then it was utterly quiet.

I wonder if it's going to happen again, thought Ash Lad.

But no, it didn't. It was quiet, and quiet it stayed. After he'd lain there for a while, he heard a sound as if a horse was chewing just outside the barn door.

The boy crept over to take a look through the door that stood open just a crack. There he saw a horse grazing. The horse was big and sturdy and splendid. Ash Lad had never seen such a horse before. The horse wore a saddle and bridle and carried full armor for a knight. All the items were made of copper and so shiny that they gleamed.

Aha! So you're the one who has been eating our grass, thought the boy. I'll soon put a stop to that!

He hurried to get his firesteel and tossed it over the horse. Then the animal was powerless to move. It grew so docile that the boy could do with it whatever he liked. He climbed on the horse's back and took it to a secret place. That's where he left it.

When he went back home, his brothers laughed and asked him how things had gone.

"You didn't stay long in the hay barn, did you? Or maybe you never even made it as far as the hay meadow," they said.

"I stayed in the hay barn until the sun came up, but I didn't hear or see a thing, no I didn't," said the boy. "God only knows what it was that frightened both of you so badly."

"Oh, we'll soon see how well you kept watch over the meadow," replied his brothers.

But when they went up to the meadow, the grass was just as tall and thick as it had been the night before.

On the next Midsummer Eve, the same thing happened. Neither of the two older brothers dared go up to the outlying meadow to keep watch over the grass. But Ash Lad said he would go.

Then the exact same thing happened as on the last Midsummer Eve. First there was a roaring and an earthquake. After a moment another, and then yet another. But this time all three earthquakes were much, much stronger than before. Then suddenly it was utterly quiet, and the boy heard something chewing outside the barn door. Moving as silently as he could, he crept over to the door opening.

Oh yes! There stood a horse right next to the wall, munching and gnawing. This one was even bigger and sturdier than the first one. This horse had a saddle too and a bridle and full armor for a knight. All of the items were made of shiny silver and as magnificent as anyone could imagine.

Aha! So you're the one who has been eating our hay in the night, thought the boy. I'll soon put a stop to that!

He picked up his firesteel and tossed it over the horse's mane. Then the animal stood there as meek as a lamb. The boy rode that horse over to the place where he'd left the other one, and then he went back home.

"We suppose it looks lovely up in the hay meadow today," said his brothers.

"Yes, I suppose it does," said Ash Lad.

They headed up there again. The grass was just as thick and tall as before, but that didn't make them any kinder toward Ash Lad.

When the third Midsummer Eve arrived, neither of the two older brothers dared stay in the barn in the outlying meadow to watch over the grass. They'd been so terrified on the night they'd spent there that they would never forget it. But Ash Lad certainly dared to go.

The exact same thing happened again. There were three earthquakes, each more vile than the one before. The last one made the boy dance from one wall of the barn to the other, but then it was utterly quiet.

After he'd lain there for a little while, he heard something chewing outside the barn door. Again he crept over to the door opening. There stood a horse close by. It was much, much bigger and sturdier than the other two he'd already caught.

Aha! So you're the one who has been eating our grass this time, thought the boy. I'll soon put a stop to that!

He grabbed his firesteel and tossed it over the horse. Then the animal stood there as if nailed to the ground, and the boy could do with it whatever he liked. He rode the horse over to the place where he'd left the other two horses. Then he walked back home.

His brothers made fun of him, just as they'd done before. They joked that he must have done a good job watching over the grass in the night, for he looked as if he was still asleep. But Ash Lad paid no mind to what they said. He merely invited them to go and see. And they did. Again the grass stood just as splendid and thick as before.

In the land where Ash Lad's father lived, the king had a daughter, and he decreed that he would give her only to someone who could ride up the glass mountain. This was a tall, tall glass mountain, as shiny as ice, that stood close to the royal palace. At the very top the king's daughter would sit with three golden apples on her lap. Whoever could ride up there and take the golden apples would have the princess and half the kingdom. The king sent word of this to all the churches in the realm and in many other kingdoms as well.

The princess was so lovely that everyone who saw her fell in love with her at once, whether they wanted to or not. And as you might well imagine, all the princes and knights wanted to win her and half the kingdom. They came riding from all corners of the world. They looked so splendid that they practically gleamed, and the horses they rode looked as if they were prancing. Every single man thought he would win the princess.

When the day arrived, as decided by the king, the area near the glass mountain was swarming with big crowds of knights and princes. Anyone who could crawl or walk wanted to be there to see who would win the king's daughter.

Ash Lad's two brothers were also about to set off, but they didn't want to take him along. They said that folks would make fun of them if they were seen in the company of such a changeling, so vile and filthy did he look after digging in the ashes all night.

"I can just as well stay here. I don't mind being on my own, no I don't," said Ash Lad.

By the time the two older brothers arrived at the glass mountain, all the princes and knights had set off at a gallop, making lather fly from their horses. But it did little good, let me tell you, for the instant the horses set their hooves on the mountain, they slid back. Not one of them could make it more than a few feet up the slope. And that was no wonder, for the mountain was as slippery as a glass windowpane and as steep as the wall of a house.

Yet everyone wanted to win the king's daughter and half the kingdom, so they kept on riding and sliding, but nothing more came of it. Finally all the horses were so worn out that they couldn't make any more attempts. They were sweating so much that the lather poured off them. Then the knights had to give up.

The king wondered whether he should make it known that the riding would begin again the next day. Maybe then things would go better. But all of a sudden a knight appeared, riding a horse so splendid that no one had ever seen such a horse before. And the knight's copper armor and copper bridle shone so bright that they gleamed.

The others shouted that he might as well save himself the trouble of trying to ride up the glass mountain, for it would do no good. But the knight paid no mind to what they said. He rode straight toward the glass mountain and then headed upward, as if it were nothing. He made it a good distance up, it might have been a third of the way. When he reached that point, he turned his horse around and rode back down.

The princess thought she'd never seen such a lovely knight. While he was riding, she thought: May God let him make it up here! When she saw him turn his horse around, she threw one of the golden apples after him, and it rolled into his shoe.

No sooner had the knight come down the mountain than he rode off, moving so fast that no one knew where he went.

That evening all the princes and knights were summoned to appear before the king. The one who had ridden the farthest up the glass mountain was supposed to present the golden apple that the princess had tossed to him. But none of them had anything to show the king. One after another they stepped forward, but no one could present the apple.

That evening when the two brothers returned, they found Ash Lad at home. His brothers talked at great length about the riding attempts that had been made up the glass mountain. At first no one had managed to get even a few paces up the slope. "But then a knight arrived with copper armor and a copper bridle so shiny that it could be seen gleaming from far away," they said. "And that fellow could certainly ride. He rode a third of the way up the glass mountain, and he could easily have gone to the top if he'd wanted to. But at that point he turned around. He probably thought that was far enough that time."

"Oh, I would have found it so amusing to see that knight, yes, I would," said Ash Lad. He was sitting next to the fireplace, digging in the ashes as he usually did.

"You!" said his brothers. "The likes of you would never be welcome among such highborn gentlemen! What a hideous creature you are, sitting there!"

The next day the two older brothers were about to set off once more. Again Ash Lad asked to go with them so he could watch them ride. But no, they refused to allow it. They said he was too hideous and too vile.

"I can just as well stay here. I don't mind being on my own, no I don't," said Ash Lad.

By the time the two brothers arrived at the glass mountain, all the princes and knights had already set off riding again. Some had even had their horses newly shod. But it did no good. They were riding and sliding, just like the day before. None of them managed to get more than a few feet up the slope. When all of them had worn out their horses until they could do no more, they had to stop.

Then the king wondered whether he should make it known that the riding would continue for the last time on the following day. Maybe then things would go better. But he changed his mind. He thought he would wait a little while to see whether the copper knight might show up again.

There was no sign of the knight. But all of a sudden a knight appeared riding a horse that was much, much more splendid than the one the knight in copper armor had ridden. This man had silver armor and a silver saddle and bridle, all of them so shiny that they could be seen gleaming and glittering from far away.

Again the others shouted to him. They told him he might as well save himself the trouble of trying to ride up the glass mountain, for it would do no good.

The knight paid no mind to what they said. He rode right over to the glass mountain and then went up even higher than the knight in copper armor. But when he was two-thirds of the way up, he turned his horse around and rode back down.

The princess liked this knight even better than first one. She sat there wishing that he would ride to the top. When she saw him turn around, she tossed the second apple after him, and it rolled down into his shoe.

As soon as the knight reached the bottom of the glass mountain, he rode off so fast that no one could see where he went.

That evening everyone was summoned to appear before the king and the princess. Whoever had the golden apple was supposed to present it. One after the other the men stepped forward, but none of them had the golden apple.

Just as on the previous day, the two brothers went home that evening and talked about what had happened, about everyone who had tried to ride up the mountain but failed. "Then at long last a knight appeared with silver armor, and he had a silver bridle and saddle too," they said. "And he certainly could ride. He made it at least two-thirds of the way up, but then he turned around. That was some fellow! And the princess tossed him the second golden apple," said the brothers.

"Oh, I would have found it so amusing to see that knight," said Ash Lad.

"Well, he was certainly shinier than the ashes you're sitting there digging in, you hideous, filthy creature!" said his brothers.

On the third day everything went exactly as it had before. Ash Lad wanted to go along to watch the riding, but his brothers refused to take him. When they got to the glass mountain, no one was able to ride even two feet up the slope.

Everyone was now waiting for the knight in the silver armor, but he wasn't to be seen or heard. At long last a knight appeared riding a horse so splendid that nobody had ever seen the likes of such a steed. The man wore golden armor, and he had a golden saddle and golden bridle that were so shiny, so shiny. They could be seen glittering and gleaming from far away.

The other knights and princes didn't even manage to shout that it would do no good to try to ride up the mountain, so astonished were they to see such a splendid knight.

He rode right over to the glass mountain and raced up the slope as if it were nothing. The princess didn't even have time to wish that he might make it all the way up. The moment the knight reached the top, he grabbed the third golden apple from the lap of the princess. Then he turned his horse around and rode back down. The next second, before anyone knew it, he had vanished from sight.

When the two brothers returned home that evening, they talked at great length about how the riding had gone that day. Finally they also mentioned the knight in the golden armor.

"That was certainly some fellow! Another knight as splendid as that can't be found in all the world!" said the brothers.

"Oh, I too would have found it so amusing to see that knight," said Ash Lad.

"Well, he gleamed far more brightly than that bed of embers you're sitting there digging in, you hideous, filthy creature!" said his brothers.

The next day all the knights and princes were to appear before the king and the king's daughter—I think it had grown too late the night before. The one who had the golden apple was supposed to present it. One after another, the men stepped forward, first the princes and then the knights, but none of them had the golden apple.

"One of them must have it," said the king, "for we all saw someone ride up the mountain and grab the apple."

Then he decreed that everyone in the whole kingdom should come up to the castle and try to present the apple. Well, come they did, one after another, but no one had the golden apple.

Finally, Ash Lad's two brothers also appeared. They were the very last ones. Then the king asked them whether it was true that there was no one else in the realm.

"Well, we do have a brother," they said. "But he certainly didn't take the golden apple. He hasn't been away from his heap of ashes on any of these past days."

"Oh, that's neither here nor there," said the king. "Everyone else has come to the castle, so he must come here too."

Then Ash Lad had to go to the royal palace.

"Do you have the golden apple? Do you?" asked the king.

"Yes. Here's the first one, here's the second one, and here's the third one too," said Ash Lad. He took out of his pocket all three golden apples. Then he cast off his soot-covered rags. There he stood in his golden armor, looking so splendid that he gleamed.

"Then you shall have my daughter and half the kingdom. You have certainly earned both," said the king.

And so they were wed. Ash Lad married the king's daughter, and their wedding was joyously celebrated, for everyone knew how to celebrate even if they couldn't ride up the glass mountain. And if they haven't stopped celebrating, then they're still celebrating today.

Butterball

There once was a woman who was baking. She had a little boy who was so chubby and plump, and he was always asking for good food. That's why she called him Butterball. She also had a dog they called Goldtooth. All of a sudden the dog began barking.

"Run outside, my Butterball," said the woman, "and find out who Goldtooth is barking at."

The boy ran outside. When he came back, he said, "Oh, God save me, there's a big, tall troll woman coming here. She has her head under one arm and a sack on her back."

"Hurry up and hide under the baking table," said his mother.

Then the big troll came in.

"Good day!" she said.

"God bless you!" said the mother of Butterball.

"Isn't Butterball home today?" asked the troll.

"No, he's in the forest with his father, hunting grouse," replied the woman.

"Blast it!" said the troll woman. "I have such a nice little silver knife that I want to give him."

"Hey! Here I am!" said Butterball from under the baking table. Then he came out.

"I'm so old and my back is so stiff," said the troll. "You'll have to slip inside my sack and get the knife yourself."

When Butterball climbed into the sack, the troll flung it over her shoulder and dashed out.

After they'd gone a good distance along the road, the troll grew tired and said, "How far is it until we find somewhere to sleep?"

"Half a mile," replied Butterball.

The troll put down the sack next to the road. Then she went over to a small grove of trees and lay down to sleep.

In the meantime, Butterball picked up the knife and cut open the sack. Then he slipped out, put a big pine root in his place, and hurried home to his mother.

When the troll got home and saw what was in the sack, she was terribly angry.

The next day the woman was again baking. All of a sudden the dog began barking. "Run outside, my Butterball," she said, "and find out what Goldtooth is barking at."

"Oh no, oh no, it's that horrible creature!" said Butterball. "She's back again, with her head under one arm and a big sack on her back."

"Hurry up and hide under the baking table," said his mother.

"Good day!" said the troll. "Is Butterball home today?"

"No, he's not," said his mother. "He's out in the forest with his father, hunting grouse."

"Blast it!" said the troll woman. "I have a lovely little fork that I want to give him."

"Hey! Here I am!" said Butterball, and he came out.

"My back is so stiff," said the troll. "You'll have to slip inside the sack and get the fork yourself."

When Butterball was inside the sack, the troll flung it over her shoulder and took off.

After they'd gone a good distance along the road, the troll grew tired and asked, "How far is it until we find somewhere to sleep?"

"Three miles," replied Butterball.

The troll set her sack down next to road. Then she went into the forest and lay down to sleep.

While the troll was doing that, Butterball made a hole in the sack and climbed out. Then he put a big rock in his place.

When the troll got home, she made a big fire in the fireplace and set a big kettle over the flames so she could boil Butterball. Then she picked up the sack. She was going to slide Butterball into the kettle, but the rock fell out instead and knocked a hole in the bottom. Then all the water in the kettle ran out and doused the fire. The troll grew angry and said, "No matter how heavy he makes himself, I'm going to get him."

The third time the exact same thing happened as twice before. Goldtooth began barking, and then Butterball's mother said to her son, "Run outside, my Butterball, and find out who Goldtooth is barking at."

So Butterball ran outside. When he came back in, he said, "Oh, God save and preserve me! It's that troll woman again. She has her head under one arm and a sack on her back."

"Hurry up and hide under the baking table," said his mother.

"Good day!" said the troll as she came through the door. "Is Butterball home today?"

"No, he's not," said his mother. "He's out in the forest with his father, hunting grouse."

"Blast it!" said the troll woman. "I have a lovely little silver spoon that I want to give him."

"Hey! Here I am!" said Butterball, and he came out from under the baking table.

"My back is so stiff," said the troll woman. "You'll have to slip inside the sack and get the spoon yourself."

When Butterball climbed inside the sack, the troll flung it over her shoulder and took off.

This time the troll didn't go off by herself to sleep. Instead she went straight home with Butterball inside the sack. When they got there, it was a Sunday.

The troll woman said to her daughter, "Take Butterball out of the sack and slaughter him. Then cook him in soup until I get back. I'm heading for the church to invite guests to dinner."

After the servants had left too, the daughter took Butterball out to slaughter him, though she didn't really know how to go about it.

"Wait a minute, and I'll show you what you're supposed to do. Yes, I will," said Butterball. "Lay your head down on the stool, and I'll show you."

That's what she did, the poor thing.

Butterball picked up an axe and chopped off her head as if she were a chicken. Then he put her head in the bed and her carcass in the pot to make soup from the troll's daughter. After he'd done that, he went out and clambered out onto the roof, taking along the pine root and the rock. He placed one above the door and the other on the troll woman's chimney.

When everyone came back from church and saw the head in the bed, they thought the daughter lay there sleeping. Then they went over to taste the soup.

"Should taste good—Butterball soup!" said the troll woman.

"Should taste good—daughter soup!" said Butterball. But no one paid him any mind.

Then the troll woman picked up a spoon to have a taste.

"Should taste good—Butterball soup!" she said.

"Should taste good—daughter soup!" said Butterball from the chimney.

By now everyone had begun to wonder who was talking, so they decided to go outside and find out. As they came out the door, Butterball threw the pine root and the rock at their heads and killed them dead.

He took all the gold and silver he could find in the house, and with that he was certainly rich. Then he went home to his mother.

Big Per and Little Per

There once were two brothers, and both were named Per, so they called the older one Big Per and the younger one Little Per.

When their father died, Big Per inherited the farm and married a woman who had a great deal of money. Little Per stayed at home with his mother. Until he came of age, he lived off the pension she was given when the farm passed to the older son.

When Little Per came of age, he received his inheritance. Then Big Per said that his brother could no longer stay on the farm, living off his mother's pension. It would be better if he went out into the world to find work.

Little Per thought that wasn't such a bad idea. He bought himself a fine horse and filled a wagon with meat, butter, and cheese. Then he headed for town. There he sold everything and used the money to buy liquor and spirits.

No sooner did he get home than he invited folks over to share what he had brought back. He poured and served drinks for neighbors and kin, and they poured and served drinks for him in turn.

He lived it up for as long as the money lasted. But when the *skillinger* were gone and Little Per's purse was empty, he went back home to his old mother. By then he owned nothing more than a calf.

When spring arrived, he let the calf out to graze in the meadow that belonged to Big Per. Then Big Per got mad and killed the calf.

Little Per flayed the hide off the calf and hung it in the bathhouse until it was properly dry. Then he rolled it up, stuffed it in a sack, and headed out to sell it. But wherever he went, folks just laughed at him and said they had no use for a dried calf hide.

After he had walked a long way, he came to another farm. There he went inside to ask for lodging for the night.

"No, I can't very well offer you lodging," said the woman. "My husband is up in the mountain pasture, and I'm home alone. You'll have to ask for lodging at the neighboring farm. But if they won't take you in, you're welcome to come back. You shouldn't be without a place to stay."

As Per went past the alcove window, he saw a pastor sitting inside the room. The woman seemed to be keeping company with him. She set ale and liquor on the table along with a big pot of sour cream porridge.

The pastor sat down at the table to eat and drink, but then the man of the house came home. When the woman heard her husband on the porch, she quickly picked up the porridge pot and set it behind the stone hearth guard. She put the ale and the liquor in the cellar, and she stuffed the pastor into a big chest that stood nearby.

All this Little Per saw from outside. After the husband had gone in, he followed and asked if he might find lodging for the night.

"Yes," said the husband. "We will give you lodging." Then he invited Per to sit down at the table and have something to eat.

Little Per sat down at the table. He'd brought along the calf hide, and now he placed it at his feet.

After they had been sitting there for a while, Little Per started stepping on the hide.

"What are you saying now? Can't you keep still?" said Little Per.

"Who are you talking to?" asked the husband.

"Oh, it's just a maiden soothsayer inside this calf hide of mine," said Per.

"What is she telling you?" said the husband.

"She says there's plenty of sour cream porridge behind the hearth guard," said Little Per.

"She's not much of a soothsayer. There hasn't been any sour cream porridge in this house for a year and a day," said the husband.

Per told him to take a look.

So that's what he did. And there he found the pot of sour cream porridge.

They began helping themselves. As they sat there, Per again stepped on the calf hide.

"Shush!" he said. "Can't you keep your mouth shut?"

"What is your soothsayer telling you now?" said the husband.

"She says there's plenty of ale and liquor under the cellar steps," replied Per.

"She may never have spoken falsely before, but that's what she's doing now," said the husband. "Ale and liquor? I can't remember ever having anything like that in the house."

"Take a look!" said Per.

That's what the husband did. And true enough, he found both ale and liquor. The man was overjoyed.

"What did you pay for that soothsayer of yours? I must have her, no matter what you want in payment," said the husband.

"I inherited her from my father's estate, so she didn't cost me much," said Per. "To be honest, I don't really want to part with her. But that's neither here nor there. If you let me have the old chest standing in the alcove, I'll let you have the soothsayer."

"The key to the chest is missing!" cried the woman.

"Oh, I'll take the chest without the key," said Per.

Then he and the husband quickly agreed on the trade. Per got a rope instead of the key, and the husband helped him to hoist the chest onto his back. With that, he set off.

After Per had walked a good distance, he came to a bridge. Underneath rushed a river so fierce that it frothed and foamed. And it roared so loudly that the whole bridge shook.

"Oh, so much liquor, so much liquor!" said Per. "I can tell I've been drinking more and more. Why should I keep lugging this chest with me? If I hadn't been drunk and foolish, I would never have traded it for my soothsayer. I'm just going to dump this chest in the river, right here on the spot!" And he began to untie the rope.

"Wait! Wait! Save me, for God's sake! It's the parish pastor you have here in this chest!" cried the man from inside.

"It must be the Devil himself who's trying to make me think he's a pastor," said Per. "But whether he pretends to be a pastor or a parish clerk, he's going into the river."

"Oh no! Oh no! I really am the parish pastor. I was carrying out my clergyman duties and paying a visit to that woman. Her husband is a brutish and crazy man. That's why she had to hide me inside the chest. I'm wearing both a silver watch and a gold watch. I'll give both of them to you, along with eight hundred *daler*. Just let me out of here!" shouted the pastor.

"Oh my! Is that really you, Pastor?" said Per. He picked up a rock and smashed open the lid of the chest to let the pastor out.

The man set off at once for the parsonage. He moved swiftly and easily, for he no longer had the watches or the money to weigh him down.

When Little Per went back home, he told Big Per, "Calf hides are certainly worth a lot at the marketplace right now!"

"What did you get for your calf hide?" asked Big Per.

"No less than it was worth. I got eight hundred *daler*. But for bigger and fatter calves, the hides are worth double that amount," said Little Per. He showed his brother the money.

"Good you told me that," said Big Per.

He killed all the calves and cows that he owned. Then he set off for town with the skins and hides. When he got to the marketplace and the tanners asked him the price of the hides, Big Per said, "Eight hundred for the small ones, and twice that for the big ones."

But everyone just laughed and made fun of him. They said there was no need for him to behave in that way. He could slip inside the madhouse for much less than that. Then Big Per understood what had happened and how he'd been fooled.

When he got back home, he was in a foul temper. He cursed and swore that he would kill his brother that very night. Little Per heard what he was saying.

When it was getting late, Little Per climbed into the bed that he shared with their mother. After a while he asked her to change places with him. He said he was freezing, and her spot next to the wall was much warmer than his. She agreed to change places.

A short time later Big Per came in carrying an axe and crept over to the bed. With one blow he chopped off their mother's head.

In the morning Little Per went into the living room to find Big Per.

"God save and preserve me! Someone has killed our mother!" he said. "The sheriff probably won't be pleased about how you got back the pension you've been paying Mother."

Then Big Per was frightened. He told Little Per, for God's sake, not to tell anyone what he knew. If he would keep quiet, he would get eight hundred *daler*.

Little Per took the money. Then he set their mother's head back on her body, put her in a sled, and set off for the marketplace. There he hung a basket of apples on each of her arms, and he put an apple in each of her hands.

A ship's captain came over, for he thought she was a market woman. He asked if she had apples for sale and how many he could buy for a *skilling*. But the old woman didn't reply.

The captain asked her again. She didn't reply.

"How many can I buy for a *skilling*?" he shouted for the third time. But the woman just sat there as if she didn't hear or see him.

The captain grew so angry that he struck her under her ear. Then her head fell off and rolled across the marketplace.

At that instant, Little Per came running. He wept and carried on and threatened to bring great misfortune on the captain, for the man had killed his old mother.

"My dear sir, if you don't tell anyone what you know, I'll give you eight hundred *daler*," said the captain. And that's what they agreed on.

When Little Per got back home, he told Big Per, "Old women are certainly worth a great deal at the marketplace today! I got eight hundred *daler* for our mother." And he showed his brother the money.

"That's good to know," said Big Per.

He had an old mother-in-law, so he killed her at once. Then he set off to sell her. But when folks heard that he was offering dead people for sale, they reported him to the sheriff. And it was only by the skin of his teeth that he escaped arrest.

When Big Per got back, he was so angry and enraged that he threatened to kill Little Per on the spot. There was no need to wait.

"Yes, well, we're all headed down that same path," said Little Per. "And there's only night between today and tomorrow. But if I'm about to leave this life right now, I have one request. Put me in the sack hanging up over there and carry me to the river."

Big Per didn't refuse. He stuffed his brother in the sack and set off. But no sooner had he gone a short distance than he remembered something he had forgotten. He had to go back to get it. In the meantime he set the sack down next to the road.

A man happened to come past, herding a splendid flock of sheep.

"To heaven, to paradise! To heaven, to paradise!" shouted Little Per from inside the sack. He kept on chanting and calling those words.

"Could I be allowed to go there too?" said the man with the flock of sheep.

"Yes, just untie the cord on the sack and climb in. Then you can take my place and go there yourself," said Little Per. "I'll gladly wait until another time. Yes, I will. But you'll have to shout the same words I'm saying, or else you won't end up in the right place."

The man untied the cord on the sack and got in to take Little Per's place. Per retied the cord.

Then the man began shouting, "To heaven, to paradise! To heaven, to paradise!" And he kept on chanting the same words.

After Per put the man inside the sack, he wasted no time. He hurried off with the flock of sheep, rushing at a good pace down the road.

In the meantime, Big Per returned. He hoisted the sack over his shoulder and carried it to the river. The whole time the sheep farmer inside the sack shouted, "To heaven! To paradise!"

"Yes, well, go ahead and see if you can find the way there," said Big Per. And he threw the sack in the river.

After that, Big Per headed for home. Along the way he met his brother, who was herding a big flock of sheep. Big Per was very surprised. He asked Little Per how he had managed to get out of the river and where he had found such a splendid flock of sheep.

"You certainly did me a brotherly service by throwing me in the river," replied Little Per. "I sank like a rock straight to the bottom, and there I saw so many flocks of sheep, let me tell you. Thousands of sheep are down there, each flock bigger than the next. And as you can see: sheep for shearing!" said Per.

"Good you told me that," said Big Per.

He rushed home to get his wife and then took her to the river. There he crawled into a sack. He told her to hurry up and tie the cord and then throw him off the bridge.

"I'm going to get a flock of sheep. But if I stay too long and you see that I can't manage the flock on my own, then jump in after me and help out," said Big Per.

"Well, don't take too long, for I'm yearning to see those sheep," said his wife.

She stood there and waited for a while. Then she thought to herself that her husband wouldn't be able to manage rounding up a flock of sheep. So she jumped in after him.

And with that, Little Per was rid of them both. He inherited the farm and land, the horses and tools. And he had enough money of his own to buy himself a yoke of oxen.

Ragged Cap

here once was a king and a queen who had no children. The queen was so distressed by this that she hardly had even an hour of joy. She was always complaining that it was too lonely and quiet in the royal palace.

"If only we had children, I'm sure things would be livelier," she said.

No matter where she traveled in her kingdom, she found that God had blessed everyone with children, even in the most wretched of hovels. And wherever she went, she would hear the women of the house scolding their children and saying that now they'd done something bad again, whatever it might be. The queen found that amusing, and she yearned to do the same.

Finally the king and queen took in a little girl, a stranger. They decided to raise her at the royal palace, and they would scold her as if she were their own.

One day the little maiden was running around in the courtyard in front of the castle. She was playing with a golden apple. Then a poor beggar woman appeared. She had a little girl with her, and it didn't take long before the girl and the little maiden became friends. They began playing together, rolling the golden apple back and forth.

The queen was sitting at a window in the castle, and she saw the children playing. She tapped on the window as a signal to her foster daughter to come inside. The maiden obeyed, but the beggar girl went with her. The two of them were holding hands when they stepped into the hall to see the queen.

The queen scolded the little maiden. "You mustn't run around playing with a ragged beggar girl," she said. She wanted to chase the girl back outside.

"If the queen knew what my mother can do, she wouldn't chase me away," said the little girl. When the queen asked her what she meant, the child said that her mother could get the queen a child of her own.

The queen didn't believe her, but the beggar girl held her ground. She said every word of it was true. The queen should ask her mother. So the queen told the little girl to go and get her mother.

"Do you know what your daughter has been saying?" the queen asked the woman when she came in.

No, the beggar woman didn't know.

"She said that if you wanted to, you could get me a child," said the queen.

"The queen should pay no attention to what a beggar child might say," said the woman, and she dashed out of the room.

The queen grew angry and once again tried to chase the little girl out. But she insisted that every word she'd said was true.

"The queen should serve my mother enough drink to make her merry. Then she'll find out what needs to be done," said the girl.

The queen decided to try it. The beggar woman was brought back inside the castle. There she was served both wine and mead, as much as she liked. And it didn't take long before the drink loosened her tongue.

Then the queen again asked her the question.

"I suppose I do know a way," said the beggar woman. "The queen should have two basins of water brought in one evening before bedtime. She should wash herself with the water and then shove the basins under her bed. When she looks under there in the morning, she will see that two flowers have sprouted. One will be beautiful, the other hideous. Eat the beautiful flower but don't touch the hideous one. Don't forget that part," said the beggar woman.

The queen did what the woman had told her to do. She had water brought up in two basins. She washed herself with the water and then shoved the basins under her bed. When she looked underneath in the morning, she saw two flowers. One of them was hideous and vile with black petals. The other was brighter and lovelier than any she had ever seen before. She ate it at once.

But the beautiful flower tasted so good that she couldn't help herself. She ate the other flower too. Surely it won't make any difference, she thought.

After a time the queen took to her bed to give birth. First she gave birth to a little girl who was holding a ladle in her hand and riding a goat. Hideous and vile was she. The moment she came into the world, she shouted, "Mamma!"

"If I'm your mamma, may God save and preserve me!" said the queen.

"Don't worry, another child will soon appear who is much more beautiful," said the girl on the goat.

A short time later the queen gave birth to another little girl. This one was so beautiful and fair that nobody had ever seen a lovelier child. And the queen was happy with her, as you might well imagine.

The older girl they called Ragged Cap, for she was so vile and ragged, and on her head she wore a cap that hung in tatters. The queen had no desire even to look at her, so the maids tried to lock the child in another room. But it did no good. The older girl wanted to be wherever her younger sister was, and they could not be kept apart.

On Christmas Eve, when they were both half-grown, there was a great noise and commotion on the porch outside the queen's room. Ragged Cap wanted to know what could be banging around and making such a racket outdoors.

"Oh, it's never worth wondering about such things," said the queen.

But Ragged Cap refused to give up. She wanted to know what it was. So the queen told her that the troll women were out there playing Christmas games.

Ragged Cap said she'd go out and chase them away. And no matter how much they begged her not to go, she said that she would and she must chase the troll women away. But she told the queen to keep all the doors closed tight so that not one of them was open even the slightest crack.

Then Ragged Cap took her ladle and went out to chase and shoo away the troll women. Out on the porch a great commotion arose, the likes of which you have never heard. There was a creaking and crashing, as if the timbers were about to fly apart.

It's not certain how it happened, but one of the doors was standing open just a crack. The younger sister wanted to take a peek and see how things were going for Ragged Cap. So she stuck her head out the door.

Whoosh! A troll woman came over and snapped off the girl's head. Then she put a calf's head in its place. The princess instantly began mooing as she walked around the room.

When Ragged Cap came back inside and caught sight of her sister, she fumed and scolded, for they hadn't taken proper care of the girl. She asked everyone if they thought things were better now that her sister was a calf.

"I'll just have to see about rescuing her," said Ragged Cap. She demanded from the king a ship that was well equipped and ready to sail. But she didn't want either a helmsman or a crew. She wanted to set sail with only her sister. And finally that's what they had to let her do.

Ragged Cap sailed off, heading straight for the land where the troll women lived. When she came to the dock, she told her sister to stay on board the ship and keep very quiet. In the meantime, Ragged Cap rode her goat up to the troll women's castle.

When she arrived, she found one of the windows open. There she saw her sister's head lying on the windowsill. She galloped at full speed onto the porch and snatched up the head. Then she took off.

The troll women chased after her, for they wanted to get back the girl's head. They crowded around Ragged Cap, swarming and jostling, but the goat kicked his legs and butted his horns. The girl swung and struck with her ladle. At last the throng of troll women had to give up.

When Ragged Cap got back to the ship, she took the calf's head off her sister and put the girl's head back in its place. And her sister was human again.

Then they sailed far, far away to an unknown kingdom. The king of that realm was a widower and had only one son.

When he caught sight of the strange ship, he sent messengers down to the shore to find out where the ship was from and who owned it. But when the king's servants reached the shore, the only living soul they found on board was Ragged Cap. She was riding her goat back and forth on deck. She moved so fast that her hair flew in all directions.

The servants from the royal palace were quite astonished by what they saw. They asked her if there were others on board.

Ragged Cap said that her sister was there too. The servants wanted to see her, but Ragged Cap said no. "You will see her only if the king comes here himself," she said. Then she continued riding her goat, making the deck thunder.

The servants went back to the royal palace and reported what they had heard and seen on board the ship. The king wanted to leave at once to see this girl who was riding a goat.

When he arrived, Ragged Cap brought out her sister. She was so beautiful and fair that the king instantly fell in love with her. He accompanied both girls back to the castle, and he wanted to marry the sister. But Ragged Cap said no. The king could not have her as his wife unless the king's son was willing to marry Ragged Cap.

As you might imagine, the king's son did not want to agree, for Ragged Cap was such a hideous troll. But the king and everyone at the palace spent so much time trying to persuade him that finally he had to give in. He promised to take Ragged Cap as his queen, though he did so reluctantly, and he was terribly distressed.

Then preparations were made for the weddings. They brewed and they baked, and when everything was ready, it was time to leave for the church. The prince thought it was going to be the most dreadful ride to church he had ever taken in his life.

First the king set off with his bride. She looked so lovely and so splendid that everyone stopped along the road to watch her ride past until she was out of sight. Next came the prince, riding next to Ragged Cap. She trotted along, sitting on her goat and holding the ladle in her fist. The prince looked as if he were taking part in a funeral procession rather than riding to his own wedding. That's how distressed he seemed, and he said not a word.

"Why aren't you saying anything?" asked Ragged Cap after they'd been riding a good distance.

"What is there to say?" replied the prince.

"You might ask me why I'm riding this hideous goat," said Ragged Cap.

"Why are you riding that hideous goat?" asked the king's son.

"Is this a hideous goat? No, it's the most splendid horse any bride has ever ridden," replied Ragged Cap. And at that instant the goat turned into a horse that was the most magnificent steed the prince had ever seen in his life.

Then they rode a little farther, but the prince was just as distressed as before. And he couldn't manage to say a single word.

Then Ragged Cap asked him again why he wasn't speaking. When the prince replied that he didn't know what to say, Ragged Cap told him, "You might ask me why I'm holding this hideous ladle in my fist."

"Why are you holding that hideous ladle?" asked the king's son.

"Is this a hideous ladle? No, it's the loveliest silver fan any bride has ever carried." And at that instant it turned into a silver fan so shiny that it gleamed.

Then they rode a little farther, but the prince was just as distressed as before, and he said not a word.

After a while Ragged Cap asked him again why he wasn't speaking. This time she told him to ask her why she was wearing such a hideous gray cap on her head.

"Why are you wearing that hideous gray cap on your head?" asked the prince.

"Is this a hideous cap? No, it's the shiniest golden crown any bride has ever worn," replied Ragged Cap. And that's what it was.

Then they rode for a good, long while. The prince was still so distressed that he sat on his horse without saying a word. Then his bride asked him again why he wasn't speaking. This time she told him to ask her why her face was so gray and hideous.

"Why is your face so gray and hideous?" asked the king's son.

"Am I hideous? You may think my sister is beautiful, but I'm ten times more beautiful," said his bride.

And when the prince looked at her, she was so lovely that he thought there couldn't be a lovelier woman in all the world. Then, as you can imagine, the prince got his voice back. And he no longer rode with his head hanging.

Then the weddings were celebrated both joyously and for days. After that the king and the prince set off, each with his bride, to visit the father of the princesses. There they held another wedding celebration that went on forever.

So if you hurry over to the royal palace, there may still be a little of the wedding ale left.

The Bushy Bride

There once was a widower who had one son and one daughter by his first wife. Both of them were nice children, and they were dearly fond of each other. After a while the man got married again. He wed a widow who had one daughter by her first husband. The girl was both hideous and mean, and the mother was too.

As soon as the new wife moved into the house, the husband's children could find no peace, not in a single nook or cranny. The boy thought it would be best to go out into the world and try to earn his keep.

After he'd wandered for a while, he came to the royal palace. There he found work with the stablemaster. The boy was both clever and hardworking, and the horses he tended were so stocky and glossy that they gleamed.

But for the sister, who had stayed at home, things grew much worse. Both the stepmother and her daughter were always after the girl, no matter where she went. They scolded and slapped her, and she never had a moment's peace. The hardest chores were given to her, curse words rained down on her all day long, and she had very little food to eat.

One day they sent her to the creek to get some water to bring back home. There a hideous, vile head popped up to the surface.

"Won't you wash me?" said the head.

"Yes, I will gladly wash you," said the husband's daughter. She began to rub and scrub the hideous face, though she thought it was a horrid task.

When she was done, another head popped up to the surface of the water, and it was even more vile.

"Won't you brush me?" said the face.

"Yes, I will gladly brush you," said the girl. And she set about brushing the tufts of hair. But it was not an amusing task, as you might well imagine.

When she was done, yet another head, even more vile and hideous than the others, popped up to the surface.

"Won't you kiss me?" said the head.

"Yes, I will gladly kiss you," said the husband's daughter. And that's what she did, though she thought it was the worst task she'd ever had to do in her life.

Then all the heads began talking to each other. They wondered what they should do for someone who had been so kind to them.

"I wish that she will be the most elegant girl alive and as fair as the brightest day," said the first head.

"I wish that gold will drizzle from her hair every time she uses her brush," said the second head.

"I wish that gold will spill from her lips every time she speaks," said the third head.

When the husband's daughter got home, she looked as lovely and bright as the day. That made her stepmother and stepsister even angrier. Things got worse when the girl spoke, for they saw that gold coins spilled from her lips. With that, the stepmother was beside herself with fury. She chased her husband's daughter out to the pig shed. There she would have to stay with all her golden finery. She was not allowed to set foot inside the house.

It didn't take long before the stepmother told her own daughter to go down to the creek to bring some water back home.

When the girl got there with her buckets, the first head popped up to the surface of the water.

"Won't you wash me?" it said.

"Let the Devil wash you!" replied the daughter.

Then the second head appeared.

"Won't you brush me?" it said.

"Let the Devil brush you!" said the daughter.

It sank back down. Then the third head popped up.

"Won't you kiss me?" said the head.

"Let the Devil kiss you! What an ugly snout you are!" replied the daughter.

Then the heads again talked to each other. They wondered what they should do with someone who was so callous and mean. They agreed that her nose should be eight feet long and her mouth should be six feet wide. A little pine bush should sprout on top of her head, and every time she spoke, ashes should fall from her lips.

When the girl got back to the house with her buckets of water, she called to her mother, "Open the door!"

"Open the door yourself, my daughter!" said her mother.

"I can't reach it, for my nose is so long," said the daughter.

When her mother came out and caught sight of the girl, you can well imagine what she thought and how she screamed and carried on. But that didn't make the girl's nose or mouth any smaller.

The husband's son, who was working at the royal palace, had made a drawing of his sister, and he'd brought that drawing with him. Every morning and every evening he would kneel before the drawing and pray to Our Lord for his sister. That's how fond he was of her.

The other stable boys heard him speaking. They peeked through the keyhole to his room, and there they saw him kneeling before a drawing. Then they spread the word that every morning and evening the boy was praying to the image of a false god. Finally they went to the king and asked him to peek through the keyhole to the boy's room. Then he would see for himself.

The king refused to believe what they said. But at long last they persuaded him to take a look, so he tiptoed over to the door.

Oh yes, there was the boy kneeling with his hands folded in front of a picture that hung on the wall.

"Open the door!" shouted the king.

But the boy didn't hear him.

Then the king shouted again, "I said open the door! It's me, and I want to come in!"

The boy jumped up and ran to open the door. But in his haste, he forgot to hide the drawing.

When the king came in and saw the picture, he stopped as if spellbound. He couldn't budge from the spot. That's how lovely he thought the image was.

"So beautiful a lady is not to be found in all the world," said the king.

The boy told him it was a drawing he'd made of his sister. And though she might not be more beautiful than the picture, she certainly wasn't any uglier either.

"Oh, if she's that beautiful, I want to have her as my queen," said the king. And he ordered the boy to leave for home right then and there to bring back his sister. And he must not dally along the way.

The boy promised to do his best to hurry. And with that he left the palace.

When the brother arrived home to get his sister, the stepmother and her daughter wanted to go with him too. So they all left together.

The husband's daughter took along a small chest that she filled with her gold and also a dog named Little Cavern. These were the only things she had inherited from her mother.

After they'd traveled for a while, they had to cross the sea. The brother sat at the tiller. The stepmother and both girls stood in the bow of the boat. They sailed a long way and for a long time.

A while later they caught sight of land. "There you can see the white shore, and that's where we'll dock," said the brother, pointing across the water.

"What did my brother say?" asked the husband's daughter.

"He says you should throw your little chest in the water," replied her stepmother.

"If that's what my brother says, then I must do it," said the husband's daughter. And she threw the chest in the water.

After they'd sailed some more, the brother again pointed across the water. "There you can see the castle. That's where we're going," he said.

"What did my brother say?" asked the husband's daughter.

"Now he says that you should throw your dog in the sea," replied her stepmother.

The husband's daughter wept and was terribly distressed. Little Cavern was the dearest thing she owned in the world. But finally she threw the dog overboard.

"If that's what my brother says, then I must do it. But God only knows how much I regret throwing you in the water, Little Cavern!" she said.

Then they sailed for a good distance farther.

"There you can see the king coming out to greet you," said the brother, pointing toward the shore.

"What did my brother say?" asked his sister again.

"Now he says that you should hurry up and throw yourself in the water," replied her stepmother.

The girl whimpered and wept, but if that's what her brother said, then she had to do it. So she jumped into the sea.

When they arrived at the royal palace, the king caught sight of the vile-looking bride with the eight-foot-long nose and the six-foot-wide mouth. And she had a pine bush growing from the top of her head. Then he was truly horrified. But the wedding preparations had already been made, with much brewing and baking, and the wedding guests were waiting. So the king had to take his bride as she was.

He was furious, and no one could blame him. That's why he had the boy thrown into the snake pit.

On the next Thursday evening, a lovely lady came into the kitchen of the royal palace. She asked the kitchen maid, who was sleeping there, to lend her a brush. When she brushed her hair, there was a drizzle of gold.

The woman had brought along a little dog, and she said to him, "Go outside, Little Cavern, and see whether the dawn will soon be here."

She said that three times. The third time that she sent the dog outside, the sky was growing lighter. Then it was time for her to leave. But before she went, she said:

> *Oh! You hideous bushy bride,*
> *you who shall lie in the arms of the king,*
> *While I must keep to the gravel and sand*
> *And my brother is in the snake pit, though no one weeps!*

"I'll come back twice more and then never again," the woman added.

In the morning the kitchen maid reported what she'd seen. The king said that on the following Thursday evening, he would keep watch in the kitchen to see whether what she'd said was true.

When darkness fell he went to join the maid in the kitchen. But no matter how much he rubbed his eyes and tried to stay awake, it did no good. The bushy bride hummed and sang to make his eyes close. And when the lovely lady appeared again, the king was sound asleep and snoring.

The woman borrowed a brush, just as she'd done before. And when she brushed her hair, there was a drizzle of gold. Then she sent her dog outside three times. When the sky grew light, she had to leave. But before she went, she spoke the same words.

And she added, "I'll be back once more and then never again."

On the third Thursday evening, the king again wanted to keep watch. This time he ordered two guards to hold him, one gripping each of his arms. They were supposed to shake and pinch him every time he started to fall asleep. He also ordered two guards to keep watch over the bushy bride.

But when evening came, the bushy bride again began humming and singing to make the king's eyes close and his head droop to one side.

Then the lovely lady appeared. She borrowed a brush, and when she brushed her hair, there was a drizzle of gold. Then she sent her little dog outside to see whether it would soon be dawn. She did that three times. At the third time, the sky began to lighten, and then she said:

Oh! You hideous bushy bride,
you who shall lie in the arms of the king,
While I must keep to the gravel and sand
And my brother is in the snake pit, though no one weeps!

"Now I'll never again return," she said. With that, she was about to leave.

But the two guards who were gripping the king's arms now seized hold of his hands and pressed a knife into his fist. With the knife they had him make a cut in the woman's little finger, deep enough to draw blood.

Then the proper bride was saved, and the king awoke. She told him everything that had happened and how her stepmother and stepsister had betrayed her.

Her brother was taken at once out of the snake pit. The snakes hadn't done him the least bit of harm. And in his place the guards threw in the stepmother and her daughter.

No one can ever imagine how happy the king was. Now he was rid of the hideous bushy bride. And he'd won instead a queen who was as lovely and bright as the day itself.

Now the proper wedding was held, and news of the celebration spread far and wide throughout seven kingdoms. The king and his bride rode to church, and Little Cavern sat beside them in the carriage.

When the wedding was done, they rode back home, but by then I was no longer with them.

The Tabby Cat on Dovre Mountain

There once was a man who lived way up north in Finnmark. He had captured a big polar bear that he was taking to the kingdom of Denmark.

Now, it so happened that he arrived at Dovre Mountain on Christmas Eve. There he went inside a house that belonged to a man named Halvor. He asked the man whether he could have lodging for both himself and his polar bear.

"God save us," said Halvor. "We can't offer lodging to anyone right now. Every single Christmas Eve the house is so full of trolls that we have to move out. Even we won't have a roof over our heads."

"Oh, that shouldn't stop you from offering us lodging," said the man. "My bear can sleep under the stove, and I can sleep in the alcove."

He begged for so long that finally he was granted permission. Then the folks who lived in the house left. But first they made ready for the trolls. On the table they set sour cream porridge and *lutefisk* and sausages, along with all sorts of other good food. It looked like a splendid feast.

All of a sudden, the trolls arrived. Some were big, and some were small. Some had long tails, while some had none at all. And some had long, long noses. They ate and drank and tried a taste of everything.

Then one of the young trolls caught sight of the polar bear lying under the stove. The child stuck a piece of sausage on a fork to roast the meat in the fire. Then he went over and held the sausage so close to the polar bear's nose that he burned the tip.

"Here, tabby cat, do you want some sausage?" the troll child shouted.

The polar bear leaped up and growled. Then she chased all the trolls out, both the big and the small.

The next year Halvor went into the forest on the afternoon of Christmas Eve to get some firewood for the holidays, for he was expecting the trolls to come back. As he was chopping wood, he heard someone calling from deep in the forest.

"Halvor! Halvor!"

"Yes?" said Halvor.

"Is that big tabby cat still living with you?"

"Yes, she's back home under the stove," said Halvor. "And she had a litter of kittens. Seven of them. And they're even bigger and crankier than she is."

"Then we're never coming back to your house!" shouted the troll from deep in the forest.

And ever since, the trolls have never eaten Christmas porridge at Halvor's house on Dovre Mountain.

Farmer Weather-Beard

There once was a man and a wife who had only one son. His name was Hans. The woman thought the boy should go out to find work, and she told her husband to go with him.

"You must promise me that you'll find for him such a good teacher that he will become the master of all masters," she said. Then she put food and a roll of tobacco in a sack for them.

They visited many masters, and they all said that they could train the boy to be as good as they were, but no better.

When the man went home to his wife, he told her what they'd said. Then she replied, "Well, I don't care where you take him, but this much I'll say. You must make sure that he becomes the master of all masters."

Again she put food and a roll of tobacco in a sack. Then the man and his son set off.

After they'd walked a good distance, they came out onto an ice floe. There they saw someone riding toward them on a black horse.

"Where are you headed?" said the man on horseback.

"I'm trying to apprentice my son to someone who will train him well. My wife comes from such fine folks that she wants him to learn to be the master of all masters," said the husband.

"You're in luck," said the man. "I'm the right person for the job. I've been looking for just such an apprentice." He told the boy, "Climb up behind me."

Then they set off, riding high into the air.

"No, no! Wait a minute!" shouted the father. "I should have asked you what your name is and where you live."

"Oh, I'm at home in the north and the south, in the east and the west. And my name is Farmer Weather-Beard," said the master. "Come back here in a year, and I'll tell you if the boy's any good," he added.

Then they took off and were gone.

When the man got back home, his wife asked him what had happened to their son.

"Oh, God only knows where he went," said the man. "Somewhere up in the air." And then he told his wife what happened.

When she heard that her husband had no idea when the boy would be done with his training or where he had gone, she sent him off. Again she gave him a sack of food and a roll of tobacco.

When the man had gone a good distance, he came to a big forest. There he walked all day long. When darkness fell, he caught sight of a big clearing. That's where he headed.

At long last he came upon a little hovel at the foot of a mountain. Outside stood a woman hauling water out of the well by winding the bucket up with her nose. That's how long her nose was.

"Good evening, ma'am," said the man.

"Good evening to you," said the woman. "Nobody has called me 'ma'am' in a hundred years."

"Could you give me lodging for the night?" said the man.

"No," said the woman.

But then the man took out the roll of tobacco, lit a wad, and handed the snuff to the woman.

That made her so happy that she began to dance. And then the man was allowed to stay the night.

After a while he asked about Farmer Weather-Beard.

She said she didn't know anything about him, but she was the mistress of all four-legged animals. Maybe one of them knew about this farmer.

Then she summoned the animals by blowing on a whistle she owned. She asked all the animals, but none of them knew anything about Farmer Weather-Beard.

"Well, I have two sisters," said the woman. "Maybe one of them might know where to find him. You can borrow a sled from me. Then you'll be able to get there by evening. But it's nearly two thousand miles to my nearest sister."

The man set off, and by evening he had arrived. There he found another woman hauling water up from the well by using her long nose.

"Good evening, ma'am," said the man.

"Good evening to you," said the woman. "Nobody has called me 'ma'am' in a hundred years."

"Could I have lodging for the night?" said the man.

"No," said the woman.

The man took out the roll of tobacco and lit a wad. Then he handed the woman the snuff on the back of his hand.

That made her so happy that she began to dance. And the man was allowed to stay the night.

After a while he asked the woman whether she knew Farmer Weather-Beard.

No, she knew nothing about him. But she said that she was the mistress of all the fish, and maybe one of them could tell him something.

So she summoned the fish by blowing on a whistle that she owned. She asked all of them, but none knew anything about Farmer Weather-Beard.

"Well, I have another sister," said the woman. "Maybe she knows something about him. She lives nearly four thousand miles from here, but I'll give you a sled so you'll be there by evening."

The man set off, and he did arrive by evening. There he found a woman who was raking the coals with her nose. That's how long it was.

"Good evening, ma'am," said the man.

"Good evening to you," said the woman. "Nobody has called me 'ma'am' in a hundred years."

"Could I have lodging here for the night?" said the man.

"No," said the woman.

Again the man took out the roll of tobacco to burn a wad of it. Then he covered the whole back of his hand with the snuff and gave it to the woman.

That made her so happy that she began to dance. And the man was allowed to stay the night.

After a while he asked her about Farmer Weather-Beard. She said she didn't know anything about him, but she was the mistress of all the birds. And she summoned them with her whistle.

She asked all of them, though she noticed that the eagle was missing. A little later the bird appeared. When she asked about Farmer Weather-Beard, the eagle said he had just come from his place. Then the woman told the eagle to take the man there.

First the eagle wanted to have something to eat, and then he would need to rest until the following day. He was so tired after the long journey that he could hardly lift himself off the ground.

After the eagle had rested and eaten his fill, the woman plucked a feather from the bird's tail and set the man in its place. Then the eagle took off. It was midnight by the time they reached Farmer Weather-Beard's place.

When they arrived, the eagle said, "Dead carcasses are lying outside the door, but pay them no mind. The folks inside are sleeping so soundly that they won't easily wake. Go straight over to the table and take three pieces of bread from the drawer. If you hear somebody snoring, pluck three feathers from his head. That won't wake him."

That's what the man did. After he'd taken the pieces of bread, he plucked one feather.

"Ow!" cried Farmer Weather-Beard.

When the man plucked another feather, the farmer again cried, "Ow!"

When the man plucked a third feather, Farmer Weather-Beard shouted so loudly that it seemed as if the walls would crack, both inside and out. But the farmer was still sound asleep.

Then the eagle told the man what to do next, and that's what he did.

The man went over to the cowshed. Outside the door he found a big boulder. He picked up the boulder and underneath were three pieces of tile. He picked them up too. Then he knocked on the cowshed door, and it opened at once. There he dropped the three pieces of bread. Then a hare came to eat the bread, and he picked up the hare too.

The eagle told the man to pull three feathers from his tail and put the hare, the boulder, and the tiles in their place. Then the bird would carry all of them home.

After the eagle had flown a good distance, he landed on a rock. "Do you see anything?" he asked.

"Yes, I see a flock of crows flying after us," said the man.

"We'll need to fly a little farther. Yes, we will," said the eagle. And he took off.

After a while he asked, "Do you see anything now?"

"Yes, now the crows are very close," said the man.

"Drop the three feathers you took from the farmer's head," said the eagle.

Well, that's what the man did.

The instant he dropped the feathers, they turned into a flock of ravens that chased the crows back home.

Then the eagle flew far away with the man. Finally the bird landed on a rock to rest. "Do you see anything?" he said.

"I'm not sure," said the man, "but I think I see something off in the distance that is headed this way."

"We'll have to travel a little farther then," said the eagle.

"Do you see anything now?" the eagle asked after a while.

"Yes, now he's very close," said the man.

"Drop the pieces of tile that you took from under the gray boulder near the cowshed door," said the eagle.

Well, that's what the man did.

The instant he dropped the tiles, they grew into a big, dense forest. And Farmer Weather-Beard had to go back home to get axes to chop his way through.

Then the eagle again flew a good distance. When the bird grew tired, he landed in a pine tree. "Do you see anything?" he asked.

"Yes. I can't say for sure," said the man, "but I think I can see something glimmering way off in the distance."

"We'll have to travel a little farther then," said the eagle. And they set off.

"Do you see anything now?" said the bird after a while.

"Yes, now he's very close," said the man.

"Drop the boulder that you took from outside the cowshed door," said the eagle.

That's what the man did.

The boulder turned into a big, high stone mountain. Farmer Weather-Beard had to break his way through it, but when he'd gone halfway, one of his legs broke off. Then he had to go back home to mend it.

In the meantime, the eagle flew home with both the man and the hare. When they arrived, the man went to the churchyard and sprinkled hallowed ground on the bird. Then the eagle turned back into his son, Hans.

When it was market time, the boy turned himself into a dun-colored horse. He asked his father to go with him to the marketplace.

"When someone comes over and wants to buy me, tell him that you want a hundred *daler* for me. But don't forget to take off the halter. Or else I will never escape from Farmer Weather-Beard," said the boy.

That's exactly what happened. A horse trader appeared, and he was eager to buy the horse. He wanted to pay the man a hundred *daler*. But after the price was agreed on and Hans's father got the money, the horse trader wanted the halter as well.

"No, that's not part of the agreement," said the man. "I won't give you the halter, for I have other horses that I need to bring to town.

And with that, they went separate ways.

But they hadn't gone far before Hans turned back into himself. And when the man got home, he found his son sitting on the bench next to the stove.

The next day, Hans turned himself into a brown horse. Then he asked his father to go with him to the marketplace.

"When somebody comes over and wants to buy me, tell him you want two hundred *daler*. That's what he'll pay you, and afterward he'll buy you a drink. No matter what you drink or what you may do, don't forget to take the halter off of me. Or else you'll never see me again," said Hans.

Everything happened just as he'd said. His father got two hundred *daler* for the horse, and afterward the horse trader bought him a drink. When they parted, it was only at the last minute that the man remembered to take off the horse's halter.

They hadn't gone far before the boy turned back into himself. And when the man got home, there sat Hans on the bench by the stove.

On the third day, the same thing happened. The boy turned himself into a big black horse. He told his father that somebody would come and offer him three hundred *daler*. Afterward the man would get his father good and drunk. But no matter what he did or how much he drank, he mustn't forget to take off the halter. Or else Hans would belong to Farmer Weather-Beard for the rest of his life.

Oh, he would be sure to remember, said his father.

When he got to the marketplace, he was paid three hundred *daler* for the horse. But Farmer Weather-Beard got him so drunk that he forgot to take off the halter before the horse trader left with the horse.

After Farmer Weather-Beard had gone a good distance, he wanted to stop for more liquor. In the stable he put a glowing-hot barrel lined with sharp nails under the horse's nose. Under the animal's tail he put a trough of oats. Then he went inside the inn.

The horse stood there, stamping and kicking, sniffing and snorting.

In came a girl, and she felt sorry for the horse. "Oh, you poor thing. What sort of master would treat you this way?" she said. Then she slid the halter off the stall railing so the horse could turn around and reach the oats.

"It's me! I'm his master!" shouted Farmer Weather-Beard as he rushed in the stable door.

But the horse had already shaken off the halter and thrown himself in the goose pond. There he quickly turned himself into a little fish.

Farmer Weather-Beard ran after the horse and turned himself into a big pike.

Then Hans turned himself into a dove. But Farmer Weather-Beard turned himself into a hawk and flew after the dove.

A princess was standing at the window of the royal palace, and she saw the hawk trying to grab the dove.

"If you knew as much as I do, you'd fly in the window to me," said the princess to the dove.

The dove came racing through the window. Then Hans turned back into himself and told the princess what had happened.

"Turn yourself into a golden ring and slip onto my finger," she told him.

"No, that won't do," said Hans. "Then Farmer Weather-Beard will make the king ill. No one will be able to restore him to health until the farmer comes to cure him. And in return, he will demand your golden ring."

"I'll tell him that I inherited the ring from my mother and I refuse to part with it," said the princess.

Then Hans turned himself into a golden ring and slipped onto the princess's finger. And with that, Farmer Weather-Beard couldn't get him.

But things happened just as the boy had said. The king fell ill, and no doctor was able to cure him until Farmer Weather-Beard arrived. In return he wanted the princess's golden ring.

The king sent a messenger to get the ring from the princess. But she said she refused to part with it, for she'd inherited the ring from her mother.

When the king heard this, he grew angry. He said he wanted that ring, no matter who had given it to her.

"It won't help matters for you to get angry," said the princess. "I won't take off the ring. If you want it, you'll have to take off my finger as well."

"Let me help," said Farmer Weather-Beard. "I'm sure I can get the ring off."

"No, thank you. I'll do it myself," said the princess.

She went over to the fireplace and smeared ashes on her finger. Then the ring came off and landed in the ashes.

Farmer Weather-Beard turned himself into a rooster. He kicked and pecked so hard for the ring in the fireplace that the ashes flew all around.

Then Hans turned himself into a fox and bit off the rooster's head. And if the Evil One was inside Farmer Weather-Beard, that was the end of him.

The Blue Ribbon

There once was a poor woman who went out in the countryside to beg. She took along her little boy. After her sack was full, she headed for the mountain ridge to get back to her own village.

After they had gone partway up the slope, they came upon a length of blue ribbon. It was lying on the path that packhorses traveled. The boy asked if he might take the piece of ribbon.

"No," said his mother. "It could be some sort of trickery." Then she urged the boy to keep going.

After they'd gone farther up the slope, the boy said he needed to step aside, behind some trees, for a moment. In the meantime, the woman sat down on a stump to wait.

The boy was gone a long time. As soon as he'd walked far enough into the forest that his mother couldn't see him, he ran back to where the ribbon lay on the ground. He picked it up and tied it around his waist. With that, he grew so strong that he thought he could lift the whole mountain.

When he got back, his mother was furious. She asked him what he'd been doing for so long. "You don't seem the least bit worried about the time," she said. "It will soon be evening, and you know that we have to make our way over the ridge before dark."

They walked for a while, but by the time they'd reached the middle of the slope, the woman was tired and wanted to lie down under a bush.

"Dear mother of mine," said the boy. "May I climb this tall mountain while you rest? I want to see if there's any sign of folks living nearby."

Yes, she gave him permission.

When he reached the top, the boy saw a light to the north. He ran back and said, "We should keep going, Mother. It's not far to where folks live. I can see a splendid light shining close by, just north of here."

The woman got up and grabbed her beggar's sack. She wanted to see it too. But they hadn't gone far before they came to another ridge blocking their way.

"I should have known," said the woman. "Now we can't go any farther. And this is a much worse place to rest."

But the boy put the sack under one arm and his mother under the other. Then he raced upward, carrying both of them.

"Now you can see that it's not very far to where folks live. Look at the splendid light shining there," said the boy.

The woman said the light couldn't be from folks. It had to belong to a mountain troll. She was familiar with this whole bear-infested forest, and she knew that the only folks in the area lived on the other side, at the foot of the ridge.

After they'd walked a short distance, they came to a big farm with red-painted buildings.

"We don't dare go inside," said the woman. "A mountain troll must live here."

"Oh, let's go in. Look how the light is shining. There must be folks inside," said the boy.

He led the way, and his mother followed. But the moment he opened the door, she fainted, for she'd caught sight of the big, bulky man sitting inside on the bench.

"Good evening, Grandfather," said the boy.

"I've been sitting here for three hundred years, but in all that time nobody has ever called me 'grandfather' in greeting," said the man on the bench.

The boy sat down next to him and started talking as if they were old friends.

"But what happened to your mother?" said the man after they'd been talking for a while. "I think she fainted. You should see to her."

The boy went over to his mother and dragged her inside. When she came to, she crawled over to the firewood rack and sat down. She was so frightened that she hardly dared look up.

After a while, the boy asked the man whether he would give them lodging for the night. The man said yes, he would.

They talked some more, but by then the boy had grown hungry. He asked the man whether he would also give them an evening meal. The man said yes, he certainly would.

After they'd sat there a little longer, the man stood up and put six armloads of dry pine on the fire.

The woman grew even more frightened. "Now he's going to burn us alive," she said as she sat among the firewood.

When the fire was nothing but embers, the man got up and went outside.

"God save me, how brave you are! Don't you see that we're in the home of a troll?" said the woman.

"Oh, never mind that! There's no danger," said the boy.

After a while the man came back with an ox so big and mighty that the boy had never seen its like. The man slammed his fist under the animal's ear, and with that it fell to the floor dead. Then the man picked up the ox by all four legs and placed it on the glowing coals. He twisted and turned the carcass until it was seared brown.

Then he went over to a cupboard and took out a silver platter. It was so big that the roasted ox didn't even fill it to the edges. He set the platter on the table and then went down to the cellar to get some wine in a tall wooden cask. He lopped off one end of the cask and set it on the table next to two knives that were six feet long. After he'd done that, he invited his guests to take a seat at the dinner table.

The boy went first. His mother joined him, but she began complaining and carrying on. She wondered how she would ever be able to handle such long knives.

The boy grabbed one of them and began cutting pieces of meat from the thigh of the ox. These he set on his mother's plate.

After they'd been eating for a while, the boy picked up the wine cask with both hands and set it on the floor. Then he invited his mother to come closer to have a drink.

The cask was so tall that she couldn't reach the top, so the boy lifted her up to the rim. He, in turn, climbed up and clung to the rim like a cat while he drank.

When the boy was no longer thirsty, he set the wine cask back on the table and thanked the man for the food. Then he told his mother to thank him as well. Frightened though she was, she had no choice but to thank the man for the food.

Then the boy sat down next to the man on the bench and again began talking to him.

After they'd sat there for a while, the man said, "I suppose I should also have a bite to eat this evening." He went over to the table and ate the whole ox, even the horns and bones. He picked up the wine cask and drank. Then he sat down on the bench again.

"I'm not sure where you'll sleep," he said. "I have only that cradle over there. I suppose that's where you could sleep, and your mother can share the bed with me."

"Of course. Thank you. That'll be fine," said the boy. He tore off his clothes and lay down in the cradle. It was just as big as a proper, full-size bed.

The woman, frightened though she was, had to lie down in the bed next to the man.

It wouldn't be good to fall asleep lying here, thought the boy. I'd better stay awake and listen to how things go in the night.

After a while, the man began talking to the woman. "We could live here so well and so pleasantly if only we could get rid of that son of yours," said the man.

"And do you know how to do that?" said the woman.

The man said he would give it a try. He would pretend that he wanted the woman to keep house for him for a few days. Then he would take the boy with him to the mountain to break up rocks to be used as cornerstones. There he would topple a whole heap of rocks on the boy's head.

All this the boy heard as he lay in the cradle.

The next day the troll—for a troll he was, that was easy enough to see—asked the woman whether she could keep house for him for a few days. Later in the day the troll picked up a big iron bar. Then he asked the boy to come with him to the mountain to break up rocks to be used for cornerstones.

After they'd broken up a few rocks, the troll wanted the boy to go back down and look for crevices in the mountainside. While the boy was doing that, the troll used the iron bar to break and bash until he had a whole mountain of rocks. Then he sent all the rocks toppling down the slope.

The boy fended off the avalanche until he could get away. Then the rest of the rocks rolled down the slope.

"Now I see what you mean to do with me," said the boy to the troll. "You want to kill me. But it's your turn to go down and look for crevices while I stay up here."

The troll didn't dare refuse the boy.

Then the boy broke up a mighty mountain of rocks and sent them toppling onto the troll. With that, one of the troll's thighbones broke.

"Oh, you poor thing," said the boy.

He went down and lifted up the rocks to pull the troll out. Then he had to hoist the troll on his back to carry him home. The boy raced off as fast as a horse.

The troll was tossed around so much that he screamed as if he'd been stabbed with a knife. When they reached home, the troll took to his bed. That's where he lay, feeling miserable.

When night fell, the troll again began talking to the woman. He wondered how they would get rid of the boy.

"If you don't know how to get rid of him, I certainly don't," said the woman.

The troll said he knew of a yard that held twelve lions. If only they could get the boy to go there, the lions would tear him apart.

The woman didn't think that would be any trouble. She would stay in bed and say that she was terribly weak and ill. And she wouldn't be well again unless she had lion's milk to drink.

All this the boy heard as he lay in the cradle.

When he got up in the morning, his mother told him that she felt weaker than anyone could imagine. And unless she had lion's milk to drink, she would never be well again.

"I'm afraid you're going to be weak for a very long time, Mother," said the boy. "I have no idea where to get lion's milk."

Then the troll said there was no shortage of lion's milk if only someone wanted to get it. His brothers had a yard where they kept twelve lions. He would give the boy the key to the yard if he wanted to milk them.

The boy took the key and a milk pail. Then he set off.

When he unlocked the gate and went into the yard, all twelve lions confronted him, standing on their hind legs. The boy chose the biggest of them and grabbed its front paws. Then he slammed the animal against timbers and rocks until there was nothing left but its paws.

When the other lions saw this, they were so frightened that they crept forward and lay down at the boy's feet like shame-faced dogs. After that the lions followed him wherever he went. When he got back to the troll's place, they lay down outside with their front paws on the doorstep.

"Now you'll be well again, Mother, for I've brought you some lion's milk," said the boy when he went inside. There was a little milk in the pail.

The troll, who was lying in bed, swore that it couldn't be true. It would take a different sort of lad to milk a lion.

When the boy heard this, he yanked the troll out of bed and tore open the door. The lions clawed the troll so fiercely that the boy had to step between them and loosen their grip.

When night fell, the troll again began talking to the woman.

"I don't know how we're going to kill that boy," he said. "He's much too strong. Do you have any ideas?" he asked the woman.

"No. If you don't know what to do, I certainly don't," she told him.

"Well, I have two brothers who live in a grand castle," said the troll. "They're twelve times stronger than I am. That's why I was thrown out and have to live here on this farm instead. But they still live in the castle, and there's an orchard with apple trees. Anyone who eats those apples will sleep for three days and three nights. If only we could get the boy to pick some of those apples, he wouldn't be able to resist tasting one. And once he falls asleep, my brothers will rip him to pieces."

The woman said she would claim to be ill and she would never be well again unless she had some of those apples. Then the boy would certainly be willing to go there.

All this the boy heard as he lay in the cradle.

The next morning the woman was so wan and so weak that she cried and moaned. She said she would never be well again unless she had apples from the orchard next to the castle where the man's brothers lived. But she had no one to send to the orchard.

The boy agreed to go there at once, and he took with him the eleven lions.

When he reached the orchard, he climbed up in one of the trees and ate as many apples as he could reach. The boy had hardly come back down before he fell asleep, but the lions lay down in a circle around him.

On the third day the troll's brothers appeared, but they didn't arrive in human form. Instead they were ferocious oxen. They bellowed at the boy they found lying on the ground in their orchard. They said they meant to crush him into bits the size of grain so there wouldn't be even a shred left of him. But the lions jumped up and tore the trolls into tiny pieces. It looked as if the lions had left behind a pile of trash. When they were done, they again lay down around the boy.

He didn't wake until late in the afternoon. He sat up and rubbed the sleep out of his eyes. Then he saw the traces left by the fight and wondered what had happened. The boy went over to the castle, where he found a maiden standing outside, and she had seen everything.

She said, "You can thank God that you weren't mixed up in that battle, or you would have lost your life."

"What? Lose my life? Me?" said the boy. He didn't think there was any risk of that.

Then she asked him to come inside so she could talk to him. She hadn't seen a Christian since she'd come to the castle.

When the boy opened the door, the lions wanted to follow him in. But the maiden was so frightened that she screamed and screamed. So the boy left the lions outside.

Then they talked about one thing and another. The boy asked why such a lovely maiden had chosen to stay with the hideous trolls.

She told him that she'd never wanted to stay with them. It was not by choice that she lived here at the castle. The trolls had taken her, for she was the daughter of the king of Arabia.

As they talked, she asked the boy what he wanted now. She could either go back home, or he could have her as his bride.

Of course he wanted to marry her. She was not to go back home.

Then they walked through the castle to take a look around. When they came to a big room, they saw two mighty swords that the trolls had hung on the wall.

"If only you were the sort of lad who could wield one of those swords!" said the king's daughter.

"Who? Me?" said the boy. "You don't think I could wield one of those swords? That should be easy enough!"

He stacked two, then three, chairs on top of each other. He jumped up on them and grabbed hold of the bigger sword and tossed it into the air. He caught it by the hilt and dropped it on the floor so the whole room shook. When he climbed down from the chairs, he picked up the sword and stuck it under his arm.

After they'd lived together in the castle for a while, the king's daughter thought she should go home to see her parents. She wanted to tell them what had become of her. The two of them built a ship, and then she left.

When she was gone, the boy rattled around alone in the castle. Then he remembered the reason he'd come there. He was supposed to get a remedy for his mother. But then he thought that she hadn't been very ill, and she'd probably regained her health by now. He decided, all the same, to go and see how his mother and the troll were doing.

He found that the man had recovered, and his mother had also recovered long ago.

"You poor things. Here you sit in this wretched hovel," said the boy. "Why don't you come back to my castle. Then you'll see what sort of lad I am."

They went back with him, both the man and the woman. On the way there, the boy's mother asked her son how he'd grown so strong.

Oh, it was because of the piece of ribbon they'd seen lying on the mountainside, the boy told her. That time when they'd gone out in the countryside to beg.

"Do you still have it?" said the woman.

Yes, he did, he told her. He wore the ribbon under his waistband.

The woman asked if she could see it.

The boy pulled up his vest and shirt to show her.

Then she reached out both hands, grabbed the ribbon off him, and wrapped it around her fist.

"What use are you to me? A lout like you!" she said. "I should hit you so hard that your brain splatters!"

"That would be much too easy a death for such a rogue," said the troll. "We should burn out his eyes and then put him in a little boat in the sea."

And that's what they did, no matter how much the boy wailed and whimpered.

But wherever the boat drifted, the lions followed. Finally they dragged the boat onto an island and placed the boy under a pine tree. They caught game and plucked birds for him. Then they made him a whole bed from down feathers. Yet he had to eat the food raw, and he was blind.

One day the biggest lion chased after a hare that seemed to be blind, for it kept running into timbers and rocks. Finally it ran straight into the trunk of a pine tree. Then it tumbled head over heels along the ground and into a little pond.

When the hare came back up to the surface of the water, it easily found its way. And with that the hare saved its own life.

Aha! thought the lion. He took the boy to the lake and dipped him in the water.

After he'd regained his sight, the boy went down to the sea. There he motioned for the lions to lie down next to each other to form a raft. Then he stood on their backs as they swam with him to the mainland.

When the boy came ashore, he went over to a birch-covered knoll. There he told the lions to lie down. Then he crept over to the castle like a thief to see if he could get his ribbon back.

When he reached the castle door, he peeked through the keyhole and saw it hanging above a door in the kitchen. Then he tiptoed across the room, for no one was there. But after he grabbed the ribbon, he began stomping his heels and kicking his feet as if he were crazy.

The woman came rushing in.

"Oh, my dear, you poor boy of mine, give me the ribbon," she said.

"Oh no. Now you shall suffer the same punishment that you meant for me," said the boy.

And he set about doing just that.

When the troll heard this, he came in and pleaded earnestly with the boy, asking him to spare his life.

"Yes, I'll allow you to live, but you shall suffer the same punishment that you gave to me," said the boy.

And then he burned out the troll's eyes and put him in a boat in the sea. But the troll didn't have any lions to follow him.

Now the boy was alone. He wandered around in the castle and longed for the princess. Finally he couldn't stand it anymore. He missed her so much that he had to leave. He loaded four ships with provisions and set sail for Arabia to find her.

For a while they had a good, brisk wind, but then they ended up becalmed next to a steep islet. The crew went ashore and roamed around to pass the time. There they found a big and mighty egg. It was as big as a small house. They began hitting and pounding on the egg with big rocks, but they couldn't crack it open.

The boy came to see what was causing all the noise, and he brought along his sword. When he caught sight of the egg, he thought it should be an easy matter to break it open. He swung his sword and split the egg in two. Out stepped a baby bird as big as an elephant.

"I think we may have done the wrong thing," said the boy. "This may cost us our lives," he added. Then he asked the crew whether they were man enough to sail to Arabia in twenty-four hours as soon as they had good winds.

Yes, they thought they could surely do that.

When they got good winds, they set off. And they reached the land of Arabia in twenty-three hours.

The boy ordered the crew members to go ashore at once and bury themselves so deep in a sand dune that they could just barely see the ships. The captains and the boy climbed a tall mountain and sat down under a pine tree.

An hour later the bird appeared. In its claws the bird carried the islet. Then it dropped the islet on top of the ships, and all of them sank. Next the bird went over to the sand dune and began flailing its wings so it nearly took off the heads of the seamen. Then it flew up to the pine tree so fast that the boy spun around. But he was ready with his sword. He swung the blade at the bird, and it fell to the ground dead.

Then the boy headed to town, where there was great joy, of course, for the king had his daughter back. But he'd hidden her away and decreed that whoever could find her would marry her, even though she'd already been betrothed.

As he walked, the boy met someone who was selling polar bear hides. He bought one of them and put it on. He told one of the captains to lead him around, using an iron chain as a collar and leash. Then the bear went about town performing tricks.

Finally it came to the king's attention that no one had ever seen such tricks before. The polar bear danced in all manner of ways, doing whatever it was ordered to do.

Then a messenger arrived to say that the bear should be brought to the palace to do tricks, for the king wished to see them.

When the bear came in, everyone grew frightened, for they'd never seen such an animal before. But the captain said there was no danger as long as they didn't laugh at the bear. They mustn't do that, or else the animal would kill them.

When the king heard this, he warned his courtiers not to laugh. A short time later the king's maid came in and began making fun and laughing. Then the polar bear threw itself at her and tore her to shreds.

The courtiers began wailing, but the captain wailed even louder.

"Oh, never mind that!" said the king. "She was only a maid. That's my concern, not yours."

It was late at night when all the tricks were done.

"It's no use leaving with the bear now, seeing as it's so late," said the king. "The bear can stay here for the night."

"Maybe it could sleep behind the stove?" said the captain.

"No, it shall have quilts and pillows to lie on," said the king, and he brought in a whole pile of bedding.

The captain was allowed to sleep in the room next door.

Around midnight the king appeared carrying a lantern and a big key ring. He told the bear to follow him. He walked down one corridor after another, through doorways and rooms, up stairways and down. Finally he came out onto a wharf that led straight down to the sea.

There the king began tugging and shaking sticks and poles. He pulled one up and pushed another one down until a little house floated up. That's where he'd put his daughter. He was so fond of her that he'd hidden her away where no one could find her.

He made the polar bear wait outside while he went in and told the princess about the bear and the dancing and the tricks. She said she was frightened and didn't dare see the bear. But the king persuaded her. He said there was no danger as long as she didn't laugh.

Then he let in the bear, who danced and did tricks. But all of a sudden the princess's maid began laughing. With that, the boy threw himself at her and tore her to shreds. The princess wailed and moaned.

"Oh, never mind that!" said the king. "She was only a maid. I'll find you another maid who is just as good. But now it's best if the bear stays here, for I don't feel like leading it back along all those corridors at this time of night."

Then the princess said she wouldn't dare stay there.

But the bear curled up and lay down behind the stove. And finally the princess lay down in bed, though she kept a candle burning.

After the king had left and all was quiet, the polar bear went over to the princess and asked her to loosen its collar.

The princess grew so frightened that she almost fainted, but she fumbled until she found the collar. And no sooner did she loosen the collar than the boy tore off the bear's head. Then the princess recognized him, and she was happy beyond all measure. She wanted to announce at once that he was the one who had rescued her. But he didn't want her to do that. He wanted to be her servant for a while.

The next morning they heard the king rustling the poles. Then the boy put the bear hide back on and lay down behind the stove.

"Well, did the bear lie there quietly?" asked the king.

"Yes, God save me," said the princess. "It didn't so much as lift a paw."

And the bear went back up to the castle to join the captain.

Then the boy went to a master tailor and ordered princely clothing for himself. When the clothes were ready, he went to the king and said that he wanted to look for the princess.

"There have been many who tried," said the king. "But they all lost their lives, for anyone who can't find her in twenty-four hours must give up his life."

Oh, there was no danger of that, the boy said. He wanted to look for the princess, and if he didn't find her, that would be his concern.

A fiddler had come to the castle to play, and maidens were dancing, so the boy danced too. After twelve hours the king said, "I feel sorry for you. It's so easy to distract you that you'll soon lose your life."

"Oh, never mind that! There's no danger from a corpse as long as it still can sneeze. I have plenty of time," said the boy. And he kept on dancing until there was only an hour left. That's when he wanted to begin his search.

"Oh, it's no use," said the king. "The time is almost up."

"Light a lantern and bring your big key ring," said the boy. "Then follow me. We have a whole hour left."

The boy took the same route the king had gone the night before. And he ordered the king to unlock the doors until he came to the wharf that led out to sea.

"It's no use now. The time is up, and this will take you straight out to sea," said the king.

"There are still five minutes left," said the boy. He tugged and pulled on the sticks and poles until the house floated up.

"Now the time is up!" shouted the king. "Come here, my fencing master, and chop off his head."

"No, wait," said the boy. "There are still three minutes left. Give me the key so I can go inside."

But the king stood there fumbling with the keys and said he couldn't find the right one. He was trying to use up the minutes.

"If you don't have the key, I have one of my own," said the boy. And he kicked the door so hard that it fell to the ground in pieces.

The princess greeted him on the threshold. She said that he was the one who had rescued her and he was the one she would marry.

And so she did. The boy celebrated his wedding to the daughter of the king of Arabia.

The Honest
Four-*Skilling* Coin

here once was a poor woman who lived in a miserable hovel far away from any village. She had little to eat and nothing at all to burn. That's why she sent her little son out to the forest to gather firewood.

He leaped and ran, he ran and leaped, in order to stay warm, for it was a cold and gray autumn day. Every time he put a twig or a branch in his firewood carrier, he had to wrap his arms around his chest. His fists were very cold. They were as red as the lingonberry patches he walked through.

After he'd filled his firewood carrier, he headed for home. Then he came upon a clearing with tree stumps. There he saw a misshapen white rock.

"Oh, you poor old rock. How white and pale you are. You must be terribly cold!" said the boy. He took off his sweater and wrapped it around the rock.

When he got home with the firewood, his mother asked him why he was walking around in his shirtsleeves in the cold autumn weather. The boy told her that he'd seen an old and misshapen rock that was white and pale with frost. So he'd given the rock his sweater.

"You fool!" said the woman. "Do you really think rocks get cold? Even if it was freezing and the rock was shivering, everyone has to look out for himself. It's going to cost money to put clothes on your back if you keep hanging them on rocks out in the clearings."

Then she sent the boy back to get his sweater.

When he got to the rock, he saw that it had turned around and one edge was sticking up from the ground.

"Oh, you moved after I gave you the sweater, you poor thing!" said the boy.

But when he got a better look at the rock, he saw underneath a money chest filled with shiny silver coins.

That money must have been stolen, thought the boy. No one would put money he'd earned in an honest way under a rock in the woods. Then he picked up the chest and carried it to a nearby lake. There he threw the whole chest of money into the water. But a four-*skilling* coin floated to the surface.

"That must be an honest coin. Whatever is honest would never sink," said the boy. He picked up the four-*skilling* coin and took it home, along with his sweater.

He told his mother what had happened, how the rock had turned around and how he'd found a chest filled with silver coins. And then he'd tossed the chest in the lake, for the money must have been stolen.

"But a four-*skilling* coin floated up, and I took it. That was an honest coin," said the boy.

"What a fool you are!" said his mother. She was quite angry. "If the only honest thing was what floated on water, then there wouldn't be much honesty in the world. Even if all that money had been stolen ten times, you were the one to find it, and everyone has to look out for himself. If you'd taken the money, we could have lived happily and well for the rest of our days. But you're a fool, and a fool you will always be. I don't want to stand here arguing with you anymore. You'll have to go out and earn your own keep."

Then the boy had to go out into the wide world. He walked a long way and for a long time, looking for work. But wherever he went, folks thought he was too small and too weak. They said he would be no use to them.

Finally the boy came to a merchant's house. There he was allowed to stay in the kitchen and carry firewood and water for the cook.

One day, after the boy had been there a good long while, the merchant was about to leave for a foreign land. Then he asked each of his maids what he should buy and bring home for them. When everyone else had said what they wanted, it was the boy's turn, the boy who carried firewood and water for the cook. He held out his four-*skilling* coin.

"Well, what should I buy you with that?" asked the merchant. "It's not going to be much of a purchase."

"Buy whatever you can get for it. At least I know it's honest money," said the boy.

His master promised to do just that. Then he set sail.

In the foreign land, the merchant loaded on board all the cargo and bought everything he'd promised for his maids. Then he went back to his ship and was about to pull away from the wharf. Only then did he remember the cook's boy, who had sent him off with a four-*skilling* coin to buy him something.

Must I really go back to town for the sake of that four-*skilling* coin? thought the merchant. Taking in that sort of riffraff brings nothing but trouble.

At that moment a woman came walking past with a sack on her back.

"What do you have in the sack, ma'am?" asked the merchant.

"Oh, it's only a cat that I can no longer afford to feed. I was thinking of tossing it into the sea to be done with it," replied the woman.

"The boy said I should buy whatever I could get for four *skillinger*," said the merchant to himself. So he asked the woman whether she would take four *skillinger* for her cat.

The woman was quick to agree, and the purchase was made.

After the merchant had sailed for a while, a dreadful gale came upon his ship. It was a terrible storm like no other. It tossed the ship this way and that, and he had no idea where they were.

Finally the merchant came to a land that he'd never visited before. There he went into town.

He went into an inn where the table was set with a stick next to the place of each guest. The merchant thought this was strange. He couldn't understand what all those sticks were for. He sat down and thought he would watch what the other guests did. Then he would do the same.

When the food was set on the table, he certainly saw what the sticks were for. Thousands of mice came swarming across the table, and each guest seated there had to wield his stick, swinging it and flinging it. The only sound to be heard was the striking of the sticks, each one louder than the other. Sometimes a guest would hit another person in the face, and then they had to stop and say, "Forgive me."

"Eating is a hard task in this land," said the merchant. "Why doesn't anyone keep a cat?"

"A cat?" they asked. They had no idea what that was.

Then the merchant had the cat brought to the inn. It was the cat he'd bought for the cook's boy. When the cat landed on the table, all the mice raced back to their holes, of course. Folks had never in living memory had such peace in which to eat their food.

They blessed the merchant and begged him to sell them that cat of his. At long last he promised to leave the cat with them, but he would have to have a hundred *daler* for it. That's what they gave him, along with their thanks.

Then the merchant again set sail. But no sooner had the ship come out in open waters than he saw the cat sitting high up on the main mast. Moments later a storm and a gale blew in once more, but even worse than the first time. The ship was tossed this way and that, until it came to a place that the merchant had never visited before.

Again he went into an inn. There too the table was set with sticks, but they were much bigger and longer than at the first place. And those sticks were certainly needed. Even more mice appeared, and they were twice as big as the ones he'd seen before.

Again he sold the cat. This time he got two hundred *daler* for it, and without the least bit of haggling.

After he'd sailed off and gone some distance out to sea, the merchant saw the cat sitting high up on the mast. A moment later a storm blew in again. At long last the ship came to another land that he'd never visited before.

Again he went into an inn. There the table was also set with sticks, but each one was five feet long and as thick as a small broom handle. Folks said that sitting at that table to eat was the worst trial they could imagine. Thousands of big vile rats would always appear. It was only with the greatest effort that they could get even a bite of food to their mouths. That's how hard they had to fight to fend off the rats.

The cat was once again brought from the ship, and then folks were able to eat their food in peace.

They begged and pleaded with the merchant to sell them his cat. For a long while he refused, but finally he promised to give it to them for three hundred *daler*. That's what they paid, with their thanks and their blessings.

When the ship was out at sea, the merchant thought about how much the boy had earned from the four-*skilling* coin he'd sent. Well, some of the money he shall have, thought the merchant, but not all of it. I'm the one he has to thank for the cat I bought. And everyone has to look out for himself.

The instant the merchant made that decision, such a storm and a gale blew in that they all thought the ship would sink. Then the merchant realized that he had no choice. He had to promise to give all the money to the boy. No sooner did he make that promise than the weather turned fine and the ship had good winds all the way home.

When he went ashore, the merchant gave the boy six hundred *daler* and his daughter as well. For now the cook's boy was just as rich as the merchant, maybe even richer.

After that the boy's life was both a delight and a joy. He took his mother in and treated her well. "For I don't believe that everyone should look out for himself," said the boy.

The Old Man of the House

There once was a man who lived in a forest. He had many sheep and goats, but the wolf would never leave them in peace.

"I suppose I'll have to trick old gray-paws," the man said at last. So he began digging a wolf trap.

After he'd dug it deep enough, he set a post in the middle of the trap. On that post he put a flat disk, and on top of the disk he tethered a little dog. Over the pit he placed branches and evergreen boughs and other debris. On top of all that he scattered snow so the wolf wouldn't notice the pit underneath.

When night fell, the little dog got tired of standing there. "Woof, woof, woof!" he said. Then he howled at the moon.

A fox came along, sauntering his way forward. He thought he was going to get himself a good meal, so he leaped—and fell straight into the wolf trap.

A little later that night, the little dog was so tired and so hungry that he began to whine and bark. "Woof, woof, woof!" he said.

All of a sudden a gray wolf came along, padding his way forward. He probably thought he was going to get himself a nice piece of meat, so he leaped—and fell straight into the wolf trap.

The next morning, at the gray light of dawn, the icy North Wind blew in. It was so cold that the little dog stood there shivering and shaking. By then he was very tired and hungry. "Woof, woof, woof!" he said and kept on barking.

Then a bear came along, plodding his way forward. He shook himself and thought he was certainly going to get a tasty morsel at this early hour. So he lumbered out onto the branches—and fell straight into the wolf trap.

A little later that morning, an old vagabond woman came walking along. She was wandering from one farm to another as she carried a sack on her back. When she caught sight of the little dog that was standing there barking, she went over to see if any animals had fallen into the wolf trap during the night.

She knelt at the edge and peered down.

"Did you fall into the trap, sly fox that you are?" she said to the fox, for he was the first she saw. "Serves you right, you chicken thief! And is that you, gray wolf?" she said. "If you've been stealing goats and sheep, you're going to be flogged and beaten to death. Oh, dear me, a teddy bear! Are you sitting there in the trap too, you horse slayer? Well, we're going to lash you, we're going to flay you, and your skull we'll hang up on the wall!" That's what the woman shouted at the bear, sounding so eager and threatening.

At that moment the sack she was carrying on her back slipped forward over her head, and the woman fell—straight into the wolf trap.

Then all four of them sat there and glared at each other from their separate corners. The fox in the first corner, the wolf in the second, the bear in the third, and the old woman in the fourth.

When it was bright daylight, the fox began moving about, pacing back and forth. No doubt he thought he would try to escape.

Then the woman said, "Can't you sit still, you tail wagger! Stop your swinging and swishing. Look at the old man of the house. He's sitting there as steadfast as a pastor." She was thinking that she would make friends with the bear.

Then the farmer arrived, the one who owned the wolf trap.

First he pulled out the woman. Then he killed all the animals. He didn't spare the old man of the house or the gray-paws or the sly tail wagger.

That night he certainly thought he'd made a good catch.

Foreword to the
Second Norwegian Edition

Peter Christen Asbjørnsen

THE COLLECTION OF FOLKTALES that we are now publishing, finished though not conclusive, may well seem to many readers an enterprise that
has been quite easy for the collectors and storytellers alike. Yet our experience
has taught us the opposite. The very effort of persuading the nation's storytellers to make themselves known, openly and without reservation, requires
approaching them in a unique manner. A direct appeal does not get you far,
and even the promise of payment is wasted on the best of them, meaning those
who have a love for what has been handed down to them. To convince such
people to remove the lock from their lips, it is necessary to possess an innate
tact, which is then further developed through practice and by studying the
Norwegian people. But above all, it is necessary to allow a true love for these
traditions to shine through; you need not bother with any dissembling, for it
will have either no effect or the opposite effect in terms of what you wish to
achieve. But if it proved possible to collect in a relatively short time the material for a book of folktales—which shall represent, more or less, the entire
country and not merely a specific region—the work would probably not be
terribly difficult. It would be enough to combine the abovementioned qualities
with a natural sagacity that could distinguish the genuine and original from
the false and incidental. Yet there is an additional type of stamina required
to make use of every offered opportunity, a doggedness possessed only by
someone who even as a child cherished our folklore and who later sees in the
national spirit the purest and most precise, revelatory form. Although the initial pamphlet of our folktales appeared in 1842, our first records date back to

1833; so we have now been collecting for close to twenty years. At the time we began our collections, there were undoubtedly few in Norway who regarded the tales as anything more than mere nursery-room chatter, with most viewing our attempt to collect and publish them as childish foolishness. We think that we have contributed in some manner to a recognition of what is meritorious about bringing to light everything that belongs to the nation. This recognition now ought to be considered generally accepted, even if an occasional boyish denunciation is heard regarding such efforts.

Yet it is not the collecting of material that proves the greatest difficulty for a work such as this one. Instead, it is in the retelling, namely, when this occurs through the use of a linguistic means that has become significantly distant from the popular spoken language, as is our written language today. In addition to requiring a poetic nature, which is capable of perceiving what is characteristic about the tales, the task also necessitates an intimate knowledge of the people, the utmost familiarity with their way of life and manner of expression, if such a retelling is to succeed. When someone who lacks these qualities attempts to tell our folktales, it is easy to see what will result. The narrator must stand above and yet retain a profound connection with the people.[1]

In the table of contents we have identified each of our contributions as collector and writer. As is evident, each of us is responsible for approximately half of the tales presented here. Regardless of which of our names is listed first or second on the title page, each of us has recorded and independently presented the tales listed under our name. Most often we have read them aloud to each other and made use of one another's advice and remarks, to the extent such seemed valid. Together we worked out the comments, with approximately equal contributions from each of us. For this we made use of the collections of folklore available at the University Library, though we regret that our methodology was by no means comprehensive. One of us, meaning Moe, has included an Introduction as part of his scholarly research. He regrets that this work was cut short, just when he thought he had achieved a more or less informed view of folklore, and he wishes he could have continued his

---

[1] Proof of the truth of this can be found, for instance, in Bang's "Reglo aa Rispo ifraa Valdris." Although the writer has made use of the spoken language and hence avoided the greatest difficulty of the narrative mode, it is an easy matter to point out much that is false in his recounting.

studies of the subject. Anyone who has some notion of the sort of preliminary study that is required for this type of research will not be surprised that this brief essay cannot offer anything conclusive. For that reason the author can only wish that it will soon be recognized that folklore exists as an intermediary link between our ancient literature, which is studied with great meticulousness and skill, and our own time and that therefore it does need to be studied. And when this is acknowledged, a better man must be found to continue what he alone has managed to begin.

Christiania, November 1851

From the Introduction
to the Second Norwegian Edition

Jørgen Moe

This translated excerpt covers the second half of Moe's Introduction,
starting on page xxxix of the second Norwegian edition.

IT IS EASY TO UNDERSTAND why it would be of great interest if you
could follow the history of the tales and establish their age in every culture. In
this way you could prove their independent existence in the various countries
and have the occasion to see what changes, both big and small, have occurred
over the course of time. It goes without saying that a story whose propagation
depends on the oral tradition must undergo such changes from one genera-
tion to the next. The shifting attitudes of the people will out of necessity—
gradually and imperceptibly—change and rewrite the tales. These attitudes
will often surreptitiously (for example, via tone and nuance) insert into the
tales things that were not originally there or that had a different meaning if
they did happen to exist previously.

If you could look back at a country's inherited traditions, you would generally find that in the fundamental idea and the storyline of the tales, they
remain true to themselves. Yet there are very few European countries that
have folktale collections of any significant age. It is possible that *Pentamerone,*
written in the Neapolitan dialect by Giambattista Basile and published in about
1637, may be the only collection that, without allowing any rewriting or revising, has understood and reproduced the traditions of the people. Most folktale
collections have been produced more recently, after the Grimm brothers, with
their excellent *Kinder- und Hausmärchen,* which opened our eyes to the beauty
and scholarly importance of folklore.

As for our own country of Norway, the storytellers, who are often quite advanced in age, usually refer back to their fathers or grandfathers and even more often to their grandmothers. Occasionally they add that these family members in turn had heard the tale in question from their own grandparents or from very old folks. But this will not take you very far into the past.

There are a few places in our ancient literature where the series of tales in which the stepmother's cruel relationship with the children appears in such a way as to indicate that back then these tales were similar to the ones we know. Then, as now, they presumably served as entertainment for the simplest classes of people. Thus it says in "King Sverre's Saga," chapter 7: "His condition most resembled that of royal children in the old stories, under the curses of step-mothers." [English translation is from "The Saga of King Sverri of Norway," translated by J. Stephton, MA, 1899, available on the website of the New Northvegr Center: northvegr.net.] And "stepmothers" are also mentioned in the Introduction of Odd Munk's as yet unpublished "Olav Trygveson's Saga." Of special interest here is the phrase "segja Sögur," because these words are still used in Telemark and in Sætersdalen to indicate the recounting of folktales.[1]

Yet there are two things that support the claim that folktales have long had a home in our country, even as far back as pagan times. First is the fidelity and conscientiousness with which the best storytellers have always continued the tradition. They show a great fear of omitting or adding to or merely altering in the slightest way any individual elements. This precision is so deeply ingrained that when the story is repeated, it is presented nearly word for word and with the same emphasis as the first time it was told, particularly when it comes to *the most salient points and the dialogue*. This is also apparent if you ask two different people to tell the same story, one of whom heard the story from the other. This conscientious precision insures against any deliberate revision of the original content. It also seems to indicate *an instinctual reverence for the age of the story and its domestic origins*. If you compare the oral storytelling tradition with what appears in published books, you will immediately see the difference. In the printed stories, things are omitted and added, and the whole narrative is treated with the greatest freedom.

---

[1] In addition to the aforementioned word "saga" and the term "tale," which is used most in Norway's flat southeastern regions, these traditions in Hallingdal and Valders are denoted with the Norwegian words *regle* and *rispe*. Both are given a scornful import, and the verb *telja* is associated with them. In the Bergen diocese the word *remse* is used.

There is a second thing (based on internal features) that provides an even more certain proof of the venerable age of these storytelling traditions. The fact is that many of the stories have vestiges not only of Catholicism (from medieval days in Norway) but even more frequently of pagan ideas—sometimes presented in their original form, sometimes in a Christian guise. Occasionally these ancient mythic elements even take center stage and hence cannot have been inserted from outside—not even if you should overlook how unreasonable it would be that they had survived as loose fragments in the nation's memory, as if just waiting for the opportunity to creep into a foreign tradition received from abroad.

Having asserted the age of these two types of bygone tales, I will first point out some of the ancient mythic aspects. No attempt is made to hide these myths of pagan times. They appear more or less prominently in the traditional tales themselves, as well as in certain elements of the tales.

Trolls and giants are everywhere, just as they are in the *Edda*s and in even earlier ancient writings. These denizens of the mountains are endowed with tremendous physical strength, but they are stupid and extremely trusting, which is why they can be fooled by human cleverness.[2]

The trolls have multiple heads and turn to stone when the sun shines on them. They use iron bars as weapons, just as was done in the earlier, or at least the German, ancient writings. As in the *Edda*s and in Saxo's work, they shoot glowing hot iron bars at people, they possess tremendous treasures of gold and silver, and they own iron boats like those in the fantastical sagas of the Middle Ages.[3]

Very rarely, on the other hand, are there any vestiges of elves, probably for reasons suggested in footnote 2. Yet one such vestige does seem to appear in "The Doll in the Grass" and possibly also in "Tom Thumb."

Like the dwarves Austri, Vestri, Nordri, and Sudri in the *Edda*s, the winds are personified in the tales "About the Boy Who Went to the North Wind and Demanded the Flour Back," "Soria Moria Castle," and "East of the Sun

[2] In accordance with the Christian perspective that obliterated the Æsir gods, humans take over the role of the gods in the battle against these monsters of the mountains.

[3] The trolls in our tales very often have animal pens that are used to fatten up humans who are to be slaughtered and eaten. This is a foreign element that can be found in Italian and French tales. Most likely it entered our stories from these aforementioned folk traditions in medieval times.

and West of the Moon." In the story "Lillekort," the title character is given a ship that is one and the same with the ship called Skiðblaðnir of Norse mythology. And you might even deduce that the hunchbacked and one-eyed old woman is reminiscent of the god Odin, whose divine power is manifested in the description of the ship. The hundred-year dispute of the three brothers in "The Three Princesses in White Land" may have been inspired by the Battle of the Hjathnings in the *Elder Edda* ["Skáldskaparmál," chap. 47, as cited in *The Poetic Edda*, translated by Lee M. Hollander]. In the traditions of other countries, there is no indication of such a battle lasting so long.

Earlier in this Introduction I showed that vestiges of the Sigurd myth are present in the tales "The Maiden on the Glass Mountain" and "Soria Moria Castle," just as Sigurd's mythic horse Grani reappears in the tale "Dappleband." Grimm assumes that the depiction of the Norns who spin the fates of men and gods ("Helgakviða Hundingsbana I," 2, 3) is the basis for the German "Die drei Spinnerinnen," which is comparable to our tale "The Three Aunts." If that is the case, then the ancient mythic vestige is not as evident in our tradition as in the German. In the latter, the three women are individually occupied, while in the Norwegian, they help everyone to spin. It looks as if the Nordic peoples (the Swedish tale "The Three Grand Ladies" treats the subject in the same way) felt the impact of hard and oppressive labor, and thus they wanted to create for themselves a happy day in the land of their imagination, a place without duress or strain. That's why the prince in the story vows that his queen will never have to work again. But even in our variant, at the very heart of the tale is undoubtedly the perception that fate distributes good fortune without regard for the striving of mortals to prove themselves worthy.

The tale "Why the Bear Has a Stump of a Tail" is reminiscent, however faintly, of the *Edda* fable about why the salmon has pointed tail fins. And similar to what we see in the story "Kari Stave-Skirt," the *Edda*s depict entire forests made of iron, as well as smaller groves and individual trees with golden leaves. In variant number 4 of this tale, the ox battles the troll but then loses strength when his name is mentioned. In the same way, in the sagas those who fought in animal form were changed back into humans when their names were spoken aloud, and their animal powers were then lost. (Such is the case, for instance, in "Rolf Krake's Saga.") In some of the folktales—"Sir Per," "The Twelve Wild Ducks," and "East of the Sun and West of the Moon"— magic spells are cast to turn people into animals or monsters. Yet under certain conditions they may resume their proper human form. The same thing often occurs in the fantastical sagas. In "The Bushy Bride" an enchanted song makes the king fall asleep, just as occurs in "Hørd Grimkjeldsen's Saga."

Two of the folktales are clearly based on myths. "Ash Lad, Who Competed with the Troll" contains distorted elements of Thor's journey to Utgard. The boy, who boldly agrees to a test of strength and an eating contest with the troll, represents first Thor and then Thor's companion Loki. But the folktale allows this representative of the Æsir gods to use cunning to walk away with the victory. In its principal depiction of the god Thor and his power, the tale can be said to be closer to the portrayal of the Æsir than was the old legend, which no doubt belonged to the later educated class.

"The Mill That Keeps Grinding at the Bottom of the Sea" depicts the same mill as in the *Edda*'s "The Lay of Grotti." In the latter, the mill first produces gold for King Frode of Denmark and later salt for the viking Mýsing, until his ship sinks to the bottom of the sea. In the *Younger Edda*, just as in the folktale, the sea then becomes salty, and there are hints that the mill is still grinding since it sends up whirlpools and maelstroms.

To these two folktales we should add "The Blue Ribbon." Although the storyline does not step by step retell a myth, the whole tale is based on "The Steel-Blue Belt," that is, Thor's magic belt, called *megingjörð* in Norse mythology. When the spindly-limbed boy wraps the ribbon around his waist, it gives him Thor's power to carry out astonishing feats against trolls and monsters. The dinner scene again refers to Loki's eating contest, but in this tale the troll demonstrates his superior ability to consume food.

Yet the ancient mythic elements in our Norwegian folktales are often far better disguised than merely under some sort of distortion. They are concealed under a *Christian* guise, which, upon superficial inspection, makes them completely unrecognizable. The persecution directed at those who continued to believe in the Æsir gods after the takeover of Christianity inevitably had an impact on the mythic ideas and vestiges that still lived on among the people. When any of these elements dared to make an appearance in folklore, the gods were hidden inside figures from Holy Scripture; or else the holy figures were given various traits that had once belonged to the pagan heroes and gods. Hence, under close scrutiny, many ancient mythic individuals can be recognized in the legendary tales that, at first glance, seem to have originated solely from Catholicism. Consequently, we might claim that the folktale "The Virgin Mary as Godmother" can be linked to the way in which "The Lay of

Grímnir" portrays Odin's wife, Frigg, as living here on earth and giving birth to children.

Similarly, one aspect of the tale "The Blacksmith They Didn't Dare Let into Hell" is indebted to the story (Fornm. Søg IX, 55–56 and 175) in which Odin one day goes to a blacksmith in Norway to have his horse shod. This is not some random or arbitrary hypothesis. The aforementioned Norwegian tale has cast in one narrative what the Germans have spread out through four different tales: "Bruder Lustig," "Spielhansel," "Der Teufel und seine Grossmutter," and "Das junggelühter Männlein." Yet none of the German tales depicts the shoeing of the horse, which is unique to the traditional Norwegian story.

The saga (Fornm. Søg., 37) describes how Thor, as a blacksmith, can't seem to get the smithy work done properly. The iron refuses to take shape, and he thinks the shoes will be too big. This leads Thor to proclaim that such a thing has never happened to him before. Then his visitor, Odin, tells him to let the work proceed as it will. And when they put the shoes on the horse's hooves, they fit perfectly. As you can see, Odin plays the same role with Thor—demonstrating his superiority in the art of blacksmithing—as Our Lord plays in the folktale.

Even though, as previously discussed, the storyline of "The Mill That Keeps Grinding at the Bottom of the Sea" is primarily mythic, it also contains an element that shows how people had to use subterfuge to allow them to coexist with a clergy that was on the lookout for heresy. When the mill is described as being taken *from behind the door in hell*, it is, in fact, marked as having a Christian attribute.

In the tale "The Seven Foals," pagan and Christian aspects are combined in the same manner. The transformation of the princes into animals belongs to pagan times. Yet their food and drink are portrayed as the sacramental bread and wine. By describing this type of nourishment for the humans who have been given animal form, the storyteller seems to want to atone for the pagan aspect.

On the other hand, the Christian concepts have undergone numerous alterations and assessments, in that they have taken on pagan elements and made them their own. In our Norwegian tales this is particularly apparent in the depiction of the Devil. He is never portrayed in accordance with the Christian concept of a conniving and destructive archenemy of humankind, as the mighty lord of darkness, before whom the devout person shudders. Instead, the Devil borrows traits from the giants who were the evil powers of pagan times. He is a creature of little intelligence who is easily fooled by the cunning of human beings. Even while situated in his own realm, the Devil is frightened by the blacksmith who arrives to surrender, as previously agreed in their pact. Here the pagan element is awakened even stronger by the power of imagination in the storytelling, which is well suited for underpinning what is humorous with what is terrifying—which is such a deeply entrenched and often prominent trait of the Norwegian national character.

But we also come across vestiges of Catholicism in these folktales, although far less frequently than the ancient mythic elements. This seems strange, given how much closer in time the Catholic teachings were to the storytellers. This factor seems to offer proof of what a deep and profound place the Æsir gods have had in the spiritual life of those residing in the North. The Catholic elements are present, first and foremost, in the legend-like tales, where Our Lord and Saint Peter wander the earth and personally offer human beings benevolent help and assistance or mete out punishment.

If we venture to say that surviving pagan aspects initially formed all legends, and if we can sometimes point out what these aspects are, it still must be understood that most of these figures from the past have here changed skin, so to speak. They are everywhere enveloped by a gentler and more illuminating light. Our Lord and Saint Peter appear in traditional Catholic form in "The Gjertrud Bird" and also more or less in "The Blacksmith They Didn't Dare Let into Hell." In the latter story, Saint Peter even holds the keys to heaven, which clearly indicates a link to papism.

In "The Virgin Mary As Godmother," the lovely and gentle lady takes in the newly christened girl, and through many types of travails and twists of fate, she makes the girl worthy of happiness and good fortune. The title character not only bears the name of but also the traits identified with the merciful mother of God. The astonishing clarity in the tone of this tale also seems to emanate from the godmother's noble persona.

In the children's story "The Rooster and the Hen in the Nut Forest," we also encounter the name of the Virgin Mary. I wonder whether the "red-gold ribbon" she provides might be a vestige of the holy woman's golden halo. And in the tale "The Master Thief," the fires of purgatory are named but presented in a humorously distorted manner.

However, these aspects from the past are far from the only internal proofs of the domestic origins of our folktales. We also have to look to the inherent nature of the stories and to the composition as a whole. Although the tales may be similar in content to stories from other nations, they are nevertheless not the same. They are clearly manifestations of our country's unique setting and commonly shared conditions.

In this sense, the setting—the entire stage on which a simple and ordinary story is played out while at the same time a colorful and richly varied imaginary performance takes place—is always the familiar mountainous landscape of Norway. We see the dense forests with the small green clearings where you can rest after a journey; the ridge after ridge of mountains that you must traverse; the heights where Dappleband is raised; the big, high mountain that casts a shadow over the king's courtyard; the steep, mirror-smooth slope that Ash Lad has to ride up; the sheltered cleft where the old woman sits and lures in the weary herder. These and thousands of other small details tell us that we are at home in Norway, no matter how amazing the events may be that capture our attention.

The same is true of the way in which daily life is determined by nature. Consider the house and its hearth where Ash Lad sits, with its furnishings and all the goings-on inside; the hut made of branches where Haaken Speckled-Beard wears his baggy leather coat; and the royal palace where the king stands on the steps and hires his own servants. Everything reminds us of the extremely simple and naïve customs that prevent the narrators from thinking of anything other than what can be found in their own quiet and remote mountain region.

Yet this sort of uniqueness, no matter now profoundly it may be woven into our folktales, is more of an external aspect. The deepest and most hidden distinctions, and therefore also the most difficult to show (although the easiest to feel), lie in the types of people that make their appearance in the stories. No matter how much they may have in common with those of closely related nations, they reflect unique aspects of Norway's national character. If we had in our possession the numerous as yet uncollected tales that flourish among our people, there is no doubt that the essential character traits of Norwegians would show up in the figures described.

Yet even in the tales of this collection, many of these character traits are evident. I think we can venture to say that among the Germanic peoples, our folktales favorably distinguish themselves by virtue of the boldness and confidence with which individuals are depicted. In this regard, the tales can even bear comparison with those in the Grimm brothers' excellent collection. However, the reason for such a favorable assessment is partially due to the fact that Denmark has few folktales and Sweden still hasn't finished putting together its own collection. This means that fewer character types have come to light in the folklore of these other nations.

The comic figures, in particular, appear most clearly and boldly in our Norwegian folktales. This is probably true of the tales in most countries "because the comical contains so much that is sharp and easily distinguished, and hence can be most readily shaped into indelible personalities" (Grimms' *Märchen*, Introduction, LI). In terms of our own tales, this is the case to a high degree, stemming primarily from the sense of humor that develops out of necessity among people who live under such harsh and difficult local conditions as we do in Norway.

Among the figures we often meet in our tales is the boy Ash Lad, who in Norwegian is called Askefisen or Espen Askefiis. The derisive word *fis* or *fiis* refers to someone who is considered pitiful or unlucky. In our first edition of the folktales, we felt it necessary to bow to the general reluctance (when writing) to use Norwegian names. Hence, we chose to use the purely Danish name Askepot, although in rural areas in Norway this name is apparently not common. Even in this second edition of the tales we have dared to use only one of the boy's nicknames, that is, Askeladden, or Ash Lad. Yet here in this Introduction I have ventured to cite his proper name.

This name is not nearly as offensive as it might seem. It means "the one who blows on the embers to make the flames flare up." Hence, it signifies this boy's humble and scorned position within the family. The ashes are his bed, and his job, if he has one, is merely to "make the flames flare up." For that reason he is also known in Norwegian as Tyrihans (the boy named Hans who takes care of the firewood) and Askeladden (Ash Lad, the clumsy and ragged boy who digs in the ashes). He is always the youngest of three brothers.[4] The other two, who are called Per and Paal in some regions, have the advantage of age and experience. They deeply despise the youngest boy, whom they mock and ridicule.

Yet Ash Lad possesses a hidden superior strength—a power that occasionally allows him to control and utilize supernatural forces around him. These forces lead him, and him alone, to victory in manly tests that his brothers have quickly failed. He alone wins the king's daughter and half the kingdom. Our

---

[4] Out in the countryside it's quite common for the youngest boy of a flock of siblings to be called Askefisen—and not just in farm households.

Ash Lad figure shares all of this with the German character Der Dummling and with *pinkel* in Swedish tales. But there is one thing that sets Ash Lad apart from them: the way in which his natural superiority is kept deeply concealed until he suddenly steps forth. His ability is hidden under an immobile lassitude (most strongly exemplified in the figure of Lazy-Lars, in an as yet untold story) and under an unflappable indifference to all the ridicule and mockery that his brothers fling at him. This indifference gives Ash Lad an impassive and foolish appearance, yet it's based on a profound recognition of his own strength. In this regard, he bears a close resemblance to Uffe Spage, a legendary Danish king described by Saxo but also known as Offa of Angel in Old English works. And, in some ways, he is similar to Amleth, a figure in medieval Scandinavian legend who inspired Shakespeare's Hamlet. Ash Lad's physiognomy conveys the impression of lax stupidity, yet smiling through it is his firm conviction that "I will surprise all of you when my time comes."

Although well concealed, this conviction about his own ability means that Ash Lad has at least partially ousted any of the gentle kindness that the German Der Dummling always shows. Nor does Ash Lad demonstrate the friendly helpfulness that makes the Swedish figure of *pinkel* so ridiculous in the eyes of his brothers. Ash Lad's deeply buried strength means that, in him, Der Dummling's childish faith has been favorably transformed into self-confidence. And he never loses a battle, the way his German kinsman occasionally does. Yet Ash Lad does sometimes reveal the milder traits that are described in German tales, for example, in the character of True.

Generally, however, the figure of Ash Lad bears a distinct resemblance to characters in the Icelandic sagas: *he keeps quiet and sleeps, he asks permission to test his mettle, and he wins.*[5]

In the same way, a feature of "The Blacksmith They Didn't Dare Let into Hell" differs from that portrayed in the German tales "Bruder Lustig" and "Spielhansel." Good-hearted hospitality and a frivolous, almost guileless ignorance about good and evil are the main traits in "Bruder Lustig," but they are not found in the Norwegian tale. Instead, the overriding element is once

---

[5] Compare to "Gautrek's Saga," chap. 4, in which Starkad lies in the ashes and is a *kolbitar*, i.e., a fireside historian of ancient Iceland. See also "Svarfdæla Saga," chaps. 1 and 2, in which Thorstein Svarfad, who will become a wise and powerful man, is initially depicted in the same way. Amleth is mentioned as far back as the *Younger Edda*; see Raft's edition, 126.

again a self-confidence that is not to be doubted. Bruder Lustig is a more comical figure, while the blacksmith is merely amusing.

In that sense he is closer to Spielhansel, though he is more boldly humorous, for he manages to fool the Devil. Spielhansel, on the other hand, fools only Death. The blacksmith is quite indignant when he sees the gates of hell close right in his face. This bears noting when we remember that this story was composed by the common people, who still had faith, and not by the "educated." The fact that the blacksmith calmly and sensibly decides to seek shelter and refuge, whether it be in hell or heaven, before he becomes homeless is a unique aspect that is in keeping with our national character. Spielhansel, who completely immerses himself in his passion for playing, embodies the ethical obliteration of the three aforementioned aspects. In that sense, it seems only right that an entertaining slyness allows Bruder Lustig to gain admittance through Saint Peter's gate, while Spielhansel is driven out of heaven and his soul is shattered. In the Norwegian tale we're left uncertain as to whether or not our blacksmith will be able to slip through the opening in the gate created by his sledgehammer.

Closely following the aforementioned character description and even closer to each other are the tales "The Master Thief" and "Big Per and Little Per." The figure of the master thief is not evident in the German folktales collections that have been published thus far. However, in M. Haupt's *Zeitschrift für deutsches Alterthum*, volume III (starting on p. 292), there is a tale from Thüringen that, in the general storyline, almost coincides with our tale and its variants. Yet in the German story the master thief appears to be a more carefree, affable, and civilized person. He is aware of the detestable nature of his handiwork, and he also takes a moralizing stand before his old parents, who have brought him to such a state.

In the collection of fairy tales by the sixteenth-century Italian writer Giovanni Francesco Straparola, there is a story titled "The Betrayer" that resembles our own tale. Although it is not my intention to compare character types beyond the Germanic peoples, in this case it still might be beneficial. In certain places Straparola's free treatment of the characters has allowed them to justify their stance.

In our tale, at first glance it seems as if all ethical considerations have been cast aside, as if the only thing we are supposed to appreciate is the *cunning cleverness* with which the master thief carries out his ploys. Yet this is not true. Throughout the entire story he is depicted in relation to other people who deserve to be tricked. The robbers, the bailiff, and the pastor have all boasted of an intelligence and shrewdness they do not possess. In addition, the bailiff, in his capacity as the "highest authority," is conceited and pompous, as well as cowardly and mean. The pastor is greedy, hypocritical, and superstitious.

Little Per is actually the same type as the master thief, although even tougher. Sly and wily behavior is still the main interest, but the ethical element has been pushed back to such an extent that Little Per shows traces of cruelty. This is especially evident in the section of the story where he causes his brother to kill their old mother. Then he puts her body in a sled, sets apples in her stiff hands, and goes off to town. There he causes the ship's captain to strike his dead mother so that her head falls off. It is solely because of the straightforward and naïve quality of the narrative, in which everything is portrayed as perfectly acceptable, that we are able to listen to this story. That is what elevates it to a type of black humor, which is not uncommon in the sagas and epic ballads. The slightest attempt to modulate or explain the actions would make the story unbearable.

This fearlessness that borders on cruelty is completely missing from the comparable German tale "Das Burle," as well as from Hans Christian Andersen's fairy tale "Big Klaus and Little Klaus." And we should remember that the latter story is a rewriting of a folktale. In "Das Burle," there are some elements of Little Per in evidence. The title character is disparaged by his neighbors, and to a certain extent justifiably so, because right from the start he seems to bear strong vestiges of a real, not feigned, lunacy. Little Per, on the other hand, is aware throughout the story of his own intelligence and consequently is at first content with his situation.

Finally, the same sort of hidden intelligence appears in "The Quandary," when Ash Lad gets the princess to stop talking, and in "Ash Lad, Who Got the Princess to Say He Was Lying." The difference is that it is revealed through what the boy says, while in the aforementioned stories it comes out in the actions of the characters. The servant boy in "Paal Next-Door" is primarily the same type of person, although in this case his intelligence is represented as peasant shrewdness.

It's as if the gentler and more positive character traits in these folktales have been saved for the depiction of women. It's true that we also encounter boldly comical female types—for example, in "Some Women Are Like That," "Gidske," and others. Generally, when these types of women appear, the comic effect is achieved when stupidity or foolishness is presented as sensible and clever behavior. It's as if the stories have wanted to portray women within a quieter field of action. Hence, with regard to the wife in "Gudbrand Slope," the comical aspect is muted by the fact that she is genuinely happy with everything her husband says and does—and we halfway wish that many more wives were like Gudbrand's. But this sort of comical female figure is rare in comparison to the male.

The depiction of the stepdaughter, whom the stepmother and her daughter hate and torment, is what makes our folktales brimming with favorable and gentle personality traits. This type of character is represented by Kari Stave-Skirt, by the daughter of the king's first marriage in "The Husband's Daughter and the Wife's Daughter," and by the daughter in "The Bushy Bride." In the latter tale, the husband's daughter is "as lovely and bright as the day" and as good as she is beautiful. The hateful hostility of her stepmother and stepsister does not prompt bitterness but rather a resigned sorrow. Kari, hungry and poorly dressed, is sent out to the forest to tend to the livestock, and there she pets and cares for the animals. In "The Husband's Daughter and the Wife's Daughter," the daughter is tossed into the well because the yarn she is spinning breaks before her stepsister's does. She cautiously steps on the brushwood fence so as not to break it, she carefully picks apples from a tree so its branches can right themselves, and so forth. In "The Bushy Bride," curses and scoldings rain down on the girl when she is sent to get water from the creek where hideous heads rise to the surface. Yet she agrees to wash, brush, and kiss them.

The daughter's own sorrow and anguish have not closed her heart; instead, her suffering has opened her heart and become manifest in a sensitivity and gentleness. *She thinks more about everyone else than about herself.* The cruel injustice she has endured has by no means caused her to distrust those who offer her advice and assistance. She displays a childlike sense of trust when she does what the birds advise in their song or when she believes what her stepmother claims her brother has demanded—even when it means that she has to throw her beloved little dog and then herself into the sea.

To awaken our deep sympathy, the suffering and anguish of the daughter's fate is described in lengthy detail until we are convinced of her gentle strength. Then it is transformed into the delightful rewards that only the folktale can provide. So that the daughter's goodness, both in her behavior and in her very being, might be demonstrated more clearly, she is portrayed next to the evil and ugly stepsister. This girl is her exact opposite in every way—in her appearance and temperament, her actions, and her fate.

Compared with the stories of the nations closest to us, the male characters in *our* tales are generally depicted with sharper and rougher personalities. These men have frequently suppressed any of the milder and more conciliatory traits, if not totally lacking them altogether. Similarly, the aforementioned female character—the husband's daughter—in our folktales is imagined as lovelier and more ethically exacting, if not as meticulously described.

In Matthias Winther's *Danske Folkeeventyr* (from 1823), the narrative makes do with depicting the daughter as "beautiful and good." The latter trait is shown only in one concrete example: she refrains from eating the tempting fruits outside the castle after she falls into the well. Even the German portrayal of the daughter doesn't seem to me as gentle or good as in our tales. There she is described partly as showing forbearance toward her fate and partly as demonstrating the greatest concern for the well-being of others. For example, in "Frau Holle," she chooses to jump into the well out of despair, and even though she does pick the apples from the tree, *it's only because they are ripe—not so that the branches can spring back up.* Nor does she take care to place the apples at the base of the tree. She is portrayed more beautifully in a spiritual sense in "Die drei Männlein im Walde." Yet even here she offers a mild objection before she obeys the harsh mother's command. And it's with the three little men—creatures of common sense—that she shares her bread. Nowhere is her kind consideration for others given such a lovely portrayal as in our tales *where she steps lightly so as not to damage the brushwood fence;* and nowhere is her trusting obedience as touching as *when she jumps into the sea because that's what her brother wants her to do.*

Yet it is equally in the overall narrative style, the tone, and the unique coloring that our folktales firmly set themselves apart from those of other nations and reveal the ground from which they have sprung. This is true not only when they are compared with the literature of distant lands but also when compared with the stories of Germanic countries.

The overall tone of folktales is naïve, childlike, and intimate, presenting the content with such conviction that its wonders are received as ordinary events. But this basic tone is modified in highly diverse ways. For instance, the Hindus frequently intertwine like lianas sensual images around and among the telling of simpler tales. Among the Arabs, the folktale has an advanced, almost elegant, and broadly motivated delivery, occasionally glittering with pictures. In both cases the narrative is episodically pieced together. Among the Italians (meaning Giambattista Basile, because Straparola's writing style is long-winded and not folksy), the presentation is bright, light, and quick paced. Among the French (meaning Madame d'Aulnoy), the style is delicate to the point of meticulous. By no means lacking in naïveté, this aspect seems to have been achieved through artistry—the fairyland forests reek of eau de cologne. Among the Germanic peoples there are recognizable similarities. Yet if a well-told Norwegian folktale, for example, was fortunate enough to be expertly translated into Swedish or German, the narrative style would always still reveal its homeland origin and vice versa.

Judging by the as yet unfinished fairy-tale collection of Gunnar Olaf Hyltén-Cavallius and George Stephens, the narrative style among the Swedes seems to differ definitively from our own. The aforementioned authors have shown great care in the collecting and arranging of their tales and variants, thereby erasing any doubt about their striving to convey the traditional tales as they received them. Otherwise I would have been tempted to believe that their narrative style was occasionally marked by artifice. Referring to the aforementioned collection, the style of the Swedes is stiffer, the story more chronologically presented, the characters and events supplied with a pomp that is reminiscent of the epic ballads—although in this case it seems artificially applied and hinders any freedom of movement. Finally, whatever is tender and sorrowful is depicted with a gentleness that is close to sentimental. Very rarely is there any humor. As proof of this, I will cite the following places that jump out at me while leafing through the pages. Page 83: Then the Vattuman donned opulent clothing, draped a scarlet cloak around his shoulders, set the golden crown on his head, and set off with his animals. Page 105: The vallare-man felt at ease in the golden armor and moved in a noble manner, as if he were the most highborn son of a king. Page 106: Yet the bride wept without ceasing, and her tears were so hot that they burned like fire on her cheeks. Page 110: Now he set off with his hawks and dogs to go hunting, venturing deep into the forest. Page 117: And yet she could not entirely forget her home. She would often sit down at the shore and with great longing gaze out at the sea and the waves that wandered freely between lands. Page 121: The woman replied: "My Lord King!" Page 141: It played through her memory. Page 142: A magnificent carriage, drawn by lively horses. Page 202: And the young man served the princess with deference and an honorable demeanor, as befitted a highborn maiden.

Like the "princess," the "young man" laments and weeps pitifully when he is in distress. Missing altogether is the bold and pure epic tone that allows the events to proceed unequivocally, without the interference of any sympathy offered by the narrator. I must mention one other stylistic feature of Swedish tales, and that is the frequency with which adages are presented outside of the dialogue. Our tales have the advantage in that key points are more often presented in verse form. These types of passages, containing meter and rhyme, enliven the story and in many places favorably bear witness to the age of the tradition.

Denmark does not possess any collection of folktales significant enough that specific characteristics in the narrative might be identified. As for Hans Christian Andersen's world-famous fairy tales, they owe as much to invention as to style. Even when he makes use of folk traditions, they are treated freely and disguised. Matthias Winther's *Danske Folkeeventyr* contains tales that consist mostly of fragments. They do not possess a consistent overall tone, nor are they well told, so they don't convey any sense of the unique qualities of the narrative style in Danish folktales. Aside from this collection, to my knowledge the only other recorded tales are stories in the Jutlandic tradition presented by Christian Molbech. Although Andersen includes ideas and circumstances that belong to the higher echelons of society, his *narrative style* does have links to folk traditions. And in this regard, his stories do come close to representing the folktales of the Danish islands, albeit in a more refined and cultivated form. Taking this into consideration, we can then say that the style of the Danish tale is smoother, milder, and in a certain way more sympathetic, with a more childlike sense of humor than in our tales.

Of all the European folktale collections published thus far, none can measure up to the superior style of the *Kinder- und Haus-Märchen,* told by the Grimm brothers. Here all the unique characteristics of the German tales are given full justice. The style is smooth and beautiful without being honed or polished. The comical and humorous sections are presented with an open and broad boldness, and yet *there is a heartfelt and congenial tone that resounds throughout the simple tale.*

It is, I think, this congenial and heartfelt quality—causing a person to feel so at ease when reading these tales—that sets them apart from ours. Reading the German stories, we feel as if we are sitting in a warm and comfortable middle-class home, listening to a respectable old woman speaking. There is a hint of the narrative style in the strong and clear features of the old woman's face that adorns the book like a vignette. In the High German–style tales, the narrative as a whole is also somewhat more refined than in ours. Yet I regard this to be an insignificant difference that is not an intrinsic part of the tales. Instead, it derives from the narrators' view of their task and from the approach they subsequently chose. If we turn our attention to this point, we might notice that in between the tales that are told in the commonly used written language, many others are inserted that have a spoken-dialect quality. By changing tack, the narrators have allowed themselves freer rein in those cases where their more refined style would not have allowed the full nature of the tale to shine.

In contrast to these tales from the Germanic countries, our own tales could be described as having a narrative style that is a *continuation and a further development of the sagas*. It is not my intention to claim that the folktale is the same as the saga—far from it. Rather, I am referring to the inner nature of the narrative, not to turns of phrase and external aspects. Regardless of the fact that in our tales we do not encounter a single vestige of the chronicle style, which is so prevalent in Swedish stories, I do think that ours bear a closer and more organic link to the narrative style of the sagas.

Everywhere we can see, as in the sagas, *the direct and ruthless way* in which everything is described—a means of expression that stems not from cruelty but from naïveté and lack of guile. We find the same bold and magnificent sense of humor that—like the hero in a German tale—seems to be "presented in order to teach fear." We discover everywhere *the pure epic narrative style whose sole purpose is the joy of observation*. Hence, it dwells as much on the sorrowful and terrible as it does on the bright and cheerful, but it rarely if ever reveals the disposition of the narrator as events unfold. Our tales can *always* say what the boy said as he sat and wept: "*It makes no difference to me.*" When some hint of a specific disposition is occasionally caught by an observant listener, it happens more often in a negative rather than a positive way. By this, I mean that it's not uncommon for a story to keep to itself a more gentle disposition toward life—or even, out of modesty, to seek to hide such an attitude—by giving to any poignant aspects the guise of humor. When this is done, it may be possible to hear a sympathetic tone underlying the amusing style. Compared to the German, the Norwegian tale is *told in a manly voice*.

Quite often in private, and a few times in public as well, people have criticized the folktales that were recounted to us, protesting that the traditional mode of expression was too lowly. The stories were found to be both coarse and vulgar, and there was a desire to elevate the style of the tales to a greater lightness and refinement. Such a desire is natural for the person who wishes to find in these stories solely or primarily an esthetic enjoyment and whose taste is more narrow than wide-ranging. Yet I am convinced that if my collaborator and I had obeyed this impulse to a greater extent than occurs in this edition, we would have quickly taken the wrong path. The unique quality of our nation's folktales comes to light in the narrative style and presentation, while the story-line is often quite ordinary. Consequently, you must realize that by elevating the tale beyond the expression and tone inherent in the traditional point of view, you would very easily, even inevitably, erase everything that makes them Norwegian. For the sake of the *scholarly significance* of the folktale it's very important, first and foremost, to present a *traditional* recounting. It may be that the style can also be refined and beautiful, but that should never happen at the expense of the tale's unique quality. The only form that is esthetically justified is the one that fully allows the content to come forth.

As in many similar situations, here the objection is usually raised that the characteristic nature of the tale lies in the thought itself, not in how it is ex-pressed. But you are forgetting that in all poetic manifestations, the thought is concentrated in the depiction. Another type of depiction would make it dif-ferent, or at least differently nuanced. If we were not to take the same path as the Grimm brothers—alternately using the written language and the spoken language for the narration of the tales—we would have to adapt the style so that it could genuinely convey what is inherent in the tales. I consider it per-missible to use the spoken language when presenting legends, but not folk-tales. The legend is far more closely connected not only to a specific country but also most often to an individual region. Consequently, the linguistic idiom frequently gives legends their strong local color. The folktale, on the other hand, is usually shared by the entire nation. Hence, using the spoken dialect would restrict and bind the tale to a much narrower realm than where it actu-ally belongs. Considering how widespread the folktale storyline is beyond our borders, we realized that a language more commonly shared than any specific dialect would be the right choice.

I believe that anyone who studies the tales of other countries and then turns to ours will generally be satisfied with our narrative style. It will be evident that in some tales the style is kept on a higher or—as it's usually called—purer plane. This occurs in those places where the general storyline has not assumed a guise unique to Norway and where the integrity of the events demands it. Yet in these instances as well, tradition speaks, as do we.

Christiania, January 1851

Foreword to the
Third Norwegian Edition

Peter Christen Asbjørnsen

AFTER THE FIRST TWO EDITIONS of our folktales saw the light of day, in 1842 and 1852, and especially after the latter, a great number of similar collections have been published in all the European countries, as well as in other parts of the world. The origins of folktales and legends, their dissemination, and their entire content have since that time also been explained from many different aspects—through examining the light that the numerous collections cast upon one another, through the publication of a number of ancient texts from the East and West, and through various types of learned studies and appraisals.

As a result, not only have we received the key to many of the mysteries of the tales formerly hidden undercover, so that we now, better than previously, can understand their content, which most often turns out to have roots in the childlike perception of nature, of bygone eras, of myths, or of fanciful assessments of life; but we also, based on a more thorough discussion and comparison of these mythic remnants of folklore, have created entire mythological constructs or systems. Over the past few years a better and more comprehensive explanation has been made regarding the age, origin, movement, and spread of folktales from one people to another, from one language to another. As we previously expected and surmised, it turns out that the folktale was present everywhere, that it is something shared by all peoples, and that it belongs to all ages and eras, but especially to the time of mythic comprehension, which in the life of a people and in the development of history is comparable to the childhood of an individual. Hence, in our time an extensive literature has arisen about folklore, with texts that contain examinations of their content. During several years spent abroad, this writer was fortunate enough, by means of various routes, to become more familiar with and better informed about a large number of these studies and research efforts than would have been possible here in Norway—partly through personal acquaintanceships, meetings, and interactions with many of the great experts and contributors to the work and partly through free access and the most amenable guidance offered by learned individuals who allowed me to make use of a couple of the most extensive private libraries on the subject. But since the objective of my travels and stay abroad was quite different from the study of mythology and folktales, I could devote only a few free hours in between other studies to reviving this interest of mine and seeking insight into the newer research; consequently, it was only possible to keep up with a few of the main trends and the more traveled paths.

With help from the many recent and largely excellent works and studies, it is now much easier to present a more complete and comprehensive view of the folktales than when our second edition was published; yet, from the afore-mentioned studies it must be clear that such a work would demand a scope and treatment that would make it more suitably published as a separate work of a more scholarly content than as a supplement to a collection of folktales in-tended for general readers and youths. Such a work would also—if this writer were to satisfy the demands he had set for himself—require more extensive studies and hence much more diligence and time than can now be given to such a task. A circumstance that also carries weight and ought to be mentioned here is the fact that this writer's old friend and former collaborator has devoted all his efforts to his ecclesiastical calling ever since he assumed his clergyman duties. So there can be no further cooperation from Jørgen Moe with regard to texts such as the work discussed above, a subject with which he has not con-cerned himself for the past ten years.

The fact that in Norway concepts regarding the folktale and other folklore—their content, meaning, pedagogical importance, and effect on the life of the people as superstition and as a means for combating superstition—have been so little clarified that some tales included in a text have evoked intel-lectually naïve remarks (samples of which have been publicly expressed), it would undoubtedly be more than desirable if we now could persuasively pre-sent in a thorough and extensive work all of these aspects, clarifying matters more than has previously occurred. However, given what has been explained above, this will have to be postponed to another time and occasion, if it is to be done by this writer.

This third edition of Norwegian folktales is thus published without an Introduction or any notes, containing solely the tales. This will have the greatest appeal for youths and readers in general, since for them the scholarly supplement is of lesser importance, of indifferent value, or an inexplicable burden, and it would also make such a book unreasonably expensive.

In the tales recounted by Jørgen Moe, only a number of orthographic changes have been made. Since the author did not have time to review the tales personally, he wanted them to be presented unaltered. Hence, the present edition has been prepared solely by the undersigned. With regard to his own tales, this writer has tried, as far as possible and without undertaking any drastic corrections or changes, to remove any foreign words and aberrant phrases.

For a new collection or series of folktales, there are—in addition to those tales that this writer has at various times had printed in calendars and minor publications—a not insignificant number of contributions from earlier times, which were recorded in the collections and travel accounts of both this writer and Jørgen Moe. The latter stories have now been given to the undersigned to be used freely in the publication of the new collection, which will hopefully appear next year.

Outside our own country, the Norwegian folktales—partly via translations and excerpts, partly via comments to foreign folktale collections, and partly via the learned works of scholars studying mythology and ancient times—have become so widespread and generally known that during the past few years hardly any work or text dealing with or discussing related folklore or mythic subjects has been published without quoting from, discussing, or examining the Norwegian folktale collections. To cite these instances would be both an enormous and an unnecessary task.

Christiania, October 1865

Foreword to the
Fourth Norwegian Edition

Peter Christen Asbjørnsen

FOR THIS EDITION of Norwegian folktales, I have once again gone over the tales that were told to me, with the intention of removing anything that seemed less popular in form and expression. My collaborator, who again did not have time to review his contributions to the collection, has made use of a friend's comments in certain places where the two of them together found the wording to be less in tune with the rest of the linguistic expression, and thus they attempted to make improvements. I, too, having until recently been away from the place of publication, have—with regard to the revising of the manuscript as well as the proofreading—been fortunate enough to find steadfast and knowledgeable assistance from this mutual and obliging friend, to whom I herewith offer grateful and sincere thanks from both of us.

Yet even though quite a number of changes and corrections have been made to this edition (and similar changes were made to the third edition), none of them will be obvious to the general reader unless the various editions are compared. For it is not only or exclusively a matter of removing or inserting individual words; at issue is just as much, if not more so, a careful modification of word forms and syntactical usage as well as the combination and reciprocal positioning of words; thus, it is in the form of speech, which had its expression in the first complete collection (1852), that now, in this edition and the previous one, the tales could be said to have achieved regularity and conformity and true popular color.

In the Foreword to the third edition, this writer mentioned his hope that a new collection or another volume of folktales might be published within the year. Because of other intervening and more pressing obligations, this did not occur; but in order not to delay more than necessary the publication of what had been prepared and was ready, a smaller edition of tales was published under the title *Juletræ* [Christmas Tree] in 1866. As soon as time and circumstances permit, the publication will be continued and further pursued. There is much stronger demand for it now than previously, since the folktales both here at home and abroad have evoked such a response that almost as many copies of the third edition have been disseminated in two years as of the first two editions in twenty-three years.

Regardless of all the praise that has subsequently been heaped upon our folktale and legends collections, it is in recent years that a clearer understanding of their various and more profound significance has been achieved. The tales have been characterized as "a revived treasure of national literature, in which the national direction of recent literature, especially insofar as the narrative style is concerned, has been considerably affected." It has been emphatically underscored that they, "as flesh of our flesh and bone of our bone," are of great importance for the development of our native tongue, and for that purpose they have even been introduced into the school curriculum.

This new edition is hereby offered to young and older readers alike, with hopes for a favorable reception. Youths and the general public have always held affection for the folktale, and justifiably so; for with its hale and hearty core, the folktale will forever retain its attraction, as long as the people themselves preserve their robust nature and health.

Christiania, October 1867

Notes on the
Regional Collection Sites
of the Tales

THESE NOTES give the region in Norway where each tale was collected and indicate whether it was Asbjørnsen or Moe who contributed the story to the original volume of *Norske folkeeventyr*. The geographical information, including where variant versions of the tales could be found, was compiled by Moe and published in the second edition (1852) but omitted from future Norwegian editions. So that readers might locate these regional sites on current maps of Norway, we updated the sites with present-day place names wherever possible. For those readers who might like to look at the tales in the original Norwegian, we included the Norwegian titles as they appeared in the fourth edition (1868), which was the source for this new English translation.

About Ash Lad, Who Stole the Troll's Silver Ducks, Coverlet, and Golden Harp
(Om Askeladden, som stjal Troldets Sølvænder, Sengetæppe og Guldharpe)
> Collected by Moe in Ringerike. Variants found in Kristiansand, Kvinnherad, Solør, and Hardanger.

The Gjertrud Bird (Gjertrudsfuglen)
> Collected by Moe in Ringerike. This story is also known, under a different title, in Røyken, Gudbrandsdalen, Østerdalen, Setesdal, and Hallingdal.

The Griffin (Fugl Dam)
> Collected by Asbjørnsen in Røyken. This story is not widely known.

The Quandary (Spurningen)
> Collected by Asbjørnsen in Gjerdrum. Also known in Røyken, Lom, Østerdalen, and Luster in Sogn.

Richman Peddler Per (Rige Per Kræmmer)
Collected by Asbjørnsen in Røyken. The ending is also found in a story from Hardanger.

Ash Lad, Who Competed with the Troll
(Askeladden, som kapaad med Troldet)
Collected by Moe in Ringerike. Variants found in Gausdal, Lærdal, Fåberg, and Østerdalen.

About the Boy Who Went to the North Wind and Demanded the Flour Back
(Om Gutten, som gik til Nordenvinden, og krævede Melet igjen)
Collected by Asbjørnsen in Gjerdrum. Also known in Trondheim, Gudbrandsdalen, Østerdalen, Ringerike, Valdres, Hallingdal, and Setesdal; variants found in Kvinnherad and Bygland.

The Virgin Mary As Godmother (Jomfru Maria som Gudmoder)
Collected by Moe in Ringerike. Variants found in Ådal, Odalen, and Valdres.

The Three Princesses in White Land (De tre Prindsesser i Hvidtenland)
Collected by Moe in Ringerike. Variants found in Hardanger and Hedmark.

Some Women Are Like That (Somme Kjærringer ere slige)
Collected by Asbjørnsen in Gjerdrum. Also known in Gudbrandsdalen; variant found in Ådal.

Everyone Thinks Their Own Children Are Best
(Hver synes bedst om sine Børn)
Collected by Moe in Ringerike. Variant found in Grimstad.

A Tale of Courtship (En Frierhistorie)
Collected by Moe in Ringerike.

The Three Aunts (De tre Mostre)
Collected by Moe in Ringerike. Variants found in Åseral and Lauvdal.

The Widow's Son (Enkesønnen)
Collected by Moe in Ringerike. This story is very widespread, with variants found in Gausdal and Valdres.

The Husband's Daughter and the Wife's Daughter
(Manddatteren og Kjærringdatteren)
Collected by Asbjørnsen in Romerike. This story is known in Setesdal,

Hardanger, Røyken, Vågå, Valdres, Hallingdal, Biri, Østerdalen, and other areas of the eastern mountains, sometimes under a different title.

The Rooster and the Hen in the Nut Forest
(Hanen og Hønen i Nøddeskoven)
Collected by Moe in Ringerike.

The Bear and the Fox (Bjørnen og Ræven)
Why the Bear Has a Stump of a Tail (Hvorfor Bjørnen er stubrumpet)
Collected by Moe in Ringerike. This story is known everywhere.

The Fox Cheats the Bear Out of His Christmas Meal
(Ræven snyder Bjørnen for Julekosten)
Collected by Moe in Ringerike. This story is known everywhere.

Gudbrand Slope (Gudbrand i Lien)
Collected by Moe in Ringerike. Also known in Røyken and Romerike.

Kari Stave-Skirt (Kari Træstak)
Collected by Asbjørnsen in Røyken. Also known in Romerike and Biri under a slightly different title; variants found in Sel, Bygland, Hardanger, and Kvinnherad.

The Fox As Shepherd (Ræven som Gjæter)
Collected by Asbjørnsen in Solør. This story is not widespread.

The Blacksmith They Didn't Dare Let into Hell
(Smeden, som de ikke torde slippe ind i Helvede)
Collected by Moe in Ringerike. Also known in Romerike and Østerdalen.

The Rooster and the Hen (Hanen og Hønen)
Collected by Moe in Ringerike. Like most children's tales, it is not as widespread.

The Rooster, the Cuckoo, and the Black Grouse
(Hanen, Gjøgen og Aarhanen)
Collected by Moe in Ringerike. Well known in Grimstad.

Lillekort (Lillekort)
Collected by Moe in Ringerike. Very widespread. This story should not be confused with another titled "The Fisherman"; variants found in Vågå, Biri, Hjartdal, and Evje.

The Doll in the Grass (Dukken i Græsset)
Collected by Asbjørnsen in Hedmark. This story does not seem to be found in many other places.

Paal Next-Door (Paal Andrestuen)
Collected by Asbjørnsen in Røyken. Variants found in Romerike, Biri, Toten, Gudbrandsdalen, Østerdalen, Valdres, Ringerike, Hallingdal, and Telemark.

Soria Moria Castle (Soria Moria Slot)
Collected by Asbjørnsen in Røyken. Known in Luster in Sogn under a different title.

Sir Per (Herreper)
Collected by Moe in Ringerike. This story is very widespread; variants found in Hallingdal, Telemark, Solør, and Smaalenene.

Little Aase Goosegirl (Vesle Aase Gaasepige)
Collected by Asbjørnsen in Solør. This story is widespread in the eastern mountain area; variants found in Ringerike.

The Boy and the Devil (Gutten og Fanden)
Collected by Moe in Ringerike. This story is known in Ullensaker as a separate story, though it is a section from "The Blacksmith They Didn't Dare Let into Hell."

The Seven Foals (De syv Folerne)
Collected by Moe in Ådal. Variant found in Hardanger.

Gidske (Gidske)
Collected by Asbjørnsen in Røyken. Variant found in Ringebu.

The Twelve Wild Ducks (De tolv Vildænder)
Collected by Asbjørnsen in Eidsvoll. This story is very widespread, known in Gudbrandsdalen, Østerdalen, and many other places; variants found in Biri, Grimstad, and Bygland.

The Master Thief (Mestertyven)
Collected by Asbjørnsen in Sel. Variants found in Lærdal, Gjerdrum, Vågå, Kvinnherad, Luster in Sogn, Evje, and Ullensvang.

The Three Sisters Who Were Taken into the Mountain
(De tre Søstre, som bleve indtagne i Berget)
> Collected by Moe. Generally widespread in the dioceses of Akershus and Kristiansand. Variants found in Bygland and Seljord.

About the Giant Troll Who Never Carried His Heart with Him
(Om Risen, som ikke havde noget Hjerte paa sig)
> Collected by Moe in Seljord. Variant found in Bygland.

Dappleband (Grimsborken)
> Collected by Moe in Seljord. Variant found in Fåberg and in Bygland and Rendalen.

Nothing Is Needed by the One All Women Love
(Det har ingen Nød med den, som alle Kvindfolk er forlibt i)
> Collected by Moe in Seljord. This story is known in the region around Larvik; variants found in Valle and Kristiansund.

Ash Lad, Who Got the Princess to Say He Was Lying
(Askeladden, som fik Prindsessen til at løgste sig)
> Collected by Asbjørnsen in Sel. This story is very widespread, though the beginning sometimes varies; variants found in Ringerike, Hemsedal, Vågå, and Lom.

The Three Billy Goats Gruff, Who Were Supposed to Go to the Mountain Pasture to Fatten Up
(De tre Bukkene Bruse, som skulde gaa til Sæters og gjøre sig fede)
> Collected by Asbjørnsen in Biri, although this story presumably belongs in Gausdal or Lærdal. Known in Grimstad; variant found in Luster in Sogn.

East of the Sun and West of the Moon (Østenfor Sol og vestenfor Maane)
> Collected by Asbjørnsen in Telemark. This story is widespread; in some areas it is called "Skjønheden og Bæstet" (Beauty and the Beast), presumably after the French story. Variants found in Fåberg, Ringerike, Valle, Bygland, Kvinnherad), and Åseral.

The Hen Who Had to Go to Dovre Mountain or Else the Whole World Would Perish
(Hønen, som skulde til Dovrefjeld, forat ikke Alverden skulde forgaa)
> Collected by Asbjørnsen in Telemark.

The Man Who Had to Keep House (Manden, som skulde stelle hjemme)
Collected by Asbjørnsen in Slidre in Valdres. Variant found in Hardanger.

Tom Thumb (Tommeliden)
Collected by Asbjørnsen in Telemark. Also known in Grimstad; this tale is undoubtedly very rare. We didn't find it anywhere else.

Haaken Speckled-Beard (Haaken Borkenskjæg)
Collected by Asbjørnsen in Sørum (in Romerike). Also known in Røyken; variant found in Vågå and also under a different title in Lier and Drammen.

Master Maiden (Mestermø)
Collected by Moe in Seljord. This story seems to be widespread; it is found in much the same form in Østerdalen, Gudbrandsdalen, Romerike, Ringerike, and so on; variants found in Gjerdrum, Ringerike, Fåberg, Sel, Gausdal, Østerdalen, and Ullensvang.

Well Done and Poorly Rewarded (Vel gjort og ilde lønnet)
Collected by Asbjørnsen in Slidre (in Valdres). This story is widely known in the entire Oslo diocese and also in Hardanger.

True and Untrue (Tro og Utro)
Collected by Moe in Ringerike. This story is very widespread; variants found in Hardanger, Kristiansund, Evje, and the area around Mandal.

Per and Paal and Esben Ash Lad (Per og Paal og Esben Askelad)
Collected by Moe in Nissedal.

The Mill That Keeps Grinding at the Bottom of the Sea
(Kværnen, som staar og maler paa Havsens Bund)
Collected by Moe in Ringerike. Also known in the Kongsberg region and in Østerdalen.

The Maiden on the Glass Mountain (Jomfruen paa Glasberget)
Collected by Moe in Ringerike. Also known in Kristiansund; variants found in Ringerike and Evje.

Butterball (Smørbuk)
Collected by Asbjørnsen in Hallingdal. This story is told everywhere with only minor differences and is very widespread in the entire Oslo diocese, under various names; variant found in Sel.

Big Per and Little Per (Store-Per og Vesle-Per)

Collected by Asbjørnsen and Moe. This story is a composite of one traditional tale from the Bergen diocese and two traditional tales from Vågå (in Gudbrandsdalen). Also known in Ringerike, Østerdalen, and most rural districts; variant found in Eidsborg (annex to Lårdal in Telemark).

Ragged Cap (Lurvehætte)

Collected by Moe in Åseral. Variant found in Vågå.

The Bushy Bride (Buskebruden)

Collected by Moe. This story is a composite from two quite similar traditional tales from Telemark. Variant found in Beitostølen (in Valdres), Solør, Telemark, and Gudbrandsdalen.

The Tabby Cat on Dovre Mountain (Kjætten paa Dovre)

Collected by Asbjørnsen. This story is widespread, often taking on traits specific to the region where it occurs; in many areas it is part of the Christmas legend cycle. We found it in Østerdalen, Gudbrandsdalen, Valdres, Hallingdal, Ådal, and Telemark and in the Bergen diocese in Luster in Sogn and Jostedalen. It is probably known everywhere in Norway. Usually the farm where the story takes place is called Kvam or Kvamme, and in some areas the man who arrives is identified as a pilgrim.

Farmer Weather-Beard (Bonde Veirskjæg)

Collected by Asbjørnsen. This story is a composite of two very similar tales, one from Ringerike and the other from Hedemark. Known under a different title in Smaalenene and Solør.

The Blue Ribbon (Det blaa Baandet)

Collected by Asbjørnsen in Ådal. This story, with its distinctive oddity, seems to have been influenced by and adopted traits from "A Thousand and One Nights."

The Honest Four-Skilling Coin (Den retfærdige Firskilling)

Collected by Moe. [Not included in the second edition of 1852, so there are no collection notes by Moe for this story.]

The Old Man of the House (Han Fa'r sjøl i Stua)

Collected by Asbjørnsen. [Not included in the second edition of 1852, so there are no collection notes by Moe for this story.]

PETER CHRISTEN ASBJØRNSEN (1812–1885) and
JØRGEN MOE (1813–1882) were energetic collectors
of Norwegian folklore in the nineteenth century. Their
collection *Norske folkeeventyr* (Norwegian Folktales),
first published in 1841 with many subsequent editions,
is regarded as a landmark of Norwegian literature and
culture. Their work greatly influenced the development
of the Norwegian language and made their names legendary, both at home and abroad.

TIINA NUNNALLY is an award-winning translator
of Norwegian, Danish, and Swedish literature. Her many
translations include Sigrid Undset's first novel, *Marta
Oulie,* the Minnesota Trilogy by Vidar Sundstøl, and *Swede
Hollow* by Ola Larsmo, all published by the University of
Minnesota Press. She was appointed Knight of the Royal
Norwegian Order of Merit for her efforts on behalf of
Norwegian literature in the United States.

NEIL GAIMAN is the author of such award-winning titles
as *Norse Mythology*, *American Gods*, *The Graveyard Book*,
The View from the Cheap Seats, and the *Sandman* graphic
novels. He is a prolific creator of prose, poetry, film,
journalism, comics, song lyrics, and drama. Several of his
titles have been adapted for television, including the Emmy-
nominated adaptation of *American Gods* and his miniseries
of *Good Omens*, based on the novel he cowrote with the late
Sir Terry Pratchett. Originally from England, he now lives
in the United States.